Praise for *Until the Last Star Fades*

WINNER for ROMANCE
2019 The Independent Author Network

WINNER – BEST CANADIAN AUTHOR
2019 Northern Hearts Awards,
Toronto chapter of the Romance Writers of America

3x FINALIST
2019 Contemporary Romance Writers,
Toronto Romance Writers, and Las Vegas Writers
(all chapters of the Romance Writers of America)

BEST BOOKS OF 2018 - Hypable

"Delightful contemporary romance [with] a good mix of poignancy and sexy fun." — *Kirkus Reviews*

"Hot new material with Hollywood appeal." — *The Hollywood Reporter*

"*Until the Last Star Fades* is an incredibly moving story of love, relationships, and celebrating the time you have… Read this novel and your heart will thank you." — *Hypable*

"*Until the Last Star Fades* is such a beautiful romance…this book has a lot of heart. I cried multiple times." — *Ashley Spivey*

"*Until the Last Star Fades* will make you laugh, swoon & probably cry, but that's okay. The best books are those that make you feel all the feels and Middleton's latest is no exception." — *Kaley Stewart, Books Etc.*

Praise for *London, Can You Wait?*

WINNER FOR WOMEN'S FICTION
2019 Indie Reader Discovery Awards

GOLD MEDAL FOR ROMANCE
2018 Independent Publisher Book Awards

"A winner for romance fans…with the kind of sweet nothings hopeless romantics die for." — *Kirkus Reviews*

"*London, Can You Wait?* will both break your heart and make it swell. Sometimes in rapid succession, sometimes at the same time. And you 1000% should pick it up and read it!" — *Hypable*

"A passionate, witty page-turner. Middleton has written a delightful and worldly novel with interesting characters and romantic twists and turns!"
— Renée Carlino, USA Today bestselling author of
Wish You Were Here

Praise for *London Belongs to Me*

HONORABLE MENTION
Mainstream/Literary Fiction Category
2017 Writer's Digest Self-Published Book Awards

"Middleton's novel is a love letter to London…Prepare to be seduced by engaging characters, irresistible in their own quirky way, and transported by keen descriptions of the sights, sounds, and tastes of London." — *Kirkus Reviews*

Jacquelyn Middleton is an award-winning author.
She previously worked in television
and lives in Toronto with her British husband.

Say Hello, Kiss Goodbye is her fourth novel.

Follow Jacquelyn:
Instagram @JaxMiddleton_Author
Twitter @JaxMiddleton
Facebook @JacquelynMiddletonAuthor,
or visit her webpage at www.JacquelynMiddleton.com

Also by Jacquelyn Middleton

London Belongs to Me
London, Can You Wait?
Until the Last Star Fades

Say Hello, Kiss Goodbye

Kori! Say hello to LOVE! Enjoy! Best wishes, Jackie xoxo

A NOVEL

JACQUELYN MIDDLETON

KIRKWALL BOOKS

KIRKWALL BOOKS

USA – CANADA - UK

This book is a work of fiction. Names, characters, places and incidents either are the product of the author's imagination or are used fictitiously. Any resemblance to actual persons, living or dead, business establishments, events or locales is entirely coincidental.

Say Hello, Kiss Goodbye

ISBN: 978-1-9992753-0-3
Copyright © 2020 Jacquelyn Middleton
First Paperback Edition, November 2020

For Zoey,

Ours was my favorite love story. x

DEAR READERS,

Say Hello, Kiss Goodbye is a sexy, contemporary romance.

Leia and Tarquin's story is a standalone that takes place in the same 'world' as my three previous books. Leia first appears in *Until the Last Star Fades* while Tarquin shows up in *London, Can You Wait?* —both as secondary characters.

Enjoy!

Content warnings: coarse language, open-door sex scenes, mental health challenges, and absolutely zero references to pandemics*, hand sanitizers, or face masks.

P.S. I've included a glossary at the back of the book to explain a few terms that might not be familiar to all readers.

Love music? You can find the *Say Hello, Kiss Goodbye* playlist on my website at www.JacquelynMiddleton.com under 'Extras'.

* I write contemporary romantic fiction, and as an author, I've made the choice to leave out real-life events that do not serve my story. Case in point, any references to the pandemic of 2020. Living through it has been incredibly difficult, and often, heartbreaking. Friends have lost their jobs, some have lost loved ones. I don't want to write about it, read about it, or relive it ever again. That's the joy of reading and writing FICTION; it provides an escape from real life for both my readers and me.

ONE

"If you're brave enough to say goodbye,
life will reward you with a new hello."
Paulo Coelho

LEIA

London, Monday, December 31, 2018

"Leia? *Ley?*" A tense voice pushed through the phone. "Is something wrong?"

A sharp breath caught in Leia Scott's throat. "Uh...I can't see a freakin' thing!" Heart hammering in her chest, she dug her fingernails into the blue straps of the yellow shopping bag biting into her parka's shoulder, her coat's waterproof material still speckled with raindrops from the wintery deluge outside. *Is it a power outage...or something worse? It is New Year's Eve—you never know, these days.*

Eyes wild, her glance ran riot through the murky darkness, but the windowless warehouse offered no clues except for the fuzzy hum of the ventilation system surrendering with a whirring gasp. A hard swallow bobbed her throat. "Shit!" she snarled, her curse joining a loud chorus of *Fucks* and *Bloody hells* rising around her.

Flashes of light—cell phones waking up—dotted the dark, illuminating the frowns and creased foreheads of Londoners stuck in the Swedish superstore's maze of tempting impulse buys. The wine glasses and colorful cushions would have to wait a little longer for that special someone to take them home.

"Leia, what's happening?!"

Ignoring the concerned plea, Leia's shaky hand skated over a nearby shelf bowed with scented candles, their sickly-sweet aroma

1

of vanilla and waffles teasing her nose, further unsettling her stomach. She gulped a breath, then another. *Don't panic.* Being plunged into darkness, unaware of what was happening, unleashed painful memories and long-practiced coping mechanisms, but her heart still raced and leapt into her throat. *Whatever this is, I'm getting out of here. Right now.*

"Hold on." Leia pulled her phone from her ear and swiped the screen, switching on the flashlight while boisterous comments and an infant's wail echoed around shelves congested with vases and clocks. *I think the emergency exit is over there? Walk slowly. Be careful.*

"Are you okay?" The distant voice in her phone wouldn't quit. "Ley, can you hear me?!"

"Oh, shit." Leia put it on speaker and looked up, swerving around a precarious tower of storage boxes. "Sorry, Sarah. The—"

"Don't tell me! They ran out of meatballs." Sarah chuckled at her own joke. The baby of the Scott family by eighteen months, she always knew how to lighten her big sister's discomfort.

"If only." Leia groaned and fussed with the shopping bag's straps digging into her shoulder. "No, the power's gone out. It's pitch black. There's no emergency lighting, nothing…" Seeking comfort, she tugged on the hand-knit scarf looped around her neck, a recent birthday gift from Sarah. *I'm twenty-six and still get nervous in the dark.* "I feel so silly." She half-laughed. "My heart won't stop pounding."

"It's not silly. Not after what we…well, *you know.*" Sarah cleared her throat. "Just remember, Ley: nice…deep…breaths. Don't let fear win. And *don't* crash into anything. I need those plates in one piece!"

"Yeah, all right!" Leia shook her head, smiling wryly. *Typical!* Caring one minute, all business the next, Sarah always knew what she wanted and wasn't afraid to say it out loud, even if it came off selfish or pushy.

Children's laughter bubbled up through the dark. "Daddy, does this mean we can have MORE ice cream?" The sweet English accent of the little boy was accompanied by a swell of hiccuppy giggles. Leia couldn't help but grin.

Yeah, give us ALL the ice cream. It fixes everything. Well, almost everything.

"Ooh! Let's play hide-and-seek!" Another little voice bounced over the candle display, but his boyish glee was interrupted by a gruff shout.

"Attention! Can I have your attention, please!" A guy illuminated by his own flashlight waved a beefy bicep. Dressed in a blue and yellow polo shirt that strained over his pumped-up pecs, he squinted into the abyss and cleared his throat.

"Oh, Saz, hang on." Leia paused beside a bin filled with packets of tea-lights. "They're making an announcement."

The employee scratched his bald head. "The storm has caused a power cut. Our backup generator is now running, and the lights will be back any minute. Until then, please hold tight. We don't want anyone to fall in the dark, 'kay? Your patience is appreciated. Cheers."

See? Nothing to worry about. Leia let out a breath, her eyes adjusting to the dark. She killed her flashlight and returned her phone to her ear. "Did you hear?" The tightness in her jaw eased. "It's a power failure, that's all."

"That's a relief." Sarah huffed. "Honestly, today couldn't be more of a Monday if it tried. You're stuck there, Dad's not back from his run, and Jordan's hogging the kitchen."

"Aw, he's cooking? Lucky!" Leia shifted sideways, letting an older couple totter past. "Boyfriend of the year, there, Saz."

"Hardly. He turned up twenty minutes ago, big bag of smelly laundry. I've told him four times to get his machine fixed—"

"Or it won't be repaired by New Year's. I know." Leia had heard Sarah complain about Jordan's broken washer repeatedly since she landed from the States ten days ago.

"If he uses up all my hot water, I'll kill him. We've got appetizers to prepare, dishes to wash—"

"Sarah, it's only one-thirty or—something. Why don't you go

to the gym? Burn off some adrenaline." The two little boys scampered past, one bopping the other on the head with what looked like a stuffed dinosaur. "You've got hours before anyone shows up." Leia sighed. *And I thought I was a control freak.* Sarah was taking her own rampant perfectionism to a whole New Year's Eve level.

"I know, but Dad's meeting Jordan for the first time, and my work friends are coming over. I need them on side for that promotion—you know what it's like." Sarah switched gears, rolling back into Type-A territory. "So, you got everything, right? Tea-lights, two black storage boxes, eight turquoise plates—the deep ones. Like a bowl, but *not.*"

Leia yanked on the straps of the loaded bag, deepening its groove in her shoulder. "Yes, Sarah."

"They'll be perfect for the mini portions of ramen you're making—"

Yeah, only because you wouldn't shut up about it. Leia shook her head. *I hate cooking.*

"IF you ever get out of there." Sarah tutted.

Leia rolled her eyes and picked at the sloppy stitching on the lip of the shopping bag. *I should've stuck with my original plan, should've rescheduled my flight to Italy. No New Year's Eve party, no sister drama, no fending off guys she wants to set me up with. What doesn't she understand about 'I don't want or need a boyfriend—ever'?* She cleared her throat. "Look, *you're* the one who said your back was too achy to shop and stuffed an Oyster card in my hand, sending me across London to satisfy your weird Swedish homewares obsession." *I love her and would do anything for her—but sometimes I could gladly give her a slap!* "No good deed…" Leia muttered under her breath.

"Ley…" Sarah's voice dipped. "I *do* appreciate it, you know."

The store's lights came alive, albeit dimmer than usual, eliciting relieved *ahhhs* from frustrated shoppers.

"Power's back!" Leia blurted. "I'm near the checkout. I should be out of here soon." She stood up straight, her words flying without pause. "I'll text when I'm almost home, okay?"

4

"Great! Don't get lost!"

Leia scrunched her nose. "I won't get los—"

"Oh!" Sarah interrupted. "If you see slippers near the cash, grab me a pair?"

"Uh, sure. Gotta go!" Leia stuffed her phone in her pocket and stormed through the crowded self-serve furniture warehouse, her black combat boots and long, confident strides outpacing shoppers steering carts loaded with flat-pack bookshelves. She nipped around a cluster of high-backed Poäng chairs where the hide-and-seek boys—twins, maybe seven years old—slouched, waiting for their dad, and past bins boasting discounted Christmas baubles and colorful spatulas. Sarah's coveted slippers were nowhere in sight.

Pulling her shopping bag against her hip, Leia reached the checkout first and unloaded her haul onto the conveyor belt. A lanky sales clerk, all oversized eyeglasses and carefully curated man bun, stepped behind the cash register.

Leia smiled. "Hi, how are you?" She reached into a coat pocket, digging for her wallet.

The clerk chuckled, revealing a gap-toothed smile. "Good, now the lights are back on." He logged into his terminal and picked up the product scanner.

"You and me both." Leia nodded as he rang up her purchases. *I'll be out of here in no time. Maybe I'll fit in a swim before Sarah needs me.* Behind her, a muffled movie soundtrack grew louder.

Ugh, the Star Wars *theme.* Leia wrinkled her nose and pulled out her credit card. Despite being named after one of *Star Wars'* most beloved characters, she wasn't a fan of the movies. Her sci-fi geek parents, on the other hand, couldn't get enough, and named both their daughters after kickass female heroines, *The Terminator's* Sarah Connor the inspiration for their second-born. Of course, Sarah lucked out—nobody asked annoying questions when they heard *her* name.

"Hazza! Can't you text like a normal person?" A posh male accent bursting with playfulness drifted over her shoulder. Leia set down her card and snuck a peek, catching only a blur of white plush—a gigantic stuffed unicorn with a rainbow mane and silver horn—before the store employee claimed her attention again.

"Dammit!" The clerk chewed his cheek and glared at the terminal's screen.

Leia tucked her long blonde hair behind her ear. "I'm sorry?" Something clattered along the floor, hitting her boots: a cell phone.

"Oh, for fuck's sake!" the voice behind her muttered.

Leia turned, finding the smiling unicorn bobbing and swaying while the tall guy behind it wrestled with a kids magic kit, a stuffed green dinosaur, and a large shopping bag, its clinking contents threatening to join his phone.

He needs help. She bent down and her right knee bit back, pinching its dissatisfaction inside her tights. *Ow! So stiff.* Wincing behind her hair, she retrieved the unicorn wrangler's phone and slowly stood up, placing the still-talking device in the free hand poking out from the mountain of plush.

"Here you go." She half-smiled, her glance jumping from the silver ring on his left thumb to the few days' growth of brown scruff framing his amused smile. Leia did a double take. *Whoa. Flirty dimples, tall, handsome—someone won the genetic lottery.*

"Cheers, love." The guy's appreciative grin grew wide and bright, and his green eyes glimmered with warmth as he lifted the phone to his mouth. "Harry, call you back." He ended the conversation abruptly and reached under his wool coat, stuffing the phone in his trouser pocket. His intense gaze searched her face. "Hey, I'm—"

"Miss? I'm terribly sorry." The clerk's solemn tone yanked Leia back to her purchases.

"Uh…sorry for…?"

The clerk grimaced, his eyes darting from his terminal to the growing crowd of shoppers waiting to pay. "Our card system isn't working. The power cut must've screwed it up."

A flash of yellow and blue—the store manager—swooped in. "The network's down. Not just us, most of Tottenham." He met Leia's eyes. "We can only accept cash right now."

"But…" Leia pursed her lips. "I'm lucky if I have a five-pound note."

Jamming the magic kit in his shopping bag, the unicorn whisperer leaned over his fluffy prize. "Hey mate, any idea how long it'll be down?"

The manager shook his head. "If you want to wait"—he pointed over his shoulder—"you can grab a complimentary tea or coffee in our bistro, but you'll have to take your items with you so cash-paying customers can come through."

"Ah, bollocks." The guy huffed and raked a hand through his tousled auburn hair, falling just shy of his narrowed eyes.

Leia scowled in solidarity, spinning a gold band on the fourth finger of her right hand. *All this way and I can't pay? Great. Fucking great.*

The manager strode toward the waiting throng and cupped his hands around his mouth. "Excuse me, everyone…" His booming voice elbowed into conversations, his cash-only news deflating the post-blackout glee.

Shaking her head, Leia returned Sarah's New Year's Eve necessities to the store-issued shopping bag. "Well, I have no choice, then." She tucked her wallet away and looked at the sales clerk. "Will someone come get us when it's working?"

"Definitely." With an apologetic wince, his large glasses slipped down his nose. "Sorry for the inconvenience."

Leia gave him a tight-lipped smile. "It's not your fault." Hoisting the heavy bag onto her shoulder, she stepped out of line, not sure where to go. She wandered toward the occupied benches near the exit, a gust of chilly, damp air whooshing around the sliding doors.

"Worst timing ever, eh?" The posh voice turned her head. Plush dinosaur aloft, *Star Wars* guy wedged the huge unicorn under his arm, his attention straying back to the checkout, searching.

"God yeah." Shivering, Leia tugged her unzipped parka closed around her dress as loud voices spewed their discontent at the besieged staff. *Where should I wait?* "I have somewhere I need to be, but I can't leave without this stuff." She gave the stranger a head-to-

7

toe sweep while he looked elsewhere. *Messy hair and whiskers aside, he's well-groomed, confident—extremely attractive. Bet he knows it, too.*

He glanced at Leia. "I don't want to come back either." His frown released as the two little boys raced past. "Hey, guys, hold up a second!" His greeting was drowned out by their gleeful shouts about ice cream and the snarky complaints of several shoppers pushing past.

Oh? Those boys are his?

He followed the twins toward the bistro, shooting Leia a quick grin. "I'm dying for a coffee. Want one?" He nodded to the small seating area, which was filling up quickly. "Claim a seat before the hordes descend?"

Leia smiled softly at his upside-down unicorn, squished and peeking out from under his arm. *Toys—for his twins.* A dull ache wrapped around her heart, but it was overtaken by pain searing through her right leg, short-circuiting all thoughts of children and small talk. She sucked in a sharp breath and adjusted the weight on her shoulder. *Keep standing and my knee will be a mess tonight.* She looked past the guy's unicorn, past his mussed-up hair, wind-swept from the storm outside, to the few remaining chairs. *I need to sit down. Just don't tell hot* Star Wars *dad my name.* "Yeah, okay."

His face lit up. "Brilliant! After you." He shifted his bag's weight, keeping it close as they moved through the crowd. "Oh, wait. Where are my manners?" He stopped and tucked the dinosaur into his bag. "Hello, I'm Tarquin." He offered his right hand.

Oh, crap! Leia's stomach sank to the floor. *Introductions? How very British.* She forced a smile as the *Star Wars* theme blasted from his trouser pocket. *Shit! Worst timing ever.*

"Oh, sorry! Just gotta…" Tarquin fought with his pocket, tugging his phone free.

Eyes wide, she looked over her shoulder, her fingers toying with the rose gold bracelet on her left wrist that she never took off. The checkout was choked with irate shoppers going nowhere and the sliding glass exit was stuck, inviting an umbrella-decapitating surge of wind and icy rain into the store.

I can't leave. I can't escape Star Wars *hell.* Leia glanced at Tarquin again. *But I can change how I react. Be grateful this guy's helping you grab a seat.* She zeroed in on his left hand as he pressed the red 'decline' button. *He's got kids but no wedding ring. His boys must've been born before he was twenty. He can't be much older than me.*

Stuffing his phone back in his pocket, he extended his free hand once more. "Where were we?"

Use the old standby. Tell him your name is Lisa. Taking a deep breath, Leia reached out. "I'm—"

"Excuse me! Miss?"

Leia spotted the hipster checkout clerk striding toward her, reading something in his palm. "Miss Scott?" He pushed his glasses up his nose with his index finger. Then, she saw it in his grasp—her credit card. "*Leia* Scott?"

Oh, for fuck's sake.

"*Leia*?!" Tarquin's voice soared, joining his brows in reaching for the ceiling.

Giving the employee a nod and a "Thank you," Leia swallowed heavily, cursing her luck.

Two

TARQUIN

Leia? Bloody hell! Is she for real? Joining the line of customers seeking free coffees, Tarquin's smile wouldn't quit. *She's gorgeous and blonde and named after a lifelong crush! It's like fate or something.* A rush of adrenaline surged through his chest, taking his pulse on a joyride. "So, that's really your name? Like *Star Wars* Leia?" The words flew from his tongue. *I can't screw this up. I cannot walk out of here without her number.*

She grimaced, tucking her credit card in her wallet. "Yeah. Thanks, Mom and Dad." A half-laugh left her lips. Her attention was restless, wandering back to the checkout. "People think they've heard wrong and call me Leah. Either that, or they go all *Star Wars* geek on me. They ask where my hair buns are, if Obi-Wan Kenobi was my only hope…" She glanced up, her large blue eyes free of shadow and mascara taking in the menu posted above the counter, and sighed. "If I own a gold bikini."

Well, if she's going there. Tarquin raised his brows. *If she does own one, I bet she looks smashing in it.* He cleared his throat, his gaze reuniting with the beverages menu holding her attention. "So, do you…?"

Leia's lips pushed into a pout. "Do I what?" Irritation peppered her tone. "Own a gold bikini?"

Oops. Struck a nerve. Walk it back, Balfour. "Oh, no—sorry. Do you want that free coffee—or tea?"

Her chin dropped as she looked his way. "Uh, no. Thanks." A grin flickered across her face.

Nice save—still got it.

"I don't like hot drinks." She scrunched her nose and stepped up to the counter.

What? Who doesn't like hot drinks? "Oh, really? I love the stuff. I measure my days with coffee."

"You..." Her face pinched. "I'm sorry?"

"My coffee consumption—it indicates how my day's going. If I've had two cups, the day's a winner, work's buzzing, I'm too busy for coffee. But four cups or more"—he winced—"the day's a bloody slog. I always drink more when things need a kick up the arse."

"Oh. Right." Her eyebrows relaxed and she smiled at the guy waiting to take her order. A bubbly "Hi!" burst through her lips, but her friendliness did nothing to soften the harried server's scowl. "I'll have a soft drink—the apple one, please."

Tarquin nodded. "Oh, those are good. Refreshing. I'll get a coffee." *Third one today.* "Extra milk, cheers—oh, and two of those raspberry soft drinks, please." The server pushed off the counter in search of their beverages. Tarquin scratched his stubble, weighing what to say next. "At least *your* name is universally loved, Leia. Unlike Tarquin. Tarquin is a rich twat's name. Kids named Tarquin get beat up. Only a few of us survive five years of grammar school."

"Aw, really? That's horrible!" Leia let out an abrupt giggle and dropped her pound coins into the cashier's hand. "So that's why I've never met a Tarquin before." She returned her wallet to her coat's pocket.

He paid for his order and chuckled, twirling his fingers through the unicorn's fluffy rainbow mane. "And you probably never will again. 'Survival of the fittest' and all that. It's a bloody tragedy."

The cashier handed over a tray with Tarquin's free caffeine fix and the bottled soft drinks, and they pulled away from the counter. Leia helped herself to her apple beverage and took a quick sip, a gratified smile curling her mouth. "One cool thing, though—people *never* forget my name." She led the way, past tables of frustrated customers and chairs burdened with yet-to-be-paid-for shopping, and glanced over her shoulder, her hair pooling in her parka's hood. "I stand out—for better or for worse."

"Oh, you stand out, all right," Tarquin whispered to himself. *For better. For so much better, Leia. God, her legs go on for days.* He softened his cheek-aching grin so he didn't look like a lovesick puppy trailing after her.

Passing an empty table, she smiled back at him and pointed at the overstuffed bag hanging from his shoulder. "Your kids are going to love all that."

What? "Kids? Ah, no—no kids. Just me."

"Oh?" Confusion clouded her eyes as she looked at the twins stretched across the table in front of them, saving it. *The toys? Raspberry drinks?* "But I thought...those boys—"

"Nope. Not mine! Um, can you hold this?" He handed Leia the tray, readjusted the unicorn under his arm, and pulled the dinosaur from his bag. "They dropped this in the dark." He leaned over, setting the stegosaurus on the twins' table. "Hey lads, I found your dino friend."

Their eyes lit up. "Steggy!" One of the boys snatched the toy and hugged it against his unzipped coat. "Now you can have ice cream, too, Steg."

"What do you say?" An approaching male voice grasped Leia and Tarquin's attention.

"Thank you." The twins chirped, obeying their father's command as he juggled three soft serve vanilla cones.

"You're welcome." Tarquin smiled and backed up, retrieving his tray from Leia. "Shall we?" Setting it down, he claimed the last vacant table and charmingly pulled out a chair for her.

A gasped "Oh" escaped under her breath as she placed her drink on the table and stole a peek at the checkout again. "Thanks." A spark of a smile emerged but was quickly extinguished as she sat down.

She's surprised? By a bloke offering her a chair? Tarquin cocked a brow and slid his hand in his trouser pocket, retrieving his phone and setting it on the table. *Who does she date? Neanderthals?*

Leia rested her heavy bag by her boots, her focus shifting back to the boys, two tables away. "That dinosaur can't get a word in."

"I was like that." Tarquin lowered his bag to the floor, stashed the bottled raspberry drinks inside, and laid the unicorn on top. Quickly removing his coat, he hung it on the back of his chair and took his seat. "I was always talking to my toys. Don't remember sharing ice cream with 'em, though." His fingers roamed, loosening the knot of his blue and green tartan scarf. It complemented his navy cashmere sweater and the unbuttoned collar of the white dress shirt peeking out.

"When I was little, I thought stuffed toys had feelings." Leia removed her phone from her parka's pocket, leaving it beside her drink. "I'd go to the store with my mom and make a beeline for the Beanie Babies. They looked all slouchy and sad, lonely, like they wanted me to take them home. So, I'd tell them I'd be back when I saved enough allowance." Pulling off her scarf, she shifted one arm from her parka then the other, releasing the lace butterfly sleeves of her white dress. She looked out of place, her ensemble imbued with a whimsical elegance.

Wow. Tarquin's eyes widened. *That's what she wears shopping? It's beautiful.* "And did you? Go back?" Chuckling, he sipped his lukewarm coffee as his phone lit up with a photo message, which he ignored it. "How many did you end up buying?"

"Tons! Even the ones I didn't like. I've never been good with decision-making."

"Yet, here you are in IKEA, home to decision overload."

Leia peered over the edge of the table at his stuffed shopping bag. "Well, it looks like you couldn't make up your mind, either."

"Actually, I was on a carefully planned mission. Got everything I wanted." He scooped up the unicorn and opened the bag, its bulging polypropylene smothering his polished dress shoes. "It's for my niece, Ava. She's four and has me wrapped around her little finger." He rifled through a magic kit, several masks, and glitter paints. "I felt guilty leaving yesterday. We were all up in Scotland for Christmas, but I had to come back for work. My brother sent me a voice message this morning, Ava asking when Uncle Talk would return. She can't say Tarquin or Tarq, so I'm Uncle Talk. It's rather fitting, according to my family."

Leia smiled softly. "Kids are smart. They pick up on the smallest things."

"Quite." He returned the stuffed toy to the bag. "So, after my meeting, I came here for presents. I must maintain my status as her favorite uncle—not that I have much competition these days." He gestured with his hands in an open, friendly fashion. "She's in a magic and unicorn phase right now. She's a total believer."

"Aw, I was once." Leia tucked a wisp of hair behind her ear and picked up her drink. "Ava will love her…"

Tarquin smiled. *She's beautiful. The blonde hair, American accent,* Star Wars *references—she reminds me of Alex but taller. More confident.* He picked up his coffee. *I wonder if she's single—*

"…almost as much as I hate *Star Wars.*" She smirked behind her bottle.

Ooof. The geeky half of Tarquin's heart curled up and died. *She hates it?* He gulped his drink and swallowed his enthusiasm. "Oh! Well, I can see why you would. Me, I just like…the music—for my ringtone," he blurted, the desperate coffee-fueled lie curdling in his stomach. *Time to change the subject.* "So, what's an American doing in a London IKEA on New Year's Eve?"

"I wouldn't know." She sipped her drink. "I'm Canadian."

Balfour, what are you like? Tarquin flinched. *First woman you've fancied in months, and you're getting everything wrong.* "Sorry. I'm rubbish at guessing accents."

A toothy grin burst through her lips as she watched the twins, mouths smeared with ice cream. "Don't apologize. It's fine."

"I thought Canadians hated being mistaken for Americans?"

She shrugged. "Some do, but it's an easy mistake to make. Happens a lot over here."

"So, how long have you lived in London?"

"I don't."

Oh, bugger. Really?

Leia looked at the checkout, besieged by sour-faced customers. "My sister does, in North London—Islington. Dad and I are visiting for the holidays. Then I'm off to Italy."

Fuck, fuck, fuck. Tarquin fought off a frown and set down his coffee. "Lucky you." *Unlucky me.* "Italy's much nicer than Islington."

Leia chuckled. "It'll make a nice change from New York."

Wha—New York? Her words felt like a punch to the stomach. "You live in New York?"

"Yeah. Brooklyn."

What did I do to deserve this? I meet her now—when I'm back living here? "I just spent the last three years in New York."

"Really? Doing what?"

"Land and property acquisition for Manville Developments. They're based in London, but I was their man in Manhattan for three years. I moved back to London last February, was here till July, then returned to New York to finish a project. Now I'm home again, running my own business."

"Oh, that's great. Same field?"

"Sort of." *And here's my excuse to casually hand over my contact deets.* "I buy and redevelop abandoned properties—pubs, churches, schools." He shifted in his chair and removed his wallet from his trousers, pulling out a business card. "I love old buildings. You can just feel the history, all these old stories seeped into the walls, you know? The heartbreaks, the triumphs…it's like they're all still there, in the bricks." He offered his credentials across the table with a warm smile. "I save them from the wrecking ball, give them some TLC and a new lease on life without losing what made them special in the first place. That way, I hope they'll be around for the *next* hundred years."

"Wow. I love that." Her finger skimmed over the textured Phoenix Properties logo on the luxe card, her nodding approval dissolving into a slight wince. "But I'm guessing most of your rivals don't feel the same way."

"Yeah, adaptive reuse has its critics, but I'm holding my own. I've been accused of being a hopeless romantic—like that's a bad thing—but I don't give a toss. There are too many developers out there tearing down old gems to build soulless glass skyscrapers. London's skyline is rife with them."

"Like the Shard?"

"Oh, have you been up?" Tarquin leaned in.

"Not yet." She laid his card on top of her phone. "But I'm headed there tonight—champagne and canapes in the clouds."

Ugh, I knew it. His stomach dipped. *There was no hope in hell a girl like her would be dateless tonight.* "Wow, the Shard for New Year's—someone wants to impress."

Leia gave him a tentative smile and sipped her drink.

"The Shard's great. It's innovative and the views are breathtaking…" He paused, raising his coffee to his lips, but he didn't drink. "The building it replaced was a 1970s eyesore, so no one blinked when that was torn down. But if it's an abandoned heritage building like a school or warehouse beloved by the community, someone should fight to maintain its history during redevelopment. Costs a bit more, but I reckon it's worth it."

Leia sighed, her gaze sweeping the bistro, full of slouched shoppers wishing they were anywhere but there.

God, listen to me. Biting his bottom lip, Tarquin stared into his cup. *I've bored her to tears.*

A slight nod tipped her chin. "I agree. It *is* worth it."

Yeah? A flutter filled Tarquin's chest. He looked up, meeting her confident stare.

"We're such a disposable society," said Leia, returning her drink to the table. "If it's old or imperfect, it's 'Throw it away' or 'Tear it down.' But the past matters. Second chances *matter.*"

We're so on the same page! "Exactly!" His overworked grin took a well-deserved hiatus while he sipped his coffee. "So, what do you do, Leia?"

"I'm a dress designer. It's my dream job, but it doesn't pay the bills—yet. So, I work at the Metropolitan Museum of Art."

"Oh, the Met! Love that place. What department?"

"The Costume Institute. I'm a collections management assistant. I help conserve, exhibit, and catalogue clothing. It's pretty

16

amazing. Some garments date back seven centuries."

Tarquin blew out his cheeks before his jaw dropped. "I'd be afraid to touch them."

She widened her eyes. "I am! But I put the gloves on and try my best not to destroy history." She giggled. "It's an honor taking care of them, especially for someone like me who geeks out over historical dress and beautiful fabrics. But the Met isn't my passion. Upcycling clothing design—that's my passion."

"Upcycling? That's like recycling?"

"Kinda, but there's a difference." She lifted her drink. "If I recycle this bottle, it will become another bottle—something of similar value. But if I *upcycle* something, the new product is more valuable. So, with clothes"—she pointed at her dress—"I take damaged and unwanted garments and fabrics and rework them into wearable pieces. The result is something new, and hopefully more beautiful and interesting. Also, upcycling saves discarded clothes from becoming landfill. Little goes to waste—so in my own small way, I'm helping the planet by creating unique sustainable fashion."

Creative, enterprising, and smart—my kind of woman. Shame she's taken. Tarquin leaned back in his chair. "Quality clothing with a conscience."

"Yes, totally!" She sat up straight, her voice bubbly. "I want to prove that you can create eco-friendly fashions without sacrificing style and design. It's a challenge, but it's fun. And I love giving new life to old things. Like you, with your buildings."

He grinned back at her. "I can see that. Your face lights up talking about it."

"Yeah." She tilted her head back, owning it. "What can I say… I see beauty in the broken and forgotten."

You and me both, gorgeous. "And you made that dress?"

"Yep, finished it yesterday. Trust me, I don't normally wear a party dress for errands!" She chuckled. "I'm test-driving it to see how it feels, how it moves. In a previous life, it was a vintage lace tablecloth, a torn silk blouse, and a curtain."

"You're kidding me."

"Nope, they were all headed for the trash. I used the tablecloth for the sleeves, bodice, and overlay, added the silk for the lining, and the curtain became the skirt. Voilà, a dress was born."

That frock is incredible. How does she even know how to…? Tarquin's eyes fought to stay above her sweetheart neckline. *Someone's a lucky guy.* He motioned toward her dress with an open palm. "Well, it's gorgeous, and if you don't mind me saying, you look beautiful in it. I never would've guessed!"

A grin pinched her cheeks. "Thanks." She lifted her bundled scarf off her lap and smoothed the skirt of the knee-length dress. "People are often surprised an upcycled dress can look like something in a fashion magazine, but my ideal customer is in on that secret. She's bold, resourceful, a trailblazer, a risk-taker—and not just with clothes."

That's a great pitch. I bet that's how people describe her, too. "What's your label called?"

"Frill-Seekers."

"Ha! That's brilliant."

Leia beamed. "*I* thought so. My label is all about pretty, comfortable clothes with form *and* function. They're aspirational but also practical for people on the go. There's no point in creating a dress that pinches when you reach for a subway pole or bend over to shoot pool."

Tarquin raised an eyebrow. "You? Play pool?"

"One of my hidden talents—not that I have much time for it these days." Her smile dimmed as she wound her scarf around her hands. "I've been sketching, making samples, doing special orders through word of mouth for ten years, but launching a brand and attracting customers is tough. Competition is fierce. My instructors at fashion school tried to dissuade me. They said creating limited-edition dresses wasn't financially viable, but I like to prove people wrong."

You're not the only one, sweetheart. "Do you have industry contacts?"

"A few. I interned at a major fashion house for two years, learning the ropes, and I'm hoping to work with a friend who's an actress—but nothing's definite yet. For now, it's status quo: making clothing for me, my sister, and any clients that come my way while I build my collection, piece by piece."

I could help her. For real. He grinned. *Plus, it's a reason to stay in touch.* "You know, you should meet a friend of mine, before you head off to Italy. He's a designer, French-Canadian. He's got a small shop in East London that's going gangbusters."

"Oh yeah?" Her sidelong glance snagged on a burst of activity at the checkout. She freed her hands from her scarf and slipped her arms back into her parka. "But he's probably way too busy."

"Simon? No, he's always happy to talk fashion. You could visit his shop, share stories about Canada." He picked up his phone, barely pausing for breath. *Get her number.* "Maybe Si would even stock your designs. He's a smashing fella, you'll love him."

"Wow, that's really kind of you but…" Her slight grimace flew under Tarquin's radar as he typed in her name. "I can't."

Can't? Tarquin looked up, meeting Leia's determined gaze. Her fingers were picking at the dark purple polish on her nails. *Oh, you wanker, Tarq. She's known you all of twenty minutes. We're strangers in a shop—nothing more.* His shoulders deflated as he pasted on a smile, parking his phone. *Don't make this more awkward.* "Oh, forgive me. I forgot—you've got family obligations, of course." Busying himself with his paper cup, he swirled the cold, milky dregs around the bottom. "Holiday time is sacred. Loved ones should always come before work. I'm sorry."

Leia twisted her lips. "But you left your family in Scotland for a meeting down here."

Bollocks. I did. She listens, which is nice, but… "Uh, yeah, but with my family, sometimes you can have too much of a good thing." He downed the last of his drink and winced, staring at a sticky coffee ring on the table left behind by a previous customer.

"You should be an honorary Canadian."

"Why?" asked Tarquin.

She smiled quizzically at him. "You apologize too much."

"Hello! Excuse me?" The store manager, ruddy-cheeked and perspiring, lingered at the edge of the bistro. "The card system is back up. Please join the queues and we'll get your transactions processed as quickly as possible. Thank you for your patience." He jogged back to the checkout, a cluster of relieved customers, including the twins and their father, close behind.

"Well, New Year's Eve is back on track." Leia nudged aside her unfinished drink.

Tarquin nodded. *For you, Leia—definitely. The Shard with your boyfriend, champagne, fireworks, London at your feet. For me? Nope. A second date with a friend of a friend, dinner, a club. Probably an awkward morning after...*

Leia's phone lit up with a text beneath Tarquin's business card. "My sister." She grasped her parka, closing it over her dress. "I should get going."

Tarquin pulled the knot tighter on his scarf. "Yeah, me too." *Let her leave first, don't be creepy.* A server swooped in, picking up Leia's half-full bottle and Tarquin's paper cup. "Oh, actually, sorry—I'm not finished with that." The bistro employee shot Tarquin a pinched 'Okay, loser' glare, handed back the empty cup, and walked away. "I'll let the crowd disperse first." He hid his frown behind a fake sip. "Thanks for the company, Leia. It's been lovely chatting."

"It has." She stashed her phone and his card in a pocket and stood up. "Well"—offering a kind smile, she hoisted her shopping bag onto her shoulder—"good luck with your business. And Happy New Year!"

Happy? I wish. A dull heaviness settled in Tarquin's chest. "Happy New Year." He flashed a sincere grin. "All the best to you, too, Leia."

Sweeping her hair off her forehead, she stepped away, joining the rush of customers headed to the checkout. Tarquin awkwardly raised his empty cup as a fond farewell, but Leia didn't look back.

He slumped in his chair. *And she lived happily ever after—with someone else.*

THREE

LEIA

The next day

Nursing an orange juice and listening to Diana Ross through her headphones, Leia hunched over the table in her sister's conservatory, sketching clothing designs in the back of her journal. The welcome warmth of the late-morning sun hugged the shoulders of her flannel Christmas pajamas, fending off the chill accompanying the first day of 2019. The glass-walled back room, a small addition to the one-bedroom ground-floor apartment, lay empty and still, albeit cluttered with the previous night's excess. A stack of the just-purchased IKEA plates, now dirty, congregated on a bookshelf along with burnt tea-lights and discarded party hats. Empty beer and prosecco bottles and folded cardboard stuffed the recycling box by the patio door along with leftover sparklers, waiting to burn bright another night.

Sarah was still cocooned in bed, sleeping off the festivities, while her boyfriend, Jordan, desperate to make a good impression with their father, Eddie, had popped two extra-strength painkillers and joined Mr. Scott for a frosty New Year's Day run around Islington. They'd been gone for forty-five minutes—Leia wondered if Jordan was keeping up or tossing his cookies behind a dumpster.

She flipped the pages of her journal, her eyes detouring past her snoozing laptop, Sarah's framed London marathon medals, and the neat stack of her well-thumbed gossip magazines, then down to the floor and the two storage boxes she had purchased the day before. Filled with Canadian treats—boxes of Kraft Dinner mac 'n' cheese,

Rockets candy, Coffee Crisp and Mr. Big chocolate bars, and semi-crushed bags of various flavors of potato chips—the orderly stash was courtesy of their dad, who had arrived ten days earlier. Leia hadn't lived in Oshawa, a city east of Toronto, for eight years, but such home comforts always transported her back to her parents' tree-lined backyard, *Hockey Night in Canada* on TV, and weekend shifts as a teenager at one of her family's two businesses, a bustling Tim Hortons franchise in the center of the city. Twenty-two years since opening its doors, Eddie, a former National Hockey League goalie, still stopped in daily, splitting his time with the car dealership he had founded with his wife, Jenny. For his daughters, cars took a back seat to donuts, so when Eddie walked through Sarah's door before Christmas with the chain's famous TimBits in his carry-on, the donut holes were wolfed down within minutes.

For Leia, no more TimBits meant Canadian Smarties were the next best thing. She ripped open a box and shook out a palmful of the colorful candy-coated chocolates. *You're procrastinating again. Listening to music, sketching, eating junk…stop it.* She slid the candies back into their cardboard home and stared at the words written in ink twenty minutes earlier:

> **December 31, I was grateful for:**
> 1. *the lights coming back on at IKEA.*
> 2. *celebrating New Year's with Dad, Sarah, and Jordan.*
> 3.

Forehead scrunched in thought, she absentmindedly stuck her hand in an almost empty bag of Hickory Sticks, the smoky potato snacks a childhood favorite of hers. *C'mon, what else am I grateful for? You're not hungover—you have no excuse.* She stuffed a handful of savory goodness in her mouth and chewed slowly, hoping something—anything—would pop into her head. *Why is this so hard?* She flipped a few pages to the front of the journal, desperate for inspiration, and read the first entry from Christmas Day, her birthday.

December 25, I was grateful for:
1. *spending my birthday/Christmas with Dad and Saz.*
2. *food.*
3. *no more jet lag.*

Her eyes jumped to the next entry.

December 26, I was grateful for:
1. *yummy turkey sandwiches.*
2. *binge-watching all of* Poldark. *Aidan Turner is yummier than turkey sandwiches!*
3. *a day spent in flannel Christmas pajamas. Even if they're in Saz's signature blue.*

December 27 was completely blank.

December 28 was half-assed with only *binge-watching more* Poldark *(should I visit Cornwall while I'm here?)* written on the first line.

The next two days were untouched. Leia had fallen off the gratitude wagon—but had she really been on it?

Before the holidays, Leia's therapist had made her promise one thing—to keep a gratitude journal. "It will help diminish toxic emotions. It will ease your depression and anxiety," she'd said. But finding time to do the homework stirred up more anxiety, not less, and the longer Leia sat cursing the blank lines in the cute zippered journal with the Brooklyn Bridge on the cover, the guiltier she felt. *Gotta love the irony...*

Her gaze leapt to the window sill in front of her and a glittery noisemaker, its golden streamers sadly splayed and torn. *Out with the old, in with the new, so they say.* Waking up her laptop, her fingers swept the trackpad and opened photo albums stuffed with New Year's Eve memories: 2013, 2014, and 2015 in Pittsburgh, and 2016 and 2017 in New York. Over the years, the cities, faces, and multi-million dollar homes had changed, but the parties remained much the same, offering chef-catered cuisine, premium alcohol, and decadent desserts—everything Leia and her friends desired except a midnight kiss from their partners. Such was the life of a girlfriend or wife of a NHL player when their team had a New Year's Eve road game. The league never stopped for "Auld Lang Syne" a reality Leia had endured, thanks to Tyler McClelland, her first love and recent ex-husband.

Diana Ross's "Upside Down" filled her headphones, and Leia sucked in a breath, selecting New Year's 2014—the night she sat in the stands watching twenty-two-year-old Tyler, an offensive defenseman for Pittsburgh, score the winning goal in a nail-biting 3-2 home win over Carolina. Afterward, the loved-up pair went out for a late dinner to celebrate. *Four years feels like a lifetime ago.* Leia clicked through her memories, an unsettled heaviness tightening her chest. First up, a photo brimming with youthful passion—Leia, all smiles entering her favorite Japanese restaurant, wearing a beloved upcycling design (a knee-length cocktail dress with a plunging neckline and bell sleeves created from meadow green velvet curtains), and holding hands with a beaming Tyler, immaculately dressed in a fitted charcoal gray suit, his blond hair still damp from his post-game shower. *We looked so amazing that night.*

She opened another photo: their secluded table romantically lit with candles. *They always saved that corner for us.*

Leia's finger paused over the trackpad, but her heartbeat had already broken into a sprint. *There's no stopping now.* She clicked. There he was, Tyler, the love of her life—the boy she had met at fifteen, the man she had followed to Pittsburgh for college at nineteen—on bended knee, a three-carat Tiffany dazzler in his hands. *He was my meant-to-be. The one.* Her jaw clenched as she enlarged photos of her tearful New Year's "yes" and their romantic clinch. *But I was one of many—so many—you fucking liar!*

More clicks and she careened into their 2015 wedding album and the photos of a lavish mid-July affair in Toronto's famous hilltop castle. Leia was twenty-two, Tyler a year older. *If I had known what was to come...* She landed on a black and white photo snapped while she happy-cried through her vows surrounded by teary-eyed friends and family.

I, Leia, take thee Tyler, to be my wedded husband, to have and to hold, from this day forward, for better, for worse, for richer, for poorer... A sour expression pinched her lips. *...in Pittsburgh and in New York, to love and to cheat, til divorce us do part...*

She slumped in her chair, glaring at the screen. *You heartless piece of shit.* Her pulse pounded, outpacing the music filling her ears. Together for ten years, married for three, separated for four months, and divorced for two. *You broke me. You stole the best of me and now I'm someone I don't recognize anymore—someone who believes nothing lasts forever and there's no such thing as true love.* She gulped back a sob and trembled. *At least I know better now. I won't be hurt again.*

Taking in a stuttering breath, she let it go and inhaled another, her watery eyes drifting from her laptop to Sarah's shelves, her sister's potted orchids, and a beloved childhood moment lovingly captured in a blue IKEA frame: the sisters, aged three and a half and five, hugging their mother in front of an iconic London telephone box. *I miss happier times. Just look at us in our matching Spice Girls tees. We were super cute. And Mom...so beautiful.* The wistful memory melted Leia's frown. *A guy's love isn't everything. I have the love of my sister and Dad. I have my career, my health. My an-*

ger at Tyler blinds me sometimes. I forget that I have so much. She blew out her cheeks. *I've gotta be more mindful, more grateful...I need to take these journal entries seriously, starting NOW.*

She picked up her pen. *Okay, I need one more thing. Think, Leia, think. Every entry, every line has to count, otherwise I'll—no. No, I won't slip back! This year will be different. This year will be great.*

A hand pressed the back of Leia's arm. *Fuck!* With a gasp, she jolted in her chair, her finger panic-clicking to another wedding photo.

"What are you doing?" Sarah's loud, accusatory tone infiltrated Leia's disco inferno.

She dropped her pen and yanked off her headphones. "Having a heart attack. Jesus, Saz!"

"You would've heard me if your music wasn't so loud." Pushing the hand rim of her wheelchair, Sarah rolled closer. "Diana Ross, eh? God, Mom loved her." She nudged her tortoise shell glasses up her nose and yawned. "I need caww—ffeeeee." Blinking through her sleepy daze, the younger Scott sister leaned into the screen, squinting her large doe eyes. "Wedding photos? Seriously, Ley? So much for not pining."

"I'm not. You *know* I'm not."

"So, what's this for?"

"My gratitude journal." Leia rested the headphones in her lap. "I'm stuck. I need inspiration. I thought hating Ty might spark...I don't know."

"Glad he's good for something." Sarah rubbed her puffy eyelids, her glasses bobbing into her long blonde bangs. She tilted her head back and spoke through another molar-flashing yawn. "He's...such...a douche."

Leia gathered her hair into a ponytail, a frown trespassing across her face.

Sarah pursed her lips. "Your hair's grown crazy long."

"Yeah, I desperately need a trim." Leia examined her ends and let out a long sigh, staring back at her laptop screen. "I hate living with regrets."

"I wish you'd listened to me."

"I wish I'd listened to a lot of people." She flipped her hair over her shoulder.

"Well, better late than never, eh?" Sarah's expression softened. "It was harsh, but that website *was* right." Reading American gossip blogs and magazines was a habit Sarah indulged in regularly.

Leia narrowed her eyes. "About what?"

"You *know*—dying your gorgeous red hair. No wonder you're having regrets. Those photos"—Sarah cringed, shaking out her hand and the numbness that often plagued her fingers in the morning— "not your best look, put it that way."

Says the woman who wears only blue clothes. "Jeez, thanks a lot! I was talking about Tyler, not my hair!"

"Oh." Sarah gulped. "Well, it's just—blonde, you know... washes you out."

"I know! You told me four months ago when I first did it." *I'm still not used to it—not that I'm telling her that.* Shaking her head, Leia escaped into her journal, leaving Sarah to peruse the Canadian goodies. *I dyed it to disappear, but a lot of good it did. They still tracked me down at the hospital.*

"If your sister can't tell you the truth, who can, Ley?" Sarah pulled her bathrobe closed over her blue plaid pajamas, a cozy pair that matched Leia's. Their identical bedtime apparel, purchased by Sarah, continued an annual holiday tradition begun by their mother when they were small. "I'd kill to have Mom's fiery red hair."

"I'd kill to have your boobs." Leia's glance bounced from Sarah's enviable 36Ds to her pretty face. The Scott sisters always turned heads, but it was Sarah with her cheeky brown eyes and flax-

27

en curls who'd modeled as a child. "And your nose. Mine's wider—like Dad's."

Sarah nodded, scooping up a box of KD. "You got his crappy sense of direction, too. Only you guys would get lost walking back from the Tube."

"I wasn't *lost*." Leia curled her lip mid-shrug. "My phone app sent me down the wrong street."

"*Riiight*." Sarah snickered. "And big boobs and a slim nose are better than beautiful red hair. We'll just agree to disagree on which of us is the *lucky* one." A mischievous smile toyed with her mouth as her fingers brushed her wheelchair's hand rims.

I don't need reminding. "C'mon, Saz, you know I didn't mean—"

"Just teasing ya." Sarah steered her chair away from the recycling bin crowded with bottles. "I'll get Jordan to take that out. I think he felt a little weird drinking in front of Dad last night."

"But you told him it was okay, right?" asked Leia. "Just because we didn't..." For years, the Scott sisters had watched Eddie's struggle with alcoholism brought on by the depression that descended when an injury prematurely ended his NHL career at age twenty-nine. But last week on Christmas Day, Eddie had marked a hard-fought milestone—five years of sobriety. "Dad was fine with Jordan drinking"—Leia ignored the click of the flat's front door lock—"and he said as much."

"I know, but it's confusing if you've never been around a recovering alcoholic," said Sarah. "Jordan really wants Dad to like him."

"Like *who*?" Stumbling into the conversation, Jordan Zheng swiped perspiration from his brow and yanked down the zipper on his damp hoodie, exposing a drenched Nirvana t-shirt glued to his toned chest. He waved his hands in front of his face in an attempt to cool down but gave up, his fingers flying into his short dark hair.

"You, you sweat monster!" Sarah did a double take, a giggle leaving her lips. Jordan usually showed up at her flat immaculately dressed in a suit with nary a hair out of place, his job as a sales co-ordinator at London's most esteemed auction house to blame. Daily dealings with millionaires and billionaires meant business casual and 'dress down' Fridays were as foreign to him as running with his girlfriend's father.

He wiped his palms on his black Toronto Raptors shorts (a Christmas gift from Sarah) and clutched her hand. "Hey, I jogged with your dad *and* faked my way through a hockey conversation," he croaked, his Liverpool accent still raspy from a recent bout of tonsillitis. "Man, the things I do for love." Stooping slowly, his hangover-inspired wince gave way as he met Sarah's lips.

Aw, they're cute together. Averting her eyes, Leia picked up her pen, tapping it on the paper. *Almost a year in—so far, so good. Heaven help him if he turns out like the others. He'll have me to answer to.*

"Your dad—my god, he's a machine!" said Jordan. "I could barely keep up. How old is he, anyway?"

"Fifty-three." Leia chewed the end of her pen. "Where is he?"

"Popped to the corner shop." Jordan tugged at his soaked t-shirt. "Is it okay if I have a shower?"

"Yep," said Sarah. "If you're quick, you'll be out in time for brunch."

"If I'm quick, I can help." Grinning, he took off and disappeared into Sarah's bedroom.

Pen in hand, Leia stretched toward the ceiling, letting out a groan. "Is the pool on Caledonian Road open today?"

"Not sure. Check their website." Sarah toyed with the KD box on her lap, the dry macaroni rattling with each shift of her hand. "So…last night, you and—"

"Yeah, about that…nice try, Saz." Leia returned to her journal.

"Obvious, much? There's no way in hell your friend is getting my number."

"But you love British accents! And he really likes you!" Sarah worked for a small consultancy agency that provided accessibility guidance to London companies. Her coworker, Leia's latest fan, was one of seven colleagues who rang in the new year chez Ms. Scott. He was also one of Sarah's references for the promotion she was chasing. "You've got tons in common. He loves lip sync battles, hates science fiction. Oh, did he tell you he loves to skate? And swim? No wonder he's so fit."

"He's divorced with two kids under five."

"So? You're divorced and you love kids—" The sentence stuck in Sarah's throat. "Aw, sorry." She squeezed her eyes shut.

Leia's stomach pinched. *End this now.* "How many times do I have to tell you? I'm not dating. Not now, not ever." She abandoned her journal and glared at her sister. "Your friend could be what's-his-face from *Poldark* and I still wouldn't date him."

"Now that's just messed up, saying no to Aidan Turner."

Leia slumped into a sigh.

"I'm joking!" Sarah rubbed Leia's arm. "I worry about you, Ley. You're so far away in New York—alone—while fuckface Tyler sleeps his way around the city. It's not right. I wish you'd stay here."

"And, what? Finding me a British boyfriend would make that happen?"

"Why not? A charming Brit—London's got tons. Take your pick!"

Like I care. Leia stared at her journal and tapped her pen on the page, refusing to respond.

Frustration creasing her brow, Sarah withdrew her hand. "You're doing it again."

"Doing what?"

"You're letting what happened hold you back."

I don't want to talk about this. Leia scoffed and bit the inside of her cheek.

"Hey, deny all you want, but no one knows you like I do." Sarah leaned closer. "You're scared of falling in love again. You're letting fear dictate everything you do—"

"Your amateur Dr. Phil routine is *really* stale." Shaking her head, Leia chuckled sarcastically under her breath. "Is he even on TV anymore?"

Sarah huffed. "You're doing this so your heart won't get shattered again, and I get it."

A tightness seized Leia's jaw as she squinted at her journal. *Yeah, blame Tyler. Or blame my so-called friends who knew the truth and failed to tell me.*

"But putting up walls?" Sarah covered Leia's hand with hers. "That's not living. You're closing yourself off from happiness, from meeting someone really great. You'll end up bitter and alone."

"Being alone doesn't mean you're lonely!" Leia's raised voice and sharp sideways glance told her baby sister to back off.

Sarah pulled her hand away. "Fine. Be a nun. Let Tyler win."

For fuck's sake! "I'm not. I'm just saying no to dating and feelings. I'm not saying no to sex."

"Oh, really? You, Leia Scott, a woman ruled by her emotions, are into hookups now? How's that work? You've only slept with three—"

"Five," she interjected, her eyes glued to her journal.

"*Five?*"

Leia nodded. "A trainer from my gym last month. He was number five."

"Ooh, you kept that quiet."

With a loud exhale, Leia slammed down her pen. "Sarah, I know having a boyfriend is important to you and I'm happy you've found Jordan, but that's not what *I* want—not anymore. I want to focus on my career, my needs—not someone else's." *Yes, that's it!* She scribbled in her journal:

3. my independence!

She stuffed her pen inside and zipped it closed with an assured tug. "I'm figuring out who I am and what I desire, and right now, I just want to enjoy myself! And that includes sex—without all the emotional, complicated stuff that comes with a relationship. So, no dates, no friends of yours." Leia caught her sister's frown. "No offence." She pressed her lips together and pushed up the sleeves of her robe. "You might not agree, but it's the way forward—for me. And you know I can't stay. My life—my job—is in New York."

"It's part-time!" Sarah spit back.

"Sisters." Jordan laughed, arms full of clean clothes destined for life post-shower. "You two sound like mine." Sarah threw him a dirty look, but he missed it, busy handing a business card to Leia. "This fell out of your parka when I hung up my hoodie."

Oh, yeah. Star Wars *guy with the dimples and weird name. He was hot, but...* Leia curled her hand around the Phoenix Properties card. "Thanks." Once Jordan left the room, she tossed it on the table beside the trash-bound Hickory Sticks bag.

"Who's that from?" asked Sarah.

"Oh, some guy I met in the power outage." Leia snapped up the Smarties box, tipping the candies into her palm. "His ringtone was the *Star Wars* theme. You should've seen his face when he heard my name."

Sarah cringed. "Ew, creeper alert. Guys into *Star Wars* are so predictable. And then they wonder why you'd never date them."

"Yep." Leia popped the remaining yellow and green Smarties in her mouth.

"So…why keep his card?"

"He's got this friend"—taking her time, Leia munched through her words and swallowed—"a designer with his own clothes shop. He offered to introduce me, but…" Leia shrugged and flattened the empty candy box, leaving it in her lap with her headphones. "Then *Star Wars* guy will have my number and—"

"*And* if Jabba the Hut texts you, you ghost him! Stop being a goof. His friend might have advice—or connections. He's doing what you want to do, right?"

"In London. New York is different."

"Not that different." Sarah reversed her wheelchair. "You should call him. It beats being alone here while I'm at work." The apartment's lock clicked, stealing both Sarah and Leia's attention.

"Oh, I keep forgetting Dad's flying home tomorrow." Leia smiled as a tall male in a drenched hoodie and sports shorts closed the door behind him and strode down the hall. "Hey, Dad. Good run?"

"Yeah, best so far. I didn't get lost this time." Pink-cheeked and sweaty, Eddie winked at Leia, who answered back with a defiant squint. He gulped his neon-yellow sports drink and motioned with a nod to the bathroom and its roaring shower. "How's Jordan? He looked a little green."

"Nah, he'll survive." Sarah chuckled, nudging up her glasses. "You hungry?"

"Starving!" said Eddie, his blue eyes smiling as his eldest daughter woke up her laptop. "Eggy bread, Leia?"

"Please." She nodded and typed *Cally Pool schedule* in the search bar.

"And Kraft Dinner for Sarah, just like when you were little." Eddie swept his wet dark blond hair off his forehead and bounded around the corner into the kitchen. "Jordan said he'll have dry toast and tea."

"I'll help." Sarah followed, glancing back at her sister. "Ley's got a call to make."

Bossy little sis. Leia shook her head and hit enter for her pool search, ditching the bent Smarties box beside Tarquin's business card.

Four

TARQUIN

"I'm not *that* hungover." Leaning against Tarquin's marble kitchen counter, Lucy Hardy tugged a hair tie off her wrist and gathered her box braids into a loose ponytail. "You know, I can make toast without setting your flat on fire."

"Is that a promise?" Tarquin chuckled, tying his *May the Forks Be With You* apron around his gray Henley and dark jeans. "I appreciate you wanting to help, but I've got this. Really."

"Do you...*really?*" Lucy toyed with the hem of her oversized *Hamilton* sweatshirt, stretching it over the bum of her navy sweatpants. "I thought we'd arrive this morning and find Prisha here."

Don't. Tarquin exhaled heavily and strode to the opposite end of his expansive kitchen where his full English breakfast bubbled and fried. Tongs in hand, he turned the sausages on his large flat top grill and kept an eye on the pot of simmering baked beans, bracing himself for Lucy's next onslaught.

"Tarq, you can run, but you can't hide." A knowing smirk crept across the twenty-five-year-old's pretty face as she stepped up to the sink and ran the taps. "How many is it now?" She pumped the soap dispenser twice.

Lucy, I'm not in the mood. Read the room.

She glanced over her shoulder, hands coated in soapy bubbles. "You've been back a month and gone out with, what? Six, seven women? Including two of my friends, and not one of them made it to a third date. You say you want a girlfriend, but—"

"Lucy." Abandoning the floor-to-ceiling windows of his best

35

friend's lavish riverfront penthouse, Harry Manville scratched his blond bedhead and padded into the kitchen. Harry and Tarquin were lifelong mates, literally. Born on the same day in the same upscale London hospital, their friendship remained strong through schoolboy days at Ludgrove Prep and Eton, university degrees at Cambridge (Tarquin) and Oxford (Harry), and successful careers including Tarquin's four-year stint working under Harry's dad for Manville Developments. "Why don't you hop in the bath? You've always wanted to gaze out over London from Tarq's massive tub." Harry rolled up the sleeves on his black shirt. "Now's your chance."

Ignoring her boyfriend, Lucy dried her hands and plucked her grandmother's petite ruby ring, a Jamaican family heirloom, from the counter. "You're stuck on Lex, Tarq." Lex was Alex Sinclair, an American playwright living in London who was also Lucy's best friend. She nudged her jewelry over a knuckle on her right hand. "It's time to move on. She has."

"Lucy, for the millionth time—I'm happy for her. She's meant to be with Mark." He tore open a package of bacon, his eyes boycotting hers. "And I *have* moved on."

"Then why compare every woman you date to Lex?"

"I don't." *Do I?*

Harry nuzzled Lucy from behind, kissing her ear. "Leave him be," he whispered, before letting go and opening the stainless-steel fridge, removing a paper bag of unwashed mushrooms.

"It's only because I care." Frowning, she unwrapped a loaf of bread from nearby Borough Market and plopped it on a cutting board. "Tarquin can have any woman he wants, so why is he single?" Lucy leaned conspiratorially into Harry. "Think about it."

An impatient buzz rose from the pocket of Tarquin's jeans. *Leia?* He abandoned the fry-up, and leapt down the counter to the faucet, dousing his hands before wiping them on his apron. "Harry, watch the grill." Fingers still damp, he fished out his phone, spying a poolside photo. "Ah, for fuck's sake, Mum! Not another—I don't need this."

"Ooh, but I do!" Sliding across the hardwood floor in her fuzzy socks, Lucy plowed into him. "You wouldn't share last ni"—Her jaw dropped. "Holy eff!" A prolific curser, Lucy's New Year's resolution was to stop saying fuck. "Your mum—that's bikini goals, right there!"

Tarquin winced. "*That's* your takeaway? Not that my mother is texting bikini photos to her son?" His eyes drifted to the message below her photo.

Mum: Happy New Year, darling. Must chat soon!

Harry made an 'Ugh, mate' face and hovered over the grill, nudging the smoking sausages with a fork.

"You have to introduce me to her one day." Lucy pulled the screen closer, her brown eyes studying the image of the beautiful fifty-something woman and the young stud wrapped around her. "That bloke is *hawt*—oh, jeez! He's that—"

"Yup." Tarquin chewed the inside of his cheek. "The fit male nurse on her TV series—the twenty-five-year-old. He's younger than me."

Harry scoffed. "She went on holiday with him? *The National Mail* is going to eat that up."

"Shit, yeah, but give her credit"—Lucy let go of Tarquin's phone—"Ibiza looks good on her!"

"Tell that to Ava, who missed seeing Grandma Kiki this Christmas." Tarquin chucked his phone on the counter, far from his brunch-in-progress. A neat freak, Tarquin's kitchen was tidy and crumb-free even in the midst of messy meal preparation. "It's one thing for me and my brothers to grow up in the shadow of Mum's selfishness, but..." He shook his head and glared at the bacon and sausages. "Ah, why bother? She'll never change."

Harry, always one to avoid an argument, cleared his throat and got to work, dunking the dirty mushrooms in a bowl of lukewarm water. "So, how was the club?" Every year, Harry's private members' club, Bespoke, threw a New Year's bash hosting an enviable guest list of actors, models, and royals. This year, following dinner with Lucy, Tarquin, and Prisha, the twenty-six-year-old traded his own celebration for a house party in London Fields thrown by their friends, Alex and Mark.

"We didn't make it." Using a fork, Tarquin rolled the browning sausages to the edge of the hot grill, making space for bacon, mushrooms, and tomatoes. "Prisha started to feel ill waiting for our car. She reckoned it was food poisoning and wanted to go home." He glanced at Harry, wrist-deep in water and bobbing mushrooms. "Did you feel okay after?"

"Yeah, felt great." Harry's eyes darted to his right and a nodding Lucy cutting thick slices of bread farther down the counter. "Have you heard from her?"

"I texted," said Tarquin. "She's feeling better, thank god." *But was food poisoning just an excuse to call it an early night? I don't blame her. Prisha is smart and attractive, but neither of us felt sparks. She's pining over a bloke from her work, and I can't stop thinking about the amazing girl I met in IKEA who, let's face it, I'll never see again.* Strip by strip, he transferred the bacon to the grill, the sharp sizzle a welcome distraction. "I got home at ten-thirty, had an aged Scotch, watched the fireworks from my terrace—it wasn't the worst New Year's Eve."

"Wasn't exactly the best, either," Lucy muttered under her breath, sliding bread into the expensive four-slice toaster.

"You should've come to London Fields, mate." Harry scooped the mushrooms out of the water, patting them dry with paper towel. "Alex and Mark did invite you."

"I know, but it still feels a little weird."

Lucy raised an eyebrow, her expression shouting 'I knew it!' "See! You're still hooked on Alex—"

"Lucy, please. Just drop it! This isn't about Alex, or Mark." He left the tongs on a plate and stormed to the fridge. *Wait.* He paused, his hand sliding down the handle. *Don't be a dick. It's not Lucy's fault.* "I skipped their party because I feel like the odd man out, okay? I envy what Mark has with Alex. Blimey, I envy what Harry has with you." He yanked open the door, escaping Harry's sympathetic nod. "I *do* want a girlfriend, someone I can be myself with…someone to love—someone who loves me back."

"She's out there, mate, trust me," said Harry.

"Yeah, probably in love with someone else." Tarquin shifted several yogurts and juices out of his way. "I'm tired of apps, dates that go nowhere, shagging *just because*—it's not me anymore. It feels…empty. Hookups were fun for a while, but now that everyone's pairing off, I—" *Fuck. I'm not talking about this.* He scowled at a pre-packaged red curry-for-one at the back of his fridge.

"I—what?" asked Harry. "Don't leave us hanging."

Fine. "I have this niggling fear I'll actually end up alone." *Shit. Well, that sounded sad and desperate, you tosser.* Tarquin grabbed a carton of free-range eggs. *Should've kept my mouth shut.*

"Well, you will be if you never make it to a third date. Stop being so picky!" Lucy licked butter off her finger as Tarquin's phone, wedged between his coffee maker and recipe books, burst into the *Star Wars* theme.

Mum, give it a bloody rest! Eggs in hand, Tarquin elbowed the fridge door closed and reunited with the stove. "Ignore her—"

Lucy pounced. "Good morning, Tarquin Balfour's phone! How may I direct your call?"

Her over-the-top business voice melted Tarquin's frown. He traded the eggs for tongs and checked their frying breakfast. "Don't fall for it—take away the air kisses and luvvie facade, and Mum's as East End as you."

"Pardon?" Squinting, Lucy covered her other ear. "I'm having trouble hearing…"

"Lucy, just take a message. Tell her I'll call her later."

Eyes widening, Lucy's brows slowly crept toward her hairline. "Your name's Leia?"

Leia?! Mid bacon flip, Tarquin's breath hitched.

"Bloody hell, who *is* this?" Lucy howled. "You're a freaking legend!"

"Leia?" Harry's mouth fell open. "Oh, mate, in your wet dreams!"

Pulse racing, Tarquin dropped the tongs on the counter and bounded past his best friend, his beckoning fingers urging Lucy to surrender his phone. "I'll take it."

She batted him away, skipping into the palatial living room. "Leia, sorry, it's a really bad line—are you calling from a galaxy far, far away?"

Tarquin raced after her, swerving around the bag of toys for Ava. "Lucy, quit it!" he hissed through clenched teeth. "Don't make fun of her name."

Stalling by the windows, she squinted in the sunlight and thrust the phone into his chest. "At least Leia's got a sense of humor—she's laughing."

Oh, god, I hope so. Tarquin wrenched the phone from Lucy's hand and covered the microphone, his tight lips and darting eyes throwing her a 'Go on, do one' glare.

Lucy played with her ponytail of braids. "Chill, Tarq," she whispered. "All yours, tiger!" She slapped Tarquin's ass playfully and padded back to Harry, stood in the kitchen doorway.

"Babe, your toast is burning." Spatula aloft, Harry let Lucy slip past, his gaze settling on Tarquin. "I'll take care of the fry-up," he mouthed, then he pulled the glass door separating the kitchen and the living room half-closed, gifting his friend some privacy with a conspiratorial thumbs-up.

Please still be there. The salty, comforting smell of sizzling bacon did nothing to calm the butterflies in Tarquin's stomach. Clearing his throat, he lifted the phone to his ear. "Hello?"

"Tarquin? Hi, it's Leia Scott"—a giggle infiltrated her words like she was in on the joke—"but I think you already knew that."

He inhaled a deep breath, exhaling into a wince. "Ah, yeah. Sorry about that." His free hand dug into his hair, leaving chaos in its path. "*That* being Lucy, my best mate's girlfriend. She thinks she's hilarious."

"Well, she made *me* laugh."

Thank fuck. The knot in his shoulders untied. "So, how are you?" He curved into the cool window, its chill inciting goose bumps on his arm. His finger traced Leia's New Year's venue towering over South London. "How was the Shard?"

"Still standing." She chuckled. "I hope. I didn't go."

What? With a squeak, his finger stopped its skyscraper climb. *The boyfriend fucked up? Please say yes.* His breath caught in his chest. "How come?"

"Oh, we changed our minds and stayed in at my sister's."

We? Bugger. He swallowed hard. "That's…a shame."

"Yeah, but we still had fun. What'd you do?"

"A bunch of us went for dinner. Then I watched the fireworks from Tower Bridge—it's close to where I live." *Yeah, leave it at that. Best to be safe. As much as I like her, I don't know her.*

Tarquin had found that people—so-called friends and potential girlfriends—became more interested in him when they learned of his family's jaw-dropping wealth. The 1991 sale of the Balfour's oil business had cemented the family's status as one of the wealthiest in Britain, and from his teenage years onwards, Tarquin chased atten-

tion and popularity by playing the bon viveur with reckless aban-
don, throwing decadent parties, sleeping with different women every weekend, and diving into extreme sports around the globe. As a
result, people never saw the real person underneath the drunken-
ness, flirty behavior, and bravado—until last year. Until Alex Sinclair. She was the first woman who didn't care about his money or
what it could do for her. Alex's love and respect showed Tarquin
that his kind heart and thoughtfulness mattered more than an abun-
dance of zeros attached to his bank balance. It was life-changing,
shifting his opinion of himself and what he wanted in life—no more
fake friends, no more frivolous partying, no more one-night stands.

But losing her also triggered something Tarquin had battled silently on and off his entire life—depression. Not that anyone knew
about it. Not Alex, not even Harry. To friends and family, Tarquin
was the clown, a hedonistic extrovert: partying hard and climbing
mountains, never vulnerable, always in control. But sometimes the
world became too much and he found himself struggling alone, too
ashamed to speak up, terrified of being seen as weak, and the soul-
crushing avalanche of hopelessness wiped him off the map. Friends,
though, thought nothing of his vanishing act. Tarquin would often
disappear on a whim: off paragliding, gambling, volunteering in
Senegal building hospitals—anything to shake the dark clouds.
Weeks later, bruised but determined, he'd emerge from the rubble
with false tales of derring-do and half-remembered parties. His most
recent 'getaway', fueled by the sadness over his split with Alex, was
last June. He decamped to Scotland and built a backyard playhouse
for Ava, then spent several months in New York City working for
Harry's dad until plans for his own business and a renewed sense of
purpose drew him back to London in December.

His finger skimmed down the window, following the outline of
Tower Bridge and its bascules opening for a tall ship to pass. "New
York can have Times Square and its ball drop—nothing beats Lon-

don's fireworks and Big Ben chiming in the background. Did you see it on TV?"

"I did! I can only imagine how amazing it was in pers—" A muffled voice dragged Leia away. Tarquin couldn't make out their conversation, but the person's tone pinched with impatience.

"Saz, I know." Sounding exasperated, Leia rejoined the call. "Sorry, Tarquin. I have to run. Brunch is ready." Her sigh caressed his ear. "But before I go, I was wondering if your offer's still open? To meet your designer friend?"

YES! Tarquin's pulse took off like a shot. "Absolutely!" *Flippin' heck! Eager, much?* He sucked in a breath, hitting the brakes. *Keep it in your pants, Balfour.* "Uh, just let me know when you're free and I'll arrange it with Simon."

"I'm free tomorrow after my dad leaves for the airport—so late afternoon, after work? I know it's short notice…"

Short notice is good! "Tomorrow's fine." He grinned. "I can meet you there, say around half five?"

"Perfect." Her reply was sunny and quick.

"Brilliant!" Tarquin stepped back from the window, his eyes sweeping across the river, taking in the bright blue sky. "So, you need details. Do you have a pen?"

"I do. Shoot."

"His shop is called Desjardins—that's his last name—and it's on Wilton Way in East London—Hackney. I'll text you the exact address."

"Oh, that's okay. I can Google it," said Leia. "That way I'll figure out the best route to take."

"It's not far from the Overground. Hackney Central is the closest stop, then it's a few minutes' walk." Tarquin looked across the room, catching a riveted Lucy peering between the glass door and the doorjamb, brows scrunched and a ketchup bottle in her hand. She mouthed, "Simon's shop?"

Tarquin gave her a fleeting nod then glanced back down to the swarm of tourists on the bridge. "I'll text him this afternoon and let him know to expect us."

"Thanks, Tarquin. This is really kind of you."

"Hey, happy to help. See you tomorrow." Ending the call, an easy smile monopolized his face. *Yes! So much can change in twenty-four hours.* His thumb skipped over the screen, saving Leia's contact details as a savory aroma urged him back to the kitchen. Chin up, he sprang back into the fray, stashing his phone on a shelf away from the mess of eggshells and baked bean splotches left on the counter in Harry and Lucy's wake.

"Another American, eh?" Lucy crunched a sliver of bacon and shot a look at her boyfriend frying eggs an elbow away.

"Nope." Tarquin squeezed past, checking their grilled breakfast. Another minute and it would be ready to serve. "She's Canadian."

"I'm all for unique dates, but Simon's shop?" Harry raised an eyebrow. "Balfy, that's a bit random, even for you."

"That's because it's not a date. She has a boyfriend and lives in New York." He shrugged. "She's a fashion designer, just starting out—I thought Si might be able to help her. I was just being nice."

"Yeah, because you fancy her." Lucy waved a greasy spatula his way. "She's blonde, right?"

I know where this is going. Tarquin pressed his lips together and dove into a cupboard, removing three large plates for their full English breakfast.

"Oh, god help us." Lucy smirked. "Trade fashion for playwriting and she *is* like Alex."

And what if she is? Is that so bad? Tarquin dipped his fingers underneath the neck of his t-shirt, scratching his chest. *Alex meant everything to me, but her heart was never really mine.*

"Is this that girl you met in the blackout?" Harry's question earned a terse nod from Tarquin in return.

"Bloody typical!" Lucy laughed, shoveling tomatoes and mushrooms on their plates. "Normal people go to IKEA for bookshelves and come out with tea-lights and wine glasses. Only Tarquin could stop in for a unicorn but cart away a girl named fucking Leia!"

Tarquin smiled and inched past her. He lifted the baked beans off the cooktop, setting the warm pot on a cork trivet. "Glad to see you're sticking to your New Year's resolution, *Lu*." Lucy hated when people shortened her name.

She scowled. "But how's yours going, eh? Finding a *girlfriend*, wasn't it?"

Tilting his head, he exhaled heavily and grabbed a large spoon. "She's not my girlfriend…she's not my *anything*."

"Tarquin, I only take the piss because I care. I know you're lonely and I want to help." She rubbed her eyebrow with the back of her hand. "Do you want my honest opinion?"

"Do you ever give anything but?" Tarquin snickered. Lucy rarely censored herself.

"I got goose bumps when she told me her name." She waved a spatula excitedly. "It's a freakin' *sign*, Balfour!"

Funny. That's what I thought…at first.

"Superstitious Lucy strikes again." Harry chuckled, rescuing the spatula from her grip.

"Shut up, Haribo. I'm being serious!" Lucy bumped Tarquin with her hip. "No one loves *Star Wars* more than you, right? It's like she was meant to find you, yeah? So, be there for her, help her out, and then pray she dumps the boyfriend." Lucy's bright eyes leapt to Harry, sliding eggs onto their plates. "And *fuck* the odds!" She beamed. "Sometimes a cute random can turn into the love of your bloody life."

FIVE

LEIA

Should I text him again? Walking briskly, hugging a pot of bright red, orange, and yellow primroses against her parka, Leia exited the map on her phone and checked the time—5:47 p.m. "Shoot!" Mid-shiver, a puff of warm breath escaped her lips as a jumble of jitters wrestled with the adrenaline flooding her chest. *Of all days to get lost—and be late!*

She hurried along Wilton Way, a quaint street of Victorian terrace houses and three-story buildings tucked into a sleepy corner of Hackney. The road was quiet apart from a few locals, bundled up in coats and wooly scarves, dashing into a small family-run corner shop. The evening's icy damp chilled Leia to the bone. *Twenty minutes figuring out what dress to wear and I still pick the wrong one. I wish I put on the wool A-line instead of leaving it in my suitcase.* Venturing a peek beyond her fake fur-trimmed hood, her eyes hopped along the numbers of the shops—67, 65, 61—a trendy wine merchant, a hip hair salon, and a secondhand clothing store. *The street's exactly as it appears online. Desjardins must be close.*

Two doors down, a window display depicting an eccentric Parisian garden party told her she was in the right place. *Desjardins—right! French for 'of the gardens'.* Small boxwood trees trimmed to symmetrical perfection shared the spotlight with stone pots of deep purple dahlias, their blooms complementing the lavender rosette shift dresses worn by two chic mannequins playing croquet.

This is it, then! Exhaling a deep breath, Leia slipped off her hood and pulled on the door handle. *Cute! It's shaped like scissors.*

The jingling of a silver bell hung high on the door announced her arrival, but no friendly faces or inviting music greeted her. The boutique stood eerily quiet.

Where is everybody? Her stomach tensed. She gingerly looked past two racks of colorful dresses, spotting the sales desk, tidy and deserted. No Tarquin, no Simon—no one. "Hello? Anyone here?"

The only response came from outside, a e-bike buzzing down the street.

Tarquin's doing me a favor and I pay him back by being late. Leia set the flowers on a display table and checked her phone. *No texs. Shoot.* Sweat threatening her brow, she yanked down her parka's zipper and untied her scarf. *Maybe he sent an email?* She opened her inbox and found a message from Violetta, her boss at the Costume Institute.

Full-Time Position—Collections Management

The words mocked her, raising a sour taste in her throat. That subject line had invaded her inbox twice before, and both times Leia had learned the job she desperately wanted and felt she deserved had gone to someone else—first to a younger coworker, and then to a guy with enviable contacts but questionable experience. Staring at the message, she swallowed again. *Same shit, different day? Just...find out.* She tapped the screen.

From: Violetta Hobbs
To: Leia Scott
Date: Sent today at 12:54 p.m.
Subject: Full-time Position – Collections Management

Dear Leia,
Happy New Year! I hope Italy is treating you well, but not too well because New York City needs you. We've been granted approval to hire another full-time collections management assistant

and interviews are happening this week. Would you be available for a Skype interview this Friday (January 4) at 1 p.m. ET? Please advise at your earliest convenience.

Best, Violetta

For a moment, Leia forgot AWOL Tarquin and Simon, and giddily dashed off an emailed *Yes* and *Thank you*. She then texted "I'm here" to Sarah, letting her know she had arrived safely, but the moment she hit send, butterflies swarmed her belly. Whether she'd stick around for much longer, she wasn't sure.

"Can I help you?" A sleepy Yorkshire accent quieted Leia's trepidation. A twenty-something brunette sporting a mussed-up bob and a sickly green pallor stood beside an antique glass case holding cocktail rings hostage. "Sorry, was in the back." The woman blinked her feathery false eyelashes and clutched the skirt of her long pink gown with two hands, lifting it so the material didn't drag along the tile floor. She wore a fuzzy cardigan over top—in clashing green—giving her the appearance of a little girl playing dress up with whatever random clothes she had found in her mother's closet. Leia almost expected to see her traipsing around in heels four sizes too big, but nope—she was wearing chunky platform sneakers.

"Hi." Leia smiled, adjusting the strap of her purse on her shoulder. "I'm supposed to meet Tarquin and Simon here."

The shop girl's eyebrows twitched. "Oh, *you're* Leia." Her response sounded like an accusation.

Not the friendliest. Leia's nod slipped into a grimace. "I'm a little late. The Overground train—"

"We were supposed to close at half five." Dress hiked up, the woman stomped past Leia and flipped the 'Closed' sign on the door.

Shoot. She had to stay because of me.

"Tarquin needed coffee. They'll be back soon. Then, I can *go*." The woman clomped behind the sales desk, planting herself on a wooden chair. She gulped a large mouthful of a neon-orange energy drink and crumpled facedown onto the desk.

O-kay. Someone's not in the mood for chit-chat.

The door's bell jangled and a burst of cold air sailed up the back of Leia's tights, the breeze flirting with the hem of her black dress.

"Ah, here you are!" Pink-cheeked and grinning above his blue and green tartan scarf, Tarquin held a steaming coffee in his hand. Behind him, a tall guy with a close-cropped moustache and beard and short brown hair shut the boutique's door.

Oh, thank god—he's not pissed off. Leia smiled. "Hi!"

Tarquin nodded. "It's so lovely—"

"Simon!" Hollering over Tarquin's greeting, the employee came alive, rising from the desk. "Freddie rang twice. Said your mobile's off." She grabbed her retro ski jacket from the coat rack, jamming her arms down the sleeves.

"Oh, right! Cheers, Spencer." Simon retrieved his phone from the pocket of his dark jeans, giving a smile and a "Sorry" to Leia, and began checking for missed voicemails. "Any sales while I was out?"

"Nope."

Yeah, 'cause you were in the back room. Leia smiled to herself, and then at Tarquin, who smirked back.

"Well, thanks for today," said Simon, listening to his message. "You're a lifesaver, Spence."

"That's me." Spencer squeezed past, ignoring Leia and Tarquin. "You can pay me in prosecco next weekend. Laters." Her hasty exit out the door ushered in another gust of brisk air from Wilton Way.

"Let's try that again." Tarquin left Simon to his messages and moved closer, a glimmer in his eyes. "It's lovely to see you—again!" He extended his right hand.

His handshake was firm—like last time—but short. "Thanks for meeting me." Leia smiled as they let go at the same time, his grin and dimples a flirty distraction. *So attractive—and so not why you're here.* She shook her head, banishing such thoughts. "I'm sorry I'm late. I thought I gave myself enough time…"

"Ah, the bane of a Londoner—you're one of us now." Tarquin's gleeful swagger and kind words put Leia at ease. "The Overground gets all mardy when the temperature plunges. It plays silly buggers with the doors." He cautiously sipped his coffee before returning for a larger gulp.

"Mardy?"

"Oh…basically, unpleasant. Grumpy." Tarquin's eyes mischievously leapt toward the door. "Bit like Si's staff!"

Simon frowned, tucking his phone into his jeans. "It's a good thing Spence only fills in occasionally, but still, I can't have her being rude—or hungover. And, god—that sweater she had on…"

"Rude staff, tardy transit—welcome to London, Leia." Tarquin chuckled, unbuttoning his coat with one hand. "Just be thankful it never snows."

"Why, what happens?" Leia's attention hopped to Simon, taking off his jacket. Fit and attractive in his black jeans and gray cashmere sweater, he looked a few years older than Tarquin, closer to forty than thirty.

"London shuts down—wimps!" Simon laughed and offered his hand, his pale blue eyes eager and welcoming. "Leia, it's great to meet another Canadian designer."

No aspiring, just designer—I like him already. Leia smiled wider and shook his hand. "Same here. Thanks so much for staying late. To show my appreciation, I brought you a touch of spring." She scooped up the pot of cheery primroses.

Simon's face lit up. "Aw, thank you!" Collecting the blossoms, he ogled their vivid red, yellow, and orange hues and gave them pride of place on his sales desk. "I was just saying I needed fresh flowers for the shop. These are perfect."

"Gorgeous colors," said Tarquin. "Happy flowers, primroses."

"Yeah, I love them." Leia dipped into her purse. "Simon, I also have a little taste from home for you." She pulled out a small bag of Canadian potato chips.

Recognizing the flavor, Simon's jaw dropped. "Oh, *you* can stay!" He squeezed the crinkly bag, his grin growing. "I haven't had these for years! Wow, I feel like I'm a kid back in Montréal. Thanks so much!"

Tarquin craned his neck, reading the package in Simon's hands. "Ketchup? Blimey, don't show Lucy."

Leia's bright eyes scanned Simon's shop. "I love your boutique. The exposed brick, the beautiful Parisian garden in the window—Desjardins—it's perfect."

"Thanks. If the last name fits, right?"

Tarquin raised his coffee toward Simon. "Leia, you surprised?"

"Uh, surprised about...?"

"Si doesn't have a French-Canadian accent."

She smiled kindly. "Oh, a lot of Montréalers don't." She glanced at Simon, still admiring his ketchup chips. "I may have Googled you...okay, I Googled both of you."

Simon scratched his beard, shooting a knowing look at his friend. "Well, that's only fair because Tarquin *definitely* Googled you—"

"Si," Tarquin interrupted, playfully slapping him on the back, "you're such a kidder. Didn't you fake it, though, on your first date with Freddie?"

"Only the accent, sweetie." Simon winked.

Leia and Tarquin burst into laughter. "I walked into that one," said Tarquin.

Simon snickered and left the bag of chips on his sales desk. "Anyway, Leia doesn't want to talk about my love life. She wants to talk shop!"

"Literally." Tarquin set his coffee on a case filled with glittery accessories and shifted out of his coat, revealing a black suit, slim fit—Saville Row style—worn with a burgundy pocket square and shirt, and a black tie. He hung his coat over his forearm and unbuttoned his suit jacket.

Leia spied a hint of silk lining—a whimsical paisley pattern. *That's no off-the-rack suit. The tapered waist, detailed craftsmanship, and contrast stitching scream bespoke. He looks like he was poured into it. It's absolute perfection.* He pulled his phone from his trouser pocket and met Leia's gape with a smile before checking the screen.

Simon laid his coat on the chair. "Leia, why don't you have a look around while I batch out the day's sales? It won't take long. Then we could chat over a bite. There's a great pub a few doors down, if that works?"

"That would be great." She nodded, eyes skimming Tarquin lost in his texts.

Leia browsed Simon's colorful gowns, some in rich jewel-toned velvet, others in delicate sherbet-hued chiffon, many embellished with sequins that sparkled beneath the shop's twinkly chandeliers. *These gowns would look stunning on a red carpet.* Around the corner, shorter slip dresses and flirty skirts with intricate hand-embroidered designs—part of his spring line—lent a more casual vibe for Sunday brunch or an afternoon wandering one of London's outdoor markets. Simon's designs were fresh, playful, and somewhat *Alice in Wonderland*-esque, perfect for the woman striving to look beautiful and unique without taking herself too seriously.

"See anything you like?" asked Tarquin, his finger tracing the beading on a sleeveless champagne-colored dress worn by a mannequin.

"What *don't* I like?" Leia gasped, lifting the hanger of a fit-and-flare cocktail dress created from elegant emerald crepe and shimmery sequined tulle. She held it against her partially unzipped parka, the dress's hem falling an inch or two above her knee. "Simon's made so many beautiful pieces." She looked up and hesitated, capturing his gaze. "Do you ever bring your girlfriend here?"

Raising his eyebrows, he stepped away from the mannequin. "Well, I would—if I had one."

He's single?! She caught her breath. *Hmm!*

His eyes slid to the striking V-neck dress in her hands. "That one would look lovely on you," he said quietly before walking away down the aisle, leaving her to peruse without interference.

She studied his square shoulders and broad back, smiling to herself as she returned the hanger to the rack.

Transactions for the day balanced, Simon joined her. Wandering through his boutique, he answered Leia's questions about schooling (he had a BA and Master's in Fashion Design Technology from University of the Arts London), financial investment (a bank loan and an early inheritance from his parents in Montréal), and how long he'd been in business (since summer 2015). Originally, he sold clothes by other designers alongside a few pieces of his own, sewn in his workroom upstairs. But as months passed, shoppers began to swoon over his pretty dresses, and eventually the small corner they occupied grew to the entire boutique. Four years on, Simon now outsourced the production of his collections to a trusted factory in South London and had a steady stream of devoted customers. More recently, he had begun winning over fashionistas in New York—two of his dresses were big sellers on the Bowery, and much to his delight, he was courting interest from three additional retailers in New York and Montréal. He regaled Leia with stories about taking his destiny into his own hands, booking meetings in the Big Apple during a holiday the previous summer, and how his 'fake it till you make it' boldness was paying off. His clothing now earned him a comfortable living, and along with the rent from the apartment above his shop, he was paying back his loans. Simon was a risk-taker, and Leia found his career path both hopeful and inspiring. She also liked him immediately, his Canadian warmth, wry humor, and love of ketchup potato chips making her feel right at home.

Forty-five minutes and thirty dresses later, the trio decamped to the Prince George pub and a table by a crackling fire where Simon bent Leia's ear with questions about her upcycled outfit—a belted black shift dress made from reclaimed scraps of silk—and her New York fashion experience. She told them about her Master of Arts in Fashion and Textiles Studies from Manhattan's Fashion Institute of Technology, and in between bites of her grilled harissa chicken and caramelized onion pilaf (*so delicious!*) shared stories about interning at one of the city's most prominent design houses.

Opening the Frill-Seekers website on her phone, she showed off her lookbook of dresses, prompting Simon to ignore his potato gnocchi to scroll and pause, scroll and pause, his grin growing as each new image settled on the screen. "Beautiful." "Bad ass." "How on earth...?" As bon mots fell from Simon's lips, Leia's smile stretched wider and wider.

Waiting for the designer to come up for air, she enjoyed her meal and made small talk about London across the table with Tarquin. They danced around anything deep, and Leia sensed he was carefully taking his conversational cues from her. If she veered off course, he'd probably follow gladly. *He's charismatic and confident and has the most captivating smile. I bet he has charmed half the women in London.*

"It's great you're loving it here," said Tarquin, cutting a bite-sized piece of steak, cooked medium rare. "If you have time, I'd recommend the Fashion and Textile Museum in Bermondsey. It was made for you, Leia. You could happily get lost in there."

"I'd love to check it out." She nodded. "But I also want to get a bird's-eye view of the city. What do you think—London Eye or the Sky Garden?"

"No! Go Shard. It's higher, better—bigger! Bigger is always best." A naughty glint in his eyes, Tarquin lowered his fork and raised his ruby-hued boulevardier for a sip. "Or so I've been told."

Cheeky! Leia laughed and swept her hands through her hair, twisting it into an improvised bun before letting it fall around her shoulders. *His playfulness is such a turn-on. Maybe I should relax my no-guys-into-Star Wars-rule. Just this once?* "I guess I'd have to see it to believe it."

Tarquin admired her for a few seconds before he licked his lips and pulled away. He set down his drink and picked up his knife and fork, but Leia's eyes lingered, stealing every chance to check him out. His hair was unruly, thanks to the wind outside and his failed attempt at taming it when they sat down. The scruff he had sported at IKEA had been shaved, and strangely, Leia missed it. *Tarquin made an effort. It can't be for me, right? He thinks I have a boyfriend.* Her attention swerved to his hands. *Nails clean, neatly trimmed with no ragged cuticles—I bet he gets manicures. I like a guy who takes care of himself.*

Looking up from his meal, he noticed her furtive glances, his mouth breaking into a cocky grin.

My face always gives me away. Leia's pulse rushed, but she held her ground, refusing to look away. *Okay, then. You wanna play, mister? Let's see what you got.* She sat up and smiled back, silently challenging him as she trailed a finger along her collar-bone…back…and forth. *Flirt with me, Tarquin.* His heavy gaze wantonly followed her fingers and drifted to her lips, the heat of his stare replacing Leia's thoughts of dresses and playing tourist with visions of slow, deep kisses, his tongue teasing, asking for more. *Tarquin Balfour, never mind our London Q&A—what do you think of no-strings sex?*

"How is everything?" The Scottish accent of an exuberant male waiter catapulted Leia from Tarquin's mouth down to her plate.

"Great!" she blurted, dropping her hand to her lap as she flashed a grin. "Really great." Her spontaneous outburst and the warm flush creeping across her cheeks roused a soft chuckle from Tarquin.

"It's all good, thanks," Simon added with a nod, his squint glued to Leia's latest photos while his veggie pasta grew cold.

Leia's glance boomeranged from Tarquin to Simon and back again. *Everything IS good. If I asked, I bet Tarquin would hook up with me.* She picked up her sparkling water, taking a long satisfying drink.

Tarquin wore an impish smile. "Someone's thirsty. Another round, I think." He ordered more beverages from the waiter and somehow got pulled into a chat about the pub's quiz night. "It's packed out *Monday* nights? That's great!" The property developer kindly indulged the waiter's giddy enthusiasm and rattled off another question, his gaze escaping to Leia every chance it could while his hands gesticulated, punctuating a sentence here, a word there. "Well, meat platters make great prizes. You can't go wrong there."

A laugh stuck in Leia's throat, her eyes sweeping over Tarquin's broad shoulders and the loosened black tie looped around his unbuttoned collar. *He talks with his hands a lot.* Free of his suit jacket, his form-fitting burgundy dress shirt skimmed over his toned arms and firm chest as he moved, hinting that Mr. Balfour wasn't a stranger to the gym now and then. *He's gorgeous, kind, charming—a bit cocky, but he's kinda goofy with it, which I like. And his passion for his work is sexy as hell.* She bit her lip. *He would be one hot hookup—*

"Leia, you naughty girl," Simon whispered conspiratorially, leaning into her right shoulder.

Shit! Leia squeezed her drink. *Caught undressing his friend.* She gulped her water, stealing a moment. *Refocus! You're here for a BUSINESS meeting. Sleeping with Tarquin isn't on the agenda. But damn those dimples…and shoulders…*

"Hiding these dresses from the world?" Simon grinned. "It's a crime against fashion."

Oh, phew. Simon didn't notice. Leia swallowed, lowering her almost empty glass. *Professional rep remains intact.*

"They don't *look* upcycled, and that's a huge selling point."

Simon likes them! "Thanks! That's my goal."

"Do you use much dead stock?" Simon scrolled through the photos again. "A lot of the fabric looks vintage."

Ending his chat with the waiter, Tarquin's gaze strayed to Leia. "What's dead stock?"

"It's surplus material from garment factories and textile mills," said Leia. "They sell it off instead of dumping it in landfills."

"Oh, that's smart." Tarquin picked up his cocktail, enjoying a long sip.

"Yeah, the fashion industry is one of the world's worst polluters." Simon squinted at the screen. "If leftover fabric can be repurposed, it helps the earth *and* designers like Leia."

She nodded. "I also have an arrangement with a factory that sorts secondhand clothes. They know what I like and put aside a lot of vintage items for me. So, I mix those materials with dead stock and biodegradable fabrics made from hemp, organic cotton, and linen. I'm hoping to work with vegan leather, too. Frill-Seekers needs to be truly sustainable, so eco-friendly textiles and upcycled materials are the way to go."

"Do you outsource production or sew everything yourself?" asked Simon.

"Right now, I sew everything. I love being hands-on, but when demand grows, I'll team up with a local factory. I've already scouted a few places who share my vision for high-quality work."

"Well, you're doing an amazing job on your own. Your tailoring is exquisite. I love the ethereal gowns for special occasions, but your daywear dresses are gorgeous, too. I can see your customers going straight from the office to drinks with their latest right-swipe." Simon enlarged the photo of the dress Leia had worn to IKEA. "This lace one is spectacular. It's romantic but has a chic contemporary edge. And the butterfly sleeves...wow." He laid her phone between their plates and picked up his fork, finally diving into his meal.

"That means so much coming from you." Smiling, Leia set down her drink. "Your designs took my breath away. I can't see those New York shops saying no to you."

"Ah, a Canadian mutual appreciation society. My job here is done!" Tarquin puffed out his chest and tossed back a self-congratulatory swig of his dwindling boulevardier.

Simon halved some gnocchi, stabbing it with his fork. "One of the things I love most about your clothes is the one-of-a-kind aspect. It's exactly what niche shoppers are craving, Leia—something exclusive, personalized, *and* ethical. The $200 to $5,000 price range means there's a dress for every budget, too. You could really make your mark."

"I hope so. I'd keep my fingers crossed, but then I wouldn't be able to sew!" She laughed, scooping up a forkful of rice and tucking it in her mouth.

"Well, if you need somewhere to create while you're here,

you're welcome to use my workroom. It's cramped, but I have cutting mats, pattern tools, dress forms, an extra sewing machine—as long as you don't mind its occasional temper tantrum." Simon's pasta finally made it beyond his lips.

Leia chewed quickly. "Really?" She covered her mouth and swallowed. "Aw, Simon, that would be amazing."

"Wait"—Tarquin scratched his temple, his eyes bouncing up from his plate—"you're not going to Italy?"

Oh, right. I told him that at IKEA. "No. I decided to stay with my sister for the remainder of my vacation."

"Ol' Islington for the win, eh? That's brilliant!" The joy in Tarquin's voice raised Simon's brow, his eyes darting between the developer and the designer.

"Yeah, my sister's happy." *And so are you, it seems.* Leia popped the last piece of chicken in her mouth, oblivious to Simon's amused glance behind a forkful of pasta.

An old-school ring blared from Simon's phone. "Man, that's loud. Sorry." He set down the untouched mouthful and picked up the call. "Freds, hey."

Leia dragged her fork through her pilaf and watched Tarquin enjoy his steak. He met her eyes again and held out his fork, offering her the final bite-size piece. *Aw, he's sweet. And so sexy. If only we were alone—but we're not, and I need to STOP this.* Her heavy stare softened into a friendly smile as she set down her cutlery on her plate. "Ooh, I wish! But I can't." She patted her stomach. "Thanks, though." As she picked up her napkin, the seriousness of Simon's voice shifted her attention away from Tarquin.

"Freddie, it'll be fine. Just…calm down, okay?" Simon exhaled heavily. "I'll be there soon. I'll grab you a burger on the way…love you." He hit disconnect and blew out his cheeks, nudging his half-eaten meal away.

"Something wrong?" asked Leia, wiping her hands.

"My fiancé. Something happened at work."

Tarquin winced. "Aw, not again. Poor sod."

Simon exhaled heavily and glanced at Leia, his brows dipping apologetically. "I have to go." He tossed back the dregs of his pint and pulled out his wallet. "But you two stay, chat…"

Leia reached out, touching his forearm. "Simon, please, put your money away. I'll get this."

"Aw, thanks Leia." Simon stood and put on his coat. "Next one is on me." He stuffed his wallet back in his pocket. "And there will be a next time, right? You'll come over, sew some dresses? I mean it. Come tomorrow! I'm open at ten and would love company."

"Okay, sure. I promise I won't be late this time."

He picked up the bag of ketchup potato chips she had gifted him earlier. "Bring more of these, darling, and I'll forgive you anything!" Simon smiled and grabbed his scarf, wrapping it around his neck.

"Done." Leia laughed and lifted her glass.

"Cheers, Si," said Tarquin. "Say hi to Freddie."

"Will do." Simon waved and then weaved through the thinning crowd, his departure stealing the table's conversation.

And three became two. Leia took a long, leisurely sip, buying time. *Should I ask him? He's incredibly hot. But sex on Saz's couch? Er…no.* She swallowed and set her water on the table, her hands retreating to the bench and her coat pooled around her hips. *I guess we could find a hotel but…walking in there with no bags, booking a room for an hour or two, staff snickering behind our backs—ugh.* Her fingers gripped her parka, gathering it over her skirt and thighs. *Could we go back to his?*

"So…" Tarquin let out a heavy sigh and rested his cutlery across his empty plate. "I guess you'll be going soon, too? Your boyfriend—"

"Doesn't exist." A slow smile teased her mouth.

Six

TARQUIN

No boyfriend? All the air sucked out of Tarquin's lungs. He flinched slightly, a smile threatening to break loose. "But at IKEA you said—"

"I was celebrating New Year's with cocktails and canapes?" Her wince slid into an apologetic grin and a slow shrug. "Yes, but I didn't say who with."

"Didn't you?" Tarquin leaned forward. *I thought...* His eyes roamed nearby tables as if his answer would be found among boisterous office workers shaking off the day with endless pints. *No, it was me. I filled in the blanks.* "Ahh...I assumed..."

"And I didn't correct you."

"Why would you? We were strangers, filling time, right?" He nodded. "For all you knew, I was just another smarmy bloke into *Star Wars.*"

"Smarmy?" Leia laughed, her fingers uncurling from her coat. "You weren't smarmy, you were nice. I enjoyed talking to you—I'm enjoying myself now."

A cocky smile wiped away the uncertainty pinching his face. "Good!" His eyes bounced to the bubbles pinging upward in her glass of fizzy water. "Let's get you another drink, then—or a dessert?"

"I—" The chorus of the Spice Girls' "Stop" burst from her phone, pulling her attention to the table. "Oh, it's my sister. I have to..." She picked it up and hit accept. "Saz, hi...yeah, I was just going to text you."

Spice Girls? Fun, nostalgic, doesn't take herself seriously...I like it. Doesn't have a boyfriend—I LOVE that.

Leia's eyebrows furrowed at something said by her sister. "Aw, really?" She gave Tarquin a tight-lipped glance. "Oh."

She has to go?

"Yeah? Okay...uh huh." She swallowed into a nod, the tension in her forehead slowly easing. "Well, we're just finishing our meals, so..." She nudged her fork farther onto her plate. "Yeah, all good here."

She's staying? YES! Tarquin traced his finger across the rim of his glass and nodded along to the indie rock playing through the pub's speakers.

"I will. Bye." Leia lowered her phone and left it on the table.

"Love the ringtone." Tarquin lifted his chin, a teasing lilt to his voice. "I bet you and your sister fought over platform trainers and Spice Girls dolls growing up. Zig-a-zig-ah!"

Leia laughed. "And you probably slept in Luke Skywalker pajamas!"

"No, Han Solo!" *Damn. That came out a little too easy. I need to cool it with the* Star Wars *stuff.* He swallowed. "Just once or twice."

"*Only* twice, eh?" She smirked. "The Spice Girls were my first concert, right here in London."

"Really? You lived here?"

"No, our family flew over for a wedding in '98 and Mom surprised us with concert tickets. My little heart exploded with glittery joy. Girl Power—in person! Life. Made!"

Tarquin's gaze slipped down her blonde waves. "You went as Baby Spice, didn't you?"

"No!" Leia cringed. "I've always had this thing about being called baby. I dunno, it's... Even now, baby—babe—makes my skin crawl. No, I was Ginger Spice." Her eyes shone. "I had the

Union Jack dress and everything. We saw them again in Toronto a few months later, but Geri had left by then. I cried buckets, but Mom bought me a bag of Hickory Sticks and a glow-in-the-dark necklace, and I was all smiles again. Turns out, I was a pretty fickle five-year-old."

"Well, Ginger, let's spice up your life." With a sly grin, he motioned subtly to the server a table away. "Let's get you something more satisfying than sparkling water."

Leia waved her hand. "Oh, I'm good. Thanks."

"No, it's only fair I get a round in." He shifted the small pot of violas on the table, moving it out of the way. "What's your poison? Prosecco, red wine, champagne?"

She shook her head. "I don't drink."

What? He froze in his chair. "Really?"

"Rarely. I can count on two hands the number of times I've had alcohol." She toyed with the napkin in her lap. "I don't like the taste or how it makes me feel. But, please—don't let me stop you."

Hmm. No coffee, no booze. Tarquin propped his elbow on the table and ran his finger back and forth over his lips. *I've never dated a non-drinker before. How would that work?*

The waiter strolled up to their table and picked up Tarquin's empty plate. He motioned to Simon's half-eaten meal and Leia's remaining rice. "You still working on...?"

"No, I'm done," she responded with a soft smile, her eyes hopping from Tarquin to the waiter. "But I'll have an orange juice mixed with lemonade, please."

"Wow, that's unexpected." Tarquin grinned. "I didn't take you for a St. Clement's gal!" He raised his dwindling drink. "I'll have one more of these. Cheers." Tossing back the remaining crimson liquid, he watched the waiter walk away, balancing their dishes with aplomb. The bittersweet taste of his cocktail raised the corners of his mouth. "I totally respect the decision not to drink. My brother is teetotal. He's never been drunk."

"You have two brothers, right? Both older?" Leia's blue eyes narrowed like she was trying to remember something. "One is… Nikolai?"

Nikolai? Tarquin's forehead creased. *Someone dived deep into Google.* "Yeah. Nick's three years older than me. Rupert—the non-drinker—is two years."

"Oh, right! Rupert!" She chuckled. "Nikolai was the name that stuck in my head."

Yeah, everyone remembers Nick.

"I promise…" She laid her hand on her chest. "I'm not a creepy stalker. I just like to know who I'm meeting, you know? Can't be too careful."

Tarquin nodded. "Who *doesn't* Google these days? I look up everyone I meet. It's silly not to." He swirled the orange twist around the bottom of his empty glass. "But despite my best Googling efforts, you, Ms. Leia, are an enigma. I found the Frill-Seekers website—and that's it. No social media. Nothing."

"Kettle—black, Han Solo!" She grinned, picking up her napkin. "All that popped up for you was a private Facebook page and your company's bio. Most of the search results were related to your mom. She's beautiful, by the way."

On the outside, sure.

"And an actress! That must be cool. Her hospital drama is getting buzz, eh?"

"Yeah, here in Britain. She's not really known anywhere else, unless you're a fan of *Equinox Ten*."

Leia shook her head, leaving her napkin on the table. "I've never heard of it."

"*E-Ten*? It was a mid-nineties sci-fi series. Mum did it for five years, shot a few British films no one saw, and then landed a soap. Her career went tits up from there. She got relegated to personal appearance work—supermarket openings, comic cons, that type of thing. She was about to sign up for *Celebrity Big Brother* when the call came through for *Shetland Medic.*"

"Lucky escape!"

"Oh, no, she would've done it." Tarquin put on an affected voice. "*Kiki loves the spotlight, darling!*" He shook his head. "Well, Kiki may love it, but I despise it. Showbiz is her thing, not ours. When we were little, she'd trot us out for all sorts of PR stunts. The worst were these pretentious magazine shoots with horses and large gardens."

A giggle burst from Leia's lips. "Oh, I saw one of those!"

He cringed. "God, you didn't." With a laugh, he rocked back in his chair, his hands fleeing into his hair. "They're bloody awful! All that fake posing and happy family bollocks? Shameless." Sliding their drinks onto the table, the server smiled at Tarquin's comments and left the final bill in between them. "Cheers, mate," said Tarquin, dropping his hands in his lap, leaving his hair wilder than it was before. "Other than Mum, I think Nick was the only one who enjoyed those shoots."

Leia grabbed her phone, her finger tapping away. "Yeah, he had a huge grin."

"Typical. Did the article say he was a child actor? Mum *loves* mentioning that."

"I don't know. The article is missing. It's just pictures. Your hair, though…" She snort-laughed, waiting for something to load on her phone screen. "Were faux hawks in style back then?"

"Hey, I was a rebel—or at least trying to be."

She tilted her head toward the bench beside her where Simon had been seated fifteen minutes earlier. "Come see. Sit here."

You don't have to ask me twice. Tarquin snatched his drink and shifted to Leia's side of the table.

Opening a webpage, she budged toward Tarquin, handing him

her phone. "Nick looks a lot like your mom."

"Yep, all dark hair, blue eyes." He placed his cocktail on the table and leaned in, skimming the article as his fingers spread across the screen, enlarging the photo. "He's got the Balfour dimples, though, see?"

Dressed in their private school uniforms the three teens flanked their glamorous mother, her enviable forty-something figure in a body-conscious, floor-dusting gown of shimmering silver sequins. Her dress, more appropriate for a London red carpet than a family photo call in a 19th-century mansion, stood out like a fur coat at a PETA rally and completely overshadowed the grand hall's antique furniture and extravagant orchid arrangements worthy of the Chelsea Flower Show. Leia seemed mesmerized.

She's looking at Mum's dress? Tarquin pointed at the two boys to Kiki's left, the taller, older one wearing eyeglasses. "Me and Rupert are like Dad's side of the family. Green eyes, a reddish tinge to our hair, but not quite ginge. We both have his bad vision, too, but I dumped my glasses for contacts." He glanced at Leia close up, captivated by the photo. *She's got freckles, sprinkled across her nose!* He couldn't tear his eyes away.

"Rupert seems…" Lost in thought, the tip of her tongue slid across her bottom lip. "Distracted."

Like I am now? He followed the slow flick of her tongue. *Leia, Leia, Leia.* A slight sigh escaped from his throat, just loud enough that a ghost of a smile flirted with Leia's cheeks. *She caught that?*

"Are you close to your brothers?" Her eyes swayed from the phone to Tarquin and back again.

"I am, yeah, but in different ways. Nico and I both love travel and restaurants, meeting new people. He works for the BBC in New York. Rupert is more…earthy. He's most at home in his Hunter wellies, herding sheep and milking cows. I share a love of the outdoors with Rupes." Tarquin chuckled at the photo. "You're right—

he *is* distracted here. I bet he was pining after the macarons on the catering table."

"Oh, I love macarons!" Leia closed her eyes and swooned. "Especially raspberry ones. They taste like heaven."

"I don't think Rupes tasted heaven or anything else. Those macarons barely touched the sides." Tarquin chuckled. "Look at him, the skinny git. I'd kill for his metabolism." He scrolled to the next image, the three Balfour boys wearing white breeches and blue polo shirts inside a luxurious horse stable with two floors, stalls as far as the eye could see, and a majestic cathedral ceiling.

"Holy—!" A mischievous snicker poked through Leia's words. "The horses have *chandeliers*?! Their stables are nicer than my apartment." She scooted closer, her bare arm grazing his sleeve as she enlarged the image. "Your eyes look a bit teary in this one."

"Yeah, I'm allergic to horses." Tarquin grimaced. "Mum was adamant we pose in there, all of us in daft polo gear."

"Aw, you look mortified...but cute." Her shoulder collided with Tarquin's and refused to leave. "I bet you broke a lot of hearts growing up." She met his gaze with a coquettish grin.

She's practically in my lap. Not that I mind! Her close warmth and the flowery scent of her perfume sent his pulse on a sprint. *She smells like summer and swimming and happy memories.* He pressed closer, inhaling. "Hey, what can I say? Girls liked me."

"I can't imagine why," she teased, her eyes bright and lingering.

Come closer and I'll show you. Tarquin swallowed, a shiver tingling down his spine as his eyes hovered over her lips. *Or help yourself. Make a move and my mouth is yours, Ginger.* "I bet you were a heartbreaker, too, Leia Scott."

She smiled and glanced back at the phone. "So, Mr. Popularity, how old are you here?"

Ah, okay. She likes to take it slow. That's fine. Some things de-

serve to be savored. Tarquin tilted in, angling toward the photos. "Fifteen, I think? I was all about skateboarding, hanging with my best mate Harry, and well, girls." *Skateboarding aside, not much has changed.*

A slow grin met her cheeks. She picked up her drink and took a long sip of the orangey lemonade.

Tarquin couldn't look away. *My god, those lips…they could unravel me.*

"Where was this, anyway?" Leia hovered over the edge of her glass. "Did you break into *Downton Abbey* for the day?"

Should I lie and say yes? He inhaled and slowly let the air leave his lungs, his body deflating into the bench. *Ugh, she's going to find out sooner or later.* "That's in Berkshire, our country house." *Quick, change the subject.* "So, where did you—"

"Wait! *House*? It looks like a castle!" Wide-eyed, she let out a strangled giggle. "So…I guess your family has more than one home, then? If this estate is the *country* one…"

Okay, here we go. Here's where her interest skyrockets for all the wrong reasons. Tarquin's heart flinched. *Might as well get it over with.* Skirting her gaze, he rubbed the back of his neck. "Uh…yeah. My family owns several in the UK…and one in France." He met her open-mouthed stare. *Fuck, there's the usual reaction. Her eyebrows can't climb any higher. Won't mention the villa in Greece, then.*

"Holy. Hell." She fell back against the bench and let out a half-laugh. "Sorry, Sir Balfour, I didn't know I had to curtsey."

"I'll let you off this time." Tarquin forced out a chuckle. *Like there's going to be a next time. Dammit, I didn't think she was the gold-digging type.* Lowering his head, he stared at the phone screen. *Brace yourself—you know she's going to ask. They always ask: What car do you drive? Which do you prefer, shopping in Knightsbridge or New Bond Street? Cristal or Moët?*

"Where's your dad?" Leia peered at the phone. "He's missing from the photos."

Oh? I didn't expect that. Her change of subject coaxed a cautious smile back to Tarquin's face. "A business trip, lucky bastard." He flicked the screen, rolling to another photo of his family in bathing suits lounging poolside on daybeds—indoors. The swimmers' paradise boasted intricate mosaic tiles, stone pillars, and floor-to-ceiling windows overlooking an expanse of green lawn. A majestic waterfall, adorned with tropical flowering plants, bubbled in the room's far corner.

Wide-eyed, Leia's head drew back, a barely audible "Wow" slipping from her lips.

"But little good it would've done if Dad had been there. Mum was the one in charge of family business. She still would've pulled us out of school and made us wear ridiculous clothes."

Leia did a double take between Tarquin and the pool of dreams. "But at least you're wearing board shorts. It could've been a lot worse."

"Speedos?!" He met her eyes and cringed. "God, yeah. I'd never live *that* down." Returning to the photo, he gently shook his head. "I missed an important Latin exam that day, but Mum didn't care. Her career always came first. Dad knew it. We all did. We were just the supporting cast."

"Nikolai, Rupert, and Tarquin Balfour." Leia shifted forward, leaving his side and returning her glass to the table. "Well, those are dramatic names!"

"It gets worse. Our full names are Nikolai Crispin, Rupert Magnus, and Tarquin Octavius."

Looking over her shoulder, she stifled a laugh. "Did your parents *hate* you or something?"

"Sometimes I think so."

"I always wanted a middle name." She dropped back against

the bench but didn't stray into his space. "Something normal. Something I could use instead of Leia."

Tarquin's jaw dropped with mock shock. "That's blasphemy!" He relaxed into a playful smile and picked up his cocktail. "You could've done what my mother did—rebrand yourself." He knocked the orange garnish riding the lip of his glass into the red liquid and took a long sip.

"I thought Kiki was short for Katherine."

He swallowed and shook his head, setting his drink on the table. "Hell no. Her real name is Tracey. Tracey Pinches."

Leia gaped.

"I know, right? She changed it when she started modeling in the mid-eighties. First, she was Kiki Lascelles, then Lascelles became Balfour when she married Dad." His fingers swept over the screen, landing on a photo depicting domestic family bliss. Kiki, dressed in an aqua Juicy Couture tracksuit, was flattening a slab of dough with a rolling pin while her three sons stuffed their faces with fresh-baked shortbread cookies. "Her personal assistant made these. Mum never baked a day in her life!" Tarquin set Leia's phone on the table. "We had a huge row when this article came out. She said I made her look like a bad mother."

"How?"

"My sneezing, my red eyes? I looked like I had been bawling. She said I damaged her image, eroded her self-esteem—so bloody melodramatic, my mother." He shook his head. "So, in typical Kiki fashion, she chipped away at mine—she took away my skateboard, told the girl I liked to stop hanging about, and yanked me out of cross-country trials. I was really good, too. I was supposed to represent Berkshire in the national championships. I never got the chance again. I was gutted, actually."

"Tarquin, I'm so sorry." Leia reached out, clutching his forearm. "That must've hurt."

His eyes flitted down to her hand, her grip soft and reassuring. *She's so lovely.* He looked up with a wistful smile and met Leia's eyes, but she abruptly pulled her hand away like she had been zapped with an electric shock.

Oh?

Leia swerved his gaze and snatched her drink, her lips desperate for her glass.

What's with the unsettled look? His stomach pinched. *Did I say something wrong? What did I do?* He ran his hand over his chin, his lips twisting. *She seems out of sorts. Say something to put her at ease.* Dropping his hand into his lap, he flashed a wry smile. "Probably for the best. I reckon those teeny tiny jogging shorts were a full-on dick slip waiting to happen."

Mid-sip, the corners of her mouth tweaked into a quick grin, then she looked away again, her eyes roaming about the pub.

Tarquin's mouth opened, but he didn't speak. *You're single. I'm single. What gives? You were into me, but now you're not?* A text woke up his phone. *Now what?* Biting his lip, he blinked and reached across the table, tilting the screen. An image of a young redheaded girl, long curls blowing in the breeze, grinned back.

Leia lowered her glass. "Is everything okay?"

I don't know, Leia. Is it? Tarquin cleared his throat. "Uh, yeah. It's just Rupert, sending a pic of Ava." A sweet smile replaced his frown. "She had a good ol' natter with me yesterday. She's going to be a big sister soon. Rupert and his wife are expecting their second child this summer, so Ava made me promise she'll still be my favorite." He chuckled, setting his phone down.

"Did she like the unicorn?" Leia's grin returned. For Tarquin, it was like the sun emerging from behind a dark cloud.

"Oh, she doesn't have it yet. Soon. They live on Orkney, the archipelago off the north coast of Scotland."

Leia's face lit up. "Really? Wow!"

Seriously? "You know it?"

"Sort of. I know a bit about Orkney's archaeological treasures. I completed a minor in museum studies along with my art history degree."

"And what'd you think?"

"It looks like a beautiful place! And I had no idea it was so rich in Neolithic sites. But we kinda skimmed the surface. I wish we'd spent more time on it."

Tarquin nodded. "There's even Norse graffiti in the chambered cairn at Maeshowe."

"Oh, I read about that! And the 5,000-year-old village at Skara Brae. But what really caught my eye was the Ring of Brodgar—I'm a sucker for ancient standing stones." Leia chuckled. "Who doesn't dream of their own *Outlander* moment?"

I'm gobsmacked that she knows Orkney—sort of. Tarquin laughed. "My dad's side were born there."

"Oh, nice! Were you?"

"No. My brothers and I are all London-born. We're the Balfour outliers, really. Everyone else is full-on Orcadian. But we'd still go up during holidays, see family. There's brilliant wreck diving there, too, so I take advantage whenever I can. Good rock climbing and surfing as well."

"Wreck diving? Like real shipwrecks?"

"Yeah, there's a scuttled German fleet from World War I. Blockships, too, near the Churchill Barriers. It's cool."

"Sounds like an amazing place. No wonder you love it so much."

"Yeah." He nodded, brushing imaginary crumbs off his lap. "So, what's your idea of fun? What are you into?"

"Lots of things. I love to read, skate…take kickboxing classes—"

"Kickboxing? That's kickass!" *And smokin' hot.*

"Yeah…if I were good at it! But I'm not. I pack a mean punch, but my kicks could be better. My balance sucks sometimes." Leia snickered. "I also like art galleries, fashion documentaries and magazines—I know, that's hardly surprising!"

"Fave designer?"

"J'adore Dior!" She lit up with a swoony smile. "His vintage stuff is so feminine and beautiful. Works of art. I also love Victoria Beckham's ready-to-wear, and Stella McCartney, too—not just for her clothes, but her respect for animals and nature as well. What else?" She swirled the ice cubes in her glass. "Oh, I volunteer for the Heart Association, and I swim. Not competitively, just for fun. It's almost therapeutic, meditative. Sewing started out like that, too. I kinda lose track of time when I'm doing it."

This is more like it. Let's keep talking, keep sharing. His shoulders relaxed. "I love that. There's nothing more freeing than surrendering to your passions. Did you always want to design?"

"No, I wanted to be a kindergarten teacher…or a tree hugger. I heard that phrase when I was a kid and actually thought that was a real job."

Tarquin laughed. "Classic! So, how did you get into making clothes? Did your mom teach you?"

"Yeah. Mom sewed a lot of our clothes growing up."

"Was she a designer, too?"

Leia shook her head. "She was a librarian, but she sewed in her spare time. One summer I made the mistake of saying I was bored, and she roped me in."

"And look at you now! She must be super proud of you."

"I guess…somewhere, somehow." Leia's voice became softer, less animated. "She died nine years ago—when I was eighteen. A heart attack." Shoulders bowed, she took a long sip again, her eyes fixating on their bill standing to attention between the salt and pepper shakers.

Jesus, that's awful. A tightness gripped Tarquin's throat. "Oh, Leia. I'm so sorry—" His phone lit up again with a text.

Lucy: Tell her about volunteering in Nepal building hospitals. YOU'RE WELCOME! x

He flipped it over, out of sight. *I'm not going to prattle on about myself, especially now. She looks so sad. But do I ask about her mom—or not? I don't want to avoid the subject and be an insensitive dick, but I don't want to make her cry, either.* Tarquin bit his lip. *Well, say something.* "Do you, uh, want to talk abou—"

"No." Her stare lifted, but she skirted his gaze. "Thanks for asking, though."

Okay. Good. He let out a soft breath. "So…will you sew at Simon's?"

With a faint nod, Leia rejoined the conversation. "I'd like to. I can only do so much by hand with a needle and thread." She sighed, returning her drink to the table. "I have a lot to catch up on"—her forehead wrinkled—"so I should probably get going." Reaching across the table, she snapped up the bill.

Going? Her words sucker-punched Tarquin's gut. *Already?*

"I have a job interview on Friday. I need time to prep." She dove into her purse.

A job interview? Here? "Oh, well done!" he blurted. "That's amazing."

"Yeah, it's for a full-time position at the Costume Institute," she replied, all trace of her flirty repartee gone as she pulled out her credit card. "Over Skype." She craned her neck and locked eyes with their server.

Bloody New York? Just my rotten luck. Tarquin's heart sank. *Bollocks.*

"I've been waiting months for this chance to come around

again." Leia's finger flicked the edge of her card as the server rushed over with the portable payment machine. "I can't mess up."

"You won't. You'll be great!" Tarquin stuffed his fingers into the pocket of his trousers, pulling out his wallet. "Leia, please—I'll get this."

"No, it's the least I can do. Seriously." Punching in her PIN, the machine's electronic beeps pierced the silence growing between them.

Three hours gone in a blink. Tarquin's chest tightened. He tucked his wallet away as the machine spit out her receipt like a petulant child sticking out his tongue. "Cheers," he said quietly, hoping she'd change her mind and suggest dessert somewhere, but she thanked the waiter and stuffed the curled piece of paper in her wallet. Tarquin didn't budge or reach for his suit jacket and coat, holding on to every last second of their time together.

A bright smile flashed across her cheeks. "I really like Simon." She picked up her phone and tapped its screen. "Now I have a friend here in the business—all thanks to you."

"My pleasure." Tarquin nodded and swallowed heavily, the ache in his chest rising into his throat, cutting off his breath. *I thought—hoped—this would be the beginning of something, not the end. We get along, right? We laughed, flirted. Shared stories—well, I did...*

She slid her arms into her parka. "I'd offer to share a taxi, but I think we're going in different directions?"

"Yeah, we are, but it's fine, really." He rose from the bench and reunited with his suit jacket and his coat, hanging on the back of his chair. "I'll walk for a bit. Get some air."

She stood up, looping her purse over her shoulder. "I had fun tonight."

Does she mean it, though? "Me too." He walked ahead of her through the thinning crowd and held open the door, the dank even-

75

ing chill of a now rainy London mirroring his mood. An idling car offered a dry escape.

"Oh, that's my ride—perfect timing." A puff of breath left Leia's lips. "Can I drop you somewhere?" She opened the door and scooted in. "You can't walk. You'll get soaked."

Tarquin ducked his head, hiding from the pelting rain. "Ah, thanks, but I'm all right." *ASK HER—before you drown!* He squinted into the warm car, the storm's cold deluge trickling down his neck and saturating his scarf. "Leia, can I see you again? Take you for dinner or a film? I promise, not *Star Wars*."

"Um." She paused, giving him a tight-lipped smile. "Sure. We could…hang out again. Soon, yeah?"

Hang out? So…not a date? He stepped back and swallowed his surprise. *No, of course not. She pulled away in the pub—twice.*

"Look…" Leia fumbled in her bag, unearthing a compact umbrella. "Take this." Her jaw tensed as her gaze flitted down his soon-to-be sopping coat. "I'll call you?"

I'll call you… How many times have I said that, knowing I never would? That's karma kicking you in the bollocks, mate. Tarquin accepted the umbrella. "Sure, okay." He nodded, a shiver racing up his wet back. "Get home safe." He pushed the door closed, on their night and on his heart.

SEVEN

LEIA

Sarah tugged on her black wheelchair gloves. "Leia, are you coming or not?" She wiped her brow, her skin pink and perspiring beneath the wintery layers of her blue wooly hat and scarf and her long navy parka. "It's almost twenty to nine! I know I start late on Thursdays, but this is pushing it—I have my presentation, remember?"

"Sorry!" Leia dropped her toothbrush in the cup beside the bathroom sink and grabbed her journal, balancing on the edge of the bathtub. She scribbled the third entry across Wednesday's page.

> ### *January 2, I was grateful for:*
> 1. *getting the Met interview.*
> 2. *Simon's offer to use his workroom.*
> 3. *flirting with Tarquin!*

She bit her cheek. *Should I call him, though? Or leave it?* Stuffing her pen inside the journal's cover, she zipped it closed and hurried into the hall. "Oh, I don't know," she mumbled, shaking her head as she yanked her chunky sweater's hem over the waist of her jeans.

"Don't know what?"

"Nothing." Leia snatched her oversized tote and dropped her journal inside where it joined her laptop, sewing tools, a homemade lunch, and another bag of ketchup potato chips for Simon.

"Ley, why don't you fill in your journal before bed?" Sarah wheeled forward and gripped the door handle with her right hand then quickly pulled backward on the rear left wheel's hand rim, her momentum yanking the door open. A burst of chilly morning air surged down the hallway. "Aren't you supposed to take your time with it?"

Says Ms. Impatient. "You *could* wait until I've got my coat on!" Leia clenched her jaw and stuffed her feet in her ankle boots, giving each zipper a sharp tug. *She's already outside. Jeez, what's one more minute?* "I fell asleep making notes for my interview last night. I *had* to finish this morning." She grabbed her garment bag from the waist-high coat hooks near the door.

Out on the walkway, Sarah looked over her shoulder and grumbled under her breath. "Always running late." A frown pinched her lips. "You were talking in your sleep again last night, by the way. Mumbling like mad."

Yeah, probably telling you off for taking my denim skirt again without asking. Leia filled her arms with her parka and scarf and followed her sister outside. "I woke up around one. I'd missed Dad's text saying he'd landed, so I called him." She slammed the door, locking it. "We ended up talking until two or so. You must be happy. He thinks Jordan's great."

"That's 'cause he IS!" Sarah swung onto the Bride Street sidewalk as Leia juggled her belongings. "Gimme your stuff and put your coat on." Shaking her head, she slowed to a stop. "What time did Dad get back?"

Leia set her bags on Sarah's lap and slipped into her coat and scarf, playing catch-up. "Six-thirty Toronto time, but they sat on the plane for *two hours* because of thunder snow!" She laughed. "Gotta love Canada in January."

"God, I don't miss Canadian winters at all." Sarah sniffed as Leia claimed her bags. "How many times did I get stuck because some idiot didn't clear the snow from their sidewalk?"

"Too many." Leia rested her garment bag over her forearm and walked quickly, keeping pace with her sister who pushed the hand rims of her wheels and sped along the pavement at a fast clip. "But Christmas here without snow felt like just another day, nothing special."

"Yeah, but you don't always get a white Christmas back home either."

"I know, but at least it's not drizzling and damp. How do you deal?" Leia scowled at the threatening sky and held up her bare palm, checking for raindrops. "It's depressing. Everything's gray and *blah*." Her eyes skipped to the street and its dead end, the high brick outer wall of Pentonville Prison.

"You get used to it. And there are so many great things here: theater, gorgeous parks, museums—and ME!" Sarah laughed, fluttering her eyelashes. "A bit of rain is a small price to pay to be with your favorite sister, right?"

Leia's heart panged. Thanks to university, Tyler, and careers, the sisters had lived in different cities for eight years. "Yeah, of course it is. I miss hanging out with you, Saz." She smiled. "When you're not pinching my clothes, or helping yourself to my dessert. That chocolate stain on your favorite dress is karma, you know."

"I have no regrets. That dessert was *heavenly*!" Sarah grinned up at her and pushed the left-hand rim, swerving right onto Roman Way, a quiet side street with low-rise red brick apartments.

"So, how do you feel? About your presentation?" asked Leia. "Nervous?"

"No, I'm more annoyed I have to wait until after lunch. I'd like to get it over with."

"Well, whenever you do it, you're gonna kill it. You know your stuff better than anyone—and they *love* you! They were all raving about you on New Year's—if you don't get the promotion, I'll be shocked! Promise you'll text me after?"

"Yep." Sarah nodded, swerving around a tree leaning over the edge of the sidewalk. "What are you sewing today?"

"I'm finishing your denim skirt so you'll stop stealing mine."

Sarah beamed. "Yours are the only ones I can get on and off easily."

"I'm also making a prom dress for my coworker's daughter. She wants 'ballerina gone bad'. It'll be sleeveless with a traditional ballerina neckline, but I'm going to scatter crystals along the bodice for some sparkle and add flirty tiers to the skirt. They'll twirl and move when she dances. It'll be badass but cute."

"Sounds adorable. That Simon guy is pretty great, eh? Letting you use his space."

"Yeah! I might even get it done before I head back to New York. He's such a nice guy."

"And what about his friend?"

Argh. She's so predictable. "What about him?" Leia looked away, her voice flat.

"Is he a candidate for your no-strings sex project?"

Well, at least she stopped being judgmental. Leia pursed her lips. "Um, maybe."

"I *knew* it! You would've been home earlier if you weren't hitting it off." Intermittent drops of rain dotted the pavement and Sarah's glasses. "So, did you two make hookup plans for later?"

"Jeez, this weather…" Leia pulled up her hood. "I grabbed your umbrella—do you want it?"

"No!" Sarah shook her head. "*Tell* me! Stop avoiding. Why didn't you arrange something?!"

Wincing, Leia gave the right of way to an older gentleman walking two Yorkshire terriers wearing matching Arsenal football club sweaters.

Sarah craned her neck, watching the tiny pups scramble past. "*Oh*…okay. I get it. He's fugly, right?"

"No! He's *very* attractive, actually. Hair to die for, killer body, and dimples for days. He was flirty and funny. Smelled incredible. Self-aware, too. That's rare these days."

"Yeah, and it's even rarer to find someone like that without a girlfriend or boyfriend." Sarah frowned. "So, he's seeing someone?"

"No, he's single. But that makes me wonder"—Leia blew out her cheeks—"what's wrong with him?"

Sarah chuckled above her scarf. "More like what's wrong with *you*, girl."

Leia threw her sister a dirty look and dove into her tote, digging out Sarah's compact umbrella, its retro rose print a much-needed touch of spring on a drizzly winter's day.

"Well, there *is* a lot of dishy gossip about you and Ty online. Maybe he Googled you? Some guys might be put off by that."

"Tarquin couldn't have seen it. He doesn't know Tyler's name or occupation." Leia unfastened the snap on the umbrella. "And all that trash is searchable under Leia McClelland, not Leia Scott. I know, I've checked."

"So, what *is* the problem? Not his *Star Wars* obsession? Oh my god, are you worried he likes to role-play?" Sarah peeked up at Leia. "He'll definitely want to show you his lightsaber."

"Shut up!" Leia laughed, settling into a sigh as she clicked the button on Sarah's flowery umbrella and it bloomed above her head. "Ah, it just sucks. I *am* attracted to him..." Her eyes trailed over a small corner shop standing shoulder to shoulder with an Ethiopian restaurant.

"But he's not that into you?"

"No, it's not that. I'm pretty sure he likes me."

"Well, you're the one with the silly 'no dating guys into *Star Wars*' rule! And you said it yourself, Ley—it's just sex. It's not like he's going to be your new husband."

"I know, but there's something else." Leia bit her lip.

81

"He's…rich."

"And that's a problem?" Sarah shook her head. "Tyler was rich, too, you know."

"Yeah, he is *now*—playing hockey—but he didn't grow up that way. Not like Tarquin. He's *old* money—there's a massive difference." She tilted the umbrella so it covered Sarah, too. "I Googled his family last night on the way home. The Balfours used to be in the oil business, but now his dad owns a sports apparel chain—Sports Now?"

"He owns *that*?" Sarah gaped as she checked for traffic and rolled down a dropped curb into MacKenzie Road. "I'm pretty sure that's Britain's biggest sporting goods retailer! Jordan buys all his basketball stuff there!"

Leia nodded, crossing the road beside her sister. "His family own huge homes all over Europe. They even have a village, a castle, and a hospital on the Orkney Islands named after them. Saz, it makes me uncomfortable. Guys like him use wealth and power to control people." She let her sister ride up onto the sidewalk first and followed. "I've seen it in New York. I know you've seen it here. Nothing comes without strings attached—especially sex. I don't want to get tangled up in that."

"Yeah, but you can more than hold your own. It's not like you're hurting for cash, either."

Leia shook her head. "Only because Tyler was a cheating, lying scumbag. And it's not like my settlement comes anywhere close to Tarquin's wealth. I can't afford to splurge on clothes or a big house. That money pays my rent and funds Frill-Seekers—for now. It won't last forever. I need that full-time Institute job *and* a financial backer. Frill-Seekers won't survive without one."

"Play your cards right, sis—maybe Tarquin could fund Frill-Seekers!"

"Uh. No." Wide-eyed, Leia whispered, holding the garment bag against her parka, away from the rain. "I can't have sex with him and then take his money. Jesus, Saz!"

"Well, it's an option." Sarah steered around a row of recycling bins and Leia dropped behind. "So, he's obnoxiously rich, impossibly single, drop-dead handsome"—Sarah looked over her shoulder—"and probably a total player."

Leia grimaced.

"That's not a bad thing, Ley. No neediness, no broken hearts. Just lots of condoms in the bedside table and toe-curling sex on demand...he's exactly the guy you're looking for, if you think about it."

Leia covered them both with the umbrella again. "Yeah, I guess." *And everything was going great until I got all touchy-feely when he seemed sad, telling me about his mom pulling him out of cross-country. I broke Rule #1: no feelings. I panicked and couldn't get out of there fast enough. Talk about sending mixed messages...*

"It's the perfect fling." Sarah smiled. "In two weeks, you'll fly back to New York, and he'll move on to his next conquest. I'm sure he's not short of admirers, not with money and good looks." She chuckled. "God, listen to me. Forget my TED Talks on ableism—I should be dishing out sex advice." Sarah stared up at her sister, who silently looked straight ahead. A black cab honked at a passing motorcycle, so she raised her voice and tried again. "Ley, I know the rich thing seems like a red flag and your brain is screaming, *Wrong guy, wrong time,* but can't you see that's good? There's no chance you'll fall in love with him."

"I don't plan to fall in love with *anyone*."

"Okay, great! So call him!"

"I feel weird, though, booty-calling him out of the blue," said Leia, fighting against a gust of wind with the umbrella. "I saw the trainer three, four times at the gym before we slept together."

"*The Trainer*—forever nameless." Sarah veered around a discarded pizza box. "Just an anonymous penis you played with for a while."

A snorty laugh burst from beneath the umbrella. "His name is Xavi—the trainer, not the penis. Happy now?" Leia squeezed the garment bag in her arms while Sarah nodded her approval. "Anyway! I feel like I have to ask Tarquin out first—but without it feeling like a date-date."

"Well, what's he into? Choose the least romantic option."

"Scuba diving and rock climbing? He mentioned those." Leia cringed. "I get hives just thinking about those things."

"Why? It's not like you'll be *doing* him on the side of a mountain." Sarah snickered. "What about an art gallery? That's safe. You'll love the Tate Modern. Lots of pop art."

"I dunno. I think he's more sporty than arty."

"Go skating, then. You brought your skates with you, right? You could show off how flexible you are."

"Saz!" Leia laughed. "Yeah, I guess we *could* go skating. Hey, remember that rink Dad found online? The Tower of London one where they used to torture and behead people? Maybe we should go there. Blood and gore definitely ticks the 'non-romantic' box."

"Nah, go to Somerset House," said Sarah. "It's this beautiful neoclassical building on the Strand, and every Christmas there's a rink in their courtyard. It's pretty and sooo London."

"Yeah, that doesn't sound romantic at all." Leia smirked.

"You've done zero sightseeing while you've been here. Go see it and have a truly London experience—before it closes for the season."

Leia bit back her grin. "I don't know. I wish this wasn't so complicated."

"It's not." Sarah squinted ahead. "You're the one complicating things."

"But what about Simon? We could be business associates,

friends. If I sleep with Tarquin, it's too close for comfort, you know? It blurs the line a bit. Flings are supposed to be just you and some guy. No mixing friends, definitely no meeting family—"

"Oh, cheers, then!" said Sarah with a huff, hanging a right onto Caledonian Road. The accessible Tube station was across the street and about a minute away.

"You know what I mean. Our lives need to be separate, otherwise it feels like a relationship." Leia smiled at the people waiting by the bus shelter as she slipped past with Sarah. "At one point, he asked about Mom, and I shut him down."

"Oh, I don't blame you. I hate telling new people she died." Sarah winced up at her sister. "You always get the pity face."

"And questions, but I give Tarquin credit—he didn't go there. The less he knows about me, the better. I don't want him becoming attached...that's IF I even see him again."

"You mean *when* you see him again." Sarah flashed a cheeky smile and pulled her Oyster card from her pocket.

Icy rain pecked the windows of Simon's second-floor apartment, sandwiched between his boutique on the ground floor and a rented apartment on the third. The steady tapping on the glass went unnoticed by Leia, alone and lost in thought as she hung her empty garment bag on a rolling clothes rack in his workroom. The cloth shell swung and gaped open like a vacated chrysalis, its precious cargo gone, already evolving into something new.

She swiveled back to Simon's worktable and the white silk Jenny Packham dress covering its surface, her hand smoothing the expensive fabric still cold from her morning journey. *I loved you once, but it's time to let you go.* A sour taste rose in her throat as her fingers lingered, tracing the embellished neckline of crystal jewels, which danced and flirted with the room's overhead spotlights. The floor-length sheath with its signature open back was elegant and modern, sexy and easy to wear—Leia's dream wedding gown come to life, but it was also a souvenir of her nightmare 'ever after'. Fingers skimming over the skirt, her nose itched and tears stung her eyes. *I can't deny it. Even now, I'd still pick you, beautiful dress.* The softness of the fabric tugged the corners of her mouth into a delicate smile. *Thank you for making me feel gorgeous and hopeful—at least for a little while.* Her heart weighed heavy as she quickly wiped her nose with the back of her hand. *Now I'll help you become the dream dress for your next owner. Here's to a new beginning and hopefully a much happier ending.* Picking up a pair of scissors, she threaded her fingers through the holes and poised the open blades at the gown's waist, her hand shaking above the luxurious fabric. *I know. This feels wrong, but...* The knot in her stomach cinched tighter. *There's no going back.* Inhaling deeply, she held the breath in her lungs. *Just do it.* Her fingers squeezed the scissor's handles.

SNIP!

Her heart flinched, but her hand flexed again and again, slicing without mercy through the skirt of the designer dress, severing her past with each cut.

See? With an audible sigh, she let go of the air bottled up in her chest and set down the scissors. *That wasn't so bad, was it?* She quickly gathered the silk cuttings and jeweled bodice into a neat pile beside her open laptop and Sarah's finished denim skirt. *Right, let's make you into a killer prom dress.*

Pulling a tissue from the box on Simon's table, she carefully dabbed her nose and glanced around the cramped workroom, the white-painted walls decorated with row upon row of photos of Simon's finished designs. *I love this space. So inspiring and creative.* It also offered all the tools she used back home, including a one-inch grid cutting board, tracing wheels, pattern shears, curved and clear rulers, two sewing machines, and several dress forms—headless, three-dimensional torso 'mannequins' used for draping and fitting clothing during the design process. Customizable with removable arms and shaping pads, they made it possible to fit clothing for women of all shapes and sizes, a designer's secret weapon.

When designing a one-of-a-kind dress, she usually skipped the flat pattern method of garment making and dove into draping: a fun, hands-on technique involving a dress form, the final fabric, and a handful of pins. Like a sculptor, Leia made her gorgeous gowns come alive through her fingertips. Wrapping and shaping the material around the curves of the form, each tuck and pinch allowed serendipity to play its role, and Leia swore these happy accidents made bolder, more unique designs. Draping was more time-consuming than other pattern-making methods, but Leia indulged whenever she could. The feel of the fabric, its softness, its stretch—there was no better way to discover a garment's beauty and temperament than by improvising on the three-dimensional form. Her current design, the flirty prom dress, wouldn't be sashaying through Manhattan until May, giving Leia plenty of time to play.

Her phone glowed with a text. *Sarah!* Stashing her balled-up tissue in a pocket, Leia picked up the phone and raced through the message.

Sarah: Boss sick. She left early so my presentation is now bumped to January 14. Grr!

"Damn, that's just before I leave." Leia sniffed and began typing a response, but another message arrived from her sister.

Sarah: Then I got roped into revising my coworker's 200-page report. Worst timing, too. My Carpal Tunnel is flaring—again.

"Shit." *Sarah's hands and wrists take such a beating with her chair.* She texted back.

Leia: That sucks! I'll grab tacos on way home to end the day on a high note.

Her sister answered right away.

Sarah: I luv you, Princess x

Leia smiled wistfully at her childhood nickname and traded her phone for one of several cotton organza pinwheels she had cut that morning from a secondhand dress. *That vintage shop next door has so many great finds! I must thank Simon for introducing me to the owner.* A creak of the wooden stairs told her she'd have her chance sooner rather than later—Simon's shift tending to customers was over, and he was free to design. *Oh! He's coming up.* Pinning the organza to a piece of silk, she sniffed one more time as the door eased open. "Hey! Good day so far?"

"Not bad—for a rainy Thursday." Wearing a pleased grin, Simon nudged the door closed with his elbow, a steaming cup of green tea and a bowl of Greek salad in his hands. "I sold two dresses before eleven. One's been slow to move, so I'm taking it as a major victory." His eyes flitted from Leia to her open garment bag to her dress form. "Looks like you've been busy, too."

"Yeah, it's taking shape—slowly." She stepped away from the future prom dress and picked up her half-eaten chicken salad sandwich, which had been keeping three rolls of colorful Rockets candy company. "Do you work downstairs every day?" She took a big bite of the soft brown bread, covering her closed mouth with her hand as she chewed quickly.

"No, just Thursday, Friday, and Saturday mornings." Simon placed his food on the table and sat down. "I'm closed on Mondays and Tuesdays, so I do most of my design work then when there's no sales staff with questions, no phone calls—well, unless it's my fiancé." Picking up his fork, he spotted the unopened bag of ketchup chips Leia had brought in, his wide grin brightening the room. "Do you have a boyfriend back in New York?" Simon dug through his bowl of greens, unearthing colorful peppers, Kalamata olives, and chunks of Feta cheese.

"Uh, no." She traded her lunch for a handful of pins and returned to the form, clearing her throat. "Too busy." She attached another organza pinwheel, adding to the prom dress's ruffled skirt. *I can't risk it, telling him about Tyler. Simon might Google him and ask a million questions—I'm not ready for that.* Peering over her shoulder, she furrowed her brows. "The other night…is Freddie okay?"

"Yeah. He works in television production, and every time there's a new job opportunity, they overlook him. This time they said he didn't get it because he's too valuable where he is." Simon stabbed some greens with his fork and stuffed them in his mouth.

I know what that feels like. The thought made Leia queasy. *It has to go well tomorrow. I need that full-time position. I just hope Tyler's affairs, the gossip, and all that notoriety won't harm my chances.* "Aw, poor guy." She tucked a hand under the skirt, working the fabric so it twirled and puffed like a silky cloud. "Have you set a wedding date?"

"Yeah"—Simon swallowed his mouthful of salad, his eyes cruising over Leia's two cut-up dresses on the table—"December 21st. Freddie's in charge, taking care of everything. I told him he can do whatever he wants as long as he doesn't ask me to cosplay. He's big into cons and sci-fi." His gaze hopped up from the silky fabric. "Have you ever cosplayed? With a name like Leia…"

"No, *Star Wars* was my parents' thing. My name is the collateral damage of their nerdiness."

"Tarquin's a huge *Star Wars* fan." Simon dug his fork through his salad, banishing the olives to the bottom of his bowl.

Huge? "Yeah, I heard his ringtone." *Now's the time to find out more about him.* "Have you been friends long?"

"Well, I've known *of* Tarquin longer than I've actually been friends with him. I met him last summer through my friend Alex." Forehead creased, he speared a pepper but didn't eat it. He settled back in his chair, his lips twisting like he was figuring something out. "Late June, I think? He seemed nice at the time."

Leia cocked an eyebrow. "At the time?"

"Oh, I barely said hi to the guy. It was at an event and they were on their way out. They actually broke up the next day. Tarquin went off to New York, and our paths didn't cross again until last month. We have mutual friends, though—Harry and Lucy—so we've hung out a few times. We always end up talking business, much to the annoyance of Freddie and Lucy."

A pin fell from Leia's hand and she stooped to retrieve it. "Does Tarquin see Alex much?" She squeezed her eyes shut. *Well, that sounded better in my head. Simon's gonna think I'm jealous or interested or...shit. Stop lying to yourself—you ARE interested!* She stood up and fussed with a ruffle, trying to appear nonchalant.

"They talk, yeah." Simon shot her a wry smile. "Why?" He nibbled on the pepper.

He's onto you. Leia shrugged, taking her time to answer. "It's...just nice when exes stay friends."

Simon shook his head. "I've never been able to manage it."

"Me neither." *But for good reason.* Leia stabbed a pin in her fabric. Before Tyler, high school Leia was in a relationship with a guy in her biology class. They broke up when he made an insensitive joke to his buddies about Sarah and her wheelchair. "I keep my

90

distance."

"Yeah. Tarquin can't, though. Alex is like a sister to Harry. That's how she met Tarq in the first place, through Harry. Their split caused ripples—Harry and Tarquin didn't speak for a few months, but now they're thick as thieves again. And Alex is back being friends with Tarq, too." He set down his fork. "I give Tarquin credit. He offered the olive branch first. It couldn't have been easy, especially with him being single and Alex happy with"—he made air quotes—"Britain's sexiest TV star."

"Oh my god." Leia stopped pinning. "Who's that?"

"Mark Keegan."

Who? She pressed her lips together and shook her head.

"The Irish actor? *Lairds and Liars*?" Simon did a double take. "It's that popular series set in 18th-century Scotland. You know, the former soldier avenging his wife's death?"

Leia shrugged. "Never seen it."

"You must've seen ads for Mark's movie, *A Promise Unspoken*, though. His face is plastered on practically every double-decker bus in London."

"Sorry." Leia winced. "I honestly don't know who he is."

Simon snorted with mirth. "Well, Mark's a huge deal here— one of the hottest actors around. Alex struggled with that at first, but they're solid now. They've been together three years, I think."

But how does Tarquin fit in?

Simon caught Leia's furrowed brow and jumped in. "Alex and Mark split for a few months last year. Don't ask—it's complicated! That's when she dated Tarquin, but the status quo has resumed— Alex is back with her soul mate Mark, and Tarquin's playing the field again. Harry jokes it's 'what he does best'." Simon picked up his tea and flashed her a knowing smirk. "But, hey, don't let *that* put you off!"

Leia half-laughed, playing innocent. "Oh, I'm not looking

to…you know."

"Leia"—Simon paused above the lip of his cup—"I'm just saying, there's nothing wrong if you were."

Walking to Hackney Central station, Leia squeezed her phone, cursing the non-stop flutters in her stomach. *This feels like I'm thirteen, calling a boy for the first time. Shouldn't this be easier? It's not a date-date. It's just sex—if I haven't put him off me, blowing hot and cold…* She stopped at the traffic light, a parade of red double-decker buses loaded with rush-hour travelers creeping along congested Mare Street. *Stop thinking. Just call him!* Tapping his contact details, she pressed the phone to her ear.

"Hey, Leia! How are you?" Cheery and warm, he answered on the second ring. No beer glasses clinking, no loud laughter—Tarquin was still at work.

Leia pictured him, a commanding presence in his perfectly tailored suit behind a slim laptop, a large coffee and important papers keeping him company on his stark desk. "I'm good. I'm just heading home from Simon's."

"Oh, you went? Good!"

Simon didn't text him? That's good, I guess. "Yeah, I started a prom dress today." *Get to it!* The traffic signal blinked green, and she followed the crowd across the street. "So, how's your day been? How many coffees did you need?" She scrunched her nose. *Chicken! You are your own worst enemy.*

He chuckled. "Ah, it's been good—a two-coffee day. I visited an old cinema I'm repurposing into a climbing gym and had two property go-sees—I put in an offer on one, a gorgeous old church. I think we might turn it into a performance space." He paused.

Is he waiting to say something? Waiting for me?

Tarquin cleared his throat. "I guess you're calling about your umbrella? I can drop—"

"No, that's…I'm—*sorry*, I didn't mean to cut you off." Leia stopped behind a pillar advertising sneakers from Sports Now and did a double take. *His dad's company.* Rubbing her temple, she blurted, "I'm calling about Somerset House." *Smooth, Leia, really smooth.* She closed her eyes and shook her head.

"Oh? Uh, okay…"

She scuffed the sidewalk with her boot. "You know their ice rink, the one with DJs and cocktails?"

"I do. It's not Christmas in London without it."

"Right! Well, I'm going to check it out before it's gone. Would you like to go Saturday night?" *As friends with benefits. Hopefully.*

He didn't answer right away. "*This* Saturday?" His tone dipped.

Shit. He's got plans. "Uh, yeah." She blew out a breath. "Look, I'm sorry. Here I am, calling last minute—again."

"No, no! It's okay. I *was* supposed to see a film with Harry and Lucy but…plans got cancelled." Through the phone, his voice carried a hint of a smile, coaxing the butterflies in Leia's belly into a full-on frenzy. "I'd like to see it too—before it's gone."

"Great! How 'bout you meet me at eight by the Christmas tree? I'm guessing it'll still be up."

"I'll be there! I'll be the Scott Moir to your Tessa Virtue."

How does he—? Leia raised her eyebrows. "You're a skating fan?"

"Hey, what can I say? I'm a sucker for cute Canadian ice dancers!" Tarquin chuckled. "What? You're surprised?"

"Well, *yeah*. You're British…and a guy."

He laughed harder. "I'm a guy full of surprises, Ginger Spice. Just you wait and see."

EIGHT

TARQUIN

Frantic blades chipped the ice, spraying snow into the air. *No! Not again! Not...* "Fuck!" Toppling sideways, Tarquin slammed shoulder-first into the waist-high plexiglass barrier hugging the Somerset House rink. *Ow—ch!* He slipped, landing with a thud on the unforgiving ice. *Oh, mate! Fuuuck.* He sucked in a stifled breath, his leather gloves clutching his arm and ribs. *I thought this would be a lot easier. Bugger. I must really like this woman, risking my neck and arse like this. Climbing was never this tricky!* Sitting up on his knees, he brushed snow from his coat's sleeve for the third time while the large illuminated letters spelling S K A T E above the south wing of Somerset House silently mocked him. *Oh, shut it! I'm trying!*

"Mate, you okay?" An orange-bibbed rink employee barely out of puberty bent down and extended a gloved hand.

Tarquin accepted it with a muted "Cheers" and slowly rose onto one blade, then the other. Straightening up, he wobbled and cursed under his breath but at least he was no longer channeling Bambi, all limbs akimbo on the ice in front of several hundred Londoners. "I will be." His ego bruised more than his body, he nudged his cashmere beanie above his tense brows and clutched the rail as the staffer glided off into the fray, searching for more skaters in peril.

Leia didn't see that, did she? His eyes shot to the rink's entrance. He let out a nervous chuckle and his ribs kicked back, unleashing a sharp twinge that stole his breath away. *Ah, flippin' heck! I didn't...* He patted the inside pocket of his coat and stuck a hand in. The flask he had squirrelled away was still screwed closed and intact despite his bone-rattling fall. *Nice one.*

His gaze coasted over the parade of smiles sailing by, but Leia's laughter was nowhere in the mix. Ten minutes earlier before they had stepped onto the ice, a broken skate lace sent her back to the cloakroom for a replacement. "Start without me!" she said, and Tarquin did, using her unexpected absence to find his groove. Unfortunately, three tumbles later, it was still nowhere to be found. But despite the wet gloves and achy arm, his spirits remained high. Sure, ice skating wasn't his forte, but being with Leia again made up for the stiff boots pinching into his ankles and the kids snickering at the large wet marks now darkening the butt of his jeans. *Come on, man. Get the hang of this before she returns. Stop white-knuckling the railing!*

Head bobbing to "Roll With It" by Oasis, his favorite band, he filled his lungs with chilly air and pushed off from the wall, straight into the surge of oncoming traffic—chatty adults, rosy-cheeked children, and rowdy teenagers effortlessly showing off. *How do I pick up speed without falling arse over tit?* Eyes glued to the approaching pack, he stood up straight and teetered, his flapping arms drawing snorty giggles from a cluster of tween girls who skimmed by as if they'd been born on blades. He ignored their snark and inhaled the festive aroma of mulled wine. *Ah, this place would be smashing at Christmas.* He peeked over his shoulder and spotted Leia. *Oh! Hello!*

Coatless and alone skating backward in the center of the rink, she gathered speed and sprung from her toe, flying into the air. She spun counterclockwise once...twice—a blur of navy, white, and black—and landed with a wobble, drifting backward on her left skate, arms aloft and her right leg extended behind her in a shaky finish.

Corrr, that was just...! Tarquin's jaw dropped. *Where was*

THIS on Google?

Leia glided along the ice, her navy fit-and-flare long-sleeved dress with preppy white stripes circling the bodice capturing Tarquin's attention. *It hugs her in all the right places. God, she's something else.* Bending over, she rubbed her right knee, cozy in black tights. She blew out a breath, then chased another.

Tarquin pulled his wide stare away and skidded into a corner. *She'll spot me soon. Be casual. Be competent.* He inched away from the boards a smidge but kept the railing within reach—just in case.

Leia straightened up and wrapped her arms around her middle, joining the approaching throng of skaters. She searched the rink, her high blonde ponytail swinging with each swivel of her head.

Tarquin fidgeted with his gloves, fighting the desire to wave. *Find me, Leia, and save me from a sad and lonely life.* He chuckled to himself, downplaying the fear that niggled constantly since his split with Alex.

Through a cluster of rambunctious teens, her eyes locked on Tarquin's wine-colored beanie then his grin. She flashed a smile and picked up speed. "Sorry!" A heavy breath flew from her lips as her skates carved to a gentle stop. "The guy with my lace got hijacked by a busload of tourists." She pulled off a red and black mitt boasting CANADA in white letters across the back of the hand and reached down, brushing snow off her right calf. "How's it going?"

"I'm gobsmacked! Did you just do a flying toe-something-or-other?"

"Oh! The double Salchow?" She straightened up and tucked an escaped piece of hair from her ponytail behind an ear. "Yeah, a sloppy one. I'm lucky I landed it."

"Sloppy my arse! That jump was a belter! C'mon, 'fess up—you skated for bloody Canada, didn't you?" His eyes widened. "Blimey! Are you friends with Tessa and Scott?"

"I wish." She giggled under her breath. "Anyway, how DO you

know about Tessa and Scott?"

"Oh, blame Ava. She watched the Winter Olympics with her mum last year, fell in love with the skaters and their sparkly costumes. She talks about Tessa Virtue like she's an older sister or something. Scott doesn't get a look in, poor sod!" He snickered and felt his left skate slip. *Shit. Note to self: don't laugh or become rink road kill.*

"Aw! Has Uncle Talk taken her skating yet?"

"I'd love to, but Orkney doesn't have any rinks. That wee problem hasn't curbed her non-stop fangirling, though. Ava's even badgering her parents to name the new baby Tessa."

Leia picked at a loose thread on her mitt. "That's way too cute."

"So, if you *don't* hang with Tessa and Scott..." A low chuckle escaped his throat. "How'd you learn those tricks?"

"I was a competitive ice dancer growing up."

"Was? Why'd you quit?" He pointed to the middle of the rink. "*That* was bloody amazing!"

"Thanks. You know how it is...you become a teenager, things happen." Glancing over her shoulder, she pouted. "You move on."

Tarquin's eyes briefly swept down Leia's body and back up again. "Yeah, but if I had your moves, I'd be showing off at every opportunity."

She flashed a playful smirk. "Why doesn't that surprise me? Jumps aren't an ice dancer's thing, though. They're forbidden, actually." Her hand dove into the fleecy interior of her mitt. "So, Simon tells me you're into kayaking, whitewater rafting, ziplining. I knew you liked climbing, but I had no idea you were a full-on adrenaline junkie. I'm impressed!"

Cheers, Si! I owe you a pint. "Yeah, I'm a bit of a daredevil. I'll try anything once. Love an adventure, me." He scratched his chin. "What else did Si tell you?"

"Uh, not a lot. We were talking about weekend plans. When I

mentioned going skating with you, he said I'd probably met my match." With a smile, she nodded toward the flow of skaters. "So, you ready?"

No! He faked a raspy cough behind his hand, delaying his answer. *Shit, Simon. Thanks for boosting her expectations. No pint for you, mate.* Patting his chest, he reined in his hacking and winced. "Sorry! The cold air makes me..." His eyes widened. "Uh, where's your coat? Do you want mine?"

"Oh, no—thanks. I checked it. I can skate better without it. Old habits..."

"You left your money and keys in the cloakroom?"

Her mitt patted the hip of her dress. "Nope. They're here." Two slanted pockets curved along each hip, adorned with three small black buttons in a row, keeping her valuables hidden and safe.

Tarquin could vaguely make out the rectangular shape of her phone pressing into the knit fabric.

"I love dresses with pockets. Most don't have them—drives me nuts—so I always include them in my designs." Her eyes shifted over the skaters swerving around them, including a woman in a wheelchair accompanied by two friends.

Look at her smile. She's itching to get out there, but if I can delay a little longer... "You designed this one?"

"Uh, no. Bought it." She looked over her shoulder. "Maybe we should..."

Fuck. He scratched his hat, a queasiness twisting his belly. "Oh...of course. After you!"

"Great! C'mon!" Smooth and elegant, Leia glided into the flurry of skaters and looked back, urging him to follow.

She's so graceful. And then there's me, lumbering about, the beast to her beauty. Tarquin's heart pummeled his chest. He pasted on a smile and stepped into her shadow, his blades click-clacking across the ice. His short, jagged strides made him waddle precariously. *Arghh, kill me now. I must look like a constipated penguin.* "Ah, so invigorating, eh? The crisp fresh air...the scent of the mulled wine..." Babbling away, his voice wavered while his arms, stiff and awkward, bobbed by his sides. "Have you ever seen anything like this in Canada?"

Leia's brow pinched as her eyes hopped from his arms to his rigid knees speckled with melting ice. "No, it's been a while."

Tarquin caught her squint. *Shit. Stop flapping your arms like a damn duck!* "I guess Rockefeller Center in Manhattan comes close, right?" Keeping his chin up, he skate-walked faster, the knot in his stomach tightening with each ankle-wobbling step. *I bet Leia could skate before I could walk! What the hell was I thinking, agreeing to this? I've dropped myself in it, for fuck's sake!* His heart thrashed beneath his coat. *All I can do now is try to stay upright, talk about New York, and maybe—just maybe—she'll pity-snog me later.* He flashed a carefree grin. "When I lived there, I never got 'round to trying out the rink, but—"

"Wait." Leia curved in front of him and pressed her mitts against his shoulders, curbing his choppy progress.

Ah, bollocks. She's onto me. A heaviness inside his chest weighed him down. *Don't let on.* He exhaled a puff of warm air. "Everything okay? Why'd you stop?"

She cocked her head, her mitts meeting her hips. "Tarquin—is this your first time?"

I can't lie to her face. Just be cheeky and hope she laughs. A glint sparkled in his eyes. "Ah, you've got me sussed. Yep, I'm a virgin."

Leia chuckled and playfully swatted his arm, barely making contact. "You are *such* a guy! Why didn't you just tell me?"

I love that little giggle she does. Smiling with delight, his dimples deepened. "You seemed so excited. And I thought, hey, I can *skateboard*—how much harder can it be to skate on ice?" He bit his lip, stifling a laugh. "The answer is: a lot!"

She wrinkled her nose, her glance breezing over a hand-holding couple skating past. "C'mon, ice virgin. I'll show you the ropes."

Ah, bless. A tingling sensation swelled in his chest. Leia bent over, giving her right leg a rub. *What's up with that?* "You okay?"

Waving away his concern, she straightened up. "I pulled something landing that jump. Told you I was out of practice." She looked over her shoulder then met his smile again, her ponytail slicing through the air. "So, skating tips. See how I'm standing? Copy what I'm doing. Avoid hunching forward or leaning back, keep your weight on the balls of your feet. Your toes should be slightly pointed out—like this."

Tarquin peered at her skates and adjusted his accordingly.

"And bend your knees a bit. It'll help with balance."

"Soft knees, just like skateboarding," he said.

"Exactly! Your arms, though—relax them by your sides and keep your head up. You'll be tempted to watch your feet, but don't. You need to be aware of where you're going so you don't crash."

"Been there, got *several* t-shirts." He groaned and rubbed his hip.

Leia grimaced. "Well, tell me if I'm going too fast or if you want to stop. I promise, I won't let you fall." A swoop of red, white, and black—her left mitt—curled tight around his right glove.

Yes! Get in! He softly squeezed her hand as the nasally whine of Oasis gave way to the frisky sixties nostalgia of "Help Yourself" by Tom Jones, all beckoning brass and toe-tapping tempo. *Ah! If Leia listens to the lyrics, tries them on for size, I'll be one happy bloke.*

She tilted her head with a squint. "You okay?"

"Oh, yeah. Brilliant! It's just this song, it's a classic..." He bit back his grin and swung her hand. "So, left skate first?"

"Sure. Let's push off with the left, then right. But just small strokes to start." She blinked up at him. "You ready?"

"Are you?" Tarquin exhaled into a laugh, sending a warm cloud of breath into the air. "This isn't what you signed up for. I really should've told you I can't skate." *But I really wanted to see you again.*

"And I shouldn't have assumed you could." She scraped a toe pick along the ice. "But we're all laced up and ready to rock, so let's make Ava proud of Uncle Talk, 'kay?"

Aw, she'd love you. He grinned. "Let's smash it."

Hand in hand, they moved forward together. Leia's strokes were slow and graceful while Tarquin's drifted toward choppy and impatient. She encouraged him along the way, but a full-on conversation was put on ice as he concentrated. *Left foot glide, right foot glide, left foot glide...*

Halfway around the large rink, Leia beamed. "You're doing great! How does it feel?"

"Uh, good." *Actually, these boots are rubbing my toes all to hell. It's blister city down there.* He kept his chin up, fighting the impulse to eyeball his skates.

"Great!" She squeezed his hand. "Try to glide more than step. See what I'm doing?"

He studied her feet, easily stroking beneath her. Coping her movements, he looked up, gawking at the blue and pink spotlights washing over Somerset House's majestic white façade.

A few wobbles, desperate hand squeezes, and one lesson in stopping later, and Tarquin's strokes were becoming less jerky and more fluid, his confidence growing with each completed lap.

This is fun! He grinned at the slightly brown but still sparkly Christmas tree, at little kids zooming past at twice his speed, but most of all, he grinned at Leia by his side, hand in hand. *She's so patient. And she's athletic as fuck—such a turn-on.*

Leia ogled Somerset House and bobbed her head to an Adele

track, her smile in no hurry to leave. "This place is so pretty. The website doesn't do it justice."

"Yeah, they do a grand job." *Oh, shit—yeah. She had a job thing yesterday.* "Hey, speaking of, how'd the interview go?"

"Good—I think. It was hard to tell."

I hope it went well, but I also hope it didn't. A tightness clenched his chest. *Maybe she'd stay here if there's bugger all to go home to?* He cleared his throat. "Yeah, especially over Skype."

Leia nodded. "My boss was wonderful, but the HR person frowned the entire time. He knows *of* me, but—" She cut herself off. "I just hope I gave good interview. A coworker texted me last night and said the daughter of the editor of *Vogue* applied. I don't know, it might be too steep a hill for someone like me to climb."

"What's with the 'someone like you'?" Rounding a corner, Tarquin dipped his chin, checking out his skates, then looked up again. "Leia, you're an amazing candidate. You're friendly and smart, good on paper, too—your master's and experience scream 'Hire me!'. I know I would."

A grin met her blush. "Aw, thanks."

"Your designs are brilliant. What more proof of your creativity and resourcefulness do they need? I bet this *Vogue* sprog doesn't get a look in."

"If only." She let out a heavy breath. "A position like this has come up twice, and twice it went to someone else. I was promised the next one, but…"

"Well, that's bollocks, but I have a feeling your luck is about to change."

Glancing at him, a warm smile lifted the corners of Leia's mouth. "Like yours? Look at you, Scott Moir, ice dancer extraordinaire! I knew you'd get the hang of it. Ready to let go?"

She wants her hand back. Dammit. "But don't ice dancers, you know…hold hands all the time?"

"Not all the time, but they do have to skate as close together as possible and in unison." She squeezed his hand. "Look, if you feel unsteady—"

"No, it's not that…" *Actually, it's exactly that. I like holding your hand. Christ, needy much, Tarq?* He gulped and looked straight ahead. *Don't be a wuss.* "Okay, let's give it a go."

Leia released his hand and scrutinized his strokes. The choppy strides and wavy arms of earlier were long gone. "See? You're a natural! We could go all night."

We could definitely go all night, no skates required. Tarquin shot her a slow smile that grew with each glide. *I mean it, Leia. Just say the word.* He grinned at the thought of an intimate soak for two in his large tub, followed by deep massages and even deeper kisses, her hands exploring, skimming down his abs and curling around him tight… He gasped, his pulse hammering in his chest and a scorching heat hardening in his jeans. *Someone is eager.* He smoothed his free hand down his long coat, keeping his predicament secret. *I can't come on too strong. I can't fuck this up.* He pushed harder, faster, sweeping around a corner with Leia matching his speed. Coming out of the turn, his skates dug in, and his left blade clipped the back of his right boot. "Jesus!" He stumbled, knocking Leia off-kilter.

"Shit!" Her sharp retort shot a burst of warm breath into the chilly breeze. Stabbing a toe pick into the ice, she swerved and cut him off. Knees clashing, blades tangling, Leia clutched his coat and shoved his shoulders back, halting his plunge. "You okay?" She swallowed a gulp of frosty air.

Tarquin pulled her in, her rapid puffs of breath skating across his cheek. *Bloody hell!* "You saved me." He chuckled, his chest rising and falling, the scent of her perfume making him deliriously dizzy. "You *sure* you're not a Jedi?"

A burst of awkward laughter split her smile. She loosened her death grip on his coat and stepped back, pulling off her mitts.

Shit. Nice one. She hates Star Wars *and you blurt out a film-related compliment? Idiot.* Tarquin followed her lead, straightening up and releasing her from his bear hug. "I'm sorry. I didn't mean to."

But Leia leaned in again, plucking a piece of fluff from his shoulder. "Well, I told you I wouldn't let you fall, didn't I?" Her soft gaze felt warm and playfully confident.

Wait—what? She's not annoyed? Tarquin's heart pounded in his chest, the giddy ache for her conspiring into a single purpose. *I'm dying to kiss you.* He swallowed thickly, refusing to let the moment fizzle—unless Leia wasn't keen—but her shallow breaths and her fixed stare, curious and wanting, hinted otherwise. "Leia...?" His raspy question hung between them as he tilted his head and dragged his eyes down to her pout...beckoning, waiting.

"CAREFUL!" A booming command cut through the air as someone rammed between them, a human bowling ball knocking Tarquin straight onto his ass.

"Oh, shi—" Leia held her balance and bent down. "Are you okay?"

Without a whine or tears, a spritely little girl dusted ice from her coat. "He's rubbish!" Blonde braids swinging, she stuck out her tongue and sprung back onto her blades, rejoining her mother, who mouthed "Sorry" through her horrified wince.

Leia snorted, fighting back laughter.

Hit and run over by a six-year-old, for fuck's sake! Can we talk emasculating? Tarquin groaned and sat up, holding his ribs. *I surf huge waves, crawl through caves, and kite ski down mountains, all without a scratch—and here I get bowled over by a hostile Cindy Lou Who in front of the woman I'm trying to impress. Bloody figures.* Waving off Leia's help, he slowly returned to his feet, the blisters inside his socks searing and tingly. *This is such a boner-killer—*

for her and me.

Leia raised her eyebrows. "You sure you're okay?" She swept snow and ice from his sleeve.

She's cringing. Great. Yeah, not the manliest of moments, was it? Kiss goodbye to a second date. He lifted his chin. "Never been better." *I can't wait to tear these flippin' skates off. My feet are gonna be a horror show.* Reaching inside his coat, he pulled out his flask, offering it to her.

"Uh, no—thanks." A passing frown dipped her lips as she cleared her throat. "I don't drink, remember?"

He unscrewed the cap. "I know. It's orange and lemonade. For you." *Not that it matters a jot. After this, I'll probably never see her again.*

Leia's expression softened. "Oh"—she tucked her mittens under her arm—"that's sweet, thanks." She accepted the flask, taking a quick sip. She licked her lips and shivered. "Our session's almost over…"

And so is our date. Tarquin nodded. *It's for the best. She lives in New York. This was never going to work.* "Yeah. Just in time too." He shrugged. "At least you've got the rest of your night—"

"What?" She glanced up, her brows furrowed as she handed back the flask. "No, it's too early to go home." Clutching her mittens in one hand, she released her ponytail with the other and fluffed her hair, letting it pool around her shoulders. "I was going to suggest heading somewhere together to warm up."

She doesn't want to cut and run? "Actually, it *would* be nice to feel my toes again." He half-laughed, screwing on the flask's cap. *Okay, here's my chance to say goodbye properly.* "I know a place across the river with an amazing view. The OXO Tower on the South Bank?"

"It sounds wonderful and…classy." Leia snapped her hair tie over her wrist and pointed at her skates. "Bet they'd love me showing up with these over my shoulder." She tugged on her mitts.

Bugger. "Ah, right. You brought them with you." *So much for taking her somewhere special.* He tucked the flask in his coat's inside pocket. "Well, we could go for noodles or sushi? Head to a pub? What do you fancy?"

She stroked closer, curling her mitts around his coat's lapels. "It's not a question of what I fancy…but *who*," she whispered, her breath sweet with orange. The unwavering stare of her blue eyes urged his surrender.

Fuck. Me. A rocket of heat pulsed through Tarquin's body. He dipped his chin toward their skates. "How quick can we get out of these things?"

NINE

LEIA

Padding into Tarquin's dark living room in her stocking feet, Leia glanced over her shoulder. *Can he see me from his coat closet? No? Be quick!* She stooped and tugged her hosiery taut while she kept an eye on the doorway. *Stupid things, always falling down.* Mid-pull, an image of Tarquin doing the opposite flashed through her mind, his strong hands peeling the tights down her thighs…past her knees, past her pedicured toes…

A feverish rush frolicked in her chest, tussling with nerves she fought to squash. *Sleeping with someone new is always a bit…argh! Being naked for the first time… Will he still be attracted to me? Will he like what I like? God, I hope he's not hairy in weird places!* She chuckled to herself. *I think I've chosen wisely. Tarquin's not a dick. He's friendly, respectful—we have amazing sexual chemistry.* She smoothed her dress as the lights came on. *And he's fit! I can't wait to explore his muscles, his happy trail…*

She bit back her smile and stood up, a low-pitched mechanical hum rising behind her. *I know that sound.* Playfully, she rolled her eyes. *Boys and their toys.* She spun toward the whirr of the rising wall of electric blinds disappearing into the ceiling. *I bet he—holy shit!* Her eyes bulged. *It's…that old bridge!* She gasped, marveling at the massive neo-Gothic towers dramatically lit against the cold, dark sky. *There's crazy rich—and then there's THIS.* A heavy swallow bobbed her throat. *He said he lived near Tower Bridge—he didn't say he lived on TOP of it!*

All thoughts of happy trail joy flittered away, replaced by the spectacular picture-postcard view. The bridge's famous Victorian towers crowded his penthouse's floor-to-ceiling windows, giving the impression that they were just another enviable trophy Tarquin had acquired along with his framed marathon medals, neon-flashing *Guardians of the Galaxy* pinball machine, and…

No way! It's not! Is it? Leia's jaw dropped.

A large framed silkscreen print stole her breath. *This one's always been my favorite. It must've set him back…well, I don't even know how much.* She loosely crossed her arms and stared wide-eyed, her fingers clutching the sleeves of her dress.

The sound of Tarquin clearing his throat turned her head. She smiled, pushing aside the stunned shock threatening to render her speechless. "Hey! Your view…*my god.* You can almost reach out and touch that bridge!"

"Yeah, it's quite something, especially at sunrise." Grinning sheepishly, he pulled off his beanie. Tufts of his auburn hair sprang to attention. "Sorry I took so long. There was a text I had to…" He scratched his temple, his gaze hopping to the bridge and back again. "So, can I get you a drink? I've got sparkling water, orange and lemonade. I might have some cola around somewhere…" He smoothed down his hair and fumbled his hat, dropping it on the hardwood floor.

I thought he seemed nervous on the way here. He didn't even try to kiss me. "Orange and lemonade would be great." She admired the view again. "Thanks."

Scooping up his beanie, Tarquin's mouth curved into a smile. "Oranges and lemons, says the bells of St. Clement's. Be right back!" He tossed the beanie onto his gray sofa, long and wide enough for two adults to lie down and cuddle in front of his massive 85" television, and slipped into the kitchen.

I should text Saz. Leia pulled her phone from her dress's pocket, typing 'At Tarquin's on Shad Thames, all good.' She hit send and tucked it away, her eyes mimicking a pinball from Tarquin's *Guardians* game, ricocheting from one surprise to another: a tall glass-windowed display case painted to look like one of those old British red telephone boxes and a life-size *Star Wars* Stormtrooper standing guard against a nearby wall. *Just the John Williams' theme, eh?* She ran her fingers along the 6'5" tall figure, its white fiberglass dust-free and buffed to a shine. *Wow, it's the real deal. Dad would flip!*

She wandered over to the red display case and patted its side. *What? Nooo! It's real, too?!* Her pulse tripped in her chest and kept its stammering beat. *Tarquin owns a telephone box!* She peered through its windows. *There are shelves inside—filled with books!* Opening the heavy cast-iron door, she studied the titles holding court where a phone used to hang. Hardback business autobiographies, Bill Bryson paperbacks, and *Star Wars* encyclopedias stood spine against spine with cookbooks, travel guides, and several children's favorites, including titles by Dr. Seuss and Maurice Sendak.

"I had to have that."

Leia glanced over her shoulder. Tarquin strolled in, his hands occupied by two colorful beverages, ice cubes tinkling.

"You know me—savior of discarded things." He laughed. "So many of these old boys are being sentenced to the scrap heap. I bought it at auction, had it restored. Looks good, doesn't it?"

"I love it. So much." She closed the weighty door and brushed her hand along its edge. "I had no idea you could buy them, though." Taking her St. Clement's from Tarquin, her smile swept the tidy living room, easily five times the size of her post-divorce studio apartment in New York. "Your home is incredible. The building is so huge and close to the Thames. Was it a warehouse before?"

"It was a brewery, dating back to 1871." He sipped his raspberry soft drink. "They converted it into flats about thirty years ago.

The views from my top floors are spectacular. Not Shard spectacular, but still nice."

"Top *floors*—plural?" She stuttered, catching a familiar face smiling up from the hardwood—Ava's fuzzy unicorn, awaiting its journey to Orkney.

"Yeah. There are five floors, outdoor terraces on every level."

Leia gulped.

He chuckled as if fully aware of how crazy that sounded. "I know. It's a lot for one person." He scratched his chest through his black sweater. "And a cat."

Eee! "You own a cat?" Her eyes scoured the room, free of toys or pet hair.

"Somewhere." His face fell. "Oh, you're not allergic…"

"No! I love cats—and dogs. It's just…you—"

"Don't seem the type? Yeah, I know. I'd LOVE a dog, but I'm not home enough, so before Christmas, I adopted a feline friend to keep me company." A grin tweaked his mouth. "She's a…dog-cat."

Tarquin's just a big ol' softie! Leia's smile grew. "A cat who thinks she's a dog?"

"Exactly! Her name's Mrs. Chuzzlewit."

Leia laughed. "What? From the Dickens novel? Oh, you didn't…"

"I wish I did! But that was the name she came with. Seemed wrong to change it." He sipped his drink, his eyes settling on her lips. "So! Want the grand tour?"

"Please!" Leia squeezed her glass. *Let's start with your bedroom!* Her stomach let out a loud growl, and she cringed. *Ugh. How sexy is that?*

Tarquin snickered. "We'll order dinner after, okay?"

Her heart sank. *Nooo. This evening is turning into a date. I don't want to be rude but…just get those trousers off!* She nodded. "Sure."

Tarquin's private elevator whisked them straight to the penthouse's second-highest floor: the tenth-floor rotunda. The steel door slid open, and he apologized in advance for the chill—"The bloody damp sneaks through the glass up here"—then, he introduced the room as "an octagon-shaped reading nook."

Nook? It's bigger than my bedroom. Leia's eyes toured the sparsely decorated, dimly lit space, home to two cobalt blue couches, a small glass table topped with neatly stacked travel and architecture books, and a well-loved drum kit. Several large framed black and white photographs of old buildings adorned the walls, but apart from the rotunda's floor-sweeping curtains and the steel ladder leading up to the domed-roof gallery, that was it. No floor lamps, no pillows, no cat...not even a whisker. Leia kept a chuckle to herself. *Nice mood lighting. Is this part of his seduction routine?*

"You're gonna love the 360-degree view...it's pretty unrivalled." Tarquin left his glass on the table and traded Leia for one of the curtains, the soaring glass windows guaranteed to show London in all its glory.

"Wow, 360, eh?" Leia glanced down at her drink. *I bet it's incredible, but that's not why I'm here. Damn. Should I make the first move?*

He grasped the weighty indigo curtain and pulled it back, revealing the distant glow of the financial district.

"Oh! It's"—Leia's eyes fell to something much closer—"ahmazing." She sucked in a breath, staring at his ass as Tarquin fussed with the curtain's tieback. *Where have YOU been hiding? Under suit jackets and long coats, that's where!*

"You've got your pick of terraces—one north, the other south." He peered beyond the glass. "Ah, bugger, it's raining"—he tossed a

111

glance over his shoulder—"but come see anyway. It's definitely worth a look."

Yeah, a closer one…preferably naked. Her heart thumped wildly, desperate to tear away his dark jeans and his confident persona to uncover what he was really made of. She set down her St. Clements beside his raspberry drink and joined him, the outside chill creeping through the windows, raising goose bumps on her skin.

"I'll never grow tired of London." Tarquin soaked up the multi-million-dollar view, his fingers restless, curling under the hem of his sweater.

Hmm. But I'll definitely grow tired of waiting. He hasn't even tried to kiss me since the rink. Leia furrowed her brow and looked out at a cluster of skyscrapers she didn't recognize across the river, twinkling like priceless jewels in the drizzly night. *If he plays the field like his friends say, why's he acting like he's sat on the sidelines?* Round and round, she spun the delicate rose gold chain around her left wrist. *Is he waiting for me to make a move? Or having second thoughts? Why even bring me here if…* She let go of her bracelet and pursed her lips. *Well, if he's not willing, I'll find someone else. I don't have time to dance around whatever this is. There are LOTS of hot guys in London.*

Staring ahead, Tarquin sighed. "Leia, I have to be honest about something."

Oh! Here we go—'I'm still in love with Alex.' Yep, got it. Jutting out her chin, she braced for his excuses to fly. *No harm, no foul. If I leave soon, I can grab late dinner with Saz.* She tugged the hair tie on her wrist and focused on the Tower of London glowering across the Thames.

Tarquin shook his head. "I can't stop thinking about you."

But… Leia's hair tie snapped against her skin.

He briefly closed his eyes then swung around, his gaze unguarded, breaths ragged. "You're smart and inspiring…and I fancy the pants off you something rotten."

The weight of his stare blazed heat through her core. *So, he does want me.* She swallowed heavily and brushed the skirt of her dress, unsure what to do with her hands. All the playful banter, the flirting, the near-kisses—it wasn't a time-wasting game at all—unless a *but* was still coming.

She angled closer, mesmerized by his soft lips gently parting, begging to be teased and explored. *Tarquin, I'll kiss you so hard you won't remember your own name.* Watching him slide his silver ring up and down his left thumb, a primal need ached between her thighs. *No feelings, just hot, uninhibited sex.*

Leia was ready to shake off her old life—her old self—with Tarquin's help.

"But I'm not sure if..." He swallowed thickly. "I don't know if I should kiss you."

Leia captured his wrist and gently drew him in, rising up on her toes to meet him. "You're not sure?" She smiled into the whisper, her lips brushing his. "If you're asking for my consent...here..." Cupping his face in her hands, she passed over his mouth again and kissed him softly, the tip of her tongue flirting with the seam of his lips. When he didn't welcome her in, she pulled back. *Seriously?* Confusion soured in her stomach "Or maybe this is a bad idea."

Tarquin let out a shuddering breath. "It's not. Look, normally, I wouldn't hesitate..." His stare wouldn't leave her lips.

Oh, Tarquin, what's holding you back? She stroked his cheek then slid her palms down to his chest, his taut muscles rousing her smile. *His heart is hammering away, raring to go, but his head is overthinking this. Is he worried I'll get attached, start texting him day and night? Nothing makes playboys run for the hills faster. But with me, he's got nothing to worry about.* Desire buzzed through Leia's body, untethering her words. "Tarquin, I don't have time for games. I'm here because I fancy you and would like to have sex with you."

A small huff left his lips, parted in surprise. "Wow. You don't pull punches."

"I would've happily skipped skating and come back here with you hours ago. We're both adults"—she curled her arms around his neck—"and I don't think you would've brought me here if you—"

Tarquin tugged her closer, answering back with deep kisses and confident strokes of his tongue, leaving Leia with no doubt about his intentions. Lost in reverence for her mouth, his kisses felt urgent and teasing but without demand.

Leia had only known one other lover who kissed like this. He was a one-off the previous year, a mistake really, but she never forgot how he made her feel respected and adored, not a plaything for his pleasure only. For months, she'd thought she would never sleep with someone like him again, a nice guy who was also fun and gorgeous, who could unravel her with a first kiss—until now.

My whole body is crying out for more. I could kiss him for hours. He's sooo good! Sliding both hands into Tarquin's hair, she kissed him harder, deeper, feeling his fingers digging into her waist as tiny gasps escaped his mouth. She smiled against his lips. *He tastes like raspberry! Sexy and sweet.*

Pressing closer, she let her hands wander, down his firm shoulders and arms until they trespassed beneath his sweater, meeting the defined curves of his chest, wide and ripped with the perfect amount of hair. *He's not crazy furry! He's toned but not bulky. Love. It.* Leia was used to athletic guys, their bodies honed to perfection in the gym and on the ice, and Tarquin didn't disappoint.

But unfortunately, *her* body was anything but perfect, the twinges in her right knee an uninvited nuisance. *Ugh, that wobbly Salchow was a big mistake.* She refocused, surrendering herself to his taste and tender touch, his delicious scent and eager moans, but each persistent throb deep in her leg pierced her bliss. *I'm making it worse, stretching like this.* She reluctantly broke away, her tights-covered heels settling back on the floor.

Tarquin smiled. "My lips are actually tingling."

Leia grinned back. "I like kissing you—a lot!" Her hands skimmed his belt and lingered in his happy trail.

Tarquin's dimples teased as his tongue flicked his bottom lip. "I can't skate for toffee, but kissing—that I can do." The thumb on his left hand stroked back and forth over her waist, his ring glinting in the dim light. "It's a shame it's not an Olympic event. I reckon I'd bag a bunch of gold medals for Britain."

Confident, much? Leia smirked and fought back a laugh, enjoying the relaxed path their tryst was taking. *He's fun—makes a refreshing change.* She dipped two of her fingers under the waistband of his boxer briefs. "But is that the best you got?" She leaned in, eager to explore more. "You don't get a medal just for showing up."

"You call that showing up?" He chuckled, scratching his temple. "Well, Judge Ginger, I plan to finish on top—so to speak."

"Are we still talking medals…or missionary? I always thought guys were more into doggie style."

"Oh, I love that, too! But sometimes nothing's better than old faithful, you know?" His weighted gaze darted to her hand edging into his underwear. "Especially the first time. It's more intimate."

Intimate? Er, should I be worried about that? Her hand stilled. "You sound like a lovesick teenager!"

"Shh! Don't tell anyone." His grin dimmed as his eyes bore into her. "Truth is, I want to watch you come."

Woah, okay! Tarquin doesn't hold back either. I knew I liked this guy for a reason. She tugged him over to one of the two blue couches. "If I didn't have performance anxiety before…" Pulling him down with her, she reveled in his delicious weight hovering above.

"You? Anxious? I don't believe it." He growled against her

skin, stopping to leave soft kisses…one, two, three…each one a little more open and wet, a little more desperate.

Leia gasped, encouraging Tarquin's mouth to roam lower down her neck. *Oh! That's…jeez, he's good at this.* His hands pushed up the skirt of her dress and skimmed her tights, sending her pulse into a frenzy. "Harder," she whispered, the twinge in her leg all but forgotten.

He looked up, all heady gaze and puffy lips. "Sorry?"

"Kiss me harder," she panted, her hands diving into his hair, twisting its softness between her fingers.

Tarquin obliged with soft bites and long sucks, his determined tongue dipping into the sweet, soft spot above her collarbone, sending shivers through her body and intensifying the hot ache pooling between her thighs.

Oh, god. Her eyes fluttered closed. *Right. There. Yes!* She bucked against him, meeting the long, hard ridge beneath the button-fly of his jeans. *Fuck!* A breathy groan escaped from deep inside her. *His clothes need to come off. Now!* She made fast work of his belt, threading it open as Tarquin pushed up from the sofa.

"What Leia wants, Leia gets." He yanked off his cashmere sweater and tore at the buttons of his jeans, shoving the denim down his legs.

Impressive! Leia glanced up from the sizeable tent in his boxer briefs.

"Uh, I'm at a bit of a disadvantage here." His lips rose into a mischievous dare she couldn't ignore. "Can I see you, too?" he asked, motioning to her dress.

It is a bit chilly in here. "I've got an idea. How 'bout we role-play? Two strangers so hot for each other she doesn't have time to take off her dress?"

"Oooh, saucy! That's a bit 'sneaky teenage shag behind the pub', isn't it?"

"I know, right?"

"You'll get no complaints from me!" Tarquin eased her back against the cushions and Leia reunited with his mouth, desperate for his sweet taste.

Kissing hard and deep, her fingertips sailed up his back and shoulders, discovering chiseled muscle, the hard-earned prize of hanging off mountains and riding waves. *If this is what extreme sports do, I'm a fan!* She swept back down and traced his hips before joining the dark hair disappearing into his boxer briefs. A quick dip under the waistband and she curled her fingers firmly around him. *He's super hard—and thick!* Tarquin groaned and rocked forward in her hand, prompting Leia to match his rhythm, her confident strokes up and down his hot silky skin pulling a loud grunt from his throat.

Leia pressed tighter, faster, her body arching, grinding against his while her mind shot off in a different direction. *Dammit. We should've discussed...we can't—fuck!* She let him go, a gasping plea on her lips. "Tarquin...wait."

She didn't have to ask twice. His hands fled her hips, his eyes dark with want and concern. "Bugger! Is everything okay?" He pressed his slightly swollen lips together and shifted back, raking a hand through his hair, tousled from Leia's adventurous fingers.

"Yes! I—it's just..." She sat up on her elbows as Tarquin rubbed his forehead like he was trying to scrub all thoughts of sex from his mind. *There's no sexy way to say this.* Leia swallowed into a twisty smile. "STIs? I've been tested—have you? Do you have *anything...?*"

His serious expression melted with relief. "Oh! Nope, no, never have I ever. I'm STI-free. My last test was before Christmas, and I always use condoms—even if my partner is on birth control. Speaking of, *are* you?"

This was easier than I thought. Gotta love a guy into hooking up. "Yep, I have an IUD, plus…" She unfastened the buttons on one of her dress's pockets, removing her phone and a foil wrapper. "I brought four. I'm up for it. Are you?" Her heavy gaze fell to the thick bulge straining against the thin cotton of his boxers.

"Ooh, you challenging me, Ginger?"

Gingah! Gimme more of those silent Rs—but they better be the only thing about him that's silent. She bit her bottom lip. *Guys who aren't quiet during sex are so hot.* "You know it."

He lay back down, gathering her in. "Well, Spice Girl"—he whispered—"tell me what you want, what you really, really want."

A giggle burst from her lips. "Be careful what you ask for."

"Don't ask, don't get." He teased with a wink.

"That's true." Condom in hand, she arched an eyebrow. "So, Tarquin"—she pulled his underwear down over his hips—"I want your cock."

"Well, he wants you, too." Tarquin yanked off his boxer briefs and tossed them to the floor, his hardness standing to attention. "I love how direct you are." He hooked his fingers under the band of her tights. "May I?"

"If you don't, I will!" she blurted.

Tarquin smiled and hurriedly peeled them from her waist. "I've been wanting to do this all night." His lustful gaze followed the black hosiery skimming along her pale skin. Down her hips, along her thighs, over her knees—where his eyes halted for a split second.

Shit. Leia tensed, feeling exposed in more ways than one. *Is he repulsed? No longer interested?* She tugged her rumpled dress back down her thighs. *Bail if you want, Tarquin. Just don't ask what happened.*

A hint of confusion dipped his brows as he liberated her manicured toes from the tights, his eyes sweeping the lengthy S-shaped scar traveling south from the top of her right knee down her shin.

I know, it's big and ugly—but it's part of me. I'm not ashamed of it.

Tarquin didn't seem alarmed or disgusted, though. Discarding Leia's tights on the floor, he stretched above her, leaving hungry kisses up her right thigh, then her left, claiming her inch by quivering inch. "My god, you're beautiful," he whispered before delivering another open, wet kiss.

He's not stopping. Leia lifted her head from the cushions, catching the playful bounce of his eyebrows.

"Hello…!" He curved forward again, his mouth warm and willing against her soft skin. Surging upward, his tongue stroked the thin strip of lace between her upper thighs. An extra intense suck and—

"Oh, GOD!" she moaned, clutching fistfuls of his hair, all her thoughts dissolving into syrupy slush.

Tarquin peered up at her, wearing a devilish grin. "I've been called many things, but cheers, love, that's a new one." He chuckled softly and shifted the lace aside, his tongue taking its time tasting, teasing her. "I've thought about this so much." Eyes never leaving hers, he licked…and coaxed, his finger pushing inside.

Leia gasped. The longer he sucked, the more she throbbed, desperate for him, desperate to give in to her wild desire. *I need more. Of him. Now.* Her mind tripped, reeling with lust.

"Tarquin?" She scooped up the condom, the sound of rain dancing on the large window filling their silence.

"You ready?" he asked, taking it from her hand.

Ready for no-strings, no-angst, ravenous sex? "Yes!" She slipped out of her panties and waited, goose bumps dotting her bare legs as he ripped open the wrapper.

Tarquin rolled on the condom and settled down between her thighs, nudging her skirt a little higher. "You're gorgeous." He smiled and pushed inside her, his eyes closing like it was almost too much. "Oh…!"

Leia sucked in a breath. *He feels so good. Thick and hot, filling me up.* Bending her legs, she squeezed them around his waist.

Tarquin began to move above her, slowly at first, making sure Leia was comfortable before picking up speed. "You good? How's London so far?"

"Amazing. I *love* London!" She hugged him, aching to taste his mouth again. *I've missed this...but it's different. He's different.* Her eager fingers scurried down his back to the swell of his ass, urging him closer, tighter, delirious with greed. "Faster," she gasped, her splayed fingers gliding over his pumping hips to where he slid deeply in and out. *This feels AMAZING. I don't want to stop. Ever. I want more...no strings, no worry. Just sex. It's such a relief...to finally give in to this.*

She inched her finger between them and touched herself, the sensations from her gentle circling and Tarquin's wild fucking pushing her head back into the couch. *A little higher, a little more—* A curse flew from her tongue.

Lost in their rhythm, Tarquin caressed her breasts through her dress and bra. If he was frustrated by the barrier of fabric and underwire, he didn't let on. "You're so fucking hot," he growled across her damp skin, his eyes smoldering with desire.

Bucking to meet him, a sharp moan escaped Leia's throat, the irresistible peak within reach. "I'm so close." She gasped, chasing her orgasm. "Are you...?"

But Leia didn't hear his answer.

Lost to a frenzy of pleasurable waves, she arched her back one last time and cried out, the delicious release trembling through her body.

"Oh!" Tarquin's frenetic movements halted into one final shuddering thrust. Head thrown back, mouth gaping, his fingers dug into the couch, anchoring him until he was spent. "Oh, bloody hell." A ghost of a smile bent his lips as he lowered himself on top of her.

I love this. Feeling his weight, his warm body, damp from exertion against mine. Pure bliss.

He pulled out and rolled onto his side. "Leia," he murmured, cuddling into her. "Now...how's *that* for just showing up?"

Sweeping her finger across his raised brow, she leaned in, her jagged breaths slowing against his flushed cheek. "I'll give you this, Tarquin: it was a damn good start." She giggled and kissed him again. "But this is a marathon, not a sprint...and I'm not done with you yet."

TEN

"Once you choose hope, anything is possible."
Christopher Reeve

TARQUIN

Howling wind and icy rain pelted the bedroom windows, wrenching tormented creaks and groans from the large panes overlooking the river, but Tarquin's smile couldn't be dampened, his king-size bed a hedonistic port in the storm. A sweeter sound held him captive— Leia's gentle breaths mid-slumber. *I don't know what's more beautiful, Leia asleep or awake.* He lay with her in his arms, heady with the scent of her long blonde hair splayed across his pillows. *How lucky am I? A week ago, we were strangers. I didn't know she existed. Now, we've had sex twice, she's in my bed hogging my duvet, and I can still taste her on my lips.* He sighed, fighting back a yawn, afraid to give in and miss a single moment. *I wasn't sure coming back here was a good idea. Of course I wanted to sleep with her, but why start something when she's leaving for New York? Why torture myself? But the way she looked at me...the way she kissed me—fuck the future. All I know is I've never wanted someone so badly and had them respond in kind. Hell, maybe she'll change plans and stay? She loves London, loves sex with me—obviously. I'd gladly take that bet. Ah, it's nice to feel hopeful for a change.*

His gaze traveled over her slightly swollen pink lips and her long lashes, eyes closed tight, smudges of eyeshadow and mascara—souvenirs from her tears of laughter when they toppled from the bed during round two—and a purple mark in the dip above her collarbone. *Sorry not sorry about that, love.* He chuckled to himself. *Maybe my New Year's resolution is coming true. Maybe she'll become—ah, quiet your mind, Balfour. You'll jinx it.*

A flash of lightning lit up the room. Leia stirred, a faint mumble escaping her lips.

"Shh, it's all right," said Tarquin, in an almost silent whisper. *Is she dreaming about our brilliant, soul-rattling sex?* He pressed a soft kiss in her hair as a crack of thunder drowned out the rain's non-stop patter on the large windows. She murmured again. *What was that? 'Wedding'...something?* He smiled. *Steady on, girl, one step at a time—*

Leia jolted awake. Mouth gasping, eyes wide, she lunged from his embrace and sat up, hauling the covers with her. "Noo!" She glared into the darkness, her fists full of duvet, her body stiff.

Blimey. Tarquin's pulse tripped in his chest. Propping himself up on an elbow, he whispered, "Leia love, you okay?"

Her eyes darted across the bed. "Ohh!" A heavy breath left her lips, loosening the tension gripping her shoulders. "*Right.*" Looking down at her dress—still on—she unclenched the comforter and retreated into the nest of pillows.

A burst of lightning strobed the room again, and within its flicker, Tarquin swore Leia's cheeks were burning pink. "Are you all right? Can I get you anything?" *Is she comfortable in that dress?*

She lay on her side and nuzzled into the duvet, her eyes softly closing. "No, it's okay. It was just a crazy dream."

"Must've been. You were chatting up a storm."

Her eyes popped open. "I was?!"

Tarquin chuckled. "Don't worry, your secret's safe."

Leia cringed. "What did I say?"

Oh, don't embarrass her more. He lay down on his side and gently brushed a strand of hair from her face. "I have no clue. You were mumbling utter bollocks."

"Oh!" A shaky laugh brought a soft smile to Leia's lips as a boom of thunder rattled the windows. "It sounds horrible outside." She yawned and glanced over Tarquin's shoulder at the bedside table. "What time is it?"

He shifted and stretched to the far side of the bed. Picking up his Rolex, his hand grazed an empty bottle of lube, making it wobble on the spot. "Just gone one a.m." He carefully placed the watch beside a half-full box of condoms and rolled back to the middle of the bed, nuzzling into Leia's neck. *Ah, this is my new happy place. I love a cuddle.* His hand slid under her skirt, the pads of his fingertips leisurely tracing circles up and down her thigh. Tarquin could feel her body relax, the tension slipping away.

"Mmm, that feels nice." Leia buried her nose in his hair as her fingers weaved through his thick, messy strands, twisting and curling. "How do you smell this amazing after sex?" She sighed, and her stomach released a long growl.

Tarquin lifted his head. "Hungry for more?"

She met his mouth eagerly, her hands holding his face. Pressing closer, she wrapped her thigh around his hip, preventing his escape—not that he wanted to.

The faint flavor of orange on her tongue, the squeeze of her thigh—skin against skin—Tarquin didn't think he'd ever be satiated where Leia was concerned. He grinned into their kiss and rolled Leia onto her back. *It's been hours since she ate something. As much as I want more of this, I want her comfortable, want her to feel at home.* He eased back from her lips, smile still intact. "How 'bout some late dinner? We never did make it to the kitchen. I'm a dreadful host—I owe you a meal, and a tour."

She smirked, running her hands along his chest. "I like what I've seen so far. I'm *very* impressed."

Me too. He pressed a smiling kiss to her lips. *But show her you have other talents, too.* "Let me make you something. Or we can wait until breakfast—it's up to you. My homemade waffles and butties are legendary! My friends swear by them."

"Butties?" She scrunched up her nose.

"Sandwiches—scrummy ones. Think bacon on thick buttery toast with brown sauce on the side. One taste and your life will never be the same." Another jag of lightning danced across the sky. "And I have Canadian maple syrup for the waffles. I know that's not exotic to you, but we could always find sexy places to lick it off of." His tongue playfully lapped her chin.

Leia squealed and her hands straying downward, settling in the line of hair on his abs.

"Aren't you glad I don't snog like that?" Tarquin chuckled and plumped up the duvet around them, creating a cozy cocoon. "So, after our sticky, steamy breakfast in bed, we can have a long soak in my huge tub with yummy-scented bath stuff. Then, when we're all blissed out, we'll curl up on the sofa for a lazy Sunday of sex and movies. Then, some more sex." A throbbing warmth grew between his thighs as her fingers caressed his stomach. *Ah, I'm getting hard again.* He brushed his lips across hers, teasing, hoping her hands would drift lower. "And later, if you fancy it, I'll cook us a proper Sunday meal: a roast with Yorkshire pudding, fresh veg, roasties. Or if you'd prefer, we could cook together..." His cheeks flushed and his words floated away, his growing ache for her derailing his thoughts. *Come on, Leia. Let's make a day of it, get to know each other better.*

"That sounds lovely, but I'm a disaster in the kitchen"—her hands slid up to his chest—"and I can't stay. My sister...she'll worry if I'm not there when she wakes up."

Whaa? Tarquin's hazy thoughts scrambled to get back on track as Leia sat up and tamed her bedhead. He rose up on an elbow. "You're gonna go *now?*" His eyes jogged down the duvet, to where he pressed hard against the sheets. "But it's bucketing outside—

you'll get drenched." He scratched his temple and looked across the bed, struggling to ignore the hot tingling in his groin. *Focus! Get back in the room!* "Uh, let me find your phone. You can text her." He flung away the duvet and leapt to his feet, the angry blisters on his toes and heels scrunching his face into a wince. "You took it out of your pocket…upstairs, right?" Mid-hobble, a flash of lightning illuminated his silhouette, showing off how eager he was for her to stay.

Leia stared, following him across the room. "Uh…yeah?"

Tarquin chuckled. *My god she's adorable when she's lost for words.*

She closed her eyes and shook her head like she was erasing his impressive erection from her mind. "But if I text now…" Her lashes flickered.

Ha! She's still gawking!

"Sarah's a light sleeper and startles easily. One time, I called her late and she fell out of bed…" She cleared her throat, and the rest of her story died a quick death.

Tarquin paused, a wry smile on his face. "Really?!"

"Tarquin…" Leia blinked into the darkness, skirting all proof he wanted her again.

"*Leia!*" He crawled onto the bed, covering himself with the duvet. "Come on, *stay*. At least until the storm passes. Then, I'll drive you home. I can't have you wandering around London in the middle of the night—or have your sister falling out of bed, bless her."

"You'd drive me all the way across London?"

Who the hell does she date? Obviously, no one with class or manners. "Yeah. Why wouldn't I? I'll even let you play DJ. Or you can fall asleep on my shoulder. That would be nice, too." He reached over and played with her hair. "Your choice."

Leia's face fell. "That's…sweet," she said under her breath.

"What's wrong?" He snickered. "Worried I'll discover you

don't *really* know all the Spice Girls lyrics?"

"Tarquin, I"—dipping her chin, she stared at the sheets—"I thought you and I were…" She let out a sigh.

"Were *what*? Hot for each other?" Smiling, he ducked his head, seeking eye contact. "Guilty as charged!"

Catching his gaze, she sucked in a breath and looked away. "You're a great guy and I like you a lot…"

Oh, no! Panic shot through his veins. *Fuck. This can't be happening! Not again—not with her.* He scrubbed his hands over his face, afraid to see her dread—or worse, pity. "Just not in *that* way, right?" Sinking into the pillows, he wished they'd swallow him whole and end his suffocating nightmare. "Was it something I did…or didn't?" The tight ache between his inner thighs began to fade. "Oh, bollocks"—he dropped his hands to the duvet—"was I too loud when we—?"

"No! You're amazing—*sex* with you is amazing. It's just…" Her shoulders slumped. "I just got divorced—in November."

"You were married?! For how long?"

"Almost four years. I should've ended it ages ago, but I couldn't do it. He was my first love, and…"

Dammit. His mouth fell open. "You still love him?"

"No! Oh *god*, no." Shifting back into the pillows, she tucked her hair behind an ear. "That ship hasn't just sailed—it sank. No survivors." Leia shook her head. "It was a horrible time. But now, I just want to enjoy myself, have fun."

Oh! Well, I can do fun! Tarquin nodded and sat up.

"I assumed you and I were on the same page." She hugged the duvet sheepishly. "I'm sorry. I didn't think you were looking for anything…serious." She offered a tight smile.

Bollocks. If you ever want to see her again, you have only one choice—LIE. "Serious? Hell, no! I get it—I mean, I haven't been married or divorced, but my heart's been broken. Fairly recently too…last summer. So, trust me, I know where you're coming from."

Leia's eyes widened. "Really? How'd you cope? It's not easy, is it?"

He shook his head. "I went up to Orkney for a week. Fresh air, old friends, family. Had a good think and decided to keep things casual from now on." *Is my nose growing? Blimey, what you'll do for a woman you fancy.* "It's been good—living in the moment, having a laugh—so, really, your timing couldn't be better. I'm all about exploring my hedonistic side."

Leia's wince softened.

If she likes that, she'll like this even more. "I'm not being cold, but I don't have time for the distractions a relationship brings. All my energy goes into growing my business."

"Oh!" She exhaled quickly. "Me too!"

Stay the course, Balfour—it's working. "And hooking up has been a real confidence boost for me post-breakup. To be honest, it's a huge relief to realize I'm still attractive to the opposite sex, that I'm still a good shag."

"That's *so* true!" Leia nodded with a half-smile. "I was with my ex for just shy of ten years, so…" She rubbed her neck and eased toward him, her fingers slipping into the overstuffed coziness of the duvet.

She's opening up. Finally. "Really? That long?"

"Yep. When I left, I had this huge fear: what if no one else wants me ever again?"

She left him? After nearly ten years. Tarquin raised his eyebrows. *What the hell happened?*

"But after my divorce, I met this guy. We hooked up a few times. It did wonders for my self-esteem, which was good because my ex basically destroyed it…" Her voice trailed off, like she had shared too much.

"Well, your ex sounds like an arsehole." Tarquin's hand moved toward hers, but he thought better of it and withdrew, pretending to brush fluff from the duvet. "You're gorgeous and smart, fun to be with. You won't have a problem finding male company—if that's what you want." *Fucking right she won't. But the thought of her with someone else...* He scratched his jaw, soothing the tightness that idea created. *You have to let it go. Don't blow it by letting your feelings for her show.*

"Yeah. I just feel out of practice, you know—meeting guys? But I love sex, so I'm not going to sit at home and wait for Prince Charming's booty call." She leaned in. "That said, I hope I wasn't too forward last night."

See! Look at the positives—she's got this healthy attitude about sex, and she wants to have it with YOU. "No, not all! I think it's great what you're doing—hooking up, enjoying yourself. Hey, if blokes can, why can't women? We think things have progressed, but the double standard is alive and well. It's unfair, really."

Leia's face lit up with the smile Tarquin couldn't get enough of. "Thank you! That's how I feel, too. A woman shouldn't have to apologize for liking sex outside of a relationship. Sex-shaming has got to stop."

"Right? As long as we respect our partners and use protection, what's the problem? We're not hurting anyone. So, not only do I get where you're coming from—I'm already there."

"Oh, good." She sighed. "I was worried I gave you mixed signals."

"Nope. I know I asked you out at the pub, but...I was hoping we'd end up here." *Technically, that is not a lie.* He brushed a lost eyelash from her cheek. "You're amazing, Leia. I had fun tonight and would love to do it again sometime—the sex, not the skating." He laughed softly. "If you're interested."

"I am." An easy smile curved her lips. "Very."

Yes! I'm quids in. His cheeks erupted into a grin. "Brilliant!"

Leia nodded. "But we need some—"

"More lube, I know! I think I've got—"

"I was gonna say rules!" She bit her lip, stifling a giggle.

"Oh. Yeah. Of course! Those too. Fucking rules."

"Is that *fucking* rules…or"—Leia made air quotes with her fingers—"fucking rules?"

"Both?" With another laugh and a curt nod, he pulled back his eye-crinkling glee, replacing it with an all-business furrowed brow. "So, how do you want to do this? Are certain nights off limits? You tell me. I'm open to all reasonable offers."

Leia smiled. "Any night is fine."

Great!

"But no gifts, no drinks, no dinner…no breakfast in the morning. No date-like activities or hanging with friends. Just sex."

No breakfast? She won't stay over, like ever? Fuck. Tarquin fought back a frown and nodded. "Well, that sounds entirely acceptable and deliciously uncomplicated. Where do I sign up? Here…?" He pressed a kiss against her collarbone, then another, the second more slow and wet than the first, like he was tasting her for the first time.

Leia trembled, her pleasurable sigh drifting past his ear. "Tarquin…"

I am GOOD! He pulled back with a self-congratulatory smile. "Sorry. Got distracted."

Her stare stalked his mouth while her hands played with his hair. "And you know it's totally fine to have sex with other people, right? Just as long as we're open about it and use condoms."

Wait? I was—other people? Tarquin's sunny grin darkened and his throat felt thick and dry like he had swallowed a lump of cotton wool. Pressing his lips tight, his gaze hopped to the incessant rain lashing his windows. He couldn't look at her, the disappointment in his eyes too raw to hide. *Even if this is a fling, I don't want sex with other people! Does she?*

"You should tell me if you want to get serious with someone else." She squinted across the pillows. "Tarquin, are you listening?"

I'm still stuck on 'sex with other people'! Raising his brows, he reunited with her stare. *Pretend you're fine with it.* "Yes! Yep!" He shifted up on his elbow. "Yes, to all of the above."

"Good, 'cause I *mean* it. I don't sleep with guys in committed relationships. I refuse to be the other woman."

She's a girl's girl—chicks before dicks. I like that. I like her. Fuck, how am I going to do this? He lifted his chin, trying to look casual and not bothered. "Well, that's another thing we've got in common. Love triangles leave me cold too, so...yeah, I'd like to know if you get serious with someone else, please and thanks." *Yeah, so I can hide in bed with a bucket of fried chicken and a bottle of Jack, sobbing my fucking eyes out.* He nodded with a tight, all-business grin.

"Oh, *that* won't happen." A chuckle left her lips as she swept her hair back off her forehead. "I'm so done with relationships. I'm happier on my own." Her words came out light and breezy, as if she'd just shared a minor detail about her life, like the elimination of skinny jeans from her wardrobe or the cancellation of her gym membership.

But the weight of that nonchalant comment pressed heavily on Tarquin's chest, her words sinking in. He forced out a laugh. "Hey, great minds think alike." He bit his cheek to keep himself from blurting out even more nonsense. *Bollocks. She's drawn a line in the proverbial sand. But surely...there's a chance I can change her mind?*

"I also wanted to ask, when we hook up, can we come back here? My sister's place is small and it would be...awkward. I don't have a bedroom."

"Whereas I have *several*," said Tarquin, trying to sound upbeat. "We could try a different one each time if you'd like?"

"So, I'll get that penthouse tour after all?"

"If you're in London long enough. When do you fly back?"

"On the eighteenth."

Less than two weeks? Tarquin's stomach plunged. *Bugger, it can't get much worse.* "That's soon."

"Yeah, but it works to our advantage, right? You said it yourself: we'll live in the moment, have a laugh, enjoy our time together, and on January 18th, we'll part without expectations or regrets." Leia grinned. "The *perfect* fling."

Tarquin faked his most sincere smile. *The perfect heartbreak, more like.*

"I'm *telling* you, my friend—angels wept, birds joyfully chirped in the dawn of a new day." Phone to his ear, Tarquin reclined slowly into his large soaker tub, a river of sweet vanilla and marshmallow-scented pink bubbles fizzing around his body, courtesy of his favorite bath bomb. "We were this perfect coming together of—"

"No. Don't." Harry chuckled through the phone, half-asleep. "I don't need to hear about you coming, together or otherwise, Balf…" His voice trailed off. "Especially at seven in the morning—on a *Sunday*. I'm chuffed you had a great time, but couldn't it wait?"

"Hazza, last night was everything. I just want to curl up in a corner and purr." Tarquin's contented grin greeted the early morning sun sneaking past the gaps in the window blind. "It's like all the mistakes, drunken shags, dates from hell—they were all worth it if they brought me to Leia." He sighed, remembering the softness of her inner thighs against his lips, her taste on his tongue, and how she cried out with pleasure, her fingers twisting in his hair. "She's exquisite."

"And leaving in two weeks. And, apparently, NOT interested in a relationship!" Harry sighed. "Mate, she left yours at four a.m. This is going to end in tears. Not hers—yours."

Jesus, Harry. Tarquin frowned and swirled his free arm through the sweet-smelling bubbles. *Can't you just play along? Let me enjoy my buzz for a few hours?* "No, it won't. I know what I'm doing. I have a good feeling about this." He glanced at the bruise on his arm, a temporary memento from crashing into the rink barrier at Somerset House. "So, how was the film? Was Lucy pissed I bailed?"

Harry ignored his questions. "Shame you didn't meet Leia last year."

"And…your point is?" With his heel, Tarquin dunked a bobbing Darth Vader rubber duck under the pink froth. He had hidden the ducks in his en suite's vanity last night so Leia wouldn't spot them.

"Well, hookups were *your* thing until Alex, and then things changed. *You* changed."

"Hmm, that's true." Tarquin winced. "Well, you know how much it pains my Slytherin arse to do this, but…fine—ten points for Gryffindor, Potter."

Harry chuckled. "Oh, you know who that reminds me of? That girl you dated before our last year at Eton. She was blonde and set up her friends based on Hogwarts Houses—"

"Oh, Pandora! Yeah, she was un-freaking-forgettable." Tarquin smiled. *That box full of sex toys under her bed…truly life-changing.*

"Didn't she go to that insane party in Wiltshire? Remember it? The outdoors one with the Ferris wheel and exotic turtles roaming the lawns."

"And strip charades by the pool! Ah, it was jolly good fun until I drunkenly got lost in their garden maze during the fireworks."

"At least you didn't take a tumble into the lake"—Harry snickered—"wearing your family's medieval suit of armor."

"I forgot about that! Blimey, yeah. Wasn't that chap Pandora's cousin or something?" Tarquin squinted, trying to pull a name from his memory. "What a twat!"

"Very nearly a dead twat if it hadn't been for the Oxford water polo team acting sharpish. Unlike his so-called uni mates who were otherwise engaged, trashing his father's wine cellar."

"I didn't know that!" Tarquin cringed. "Imagine when his parents got home from Bermuda or wherever the devil they were and found their Château Lafite 1869 smashed all to hell? I know I've done some stupid things, but I've never wrecked someone's home for shits and giggles. Wankers. I would've left had I known that. Fuck my fee."

"Oh, yeah! It was your first paid DJ gig."

"Nope, third, but still bloody great. Pandora and I...god, we were so hot and heavy behind the decks. Everyone was so pissed, nobody noticed I played the same song twice." Tarquin chuckled. "She spent half my set with her hand down my trousers. She had this fantasy about blowing a DJ while he spun, and well, you know me, making dreams come true since 1992!"

"Yeah, mostly your own!" Harry laughed.

Tarquin sank deeper into the water. "I put Fatboy Slim on, she tore open my fly and went for it. Even today, I can't hear 'Right Here, Right Now' without a blissed-out grin."

"You pillock! You've totally ruined that song for me now. Cheers, Balf."

"Hey, I didn't ask her to do it!" Tarquin reached for his first coffee of the day, balancing on the wide edge of the tub. "I was just doing my job."

"While Pandora did hers," said Harry, through a yawn. "And DJ Klimaxxx was born!"

"Oh, mate, it was *hot*." Tarquin groaned. "I couldn't wait to repay the favor, but next thing I knew, she legged it out of there."

"Didn't she leave for a birthday party or something?"

Tarquin took a quick sip. "Yep. Met up with some bloke there, according to her friend. I never heard from Pandora again. No texts, nothing."

"I remember how gutted you were. It sucks, finding out the girl you're into is seeing someone else simultaneously."

"Yeah, I thought we had something, you know? We had so much in common—indie bands, skateboarding, a penchant for rule-breaking..." Tarquin returned his coffee to the side of the bath.

"But not a desire to be in a steady relationship."

Ah, okay. I know where this is going. Tarquin shook his head slowly. "Hazza—"

"Tarq, I say this as your best friend. I love you, mate, but your potential girlfriend radar has always been rubbish. You fall too hard, too fast for women who see you as nothing more than a good time. Alex was the only exception."

He flicked bubbles off his chest. "Well, Lex *was* my most recent girlfriend, so I'd say my radar is obviously improving."

"But is it? This thing with Leia—"

"Harry—"

"You're completely deluded. Can't you see what this really is? She's getting what she wants."

"And so am I." His free hand cut through the bath water, causing the floating Darth ducky to bobble and nod over the foamy waves.

"Well, sex, yeah, but not all the great stuff that can come with it, stuff *you* said you wanted. Unless you've changed your mind?"

"I haven't changed anything. You said it yourself: hookups were my thing, remember? So, I'm doing what I do best—but as a means to an end." *It better be a happy one.* Tarquin swiped a cluster of bubbles off his bruised knee. "I *will* win her over. I'm not afraid of a challenge."

"I know you're not, but she's leaving in two weeks!"

"Her plane leaves in two weeks—doesn't mean she'll be on it." *She might be unsure about a relationship now, but give her time. She'll change her mind. Succeed or die trying, right?* Tarquin jutted out his chin. "Look, Harry, you weren't here last night. Leia's different. We understand each other. We definitely have this connection."

"Oh, Balfy. Here you go again."

"No, not again. I've been serious about *two* women, Harry. Two. That's it. Leia's only number three."

"Yeah, and the hopeless romantic in you kidnaps your brain and replaces it with candy floss. You lose all sense of reality, start booking couple's holidays, buying gifts…"

Tarquin frowned. "I haven't fallen in *love* with her, if that's what you're worried about."

"Well, good." Harry snorted. "You barely know her."

"Actually, I know more than you think."

"Sex isn't knowing someone, Tarq."

"No, but it's a good start, okay? Jesus, Harry." Tarquin swept a wet hand through this hair, slicking it off his forehead. "Despite what you think, you can learn a lot about someone in bed—like if they're giving. Or patient…if they listen. Not everyone starts off as friends like you and Lucy. Some of us take a different path. It doesn't mean a meaningful relationship is out of the question just because we slept together first. I swear, it's like someone wanted us to meet. Lucy gets it. Why don't you?"

Harry exhaled a forced breath. "Because I don't want you to go off the grid again if it doesn't work out."

What? Why is he saying—he doesn't know, does he? Dammit. It would help if I could see his face. I've never told Harry about my depression, and I'm not about to now. "Harry, I went away because *you* made it crystal clear you didn't want to be friends anymore."

A beat passed before Harry responded. "Yeah, I overreacted...but you know I had my reasons."

"Yeah, and we patched all that up, so can we drop it—please? And you can stop worrying about me. This will be the last time I fall back on hooking up. I *will* walk away with the woman of my dreams."

"Or a broken heart," said Harry.

The story of my life. Tarquin flexed his fingers under the water, his jaw tensing. "Leia's worth the risk." *Keep telling yourself that, mate.* He narrowed his eyes, staring down the morning sun creeping over the far edge of his tub. *Even if she breaks me.*

ELEVEN

LEIA

Leia carefully flipped over onto her stomach, mindful of the couch's habit of squealing under the slightest duress. *Tarquin's bed felt like a fluffy cloud. This back-breaking monstrosity should be tossed in a dumpster and set ablaze.* She hugged her pillow and closed her eyes, shutting out the brightness bursting beyond Sarah's curtains (another IKEA bargain). But no matter how tightly she scrunched her lashes, Jordan's nasally snores drilled through the morning quiet. They rose and trailed off, giving way to snorty wheezes that sounded like the raspy breathing of Leia and Sarah's childhood bulldog. *How does Saz sleep through that? He's lovely, but I would've smothered him with a pillow by now. I need to get earplugs! I keep forgetting.* She let out a long, silent yawn. *Make a note.*

Her hand skimmed over the couch and underneath Sarah's black and white knitted blanket, one of her latest masterpieces, searching…searching…until her fingers trailed over the plastic case of her phone. She dragged it to the surface and woke it up, the jarring glow piercing her sleep-deprived stupor. *Argh, it's…shit! Almost eight? I slept, what, three hours?* Mid-yawn, she punched BUY EARPLUGS into her to-do list and left her phone on her pillow. *If I'm up, I might as well get it out of the way.* Dipping her shoulder over the edge of the couch, she reached underneath, her fingers skimming dust bunnies and a forgotten gossip magazine until they met the familiar padded cover of her journal.

She rose up on her elbows and unzipped the pages, the shift

138

sliding her phone into the dip between her blanket and the back of the couch. Pen in hand, she jotted down the first three things popping into her head.

January 5, I was grateful for:
1. *landing the Salchow (wobbled but didn't fall).*
2. *Tarquin not making a fuss about my scar.*
3. *two fantastic orgasms!*

She crossed out two orgasms and wrote in three. *The second was a double.* Gnawing the end of the pen, she broke into a smile, her body aching, reliving his touch. *Tarquin, you did not disappoint.*

The vibration of her phone between the cushions earned an even bigger grin.

Hmm, I guess I didn't either! I swear his mouth might be my new favorite thing. Or his penis. A rush of heat throbbed in her panties. *Both? The man is truly gifted. And his stamina...jeez, he can last.* She stuck her fingers into the couch's gap and fished out her phone. An unexpected name glared back. *Oh! Shantelle? I haven't heard from her in weeks.* Leia pushed herself up and eased back into the cushions, shifting her journal out of the way. *It's three a.m. back home—I hope nothing's wrong.* She tapped the screen.

Shantelle: Hey, Scotty!

A scraping sound—the pocket door to Sarah's bedroom—tore Leia away as the piggish rattle of Jordan's snores escaped, reverberating down the hall. *Saz is up.* She returned to her phone, vibrating with text after text.

"Dirty stop-out!" Sarah wheeled closer, a half-laugh fighting through her yawn. "You woke me, tiptoeing in at five a.m."

"*I* woke you?" Leia scoffed above her phone. "Jordan sounds like he's swallowing his own face."

Sarah ignored the comment, motioning down the hall. "You dropped something when you snuck in."

Leia craned her neck and squinted. What looked like a flat black change purse, no larger than 2"x 3", with a kiss lock closure lay just outside the bathroom door.

"Wait a minute—is that what I think it is?" asked Sarah, a pleased smile on her lips. "Mom's mini sewing kit. You still have that?"

"Yeah. I keep it with me, just in case I need to mend something. It must've fallen out of my pocket. I'll get it in a sec." Leia returned to her phone.

"Who's that? Tarquin?"

"No. Shantelle."

"Shantelle Joy? You're still friends? I thought you lost touch." Sarah whipped off her glasses and cleaned the lenses with her pajama top. "Didn't she move or something?"

"Yeah, she quit Tiffany's and moved four times, but we're always texting, even when she's busy on set."

"Of what? Her bedroom? She's a YouTuber!"

"She *was* a YouTuber," said Leia, her brow creasing as another text landed. "She caught the eye of a talent scout and is acting now. A Netflix series."

"I don't have time for Netflix." Sarah punctuated her disdain with an emphatic nudge of her glasses back up her nose.

"Well, she's amazing in it—so amazing she got cast in her first movie straight after." Leia lowered her phone and gave yawning Sarah a flash of side-eye. "She's a good friend. Don't be mean."

"I'm not!" Her sister's sleepy gape morphed into a pinched grimace. "I'm just saying I don't watch as much TV as you do."

At least I don't read trashy magazines like you do. Leia shook her head. "Shantelle used to be scared to act in front of people. Now

140

look at her, the female lead in a film with a major studio. It's called *Lost for Breath*. Apparently, it's *Twilight* meets *Erin Brockovich*!"

A smirk toyed with Sarah's mouth. "Eco-friendly vampires? Sounds like a winning mashup."

"Joke all you want, but it's getting A LOT of buzz and it's not even out until August." Leia beamed. "Best of all, Shantelle promised to wear one of my gowns on the red carpet."

"Really? She said that? When? *Now?*"

"No, ages ago. And she wants me to style her, too. She could hire anyone, but she wants someone she knows, someone she trusts. This could be massive for me. It could lead to new clients, maybe an investor or two."

"I had *no* idea." The surprise on Sarah's face dissolved into a faint frown. "Why didn't you tell me?"

"Because I knew you'd be weird—I know you don't like her."

"I never said that!"

"You didn't have to!"

"Well, it's not that I don't *like* her, it's just"—Sarah snickered—"what's with the hippy-dippy horoscope shit she's into?"

"Oh, that's just for fun." *I think?*

"That one time I met her, she talked non-stop about her psychic advisor and astrologer and how they changed her life. If that's not annoying…" Sarah's puffy eyes trailed away, skimming over the tiny coffee table and her Will and Kate royal wedding mug. A fuchsia lipstick stain kissed its rim. "So, what does she want, then? To drag you to a tarot reading when you get back?"

Leia shrugged and resumed reading the growing stack of texts climbing her screen.

Shantelle: My horoscope nailed it! It said I'd meet a tall stranger tonite and I have! I'm at a gorgeous party eating shrimp tacos with an elf! Take a guess! Where am I?

Leia's half-mast eyes blinked lazily, the cobwebs refusing to clear. *A tall elf? Gawd, Shantelle! I hate when you drunk-text me.* She broke into a breath-halting yawn and read on.

Shantelle: Are you sleeping? God, time zones are the worst! Okay, I'll TELL you then. I'm at a party with Will Ferrell—you know, ELF! Live...from New York...

Leia's head snapped back. *What?* She squinted at the screen, re-reading Shantelle's words. *Live from New York? Oh!* Her jaw dropped. "Oh, Saz! Shantelle's at an *SNL* after-party!"

Sarah's eyes bulged. "*Saturday Night Live*? How on earth did *she* get in?"

"I told you, didn't I? She's having a *moment*."

"I HATE when people say that!" Sarah stuck out her tongue. "It's right up there with 'She's living her best life.' What else does she say?"

"I'll read it to you." Leia cleared her throat.

Shantelle: Crazy, right? We're surrounded by celebs! It all started when the guys won tonight—Morgan scored the OT winner! SO PROUD of my man! An SNL producer texted him after the game & invited us here. You'd laugh. Ty's losing to Kristen Wiig in beer pong!

Leia paused, her nose scrunching like she smelled something rotten.

"Tyler's there too?" Sarah craned her neck, angling toward the tiny screen in her sister's hands. "Shantelle's socializing with him?"

Leia nodded, immersed in her phone. "Well, Morgan *is* Tyler's defense partner. They're best friends, pretty much."

SAY HELLO, KISS GOODBYE

"Like that's not super awkward."

I knew she'd say that. "I *can* be friends with Shantelle and Morgan without seeing Ty, you know. She's always had my back." Scrolling, scrolling, Leia's thumb was on a mission. "She was there for me when it mattered, after the fire. No one else was."

"I was!" Sarah protested. "And Dad."

"I didn't mean you guys—of course you were amazing. I meant Erika, the other wives—*they* weren't there for me." A stinging sensation prickled the back of Leia's nose as her finger slowed its wild scrolling, nudging away Shantelle's rambling mentions of Lizzo and chopitos. "One whiff of scandal and I was on my—" Her eyes popped. "Oh?!" *No, really?* She blinked at the screen and read the words again.

upcycled gown…red carpet…March 28

A burst of adrenaline shot through her. "Holy shit!" Sniffing her nose, she looked up from the screen, her mouth agape. "She meant it! She *really* meant it! Shantelle wants me to dress her for a premiere in March!"

"Seriously?!" Sarah's gleeful stare collapsed. "But—I though you said her movie wasn't out for months?"

"The gown isn't for *her* premiere, it's—I'll read it to you." Leia licked her lips, her smile reflecting back from the screen.

Shantelle: Scotty, please tell me you're home soon? I need an upcycled gown for the New York red carpet of *A Promise Unspoken* on March 28.

Leia glanced at her sister. "This is bananas! Simon's actor friend is in that movie." She dove back in, reading aloud.

143

Shantelle: The film's director is friends with my director & the studio wants me to BE SEEN. I want to look cute! But can we scrap what we discussed before? I've kinda changed my mind. Please don't hate me!

"She changed her mind?" Sarah arched a brow. "How considerate."

Leia shook her head. "No, it's fine. We talked red carpet looks *ages* ago. Shantelle used to love short hems and sequins…" She dipped her chin and resumed reading the messages out loud.

Shantelle: I'd like floor-length, no sparkle. Make my ass look fierce & everything else is up to you. I TRUST you! You've got my measurements, right? Let me know if you need anything else. Btw, if you style me that night, too, I can make sure you get a nice payday from the film studio! Plus, I need you there by my side!

Leia's smile crinkled her eyes. "Yesssssss, she shoots, she scores!" Squeezing her phone, she punched the air in triumph, a playful laugh escaping her lips. "I *knew* she'd come through! She might be hard to pin down sometimes, but when she makes a promise…"

"So, you'll get paid for styling her, but not for the actual gown?" asked Sarah.

"Yeah. Most designers loan their dresses to celebs for big events. They rarely get paid. It's all about exposure and press coverage. A single mention of a designer's name on the red carpet can result in thousands of dollars in future sales."

Falling back into the couch's cushions, Leia dropped her phone on the blanket and let out a breathy sigh, her lips sliding into another massive smile. *This could change everything.* "Just imagine,

Shan posing in my gown, cameras snapping away as she tells reporters she's wearing sustainable fashion from Frill-Seekers. Celebs will see my gown. The fashion world will see my gown! What if they want to meet me, collaborate, interview me for *Vogue*...?!"

Sarah's concerned frown didn't stand a chance against Leia's cheek-aching grin. She gave in and flashed the smile Leia loved, all shiny brown eyes and almost perfect teeth. "I can see it now: my sister, fashion's new IT girl! Captivating buyers, seducing shoppers, sharing her passion for clothing with a conscience in celebrity gossip columns—" Sarah froze, her face souring over the words she couldn't take back. "I mean"—she cleared her throat—"I know you've been featured before, but..."

Yeah—for all the wrong reasons. A tingling sensation unsettled Leia's heart and her sunny smile faded as colorful Manhattan gossip pages scrolled through her mind, memories of being hounded, of her self-esteem being torn to shreds. All those photos—private moments and embarrassing revelations splashed across the web for strangers to devour. *Erika's wedding reception...the police car on our curb...* Her jaw tensed. *The babies.*

Scrunching her eyes, Leia bowed her head and swallowed hard. *What if they dig for more dirt? Or make shit up?* She shifted back on Sarah's couch, its groaning springs in unison with Jordan's sharp snores. *Could I survive that again? Maybe putting myself out there in public with my designs isn't the smartest idea.* Her gaze lingered over Shantelle's texts. *Oh, I know what you'd say, Ms. Joy: "Take a deep breath, give fear the middle finger, and jump in!"* Leia toyed with her phone. *Shantelle is always offering 'carpe diem' advice. And she's right—I can't let what-ifs derail Frill-Seekers. Not when I've overcome so much.* A flutter of purpose filled her chest. "This time will be different. It'll have nothing to do with Tyler or the fire—" She cut herself off, her face softening. "I'll be on those pages because I did something special, something Mom would be proud of." Her eyes skipped to her sister. "Saz, I want that more than any-thing. I want you guys to be proud of me."

"Aw, we are proud of you, Ley! We never stopped, you silly boo." Sarah inched her chair closer and clasped Leia's hand. "I know it's been shit, but you got through it. I wouldn't have coped half as well."

"But that's the thing—I didn't cope. I was a total mess. I broke down completely."

"And you're surprised?" Sarah widened her eyes. "After what he did to you? Lots of guys cheat, but Tyler"—she shook her head—"Tyler dropped a nuclear bomb in more ways than one. You've got nothing to be ashamed of."

"Yeah, but…" Leia twisted her lips. "Punching him in the face wasn't my finest moment."

"Like hell it wasn't!" Sarah squeezed her sister's hand and let go. "You broke the asshole's nose and made him squeal! I would've paid good money to see that, and I know I'm not the only one."

Leia let out a small chuckle before falling silent, her fingers tugging a loose thread on the sleeve of her pajamas. "You know, this is it, Saz…the chance I've been waiting for since Brooke." The mere mention of that name stole the air from Leia's lungs. She took a moment and started again. "Dressing Shantelle might help salvage my reputation."

"You *will* salvage it, Ley. But this turnaround—is it doable? Two months…"

"It'll be tough, but I'm up for the challenge," said Leia. "I've been sketching ideas for weeks, so I'm ahead of the game. I'll plug her measurements into CAD, use a 3D model, and tweak my top five choices. Then, I'll email Shan the mock-ups so she can pick her favorite."

"All without sewing a single stitch. Technology, eh?"

"I know, right?" Leia let out a heavy breath. "Once she chooses,

I'll start draping—provided I've found the right fabric. I'll search online later. There's bound to be dead stock suppliers nearby. I can't waste a second. It's gotta be go, go, go."

"Little Miss Busy is back in business." Sarah smiled. "I guess you won't have time for much else. It's good last night's sex adventure was a bust."

What? Leia furrowed her brow. "No, it wasn't a bust." She scratched her bedhead. "Tarquin was amazing. He's definitely talented—in more ways than one." She sat back, remembering him between her thighs, his tongue warm and persistent, making her climax again and again. A blush rose on her cheeks. "Why'd you think last night was *meh*?"

"You came home early. I hope you took a cab—the Night Tube can be sketchy."

"Tarquin drove me."

"Drove you?" Sarah's voice rose, a soft smile tweaking the corners of her mouth. "From Shad Thames? That's easily an hour-long round trip."

Leia nodded, her eyes falling to the floor and the umbrella she had lent him days earlier. "Well, he offered…"

"Sweet! How many guys would leave a warm bed in the middle of the night for a girl they barely know?"

"In my experience, none." Leia plucked the pen from her gratitude journal. *He was lovely. Ignoring my scar, wanting to spend the day with me, wanting to cook for me…so attentive and caring like— oh. Shit! Like he was auditioning to be my boyfriend.* She bit her cheek. *I can't tell Sarah all this. She'll get more excited and have us married off before I fly home.*

"So, why kiss goodbye to a kind, hot Brit with amazing stamina and morning wood?"

"Oh my god!" Leia swept her hair off her shoulders, twisting it into a bun. "I'm so not talking to you about *that*!" She stabbed her pen through her messy up-do, keeping it in place. "I left because cuddling and staying for breakfast are things couples do, and we are *not* a couple."

Sarah lifted her chin, her eyes narrowing into a squint behind her glasses. "Nice hickey."

What? Leia winced. "Where?!" Her hands flew to her throat. "I didn't see it last night."

"The hollow by your collarbone. Left side," said Sarah. "He's a bit of a keener, eh?"

Fuck. Leia grabbed her phone and opened the camera app. *How bad is it?*

"When are you seeing him again?"

Reversing the camera, Leia angled the screen in front of her neck. "I dunno." She tilted her head and tugged her pajamas aside. *Ah, jeez!* Tarquin's amorous souvenir earned a frown and a terse "Ugh." *This is my fault, telling him to kiss me hard.* She closed her eyes tight for a beat and dropped her phone in her lap, but her fingers fled back up to her stretched collar, yanking it over the purple mark. "We had fun, but…I think we want different things."

"What? Anal?"

Leia snorted out a laugh. "*Saz*! No! I think he might be looking for something more than sex."

"Didn't you discuss that?"

"Yeah, but still. It's just a feeling I have." Leia closed the neck of her pajamas one button at a time ensuring that Jordan—when he snored himself awake—wouldn't spot Tarquin's love bite and piggyback on Sarah's teasing.

Sarah scooped up her Will and Kate mug. "I think you're overreacting." She peered inside and sneered at the cold dregs of last night's milky tea swirling in the bottom of the cup.

"No, I'm being cautious. I can't get involved with someone who wants something I can't give."

"Just because Tarquin was a gentleman last night doesn't mean he's catching feelings, Ley. It means he's nice! You've just forgotten what that's like. Seriously, your alarm bells are triggered too easily. Not every guy is an asshole, you know."

No, just the ones I get mixed up with.

"What was his place like?"

"Like a castle in the sky—no joke." Leia slumped back into the couch. "Imagine a historic warehouse converted into apartments, and his place is the lavish penthouse with *five* massive floors."

Sarah's eyebrows disappeared into her bangs. "*Five?*"

"Yep! We took his private elevator to get to the top one."

Mouth agape, Sarah curved forward in her wheelchair. "He has his own elevator? God, he's a man after my own heart."

I knew she'd love that. Leia chuckled. "I wasn't surprised he has lots of man-toys, but I didn't expect so many books. They're everywhere! On shelves, coffee tables, all neatly stacked—even inside a red telephone box."

"What? Like a *real* one?" Sarah giggled. "You took a selfie with it, didn't you?"

"No!"

Sarah reached out. "Let me see your phone."

"I didn't!"

"Well, it must be the only one in London you haven't snapped."

Leia shrugged. "So, I like them."

"You *love* them!"

I do. I'm obsessed. "Tarquin's also got a baby grand piano and a pop art collection. And he loves to cook."

"Jeez, Ley, you read him all wrong."

She picked at the case on her phone. "Yeah, I couldn't believe it when I spotted Warhol and Lichtenstein originals in his place."

"Christ on a bike! Jordan's gonna freak when he hears that! They're having a huge Warhol auction at his work."

"Well, it gets better," said Leia. "He owns an original signed Banksy, too."

Sarah's jaw dropped. "You *love* him!"

"Yeah, and his print is my favorite: the young girl reaching for the heart-shaped red balloon—"

"Drifting out of her grasp!" Sarah finished Leia's sentence. "Wow, I hate to think what that must've cost. Where does he keep it?"

"It's in his living room overlooking that gorgeous bridge. You know, the old one that looks part castle, part bridge?"

Her sister squeezed the mug in her grasp. "Tower Bridge? That's his view?! Oh, man. That's just—wow. A view you could fall in love with, and despite all that, you *still* don't want to date him?"

Leia rolled her eyes. "Saz, if you like him so much, maybe you should."

"He sounds perfect for you, that's all. I'd hate for you to kiss him goodbye just because—"

"Tyler sounded perfect, too, remember?" She shook her head. "I uprooted my entire life for him—twice. I won't let myself go down that road again." Her sister opened her mouth to say something, but Leia cut her off. "Even for great sex with a rich British guy with a castle in the sky."

150

TWELVE

TARQUIN

One week later

Fighting the heaviness squeezing his chest, Tarquin peered through a floating veil of dust and ash, his polished shoes crunching shattered glass and scorched beer mats with each step. He rubbed his stingy eyes and swung his flashlight once more over the charred remains of what used to be a maze of tables and chairs as a wheezy tickle stole his breath. He sputtered and coughed, the eerie essence of the derelict Spitalfields pub creeping into his lungs. *It sucks to be forgotten, eh, old boozer? You must've been a showstopper once upon a time.* Built in 1860 but shuttered in 2012, the abandoned property had recently survived an arson attack and two failed demolition orders. If the price was right, Tarquin hoped to return the once popular tavern to its former glory and save it from being flattened to make way for another soulless fast food joint or pound shop.

Fuck. I'll pop a contact lens if I'm not careful. I should've worn my glasses. I wasn't thinking this morning...my head's all over the place. He closed his eyes briefly but found no relief, the itchy burn conspiring with the churning in his stomach. *I can't stop thinking about Leia.* A cough hijacked his lungs. *Shit. I promised myself I'd let her reach out to me, let her call the shots—but what if I don't hear from her? It's been a week and still no texts.* On the far wall, the bright beam of his flashlight crawled across a barely recognizable dartboard, its wires and numbers melted and twisted from unimaginable heat. *Is she ghosting me? Or playing hard to get?* He fussed with his hard hat digging into his scalp and scrunched his

151

eyes at the water-damaged walls and boarded-up windows blocking the midday sun. *Fuck it, there's only one thing for it.* He secured his lit flashlight under the arm of his suit jacket and tugged his phone from his trouser pocket, quickly typing out a text.

Tarquin: Simon, quick FaceTime call? Only if Leia's not there.

A minute passed. *No response, nothing.* Tarquin chewed his lip. *Maybe Si's at yoga?* He set down his flashlight on a wobbly table with three legs, its surface a ghostly pallor of ash and chunks of fallen plaster. *Or out with Leia for lunch?* He collected his reusable coffee cup, recently purchased in the hopes of showing Leia he could be eco-friendly, too. *Bloody hell, I miss her. That cute laugh, her beautiful blonde hair, her lips…on me. Ahh, what are you up to, Leia?*

Downing the dregs of his fourth coffee of the day, his tired eyes pored over the singed wooden bar and the cracked mirror hanging behind the long-forgotten (and long-ago-drained) liquor bottles coated with swirls of caked-on soot. A ratty plastic bag, half-melted and clung to a nearby beer tap, its chunky red font faded but still readable, snapped Tarquin to attention. *SPORTS NOW? Dammit, Balfour! Get your head back in the game! You'll never prove Dad wrong carrying on like this.* He sniffed sharply, the stench of burnt rubber irritating his sinuses. *Okay, so the question I should be asking is: Can I bring this pub back to life without destroying its history and old-fashioned charm?*

A high-pitched squeak jerked the cup away from his lips. The kitchen door mid-swing spit out the fifty-something real estate broker, the blazing headlamp on his hard hat glaring like a third eye. Barrel-chested with thick biceps bulging through his polyester suit and a crooked nose you'd need a roadmap to follow, he looked just as happy to give you a fat lip as a property sale. "So, Mr. Balfour," he said, plucking a stubby pencil from behind his ear. "Made a decision yet?" He raised the two fuzzy gray caterpillars he called eyebrows and pushed out his lips, his hard stare and glowing headlamp landing on his clipboard, the papers discolored with cigarette ash and smears of Worcestershire sauce. "Give me the magic number and I'll call off the other bloke. He's due at half-three. He's bringing an offer—and blueprints."

"Blueprints?" Tarquin snorted, fighting back a sneeze. "For what?"

"A takeaway. Tacos, I reckon." The guy's sneer hinted that Mexican cuisine wasn't his favorite. "He's dying to tear this shithole down."

The cheeky bugger. "Not if I can help it." Skirting a trail of mouse droppings on the bar, Tarquin slammed down his empty cup and looked at his Rolex. *15:10. Shit, blueprint bloke will be here in twenty minutes.* His pulse continued to gallop. *Think with your HEAD, not your heart. Can you really save this place? Or is it too far gone? Fuck, I need to crunch more numbers.* He pressed his lips together, the weight of the pub's future leaning heavily on his shoulders. *I need more time.* Wiping his brow, he clocked a half-peeled West Ham football club sticker on the side of the broker's hard hat. Tarquin's wide eyes went unnoticed—the property guy/Hammers supporter was scratching something illegible in pencil across his papers. *It's worth a shot. If there ever was a bloke into footy and pints, surely he's it!*

The knot in Tarquin's throat loosened along with his tight smile. "I'd love to restore this place, bring back football for the punters. Big screens, cheap pints, pies and sausages—none of that posh nosh or tasteless fast food other places serve up. Just proper British pub grub, you know?"

"Yep. You've got twenty minutes." The West Ham fan kept writing, ignoring Tarquin's idealism.

Someone woke up on the wrong side of the bed. Tarquin frowned. *Go full-on footy.* "So, Hammers, eh? Me, too! Been to a match this season?"

"Not yet. I promised my grandkid, but…" He shrugged and flipped a page on his clipboard.

"Aw, that's a shame. Your grandson would love it."

"Granddaughter!" The broker snarled and tore away from his notes, his headlamp's glare blazing across Tarquin's face.

Jesus! He flinched, his eyelids scrunching shut. *How was I to know?* Tarquin cautiously blinked his sore eyes open and slipped into an earnest smile. *Gimme a break, mate. I'm trying here.* "Oh. Well, that's great you have footy in common…it's an important bond, that."

Returning to his clipboard, the broker's nostrils flared as he scrawled a jumble of messy letters across his papers.

Okay, last chance. Hit 'em in the feels. Tarquin scratched his temple. "You know, my mum's dad was a huge football fan. He took me to my first match—the Hammers at Upton Park! I was five, maybe six, and completely gobsmacked by the match day buzz. He got me a program, a bag of chips drenched in vinegar, then he let me sing along to all the dirty footy chants. It was heaven." The memory made Tarquin genuinely chuckle.

The broker sucked his teeth and frowned at his watch as if Tarquin wasn't there.

"Grandpa was a builder, worked in the Docklands. He was always grafting, so I loved every chance to be with him, you know? Sitting in the stands watching West Ham, just me and him—it was everything." Tarquin dipped his head, seeking a reaction beneath the brim of the other hard hat. *Nothing? Come on, guy! Feel something.* "I wanted to be just like him. That's why I build things. Looking back, I thank my lucky stars he took me to that match. We lost him a year later." *If that doesn't warm his cold, dead heart…*

His story earned a flicker of stony side-eye.

That's all I get? Tarquin straightened up and choked back a sneeze, his eyes scratchy from dust and ash overload. *Gramps, please forgive me for what I'm about to say.* His attention circled back to the broker, digging through the pages curled over the top of his clipboard. "Actually, you remind me of him." The words had barely left Tarquin's lips when he choked into a cough. *I know! It's an ugly lie, but I need to buy more time!*

The cyclops tilted his head toward Tarquin once more.

Is that a smile? Tarquin grinned. "Making memories with your granddaughter…you can't put a price on that." He woke up his phone. "Look, I know some people. How 'bout I call them up, get you some great tickets—"

"Oh, mate!" The widening smile rippled through the broker's graying stubble as he slapped his clipboard on the bar. A nasty cloud of ash and plaster swirled into the musty air. "You honestly think I'd fall for that gobshite? I wasn't born yesterday." He sneered at his watch.

Tarquin's face fell. "It's not gobshite—"

"Now you've got *fifteen* minutes."

The *Star Wars* theme wailed from Tarquin's palm. *Fuck. When it rains…* He glanced down, catching a full-screen image of himself with a little photo bubble in the top corner. *Simon, FaceTiming.* He threw a glare in the broker's direction. "I've gotta take this—I'll be back in five."

Tarquin whipped off his hard hat and rushed outside, the unrelenting mid-January sunshine stabbing his sore eyes into a squint. Along the curb, a double-decker bus rumbled to a stop, so he hit accept and cranked the volume, but the sun's cheery glow obliterated much of Simon and the shoulder of the person sat beside him. *Who's he with?* "Hey, Si!" he shouted over the traffic. "How's tricks?"

155

Simon glanced off screen. "Don't you mean how's Leia?"

Oh, mate! She's right there?! Tarquin's heart kicked against his ribs as he held back a breath. *Bollocks.* His cringe twisted into a sheepish smile. "Oh, *hey*, Leia—"

Simon tilted his phone, the picture zooming over the woman sat to his right wearing a frilly blouse and a blank facial expression. "It's a mannequin, silly."

A hard exhale pushed through Tarquin's lips. "Well, I couldn't tell."

Simon's live feed shifted back to his face again, and his fake friend left the conversation. "Leia's out running errands, and yes, I *know*."

Fuck. "Erm…she told you?" Tarquin veered into the narrow alley between the pub and a fish and chips shop, trading the sun and most of the street noise for the reek of grease and rotting haddock wafting from a small dumpster. *Jesus, that's rank!* "Gimme a moment." He grimaced and held his phone aloft, squeezing past the overflowing bin, putting distance between himself and the stench. "Sorry…" His stare returned to the screen as he rested his hard hat upside down on the dented lid of a recycling bin. "What did she say?"

"A week has passed and you haven't heard from her." Simon smirked. "So, how does it feel, eh, Tarq? Being the one waiting, wondering, thinking *why hasn't she called*?"

"You're loving this, aren't you?" Tarquin nodded, an anxious chuckle behind his tight lips. "Look, mate, just put me out of my misery. If she's said something—"

"She didn't."

She didn't mention me? That can't be good, either.

"I asked about her weekend and she got tongue-tied, so I put two and two together…her blush pretty much confirmed it."

"And? What did she say?"

Simon laughed like he was reveling in every minute, torturing his friend. "I think it's great. Two of my friends hooking up, enjoying each other's company."

"So, she enjoyed herself? I wasn't sure."

Simon took a long sip from a colorful juice and shook his head. "Tarq, you of all people couldn't, you know, *tell...*?"

"Of course I could tell! I *know* she..." *Unless she faked it?* He pressed his lips together. "What I mean is, I'm not sure she wants to see me again. I drove her home after, but she was quiet, seemed lost in thought." He glanced down the graffiti-sprayed alley, spotting a rat eating something from a discarded Styrofoam container. A frown soured his expression as he shuffled sideways back toward the smelly bins, leaving the rodent to dine in peace. "Hopefully, she wasn't having regrets."

"Oh, I didn't get that impression." Simon hid his grin behind a sip of a bright red juice.

"Did she *say* she wasn't?"

"She didn't say a whole lot, okay? But she did say she 'had fun'," said Simon.

His face pinched.

"Tarq, stop doing a Freddie! Don't overanalyze it! From what I've seen, Leia values her privacy, so if I were you, I wouldn't take it personally if she's hesitant to open up. She said she had a good time, so stop worrying. And for what it's worth, I'm pretty sure she hasn't been out with anyone since."

Thank Christ. Tarquin blew out a breath. *That 'sex with other people' thing was doing my head in.*

"In fact, she hasn't been out full stop—not with her sister, not with me, no one."

"Really? Why?"

"She got a last-minute commission—a red carpet gown. Funnily enough, it's for a client going to Mark's New York premiere of *A*

157

Promise Unspoken."

Erghhh. Must everything come back to Keegan? Tarquin forced a grin. "Wow, small world. Is Mark going?"

"No, his play here doesn't end until mid-April, and the film premiere is late March. Leia's been laser-focused, traveling around sourcing material and draping fabric day and night. Two mornings last week, I woke up and found her face down, asleep on my work table."

"Blimey. She *slept* there?"

Simon nodded. "She's skipping meals, doing whatever it takes to get the job done. But two days ago, she trashed everything— started over from scratch. She was cursing a blue streak, pulling out pins and stitches, swearing at Liam."

Bollocks. There's a guy? The pungent stench from the dumpster, the breezy mention of another guy…Tarquin's stomach rolled with nausea. "And Liam is…?"

"Do I detect a hint of jealousy, Monsieur Balfour?"

A sour taste tormented his throat. "Si—"

"Relax! Liam is my spare sewing machine."

Oh, for fuck's sake! The tension in his jaw let go as he chuckled. "You named your sewing machine?"

"Don't judge! You named your car."

"Yeah, because a gorgeous '66 Alfa Romeo Spider deserves a name!"

"*Millie*? Yeah, that's très sexy, Tarq."

"I didn't call it Millie! It's the *Millennium Falcon*! Lucy calls it *Millie* to get on my wick."

"Nice to see it's working." Simon's sarcastic grin dissolved. "But…this week's been hard for Leia. I feel terrible, watching her struggle, knowing I played a part. I should've trashed Liam ages ago. He's stubborn and belligerent just like his stupid namesake."

Belligerent Liam. Of course. Tarquin squinted at his phone. "By chance, would that be Liam from Oasis? You're a fan? Since *when*?"

"Freddie's the fan. He named it!" Simon smiled. "And yes, he named the other machine Noel. Noel's more reliable than Liam, less prone to throwing a hissy fit. Anyway, I made Leia swap with me."

"That was kind of you," said Tarquin, glancing anxiously at his Rolex.

"Yeah, too kind. The day after, I was pulling *my* hair out. But you'll never guess what Leia did?!" Simon looked away.

"Er...swapped back and sewed by hand?"

"See for yourself..." Simon flipped his phone's camera around, his feed landing on a bolt of cerise pink chiffon sprawled beside a sewing machine.

Tarquin stared blankly at the screen. "Uh...Si, I don't know what I'm looking at."

"Leia bought me a new machine." Simon's pointing finger invaded the screen. "This is it!"

Tarquin's eyes widened. "She bought you that?"

"I know! It showed up this morning and my jaw hit the floor!"

That's so generous of her. "You naming this one, too?" Tarquin joked.

Simon's off-camera snicker was barely audible over the thundering bang of a recycling truck hitting a pothole beyond the alley. "I insisted on paying her back, but she refused, said it's a thank you gift for my hospitality."

A thank you gift? Already? Tarquin leaned in, seeking clarity. *But she's only been at Si's for a week or so. Why is she thanking him now?* "Is she headed back to New York *before* the 18th?"

"No." Simon reversed his camera, capturing his head shake. "Don't think so."

"But she's heard back about that full-time museum job by now, yeah"

"Nope. Not a word, not even about a second interview. Every day she comes in, waiting, hoping. I feel bad for her. I wish they'd just tell her she didn't get it so she can move on."

"So, you think she'll *stay*?"

Simon shrugged. "I guess it depends. I know she's happy being with her sister and she likes London...why don't you drop in and ask her? She could use a break. If that blush was anything to go by, I think she'd be pleased to see you."

I'd love to see her. Tarquin winced. "But I can't just drop in. You know how hookups work, mate. Leia set some pretty strict rules."

"Since when do *you* follow rules?"

Since Leia made them. I want to respect her wishes. "She was pretty clear about what she wanted, Si. Socializing together with friends—you—is a no-go. I don't want to do anything that'll fuck things up."

Simon's purposeful smile beamed through the screen. "I think the only way you'll fuck it up is if you keep your distance."

He's got a point.

"So, get your ass over here," said Simon. "If you leave now, you'll catch her before she's done for the day."

A jolt of movement caught the corner of Tarquin's eye. A man, phone aloft, was backing up on the sidewalk, snapping photos of the pub. *Is that blueprint bloke?* Stretching his wrist, Tarquin checked the time. *Bugger! He's early!*

"You won't have many chances left, Tarq. She's flying home in four days."

"I know, but..." The photographer hurried away, vanishing from Tarquin's view. *Shit! I can't lose this deal. I need this pub!* He grabbed his hard hat and rushed down the alley, squeezing past the smelly dumpster, and reemerged on the sun-drenched sidewalk, the bustle of hungry Londoners on their lunchbreak swallowing him up.

"Hey?" Simon squinted. "You okay?"

Tarquin pushed through the crowd. "Si, I've got a work emergency. Talk later." Stashing his phone in his suit jacket, his hard stare flitted up, catching the Tex-Mex franchisee and the joyless broker, clipboard stuffed under his arm, shaking hands in the pub's doorway.

THIRTEEN

LEIA

The next day

Leia stifled another yawn and tilted her head, studying the cerise pink chiffon draped over the curves of her dress form. Showcasing a gathered bodice with a plunging V-shaped neckline, the floor-length gown was elegant and glamorous, temporarily sleeveless, and held together with an army of pins. *Is it too much boob? Shantelle wants a killer ass, but I think she can pull off both.* Twisting her lips, Leia fussed with the silk again and stepped back, glancing over her shoulder. "Simon, what do you think? Was the heart-shaped neckline better?" She stared at her work in progress and nibbled her fingernail. "I'm torn."

Mid-sketch, Simon set down his stylus pen and looked up from his drawing tablet, a jumpsuit sketch destined for a video conference call with a New York store nicely taking shape on his laptop screen. "Oh, I like this one"—he nodded enthusiastically, the pitter-patter of cold rain on the windows filling his pause—"a lot!" He leaned over the work table, littered with pins, splayed scissors, and two nearly empty bottles of cola—Leia's pick-me-up of choice. He scratched his beard. "Is this the dead stock you found in Reading?"

"No, the other place you told me about—in Nottingham? Feel it!" Leia handed him a piece and stuck her hands in the pockets of her old University of Pittsburgh hoodie. Paired with her favorite pair of faded boyfriend jeans and her chunky-soled combat boots, the cozy zip-up from her alma mater was the perfect outfit for a damp, blustery day. It also didn't hurt that it kept Tarquin's fading hickey a secret. Each day, the love bite paled a little more, along with her hopes of hearing from him again. "They had tons of it, no dyeing required."

"It was *already* this color? That's a time-saver." Simon's forehead creased as his thumb sailed along the fabric. "It's great quality. Soft and light, will cling in all the right places. Shantelle will feel *and* look amazing in it."

"Yeah, I totally lucked out. I showed it to her last night over FaceTime and she signed off on the color and heart-shaped neckline, but"—Leia's hands burrowed farther into her hoodie's pockets as her stomach let out a long, snarly growl—"I'm having second thoughts. This design feels...too *safe*, maybe? You only debut on the red carpet once. I think she should make more of a splash, be the actress everyone's talking about."

Simon set the fabric sample on the table and stood up, joining Leia in front of her rough design. He crossed his arms, the sleeves of his white dress shirt rolled up to his elbows. "The deep neckline will draw lots of attention. Can Shantelle carry it off? What's she like—is she shy or outgoing?"

"She's quiet one on one, but get her to a party and she lights up like the Vegas strip." Leia laughed, removing her hands from her hoodie. "She becomes another person. It's kinda scary. Actresses, right?" She pulled out a pin and deepened the neckline. "Shantelle doesn't usually wear anything low-cut, but her body is curvy and athletic, so beautiful. If anyone could pull this off..." She squinted at the fabric and stuck the pin in again.

Simon spun the form around, examining the back of the pinned garment. A panel of pink lace covered the upper back, offering a discreet glimpse of the mannequin's 'skin' beneath. Leia had salvaged the intricate needlework from a damaged vintage dress and had it dyed to match the rest of Shantelle's gown. Simon twirled the dress form again, admiring the elegant material accentuating the figure's décolletage. "I'd go with your gut. Keep the plunging V." He nodded. "Sexy but tasteful. Bit of boob tape on the day and she won't feel like everything is on display."

I've missed this, having someone to bounce ideas around with. Leia smiled as he returned to his chair. "That's what I thought. Thanks!"

"Any time." His eyes trailed down the draped cerise fabric as Leia fussed with it, a smoothing of a crease here, a pinch with a pin there. "I can't get enough of that color. Really pops." He picked up his 'energizer juice', a concoction of apple, orange, carrot, and ginger purchased from the café on the corner.

"That's what sold me." Leia swept her misbehaving hair off her forehead. Wild and temperamental, it kept falling into her face. She yanked a hair tie from her wrist and corralled her blonde locks. "I hope I have some left over. I'd love to make a skirt for myself."

"If you have time." He sipped slowly, savoring his healthy drink.

Huh? Leia twisted, her perky ponytail playing catch-up, landing on her shoulder. "Why wouldn't I?"

Lowering his beverage, Simon pulled his chair closer to the table. "You might be swamped with orders after Shantelle slays in your gown. You know, like the Kate Middleton effect."

"Oh, I'd gladly give up my skirt to have *that* problem!" Leia scooped up two smaller pieces of lace from the table. "If only, eh?"

"A boy can dream," said Simon, picking up his stylus. He sailed it across his drawing pad, the flourish creating the beginnings of a sleeve on his laptop screen.

"Yeah." Her fingers dipped into the holes stitched into the lace's flower pattern. "But I have to be realistic. I've only ever planned on winning one customer at a time. I know there are smart shoppers out there who want limited-edition dresses that look good *and* help the planet. I just have to find them."

"How's it going finding a financial backer?"

Leia's smile wavered. "It's not. The words 'limited-edition' and 'custom-made' send them running for the hills. They worry I won't earn as much as someone with a large production run, so apparently, I'm not a good 'return on investment'. Sustainability might be buzz-worthy, but when it comes down to it, backers would rather fund designers who swerve green initiatives and flood the market with clothes. But I don't want that for Frill-Seekers. Upcycling is about *quality*, not quantity. I need someone who understands that and be-lieves in repurposing old things as much as I do." She pressed her lips together. *Shit. I literally just described Tarquin...*

Leaving the lace on the table, she dug into her hoodie pocket and pulled out her phone. *Still not a peep.* The text-free screen felt like a kick to her gut. *Did my rules scare him off? Is he one of those guys after all, the kind who insist on 'being in charge'? Well, what-ever. I'm not changing who I am just so I can get laid.* Her forehead creased. *If it's not my rules, maybe he met someone. I wouldn't be surprised—a guy like him won't stay single for long.*

She tucked her phone in the back pocket of her jeans and revis-ited the lace, laying a swath over each shoulder of the dress form, making flirty, albeit temporary, short pink sleeves. Her stomach grumbled again, loud enough to earn a concerned squint from Si-mon.

"Feel free to tell me to mind my own business, Leia, but how *are* you supporting yourself? A part-time job can't put food on the table, let alone fund a fashion line."

Simon kills me. He's like Sarah, comes right out and says what other people only think. Letting out a sigh, she stopped fiddling with the lace. "It doesn't. That's why I need that full-time position." *And?* She bit her cheek. *Go on, tell him. You've got nothing to be ashamed about, remember?* "But I have some help, too...from my divorce settlement."

165

"Oh, *really*?!" Simon's face lit up above his drawing tablet and laptop screen. "Hey, you go, girl! I hope you took him for everything."

Leia laughed. "Well, not *everything*. I gave some of the cash to a friend who needed it more than I did. What's left covers rent on my one-bedroom apartment in Brooklyn, which doubles as my workroom. It also funds some Frill-Seekers costs, but my other expenses are paid out of what I earn. I have a side hustle, too—I mend vintage clothing and do alterations."

"With what time? When do you sleep?"

"You sound like my dad!" Leia scoffed. "He says I put him to shame, but honestly, no one works harder than he does. He runs two businesses, oversees my mom's literacy charity, helps out with the NHL alumni association, and does commentary on Saturday night hockey broadcasts."

"You serious?" Simon set down his stylus, leaving his jumpsuit sketch with half a sleeve. "He played in the NHL?"

"Yeah, for nine years—for Vancouver, Calgary, and Chicago."

Simon picked up his juice, taking a quick sip. "I grew up watching *Hockey Night in Canada* on the CBC every Saturday…"

Simon likes hockey?

"…and your dad is on it now. How fun is that?"

Leia smiled. "So, being a Montréaler, you must be a Habs fan."

"Ah, good guess, but nope. Isles all the way."

What? The New York Islanders? A sour taste rose in Leia's throat. *Out of all the teams, he cheers for Tyler's? There's no way I can tell him my married name was McClelland. Heaven help me if he's up on all the gossip. I couldn't deal with his pity.*

"Imagine how that went down growing up in Montré—" His phone erupted beside his drawing tablet. "Just a sec." He casually picked up. "Hey, Spence." Simon's eyes pinched—then opened wide, brimming with joy. "Oh! Be right there." Pushing back his chair, he abandoned his phone on the table. "There's a delivery downstairs."

Thank god. Leia nodded in relief.

Stairs groaning under Simon's pounding size elevens, she worked her dress form, pinning lace tiers to the shoulders before fiddling with the neckline again. She whipped out her phone from her jeans and stood back, fitting the full silhouette into frame. *If Shantelle likes these changes, I can start sewing tonight.* She snapped photos from different angles and began to record a video, but a text interrupted her fashion shoot.

Sarah: I GOT IT!

Leia's heart leapt into her throat. "Saz!" She squealed as she typed.

Leia: I knew you would! So proud! xo

A second text bubble bumped Sarah's first message up the screen.

Sarah: Let's celebrate! Meet at 7. St. Bart's Brewery on West Smithfield.

Leia snickered. "Yes, Saz." She selected the thumbs-up emoji and hit send as Simon, barely winded from his sprint up the stairs, strode through the doorway with a large wicker box in his arms. *What the?* Her stare zeroed in on the metal buckles and leather ties holding the lid closed. "What is THAT?"

"Lunch!" Simon grinned, resting his weighty bounty on the table. "Just in time, too. With all that growling coming from your stomach, I thought an alien was about to burst from your belly."

Leia chuckled and slid her phone into her hoodie's pocket. "You sure it's not lunch *and* dinner?" She tilted her head, examining the black F & M stenciled on the wicker's front. "It's massive!"

"Heavy, too. It's a hamper from Fortnum & Mason on Piccadilly. Crazy, eh?"

Piccadilly? Sounds expensive. "Isn't Fortnum & Mason like Harrods?"

"Yeah, they're both upscale stores, but Fortnum's specializes in food, wine, and homewares from around the world. Even the Queen shops there." Simon threaded the ties through the buckles. "If you're looking for fancy cookies, teas, or jams, Fortnum's is the place. They do a gorgeous afternoon tea, too. You'd love all the baked goods and fancy sandwiches."

"Maybe, yeah." Leia ran her finger along the edge of the wicker box. "Looks like I picked the perfect day to forget my lunch. Simon, you really didn't have to."

"Hold your horses, girl—it's not from me." The stairs creaked as he flipped open the lid and reached inside.

A satisfied client, then? Her eyes narrowed. *Is that prosecco? Spencer's gonna love that.*

"Tarquin sent it." Simon glanced over his shoulder, his smile greeting someone blonde—someone who wasn't Spencer.

"That's Tarquin, Mr. Generous!" The blue-eyed arrival whisked off her knit hat, her long bangs and tresses speckled with mist from the wintery mayhem outdoors. "He can't help it. Giving is in his DNA."

Tarquin sent it? And...who's she? Leia's eyes widened. *She's American. Pretty. Obviously knows Tarquin.*

Simon met her gape. "Leia..."

A flicker of surprise washed over the American visitor's face. She looked at Leia and her baggy Pitt hoodie.

"Meet one of my closest friends. Alex Sinclair, playwright and

Twizzler aficionado."

Tarquin's ex, Alex? Oh, shit! Leia's breath hitched. *I knew I should've made an effort. I look like a college kid who fell out of bed.* She painted on a polite smile. "Hi! Simon's told me a lot about you."

"And you!" said Alex. "This guy can't stop talking about the new sewing machine you gave him."

"I can't." Simon nodded, lifting bowls of sliced veggies and dips from the filled-to-the-brim hamper. "I'm officially a card-carrying member of the Leia Scott fan club."

Leia chuckled and tucked a loose strand from her ponytail behind her ear, a blush blooming on her cheeks. *So, Tarquin has a thing for American blondes?*

Alex grinned, her fingers bunching up her woolly hat. "And I love your name—Leia. It's so pretty." Her gaze flitted to Simon.

Leia blurted out a quick "Thanks." Lost for more words, she remained silent, lending their conversation a pregnant pause. *Hmm. What else did Simon tell her? About Tarquin—and me?* She played with her ponytail and let it go, unsettled. *Alex is being super polite. No* Star Wars *jokes, no mention of Tarquin—and she's white-knuckling her hat.* Leia gulped. *Pretty sure she knows...but so what? Why does that make me feel awkward?*

Simon placed a square container labelled 'smoked salmon platter' and another bursting with colorful fruit beside the veggie bowls. "Leia is a fashion designer. She's Canadian but lives in New York."

"Oh, cool. I'm headed there in April for my play," said Alex. "It opens in late May."

"Oh, really? That's amazing," said Leia, spinning the gold band on her right hand, unaware she was doing it. "Which theater? I love Broadway."

Alex's face briefly pinched. "Uh, actually, it's off-Broadway. If it does well, it might get a transfer."

Shit. Waves rolled in Leia's stomach, her once-ravenous appetite lost in the undertow. *I've insulted her. I've slept with her ex—who's still her friend—and insulted her. She's gonna hate me. At least this hell will be over in a few minutes.*

Simon popped open a clamshell container filled with cocktail sausages, the aroma of honey Dijon dressing infusing the air with a zesty zing. "Alex, stay for lunch?"

Oh, good god, no.

Simon grinned. "There's enough to feed all of Hackney."

"Um, well, I only stopped in to return Spencer's fondue pot…" Alex squeezed the strap of her laptop bag, her eyes darting to Leia.

Oh, shit. Do I look like I don't want her here? She beamed a friendly smile, her reply bright and breezy. "Oh, stay!" Leia wasted no time, eagerly shifting her cola bottles, fabric, and sewing tools to the far end of the table so their party of three could dine without getting pricked by rogue pins. A nervous giggle escaped her throat, but it went unnoticed thanks to the squeaky plastic lid Simon was opening on one of the serving trays. *You're about to break the first rule of flings without strings—don't hang with their friends! Or worse, exes.*

"Lex, there's a cheese tray!" Simon set down the noisy platter. "And brownies," he teased, waving the wrapped-up chocolate treats. "Your two favorites!"

Alex's smile bloomed. "Okay, I'll stay. Thanks. Saves stopping at Pret!" She lowered her laptop bag to the floor and unbuttoned her wool coat, a flash of sky blue, making Leia do a double take.

It's that dress!

Coat off, Alex smoothed the flattering skirt, its hem floating just shy of her knees. The garment's fit-and-flare silhouette and elegant crepe material drew an appreciative smile and a wink from Simon. For good reason, too. The dress's emerald twin, glammed up with dazzling sequins and a plunging bodice, graced a mannequin in his latest shop window display, one Leia ogled every day on Wilton Way.

It's even more gorgeous on her. Leia picked up one of the cola bottles, a splash of soft drink swirling around the bottom. "You look so pretty." She grinned and meant it as she surveyed her college hoodie and ripped jeans. *And I look a hot mess. Alex must be thinking, 'Some designer you are. You can't even dress yourself.'*

"Thanks!" Alex smoothed the skirt. "I treated myself."

"And I'm glad you did," said Simon, elbow-deep in Tarquin's lunch delivery. "Do you have a meeting today?" Bottles of prosecco and sparkling water clinked as he removed them from the hamper.

"At three." Alex played with the charm on her necklace. To Leia, it looked like a tiny blue and silver motorcycle or maybe a Vespa, the retro type she'd seen zooming through London traffic. "I'm a bit anxious about it. It's at the Young Vic."

Simon stopped rooting around in the wicker, his jaw slack. "They called you back?"

Leia twisted the cap on her cola bottle open and closed, her gaze volleying between the two friends.

"Yup," said Alex, smothering a spare chair with her coat. "Fingers crossed, *Waterloo Bridge* will be on stage eighteen months from now."

"Alex, that's *fantastic!*" Simon lifted out another large container. "Leia, Alex's play is about the women who built Waterloo Bridge during World War II. It's *really* good." Snapping open the domed lid, he surveyed the table crowded with covered containers and bowls. A bemused grin creased his brow. "Did Tarquin leave anything in the actual store? We've got cheese-stuffed bell peppers, olives, crispbreads, smoked salmon. This one's pork pies." He looked up. "Alex, can you grab some dishes from the kitchen? Get four of everything. I'll make up a plate for Spence, too."

"Sure thing." Sweeping her bangs from her eyes, she strode into the kitchen.

Simon flashed a conspiratorial grin in Leia's direction, remaining silent until the jangle of cutlery from the kitchen filled the air. "So, I spoke to Tarq yesterday," he whispered.

Oh? Leia stopped tormenting the cap on her cola. *Simon doesn't want Alex to hear. She definitely knows, then.* "Oh, really? How is he?" She lowered her voice to match Simon's, listening for creaking floorboards signaling Alex's return.

"He's good. Work is keeping him on his toes. He asked after you."

He did? She fought back a smile. "I've been meaning to text him…"

"I told him how swamped you've been—too busy to sleep or eat. I have a sneaky feeling this hamper was intended as fuel for you!" Simon dove into the hamper again. "Oh, what's this?" Leia leaned in as his hand reappeared clutching a long box in Fortnum's signature blue. He lifted the fancy cardboard lid. "Ooh, nice! Pretty in pink, see?"

Macarons? Tarquin remembered?! Leia set down her cola and admired the delicate baked goods, the pink hue both familiar and thrilling. *He's been thinking about me!* Her heart tripped as a grin flirted with her lips. "They're raspberry." *My favorite. This is just too sweet and so kind. I have to thank him.*

"Feel free to take them home, share with your sister." Simon stashed the empty wicker hamper underneath the table.

The hall floorboards squeaked and Alex swerved around the doorjamb, her arms cradling a colorful stack of ceramic plates.

"Oh, let me help." Leia left the box of macarons on the table and pitched in.

"Si—mon!" Spencer's holler fought its way up the stairs. "The cash drawer is jammed! Can you fix it? It's doing my bloody 'ead in!"

Simon sighed loudly and forked a slice of eggy frittata, plunking it on a plate. "I'll take this to Spence." He swiped a knife and fork. "You ladies dig in. I'll be back in a sec." He disappeared around the doorjamb, the stairs complaining with each pounding step.

Alex sat down and plucked a piece of crumbly cheese from a tray while Leia surveyed the multiple platters of fruit, smoked meats, and fresh veggies—a delicious spread guaranteed to satisfy their bellies today and tomorrow, too. *This is amazing.* She pulled up a chair and removed her phone from her pocket, selecting Tarquin from her contacts. Thumbs flying over the keyboard, she typed then paused, re-reading her message.

Leia: Lovin' the picnic. THANKS! Especially the macarons. Shame you're not on the menu—NAKED.

Leia hit send, wondering if a cheeky response might arrive while Alex nibbled cheese just an elbow away. She laid her phone face down on the table, just in case.

The playwright flashed a kind smile. "I can't get over this spread. Tarquin's a bit of a foodie, so I guess it's not surprising."

She wants to talk Tarquin? Leia sucked in a breath. *Uh, okay.* She scooped up a stuffed pepper. *Actually, talking about him might be a good idea. Get any weirdness out of the way.* She poked the cheese peeking out from the pepper with her fork. "I'm a terrible cook, but I love to eat. This definitely beats the boring microwave meal I forgot to pack."

"Don't let Tarquin hear you say that," said Alex, toying with a cluster of grapes. "He hates microwaves. He's all about fresh ingredients from Borough Market and making meals from scratch—he's incredibly passionate and hands-on in the kitchen."

I guess she'd know. Leia's stomach clenched. *Wait...am I jeal-*

173

ous? Yeah, right!

"Oh god! I didn't mean that to sound...*you know*..." Alex let out an uneasy giggle, her attention settling on the platter of pork pies. "I have to be honest..."

Oh, shit. Here it comes. Leia froze.

"I'd trade most of this for a microwave meal in a heartbeat."

I didn't expect that. Leia disguised her rushed breath with a laugh.

"I'm such a picky eater. Most of this is lost on me..." Alex examined a grape then popped it in her mouth.

They exchanged a smile then both fell silent and ate, Alex sticking to cheese and fruit while Leia benched the stuffed pepper for a small bite of Scotch egg, a British classic she'd never eaten before. Rain drummed on the windows, but it failed to drown out Spencer and her pitch-imperfect warble destroying "Angels" by Robbie Williams playing in Simon's shop downstairs.

Alex took a sip of water, her eyes swimming over the box of macarons and the dress form draped with Leia's fabric, their combined rosy pink offering a hint of spring on a dour winter's day. "I bet you're having lots of fun with him, huh?"

Ugh. How do I answer that? "Um, yeah?" Leia nodded with a smile, wishing Simon would show up and diffuse the awkwardness suffocating the room.

Alex pitched forward. "Leia, you know—"

"It's only been the one time!"

"Huh?" Alex's brow creased.

"Over a week ago," Leia blurted. "I know this feels awkward, but it shouldn't, should it? We're all adults! You're his ex and I'm...just having some fun with him. It's nothing serious, and besides—"

Alex gaped. "Oh! I...was gonna say Simon could help you make contacts here." She winced into a giggle. "You and Tarquin...*really*?"

Oh, great! She didn't know? Leia gulped, wishing the floor would swallow her up.

"Exes can be territorial sometimes." Sarah stole the last forkful of Jordan's grilled swordfish from his discarded plate, her eyes flitting through the St. Bart's Brewery crowd. The popular bar and restaurant overlooking London's historic Smithfield Market was near her office and one of her favorite hangouts. "It's nice Alex isn't. Even better, she said go for it!"

Leia glanced at her phone, placing the text-free screen face down on the table. "I wish I told her in a more elegant manner. I basically word-vomited. It wasn't pretty."

"Meh, pretty is overrated. You got the job done *and* made her laugh before her big meeting! I wish someone made *me* laugh before my presentation," said Sarah, poking the chickpeas in Jordan's salad with his fork as she watched him talking outside on his phone. "I was so wound up."

"Yeah, but you still got the promotion and a new office—with a window. You could grow your orchids on the sill. I'm so proud of you, Saz. So is Dad. I called him before I left Simon's and he's been telling all the neighbors." She laughed.

"It's times like this he feels so far away," said Sarah. "I'll FaceTime him again tomorrow, give him a tour of my new space." She picked up Leia's box of raspberry macarons and peeked inside. Only one of the six cookies remained. "So gorgeous! I bet they taste as good as they look. How'd he know about macarons?"

Leia stuffed her hands in her hoodie's pocket. "I mentioned them once."

"And he remembered? Tarquin *likes* you." Sarah stared at her sister. "And *you* like him."

"Of course I like him." Leia pushed aside her half-eaten sun-dried tomato flatbread. "I wouldn't sleep with someone I found repulsive."

"No. It's more than that. Your cheeks flush when you talk about him."

Leia flapped a hand at her face. "That's because it's warm in here."

"If you say so." Sarah gently tipped the box, and the lone macaron rolled into the corner. "So, why haven't you texted him?"

"I did! Right after the hamper arrived."

"That's too little, too late. You're flying to New York in three days!"

Leia pulled her hair free from her ponytail. "Well, he didn't text me, either." She ran her hands through her blonde tresses, smoothing the dent left behind from the coated elastic. "I figured he wasn't interested in meeting up again."

"Until he sent you raspberry macarons!" Sarah swooned over the box, handing it back to Leia. "Those are better than a text any day, so romantic and yummy."

"Don't get all gooey-eyed, Saz! I don't want to *marry* the guy. I'd just like to sleep with him again. Who knows when I'll have sex that great back in New York." Leia admired the last macaron.

"Crisis averted!" Jordan plunked his phone on the table and dropped into the chair beside Sarah. The shoulders of his suit were dappled with raindrops.

Sarah covered his hand with hers. "Everything okay?"

"There was a blunder with today's auction. My boss needed some translating done to seal the deal." He pushed away his plate and stifled a burp. "Oh, man, I can't wait to head to yours and get comfy in jeans and a t-shirt."

"Oh, but not yet?" begged Leia, setting down the macarons.

"Saz, don't get mad. I know you hate surprises, but I bought a cake."

"Aw, you didn't! Is it the caterpillar cake from Tesco?" Sarah chair-danced like a sugar-jacked six-year-old celebrating a birthday. "I luvvvve him."

Caterpillar? Leia snickered, tugging her hair tie over her wrist. "You're such a goof. No, I didn't buy a weird bug cake. It's a pretty one from Soho, s'mores flavor."

Jordan cuddled his girlfriend. "Oh, go on, treat yourself! We could share a small piece."

"Don't look at Leia. She *never* shares her dessert," Sarah joked. "Come to think of it, she doesn't like to share anything."

Leia made a face.

"You know it's true. You get mad every time I borrow your clothes."

"That's because you don't ask. Borrowing implies *consent*. You just nick 'em!" Leia slowly shook her head, eyeballing Sarah's blue sweater, which rightfully lived in her own wardrobe. "Anyway, no one has to share tonight. This cake could feed half this bar." She dropped her napkin on the table and stood up. "The manager stored it for me. I'll be right back!"

Halfway to the bar, her phone—face down on the table—lit up with a text.

Tarquin: I'm liking THAT visual a little too much. I'm getting hard just thinking about you. I wonder...what tastes sweeter— you or the macarons? Fancy finding out?

Fourteen

TARQUIN

I'd know that gorgeous long blonde hair anywhere.

Swerving around a pillar and a high-spirited huddle of city bankers slamming back blue shots, Tarquin clutched a pint and a bouquet of red and orange primroses. *What's she wearing?* He approached her table crowded with dwindling drinks and half-eaten slices of chocolatey cake. *A uni hoodie and jeans? Ooh, fun! Are we role-playing freshers week? Me the inexperienced shy nerd, her the sexy first-year student.* "Leia?" He broke into a smile that could be seen a block away. "Hi!"

She did a sharp double take and slowly stiffened, her forkful of chocolate and marshmallow cake halting midair between her mouth and the table. "Tarquin?" Her Canadian accent jumped an octave higher. "What are—you working nearby?" Barely blinking, she returned the last mouthful of dessert to her plate and fussed with the hem of her Pitt hoodie, a tentative smile twitching her cheeks. Her gaze flitted to the cellophane-wrapped flowers, then her sister.

You know I was. Tarquin's brow briefly pinched as he squeezed the glass in his hand. "Erm, yeah." He swooped down, kissing her on both cheeks. "I thought you might like these," he whispered, offering the bright bouquet.

"Primroses!" Sarah swooned. "Red ones, Ley! Your fave." The younger Scott's eyes swept down his suit and back up again, her welcoming grin showing no signs of letting up. "Tarquin, hey! I'm Sarah, Leia's sister, and this guy here is my boyfriend, Jordan." After squeezing her paramour's shoulder, Sarah gestured to the vacant chair beside Leia. "Please, join us…it's great to meet one of Ley's London friends."

"Thanks." He nodded and sat down. "It's a pleasure to meet you as well." Narrowing his eyes, his mind raced. *I had no idea her sister was in a wheelchair. She looks familiar, though. Where do I know her from?* He placed his pint on the table, his gaze skimming over the cake before it tracked back to a quiet Leia, sniffing the flowers. The open macaron box from Fortnum & Mason kept her water glass company. *She looks like she swallowed a fly. What's going on? Does she regret inviting me?*

She leaned in, her surprised expression loosening. "The primroses are beautiful, thank you."

"Tarquin, have some cake. I won't take no for an answer!" Sarah grabbed a knife dabbed with custard, gooey marshmallow, and chocolate buttercream. "You have to celebrate with us!" She skewered the sumptuous gateau, slicing through decadent frosting, thick chocolate sauce, and a generous mountain of chunky toasted marshmallow crowning the top.

They're celebrating? Oh, bollocks! So, Leia got the New York job. His stomach dropped. *That's why she wanted to see me—a farewell fuck?* Tarquin chuckled uneasily, his eyes settling on Leia as her brows drew together. "What's the occasion?"

"Saz got a promotion," said Leia, swapping the bouquet for her phone.

Sarah?! Tarquin's chest relaxed, his face lighting up with relieved glee. "Congratulations! What will you be doing?" He glanced down at the celebratory cake slice slid across the table by Jordan. *Chocolate and marshmallow, me and Leia—perfect pairings.*

Sarah licked digestive cookie buttercream off her thumb. "I'm the new Inclusive Environments Specialist at Accessible London." She set down the knife and paused, her focus pinching as it strayed to her sister.

Tarquin followed her gaze. Leia reclined away from the table, silently poring over her phone.

"It's a consultancy agency"—Sarah's voice drew him back—"that offers accessibility guidance to construction organizations, developers, building managers—you name it." Picking up her fork, she gave him a confident grin. "Our goal is to make London accessible for *everyone*. Kind of a passion of mine."

That's how I know her! Tarquin broke into an open-mouthed smile and pointed a knowing finger. "I saw you speak! Two or three years back. You did a TED Talk at the urban planning convention at the ExCel—on wheelchair accessibility. You were fantastic, really great!"

Sarah's eyes lit up like a Christmas tree, her cheeks blushing slightly. "Oh, wow! Yeah, that was me—*thank you!*" She scooped frosting from her cake slice. "There weren't many people there…"

Jordan rubbed her shoulder gently.

Tarquin's business mind quickly connected the dots. "I just purchased a cinema for redevelopment and could use some guidance with inclusive design. Could you help me?"

"God, yeah! We can *definitely* help with that!" Sarah beamed. "I'm so glad we met."

Leia looked up from her phone and shot daggers across the table to her sister, which didn't go unnoticed by Tarquin.

O-kay. That was weird. A wrinkle flirted with his forehead. *Obviously, I've interrupted something between these two.* "Uh, Sarah, do you have a business card?" He tugged his wallet from his trouser pocket.

"I do!" Sarah dropped her fork and pulled a blue card from her purse. "It's my old one, but my contact info is the same."

"Cheers." Tarquin smiled, trading his details for hers.

Sarah let out a breath, avoiding Leia's glare. "Right. Jordan, you ready?"

SAY HELLO, KISS GOODBYE

"What?" Leia leaned over the decimated slice on her plate. "You're leaving? Tarquin just got here, and you've barely touched your cake."

Tarquin shifted backward out of the line of fire, taking his pint with him. *If looks could kill.*

"I'm saving mine for breakfast," said Jordan, reassembling the splayed-open box.

"Sorry, Ley," said Sarah, planting several ten-pound notes amidst the empty glasses and discarded plates. "Didn't I mention my early conference call? They're totally throwing me into the deep end!" Dodging Leia's unrelenting frown, she shrugged into the sleeves of her coat.

Jordan caught the elder Scott's headshake. "Oh, do you want another slice?"

"No, but I'd like another sister," Leia grumbled under her breath.

Remind me not to make you angry. Tarquin took a long sip of his pint, staying out of the exchange.

Sarah ducked under the strap of her purse, hanging it across her body. "Tarquin, we'll be in touch?"

He lowered the rim of the glass from his lips, his gaze stuttering away from Leia, her cheeks burning pink. "Yes! Very soon."

"Great!" Sarah smiled, unlocking her chair's brakes. "Ley, text me if you're gonna be late." She reversed and curved sharply, following Jordan, who looked over his shoulder and waved, the cake box cradled in his grasp.

I can feel Leia prickling with anger. Tarquin looked away from the lively Tuesday night crowd and snuck a sidelong glance. *Holy death stare. She's about to explode.*

"I'm gonna kill her!"

Why? Because she left us alone? Tarquin's chest pinched. "What's she done?"

Leia shook her phone. "My texts tonight? They weren't from me—no. Sarah sent them. *She* invited you here."

"What?" *Oh, shit!* Tarquin's face began to prickle with heat. *Bollocks! Her sister...saw my sext?!* He gulped and cleared his throat. "Uh...she did?"

"Yeah." Leia plowed her free hand through her hair. "She must've done it when I got up to get the cake. See for yourself..." She offered him her phone.

Tarquin squinted at the conversation, starting with Leia's message from the afternoon.

Leia: Lovin' the picnic. THANKS! Especially the macarons. Shame you're not on the menu—NAKED.

Tarquin: I'm liking THAT visual a little too much. I'm getting hard just thinking about you. I wonder...what tastes sweeter—you or the macarons? Fancy finding out?

Leia: Like you have to ask, big boy! I've missed that sexy body of yours. I'm gagging for it. Come meet me at St. Bart's Brewery on West Smithfield, across from the market. xo

Tarquin: Blimey, that's convenient! I'm on site in Clerkenwell. Be there in ten!

Leia: Hell to the yeah! Get that sexy ass down here! Grab a pint and come find me. I'm near the back with friends. xo

Tarquin let out a sharp exhale and handed back her phone. "Wow. That's bloody embarrassing. Looks like we were set up."

"'*I'm gagging for it*'—gimme a break! I would *never* say that."

Leia seethed. "Fucking Saz! I would've told you but—I didn't want to embarrass you, or make a scene. And she knew it! Jesus! I hate when she plays me."

"Well, I feel stupid, too." Tarquin nudged away his untouched cake slice. "I should've listened to my gut."

"What do you mean?"

"It's just, you"—he shook his head, trying to course-correct—"I mean, *Sarah* mentioned hanging with friends. You and I agreed—no friends, no family."

Leia nodded. "Funny enough, I met Alex today. She dropped in at Simon's."

Really? Tarquin's head snapped back. "Uh...?!"

"She's lovely. Thinks highly of you."

"Yeah? Well, the feeling's mutual. She's a good friend." Tarquin cleared his throat. "Leia, I know Sarah's message should've been a red flag, but..." He offered a disappointed smile. "I wanted to see you. I thought—when I saw the *xo*s...maybe you'd changed your mind about those rules."

"I'm sorry, Tarquin." She avoided eye contact, shifting the flowers aside. "I haven't."

Her admission felt like a fifty-pound barbell had fallen on his chest, cutting off his breath. *I really thought we had something. Fuck! I shouldn't have come. It's made everything worse.* He loosened his tie. *Looks like my night's over.* "Ah. Okay..." With a tight-lipped smile, he pushed his chair back. "I'll leave you to it. And don't worry, I won't text you again—"

"No!" Leia grabbed his suit's sleeve. "Stay. *Please*?" Her grip loosened. "If you want to."

"Do *you* want me to?"

"Yes." She released his arm and tossed her phone on the table. "I have to tell you something."

Oh? Is this good or bad? He sat back down. "Shoot."

Leia closed her eyes in frustration. "I'm sorry I'm such a hot-headed freak. None of this is your fault, okay?" Her eyelashes flitted open. "Saz always meddles, thinks she knows better than me."

"Is she older?"

"Younger." Leia yanked the gold band on her right hand round and round her finger like each rough twist would help crank the words out. "I'm sorry I made you feel unwelcome. I just…didn't want you to meet Sarah. I *knew* if she set eyes on you, she'd"—Leia pressed her lips together—"she'd push me even harder to date you."

A slow grin roused his dimples. "So, you've been talking about me, Ginger?"

"Don't let it go to your head!" Leia giggled. "You should know if I *had* gotten to your text before Saz, I would've replied." She offered him an alluring smile. "I really wanted to see you tonight."

"Yeah? Me too." Tarquin inched his chair closer and lost control of his grin, sprinting through his stubble. "I had to redo a development proposal with my assistant three times because of your flirty text—the 'naked' bit. Jesus, Leia, thank god I was sat behind my desk."

A blush began to brighten her cheeks. "Well, I'm pleased it had the right effect, but…" Her smile dimmed. "I'm…worried."

"Why?"

"I don't want to hurt you—"

"You won't!" he blurted back on auto-pilot. "No strings, right? I get it. It's cool. That's what I signed up for."

"You say that"—Leia picked up the flowers—"but did you…*really*?" She studied the petals, then met his eyes again. "I think you might want more."

I do, but I'll go along with whatever this is. Maybe, if I'm lucky, there will be a chance to change her mind. He smiled. "I'm not dropping on bended knee any time soon, for *anyone*, okay? You don't want serious—I don't either."

"You sure?"

"I just like being with you."

Leia returned the primroses to the table. "I just like being with you, too."

Tarquin's heart tingled, giddy with hope and anticipation. "Well, good!" He tilted in, sweeping a piece of hair from her eyes. "Glad that's all sorted, then!"

"So..." Leia whispered teasingly, her gaze tangling with his. "What shall we do now...?"

Christ, she's killing me. "Don't know. What do *you* want to do?"

Close enough to kiss, Leia smiled and brushed a lascivious finger across his lips. "I'm GAGGING for it, big boy."

Tarquin burst into laughter, and Leia gave him a playful shove.

"But seriously, what's that saying?" She giggled. "The one you British blokes use?"

"Grab your coat, sweetheart." He smiled. "You've *pulled*!"

Pressing Leia against the wall, the cellophane-covered bouquet crinkling between them, Tarquin lingered over her mouth, her fingers lost to the warmth beneath his half-buttoned dress shirt. "Let's get comfortable," he whispered. "Come." He clutched the flowers and captured her hand, leading the way down his main floor's hallway, but something caught Leia's eye.

"Oh! Hang on..." She tugged him back and ducked around the doorjamb, her easy smile lighting up the dark room. "A *snooker* table!" She dropped his hand. "Why didn't you say?"

She knows the difference? Tarquin flipped the switch, and several pendant lights cast a soft glow, revealing the large room's fully stocked bar, massive wall-mounted flatscreen television, and another expansive window overlooking the River Thames. "I knew you liked pool, but—"

"My dad watched snooker on TV when I was growing up. He found it relaxing." Leia swerved around a long black leather couch and plunked her oversized tote on the floor, the almost empty macaron box tumbling out. She bounced to the far end of the table where fifteen red balls arranged in a triangular formation sat on its green felt surface. "It's been ages since I had a game!"

Tarquin chuckled and picked up the macaron box, setting it on the table's top rail. "Don't get too excited." He rested the flowers on the arm of the couch and whipped off his suit jacket, laying it neatly beside the blooms. "The only balls you'll be playing with are mine."

"That is *soooo* cheesy." She snickered, picking up the white cue ball.

"I aim to please." *I swear, next to you coming, your laughter is my favorite sound.*

He closed their distance, passing framed photos on the walls of his younger self, pink-cheeked and smiling with friends atop a snowy mountain and relaxing in an après-ski hot tub.

Leia squeezed the cue ball and returned it to the playing surface. "You're just worried I'll kick your ass."

"You promise?"

She cocked an eyebrow and bent over, pretending to take aim with an invisible snooker cue. "I'm quite the expert with a slippery shaft." She bit back a giggle, letting her dirty joke hang in the air while she completed her fake shot.

Now there's a picture. A groan strangled in Tarquin's throat, his heated gaze skimming the soft curves of her jeans-clad ass. "I *know* you are." *I can't wait for you to sink down and ride me.* Breaths grew ragged in his chest and a hot pulse in his trousers grew hard and eager. *Game fucking on.*

Leia spun around, catching his gape and the straining erection in his pants. A saucy grin owned her lips as she pulled herself up onto the table's edge, her long legs dangling, spreading, welcoming him in. "You need a reminder..." She grabbed his loose tie and reeled him in between her open thighs.

"You need fewer clothes." Tarquin's warm breath feathered her neck, his hands finding their way underneath her hoodie, teasing the button on her jeans. She stretched back on the snooker table, just shy of the carefully arranged billiard balls, and raised her hips, allowing Tarquin to whisk the old Levi's over her thighs and down her legs, the denim falling to the floor in a heap.

Sitting up, she widened her legs again and fussed with his belt buckle. "I have condoms in my bag—berry-flavored." She slid his zipper down, her nails grazing his boxer briefs and his rock-hard heat, her mere touch triggering an explosion of achy throbs in Tarquin's pants.

I want her so much. "Good. I like a woman who plans ahead." Tarquin tugged off his trousers and socks then lunged forward, pulling her toward him, their bodies meeting in a clash of lips and teeth and frantic hands. He coaxed the cozy layers of her hoodie and t-shirt up...up, over her bra, and broke their kiss, a smile on his lips as Leia helped the clothes sail over her head. *My love bite! It's faded but still there.* "Just look at you!" He gasped. "Perfect in so many ways."

On first try, Tarquin unhooked the intricate lace and satin hugging her breasts while Leia's feverish hands freed the remaining buttons on his shirt, dragging it down his arms. He tore at the cuffs, yanking the designer shirt from his wrists and tossing it on the couch behind them. He pressed closer, delirious for her mouth.

That's when he saw it, woven into her skin.

The faded line originated just below her navel and veered around her belly button, where it crept up the center of her abdomen, halting an inch or two beneath her breasts.

Oh, Christ...what the hell? A hard swallow bobbed his throat, the cocky cheekiness of his gaze gone. He pulled Leia in, pressing soft kisses against her forehead, the urge to hold her, to protect her greater than his unbridled lust. *She looks stitched back together. First the leg scar, now this? I assumed that one was a skating injury, but maybe not?*

Leia stiffened slightly and looped her arms around his neck, her fingers lacing through his hair. She held on like she was offering *him* comfort, not the other way around.

Tarquin blinked, all sorts of fears and accusations whirling through his mind. *Did someone hurt her? Her ex, maybe?* He pulled back with a tight smile and tenderly swept the hair from her face, the throbbing ache in his boxer briefs fading. Sex was no longer top of mind. *Obviously, she survived something major—something life-changing. But how do I ask...without sounding like a nosey prat? Or making her feel self-conscious?* He ran his thumb down her cheek, hoping the right words would come. "Leia, I..." *I really hope she doesn't mind.* "Is it okay to ask...what happened?"

A flicker of a grin played with her mouth. "Of course! Ask away. I wish more people did. I can't tell you how many times I've been at the beach and all eyes seem to be on my stomach. Not that it's ever stopped me from wearing a cute bikini." She fluttered her eyelashes, showing no signs of apprehension or embarrassment. "My spleen ruptured years ago. I needed emergency surgery to remove it."

Ah, thank fuck it wasn't her ex who hurt her. The tension pinching Tarquin's brow eased. *But still...the pain she must've been in.* He softly caressed her jaw. "God, that's awful."

"I now have an increased risk of catching infections without it, so"—she lifted her arm, showing off a tiny charm dangling from the delicate rose gold bracelet on her left wrist—"I have to wear this in case of an emergency. It's not the sexiest of inscriptions—NO

SPLEEN." She chuckled.

"But you're okay *now*?"

A smile bloomed across her cheeks. "Yeah." She looked down and grazed a finger along the faded white seam. "In a weird way, I've grown to like my scars. They make me feel badass, like I can survive anything. They're a reminder of my resilience. But I'm never sure how guys will react, especially with this one." A gentle shrug raised her shoulders. "That's why I wore my dress the first time we had sex."

"And the second time..." *Doggie style from behind—fucking incredible.* The semi in his underwear throbbed, growing firmer with the memory.

"Yeah. That was *good*!" She bit her lip, meeting his eyes again. "I didn't know if I'd see you again, so I thought I'd spare us any awkwardness. And trust me, it can get awkward." Her fingers skimmed up his happy trail, sparking goose bumps in their wake. "Guys get squeamish. They zip up, make excuses..."

"You're kidding?"

"Well, not that I have a huge number of hookups to go by but...yeah, it's happened. People want perfection."

So true. I only thought she was perfect because...well, she's perfect for ME. I didn't mean she's flawless. I'm not; no one is.

Leia sat back, clearly comfortable with her scars and being naked, apart from her barely-there lace panties. "So, what about you, Tarquin Octavius Balfour?" She shifted the macaron box closer. "What are your thoughts on the perfectly imperfect?" Leia glanced down at the last cookie, her expression darkening. "Oh! Speaking of which..." She tilted the container, sending macaron pieces sliding into its cardboard corner.

It must've shattered when it fell from her bag. Licking his lips, Tarquin curved forward, plucking the largest shard from the box. "I bet it's still delicious, though." He looked up through his hair, offering the half shell of pink cookie.

Her lips, warm and full, brushed Tarquin's fingers, taking the broken macaron onto her tongue.

Those soft lips will be the death of me.

Chewing slowly, her eyes never wavered from his. She scooped up a drop of buttercream from the box. "It's *so* sweet and tart." She flashed a suggestive smile and offered her finger. "Want a taste?"

"Please." His pulse throttling in his chest, he slowly took her finger in his mouth and sucked, savoring the tangy sweetness mixed with the saltiness of her skin. She arched toward him, her nipples hard and beckoning. *Come here, gorgeous! I want to lick every inch of you.* Heat pulsed in his boxer briefs, his erection fighting the constraints of the cotton. He pulled his mouth away, craving more. "Macarons are delicious, but there's something even better..." He cupped her face, his thumbs caressing her silky skin. "You."

Leia dropped the box on the table's green felt and drew his shoulders toward her, meeting his mouth with renewed passion. Their tongues danced and tasted, their hunger for each other growing hotter with each sigh and tightening grasp.

Tarquin left her lips, leaning his forehead against hers. "You're beautiful." He smiled softly. "Every freckle, every scar—every inch." He bowed his head and took her nipple in his mouth, his tongue and teeth gently teasing, coaxing a moan from Leia. She dug her fingers into his bare back, pulling him in tight, burying her nose in his hair.

I'm pressing hard against her thigh—she can't have any doubts about how much I want her.

"Your condoms or mine?" she whispered.

"I'll do the honors." Tarquin let her go and ducked to the floor, rifling through his trouser pockets while Leia shimmied out of her panties, letting them slide down her bare legs to her toes. She kicked them off and flicked open the macaron box, helping herself to the last broken layer of pink shell, her eyes closing halfway in rapturous bliss.

Tarquin stood up, stepping out of his boxers. He rolled on the condom, his darkening gaze returning to the leggy blonde, mesmerized by her open thighs and tongue swirling around her fingers, licking sugary meringue. *I adore her…so happy and carefree, a bit cheeky and naked as fuck.*

"Want another suck?" An impish grin pinched her cheeks. She swayed her knee back and forth, inviting him in.

Tarquin swooped his arms around her waist and claimed her open mouth, kissing her hard and deep, the taste of raspberry fueling his hunger. *She's sweet and sinful and I can't get enough.* Leia cupped his balls while her other hand closed around his hard length, bringing him to where she waited wet and ready. *Oh, dear god! I need to be inside her like I need to breathe.* Squeezing her ass, tightness grew in the pit of his stomach as a low groan growled in his throat. "Leia, you're so—"

"Yeah, look what you do to me." She shifted and guided him inside, her breath catching as he sank in deep.

Christ. She's hot and tight. Nothing is better than this. He gripped her waist and moaned, her urgent puffs of breath skating across his skin.

"Fuck me, Tarquin," she begged in his ear, daring him as she teased his balls, stroking and gently squeezing. "Fuck me fast, so we can do it again…and again…" As she slipped her tongue along the nape of his neck, Tarquin shivered, desire quaking through his body. "Let's set a new record," she purred, digging the nails of her free hand into his ass. "Think we can beat three times?"

"Better believe it. I could do it with both hands tied behind my back."

"Ooh, I'll file that for later."

"Good thing I have ropes from rock climbing, then." Tarquin

raised a speculative brow as he began to roll his hips. "A smart, beautiful woman once told me, 'Be careful what you ask for.'"

Leia rode each slow thrust, a grin breaking through her gasps. "I always ask for *exactly* what I want." She tightened her grip on his balls then released them, sinking her teeth into his shoulder. She playfully nibbled and then sucked—hard.

Oh, mother of... The pleasure of her wicked mouth rocketed straight to his throbbing penis as it slid deep in and out. *Two can play at that game.* Tarquin drew in a heady breath, his finger rounding the curve of her hip. He swept between her thighs and Leia pushed against his hand, his gentle touch, stroking, teasing a vulnerable whimper through her lips, parting with need.

"Make me come…"

Capturing his mouth, Leia's tongue parted his willing lips, their kiss frenzied and deepening, hands grabbing, their passion chasing the same goal as Tarquin thrust faster.

Going at it like this, we won't last long. Sucking and kissing, an uncontrollable rush of heat and urgency pressed heavy in Tarquin's core. *She feels so good.*

Leia left his lips with a growl, her gaze wild and determined, watching where their bodies met again and again. She writhed against him, grinding, swiveling her hips, her hands gripping his shoulders, which glistened with sweat.

God, she's unreal. She's right here with me, not backing down, giving as good as she gets. Tarquin held her waist, kissing her again, tasting her as his hips slammed—forward and back, faster, deeper—reveling in her hot, slick skin and breathy moans growing louder with each thrust. It was almost too much, her sounds, her heat lighting his fuse. His thighs burned, aching for release.

I can't come first. I have to keep climbing so I can watch her, see her finish. He left her lips and dug his fingers into the curve of her ass, fighting to focus, desperate to hang on. *I can't surrender first.*

Tarquin barely got his wish.

"Oh, god!" Thighs squeezing tight, a silent groan stalled in Leia's throat. She shook and clung to him, her whole being coming apart in his arms—and pulling him down with her.

Tarquin moaned, Leia's open lips and sweet gasps pushing him beyond the brink. *I'm in trouble. I'm in freefall, losing myself completely. I...I love this girl.* "Fuuuck!" He plunged over the edge, jerking with each intoxicating wave rolling through his body. Holding Leia tightly, his legs trembled with relief as the sweet ecstasy of learning her body's secrets and earning her trust stole his breath—and his heart.

FIFTEEN

LEIA

I love it! This room looks like a hip bookstore meets Soho coffee shop—but tidier. He's way too neat! Wrapped in Tarquin's thick cotton robe, Leia sank into his luxurious sofa, a modern oasis of curved edges and sumptuous mulberry velvet, and admired the towering walnut bookshelves framing the room. Their contemporary design was comprised of one hundred and two (Leia had counted) open squares and rectangles of various sizes, stacked and arranged to best showcase Tarquin's enviable collection of trade fiction paperbacks and hardbacks—all organized in a rainbow of candy-colored spines. *I can't get over all this! Tarquin should be a Bookstagrammer.* She sipped her chilled orange juice and sat back, marveling at his knack for bookish flare.

The only wall spared of books was actually a window, yet another of the vertigo-inducing variety overlooking London's jewels—in this case, literally. Leia had read about the Crown Jewels being kept under lock and key in the Tower of London, and the eighth-floor library offered an impressive cross-Thames view as well as a front-row seat to the morning's spectacular sunrise.

She stretched against the sofa, careful not to aggravate last night's injury—a pulled muscle in her back. *Ugh, it pinches. Turns out, sex against his phone booth wasn't one of my brightest ideas.* She giggled quietly, filing away the long-held fantasy finally come to life. *That orgasm was totally worth this morning's bruises, though.*

A loud text tone sounded and she fumbled her phone, determined to keep noise to a minimum while Tarquin dozed in the master bedroom next door. She took another sip, peeked at the screen—a bunch of eggplant and crying-with-laughter emojis along with…

Sarah: He's SO into you!

Leia smiled. *Saz, you're so lucky I had a great time last night. Otherwise, I'd be cursing a blue streak over that stunt you pulled.*

She hit rewind on her mind's highlight reel of their frenzied overnight adventures. Tarquin had made good in more ways than one, giving her a grand tour of both his penthouse and his body. What started in the snooker room moved down to the living room (with a brief sojourn for mind-blowing oral in the kitchen), then back up to his bed where, satiated after a fourth orgasm, his fingers tenderly drew London landmarks on Leia's stomach and thighs until sleep whisked them both away. *He's totally to blame for my dream: sex with him on the London Eye…*

Her skin still tingled from his touch. *His hands! To die for! Hands that climb mountains, build schools, save theaters…holding me down and lifting me up, taking me higher and higher until I shatter and float back to earth…heavenly.*

But their evening wasn't all peel-me-off-the-ceiling sexcapades. *That second time on the snooker table, though…me on top, straddling him…I totally cracked up when our bouncing sent the snooker balls clacking and spinning into different pockets.* She bit her lip, killing a burst of laughter bubbling up her throat. *Then, Tarquin got the giggles and neither of us could come. It's so sexy being with someone who has a sense of humor in bed. I've never had that before.* An aching yearning flirted inside her panties. *Oh, Leia. This isn't good.* Her tired eyes followed a plane slicing through the pink clouds above Tower Bridge. *You're starting to like him—a lot.*

Leia missed the give and take between the sheets, the savage need and playful pillow talk of her early years with Tyler...all things Tarquin offered, all wrapped up in a sexy smile and a generous heart. And it wasn't just her imagination. Every tender caress, each desperate, steamy kiss was like a blowtorch melting the ice she'd carefully packed around her heart.

But am I falling for him—really? Or is it the orgasms? They trick you, orgasms...make you feel like you're falling in love when it's really just feel-good chemicals in your brain. Staring at her primroses happily on display in a squat square vase, she swirled the juice in her glass. *Sometimes I miss the old Leia. She was joyful, romantic. Believed in happily ever afters...* Her heart pinched. *No. Stop it. I can't get sucked down that rabbit hole just because Tarquin's gifted in bed. I didn't fall for Xavi and I won't for Tarquin. Although, to be fair, Xavi likes to check his Instagram during sex, so the bar wasn't set very high there.* She cringed and took a long sip. *I'm leaving in two days so...I'll just enjoy this for what it is—a brief infatuation, a lovely London fling. And that's all!*

She set down her juice and opened the notes app on her phone, her thumbs flying easily over the small keyboard.

January 15, I was grateful for:
1. *Saz getting her promotion. So deserved!*
2. *that massive lunch hamper from Tarquin. Simon and I have leftovers today. Yay!*
3. *FOUR soul-rattling orgasms and tons of laughs. I haven't laughed like that in months.*

She pressed 'save', planning on transferring the entry to her journal when she got home. *I should get going soon. I need to shower, change clothes.*

"This is my fave room."

Leia looked up, finding Tarquin dressed in a fresh pair of snug boxer briefs and a gray *Horton Hears a Who* t-shirt, faded and obviously much loved. *His fondness for Dr. Seuss is cute—unexpected, too!* "I hope you don't mind…" She raised her glass of OJ. "I made myself at home."

"Good! You hungry, too? I can make waffles or eggs, a brekkie burrito?"

"You are such a rule breaker!"

"You're only finding out now?" He yawned and reached under his tee. The scratching motion lifted his shirt, gifting Leia a tease of glorious six-pack. "Or we could go back to bed? I'm an awesome cuddler. 'Spooner of the Year', me."

I'd love to be wrapped in his warmth again, but one thing will definitely lead to another… "No, 'cause we won't just spoon!" She chuckled, pulling her eyes away from what she really craved for breakfast. *I need to hit the brakes here. I'm in way over my head. I can't let whatever this is veer out of my control.*

"Yeah, probably not." A sly smile danced across his lips. "How was the sunrise?"

"Stunning. All bright pinks and oranges. You were right about the bridge, too. It looked magical."

With a lazy nod, he rubbed his eyes then blinked several times, his focus drifting away.

"You okay?"

"Yeah. I fell asleep with my contacts in. I swapped 'em for a fresh pair, but my eyes aren't having it." He laid beside her on the sofa and happily nuzzled into her hair. "Mmm, the smell of my favorite things—salted caramel, sex, Leia." He slipped his fingers through the opening of her bathrobe.

"In that order?"

"Well, you have to admit"—he traced a path up her thigh—"that salted caramel lube…"

Mm, those hands of his should come with a health warning—

may cause shortness of breath, dizziness, heart palpitations…
Leia's pulse picked up as she returned the favor, fingers splayed and lingering, toying with his chest hair underneath the soft cotton of his t-shirt. "I've never been a caramel fan—until now!"

"I'll take that as a compliment." Gaze falling heavy, he left a kiss in her hair and whispered against her skin, his stubble tickling and his breath warm and quickening. "Tell you what, how about we peel ourselves off this sofa and curl up together in a warm bubble bath? We'll have a proper soak. You know, candles, the works…"

Did he buy all that for me? It's romantic and lovely, but edging a little too close into boyfriend territory. I like you, Tarquin. I love sleeping with you, but you can't have my heart. Leia pulled her hands out from his shirt. "You don't have to do the whole seduction thing."

"What thing? I just love bubbly baths."

Leia raised a skeptical brow.

"I do! Go, look in the cupboards in my en suite. You'll find six different bath bombs, loads of body washes…"

To be fair, I did see body washes on the side of his tub.

"…and my rubber duck collection."

"You collect rubber ducks?"

"Not just any ducks—*Star Wars* ducks!"

"Of course!" Leia smiled and played with a piece of hair sticking up straight above his forehead. *He's just a big kid.* "Stupid question, I know, but do you have a Princess Leia duck?"

"No. Strangely." His finger trailed back down her leg. "But that's never stopped me from a good soak. I read ebooks or watch football on my tablet…"

Okay, I get it—baths are his way of unwinding, chilling out.

"…or have knee-wobbling sex with a *gorgeous* Canadian designer." The hardness prodding Leia's hip suggested that Tarquin liked that idea—a lot. His lips curved at the corners into a 'You can have me again if you want' cheeky smile that set off his dimples and a heavy ache high between Leia's thighs.

This man! His mischievous charm will be my undoing.

"Shall we make up for the orgasms we lost on the snooker table?"

Tempting. I need to finish Shantelle's gown, though. "I'd love to, but duty calls"—she stroked his cheek—"and I have to shower and change at Saz's before I head to Simon's."

Tarquin sat up and Leia followed, planting her bare feet on the floor. "You could shower here." He scratched his bedhead, a smoldering urgency lingering in his gaze. "Have breakfast…"

Nice try. She giggled. "Don't you have meetings this morning? Architects to order around?"

"Yeah, but I don't have to be suited and booted for another three hours. Plus, my office is right there." He waved a dismissive hand toward the window. "In the Shard."

Why doesn't that surprise me?

"But I understand. You've got a lot farther to go than I do." He rubbed his eyes again, his disappointment only evident by the slight sigh on his lips as Leia downed the rest of her juice. "You know, I wasn't just blowing smoke about your sister. That TED Talk she gave on accessibility really stuck with me. I couldn't place her right away, but when she mentioned her job, it clicked." He smiled. "So, *both* Scott sisters are forces to be reckoned with, eh?"

"Yeah, I guess. Sarah calls it as she sees it. How can she not? She lives it every day. Places she can't enter, transit she can't use—it's a never-ending battle—but instead of complaining, she's pushing for real change, making sure voices like hers are heard. I couldn't be prouder."

"I can't wait to work with her," said Tarquin. "I want my properties to have ramps and automatic doors, braille on elevator keypads, visual fire alarms, voice announcements…"

"Well, Sarah's your woman." Leia left her empty glass on his coffee table. "She knows all that inside out. She's really building a reputation as the go-to person here in London."

"So, how long has she lived here?"

"Three years." Leia glanced across the room, her eyes catching a cluster of photos on the monster bookcase: shirtless Tarquin, arm wrapped around a surfboard on a beach, and another atop Sydney Harbour Bridge. Shoulder to shoulder, the teen Balfours brothers wore frumpy, baggy onesies and safety harnesses. "She did her final year of university in Oxford, then moved home. But she's a total Anglophile, loves the royals and winters without snow, so she came back in 2016."

"Your poor dad, though. Both girls far away."

"Yeah. He misses us, but it gives him an excuse to travel."

"What about you? Do you visit Sarah often?"

Is he trying to tease out of me when I might be back? Leia ran a hand through her unruly hair. "Dad's here more frequently than I am. The last time I visited was"—she looked up at the ceiling, calculating dates—"eighteen months ago."

Tarquin widened his eyes. "Oh."

"But we talk all the time. Sarah's my best friend." *One he'll be working with closely. And they'll chat—they're bound to. I didn't want to share so much, but I don't really have a choice. He's already seen my scars…*

Leia cleared her throat. "It's hard to believe we almost lost her."

Tarquin's brow furrowed. "*Lost* her?"

"Yeah." Leia tightened her robe. "Sarah was nine—almost ten. I was eleven."

Tarquin nodded attentively.

"Skating was our thing. If we weren't at the rink, we were helping Mom sew our costumes or practicing choreography at home. I

200

was pretty good on the ice, but I had to work at it. Sarah, though, was a natural. I swear, every month she came home with something—a ribbon, a trophy. That afternoon, she added another first-place medal to her collection."

A warm smile brightened his face. "Was she an ice dancer, too?"

"No, singles. She was like a ballerina on ice, so graceful. Her artistry blew everyone away. Mine, not so much!"

"Oh, come on! I saw you gliding about, putting everyone to shame."

Leia shook her head. "I was okay at best. Not like Sarah. She had the potential to be world-class. And her *jumps*! God, she could leap rings around everyone in her age group. I was all long legs and wobbly ankles back then. It's a miracle my partner didn't ditch me after our first comp." She smiled at the memory. "Anyway, one weekend we had a skating competition about ninety minutes away from where we lived. Mom and Dad were there, cheering us on as usual. Saz and I wanted to hang out with the other kids after the competition, the last big meet of the season. It was getting colder and a snowstorm was forecast for later that night, so Mom and Dad headed home in the car, letting me and Saz take the bus back with the other skaters as a treat.

"Our team hung around for a bit to celebrate, said goodbye to the kids from the other skating clubs, and then we set off. We were singing, yelling, having a great time in the middle of nowhere. Our coaches had the driver pull over at a diner on this country road so we could pick up dinner—burgers and fries for our celebration trip back. Half our team wasn't returning in the fall so we wanted to make the most of it…" Leia paused, pulling Tarquin's robe tighter. "So, we got our food. Climbed back on the bus, heading home to our rink. Eating, singing songs. Then, maybe ten minutes later, a truck strayed into our lane and hit us."

201

Tarquin flinched. "Oh, god!" He blinked several times, his mouth falling open, searching for words. "Who…?"

He looks horrified. "A drunk trucker. The impact rolled the bus, tossed us around like dolls. I can still remember the sounds—the metal crunching, glass shattering. Screams. I smashed into the ceiling and blacked out."

"Oh, Leia…" His brow tense, Tarquin scooped up her hand, holding it tight.

"When I came to, the bus was on its side and I was wedged between seats. I was dizzy and nauseous, had a crushing headache. It felt like I'd been stabbed in the stomach and hurt to breathe. And I was gagging. I had this thick, metallic taste in my mouth."

"Blood?" He winced.

Leia nodded. "I looked for Sarah, but it was *so* dark, and still. I could only see a few feet ahead of me. I thought the crumpled shapes nearby were torn up seats…until they moaned. I called out for Sarah, but she didn't answer. That's when I started to panic. I had to get out of there. I had to find her.

"My leg was killing me, bleeding pretty bad, but I dragged myself into the aisle. All our stuff was scattered: skates, iPods, burgers—everywhere. I heard friends crying, scrambling to get out. And that's when I spotted Sarah's new medal, wedged under me. Just seeing it made me feel less panicked, like it meant she must be close by, you know? I picked it up and put it in my pocket to keep it clean. I remember thinking she'd kill me if I got blood all over it."

Tarquin squeezed her hand. "Where'd you find her?"

The sting in Leia's eyes begged her to blink. "I didn't. It was only when the fire department rescued me that I heard where they found her—alone in a snowy ditch. She'd been thrown clear."

"Holy shit."

"I wanted to see her, but she was surrounded by paramedics." Leia's voice wavered as she gulped back a sob. "I-I heard her crying..." Tears spilled through her lashes and trickled down her cheeks.

Tarquin drew her in and rubbed her back softly.

"I still feel guilty that I wasn't there for her. I should have been *with* her."

"But you were hurt, too! You were trapped—it's a miracle you both survived. Did anyone..."

She nodded through her tears. "Four people died—the bus driver, two coaches, our friend Clara. It was awful. No one walked away unscathed."

"Your scars...?"

"Yeah. I had deep cuts, a chipped tooth, a concussion, a ruptured spleen. My right shin bone was sticking out of my leg."

Tarquin winced. "Jesus."

"But compared to Sarah"—a sob stuck in Leia's throat—"Sarah suffered a bunch of puncture wounds, a concussion, a crushed kidney, a broken collarbone. Then, they told us she had shattered vertebrae in her back. She'd never walk again, let alone skate."

Tarquin looked sick. "What you both went through...at such a young age. I'm so, so sorry."

There's so much kindness and empathy in his eyes. He's not just saying these things. He really means them. "Thanks. It was brutal at first. Sarah was in constant agony. You'd think being paralyzed from the waist down would mean she'd be pain-free, but that's not how all spinal cord injuries work. It's like the brain and nerves can't communicate properly. It sets off all sorts of awful sensations—burning, tingling, spasms. Her moods were all over the place, too."

Tarquin nodded.

"She was angry, depressed...to be nine years old and in hospital for months, unable to finish the school year or play with friends... She had just started to feel some independence as a little kid and it was all snatched away." She wiped tears from her cheeks. "Jeez, look at me. It's been fifteen years, but it's amazing how it all comes flooding back. The scars fade, but…" She sniffed.

"That horror stays with you, right?"

Leia looked down and found Tarquin's hand entwined with hers. "We both had nightmares, for a long time. I was scared to leave the house for a while. I wouldn't get on a bus if you paid me, even with Mom by my side. The thought alone made me nauseous." *Just like when lights go out suddenly. I still freak out in the dark.*

"Our therapist diagnosed both of us with PTSD. It took years, but we worked through it—mostly." Leia swept her hair off her forehead. "It's strange what sticks. Sarah still won't touch burgers, and we're both nervous if we see big trucks coming toward us on the road. But we moved on and learned to live with our new normal. I plan more now, worry more. When I'm somewhere new, I always check where the emergency exits are. And I cut to the chase—ask for exactly what I want. I hate being a passenger. I need to be in control…in case you haven't noticed."

Leia raised her eyes to Tarquin's, half-expecting him to jump in with a light retort, but he didn't. *No Spice Girls or* Star Wars *jokes. No sexualizing my 'in control' comment.* His respect and empathy warmed her heart. *He's all about fun and risk-taking but can be so caring and sensitive when it matters, too.*

"Well, given everything you've been through, that's totally un-derstandable." He gave her a kind smile, raised their clasped hands to his lips, and planted a barely-there kiss on her knuckles.

Leia almost gasped at his simple gesture of kindness. *Oh, god, no! Please don't be so great, Tarquin. I can't fall for you—it'll end up hurting us both so badly. Let's pretend that never happened…*

She cleared her throat suddenly as their hands returned to the sofa. "Oh, one really weird thing? Sarah came away with a love for blue clothes."

"Blue clothes?"

"Yeah! She wears blue all the time!" Leia let go of his hand. "She had blue on the day of the accident and decided a month later it was her lucky color."

"But...she almost died?"

"It's lucky because she lived."

Tarquin nodded slowly, Leia's explanation rousing a soft smile. "Right. Of course."

"Growing up, Sarah always said, 'Olympics first, then medical school.' She hoped to become a doctor, but months in hospital put her off that idea. So, she decided to make a difference another way, and nothing, not even losing the ability to walk, was gonna hold her back."

"Wow! Pretty ballsy nine-year-old kid."

"Tell me about it. Even now, if anyone uses the words 'wheel-chair-bound' or 'confined to a wheelchair' in her presence, she schools them without mercy. She's never felt stuck or restricted—her chair makes it possible for her to explore and live her life—but some people don't see it like that, for some strange reason. Anyway, she doesn't let their small-minded, ableist bullshit hold her back or change how she feels about herself. She's absolutely *killing* it at work, has an awesome boyfriend, plays in a wheelchair basketball club, does marathons twice a year—"

"The London marathon?"

"Yep. Maybe you'll see her at the finish line this year." Leia smiled wistfully. "She loves being active. When Dad was here, he tried to get her to go skating with him at the Tower of London. It's accessible, but she wasn't ready. Maybe next Christmas." Her heart leapt into her throat. "Ah, I'm going to miss her. I can't believe it's time to go. This trip flew by." *Two more days and then we're back to talking on the phone, messaging, Skyping. It's not the same as being here.* Her fingers toyed with the gold band on her right hand, their mother's wedding ring. "It's been great bingeing pizza, sharing the excitement of her job promotion, celebrating my birthday—all things we can't do with an ocean between us."

"When was your birthday?"

"Christmas Day."

Tarquin's eyes lit up. "Someone got cheated!"

"Yeah, but Saz always makes it special."

"I think it's wonderful how close you two are," said Tarquin. "Take it from personal experience, not everyone has that."

Leia nodded. "Yeah, we were never like the other sisters we knew—the ones who barely tolerated each other. If I was at a hockey game, the movies, Saz was, too. My little sister, my shadow. But don't get me wrong—it wasn't all Beanie Baby parties and dressing up as Spice Girls. We drove each other crazy, too. Still do—like last night. Saz thought she was helping, I thought she was overstepping, and—*dun, dun, dun*, storm clouds!" Leia chuckled. "I bet you thought we hated each other."

"I wouldn't say hated, but it *did* feel like I walked right into the middle of something."

"But that's just it. Saz and I can be yelling at each other one moment then cooing over a puppy the next, like nothing happened." Leia smiled. "I won the sister lottery. I'll always have her back and she mine."

"I love that." He squeezed her forearm softly and let go. "Thank you for telling me, about the accident and everything. You've been through so much."

"Yeah." Leia looked down. "At the pub, you asked why I started sewing…"

"You said you were bored…your mom roped you in, right?"

He remembered. "Yeah, but that's not the real reason. Sarah is."

"Oh. How come?"

"She really struggled with getting dressed on her own after the accident. Clothes were difficult to get on and off, and hard seams, rivets, and pockets pinched or dug into her skin. Mom scoured the mall for anything that would make Sarah's life easier but always came home frustrated and empty-handed. That's when she began upcycling Sarah's clothes."

His smile crept up to his eyes. "And you helped?"

Leia nodded. "It was a huge learning experience—for all three of us. Mom had to figure out which materials were soft but still strong enough to withstand wear and tear. She played with pieces Sarah loved, repurposing them into something better. Jeans and pants were altered to be higher in the back and more comfortable around her stomach. Mom adjusted pockets, zippers, buttons, added magnets in some cases—everything had to be pain-free and easy to get on, but still cute."

"I never thought—I guess I take getting dressed in the morning for granted."

"I know, right? We all do. But Mom made sure all of Sarah's stuff was comfy, functional, and stylish. Little girls can be so picky about what they wear!"

"There were battles?" asked Tarquin.

Leia laughed. "You have *no idea*! But seeing Sarah regain some independence made them all worth it. Some people say fashion is superficial, but they couldn't be more wrong. We're happier, more confident—ready to take on the world when we feel good in what we're wearing, and helping Saz introduced me to my passion for upcycling. I still make most of her clothes and offer adaptive pieces in every collection. I also do custom work and alterations for clients with disabilities, too."

"Wow. All because of your sister."

"Yeah. I'd do anything for that girl—including shopping during a blackout on New Year's Eve—" Something fuzzy rubbed against Leia's ankle. *Oh?* She glanced down. "Your cat! Mrs…"

"Chuzzlewit." Tarquin scooped up the chubby tabby, cuddling her on his lap. "My little tiger. Isn't she beautiful?"

"Yeah." Leia let the feline sniff her hand. "It's a good thing you showed up, Mrs. Chuzzlewit because I was beginning to think your owner made you up."

"Oh, she's just a tad standoffish. I don't think her previous person treated her very well."

I know that feeling.

"That's why I give her everything." He kissed his pet on the head. "She's worth it, aren't you, my beauty?"

Aw, he genuinely adores her. The cat pressed her fuzzy face against Leia's hand, begging to be scratched. *And I can see why— she's a total love bug.* Leia gently rubbed behind her stripy ears, and the tabby squirmed out of Tarquin's grasp, leaping onto her lap. Mrs. Chuzzlewit closed her butterscotch eyes, and her rumbly symphony of purrs grew loud as they vibrated against Leia's thigh.

"I think you've got another fan. See, even Chuzza wants you to stay."

"Oh, I see the plan now! Hey cat, did your owner put you up to this?" Leia happily scratched Mrs. Chuzzlewit's shoulders. *I'm so conflicted. The way Tarquin reacted to my scars, the accident, Sarah's story...he didn't glaze over or change the subject. He listened, asked questions. He really cared.* She glanced up at him, his warm smile easy and brimming with adoration. *I can't deny it—he's lovely. If I lived here, if I was looking for something serious—if I wasn't scared—he'd be perfect.* She grinned back but pulled away, ruffling the cat's ears. *But I can't have my heart shattered again. Even the sweetest guys don't come with a guarantee.* "I'd love to hang out, Tarquin, really, but Shantelle's gown won't sew itself. I really should get a move on."

"Oh, no worries. I'll drive you to Islington."

"You *really* don't want to work today, do you?" Leia smirked.

"I hate the boss. He's a right bastard."

A laugh burst through her lips. "Well, I can't help you with that!" She gave Mrs. Chuzzlewit one last pet. "I appreciate your offer—you're such a sweetheart—but the Tube's fine."

Tarquin lifted his cat from Leia's lap and set her gently on the floor. "How about we meet up later, then—grab a bite?"

I was gonna work late on Shantelle's gown, try to finish it.

He glanced down, catching the tabby weaving back and forth between Leia's calves. "I know we agreed not to do date-like things, but you're leaving in two days! Let me treat you to dinner." He looked up, a visible swallow bobbing his throat. "How 'bout it, Ms. Frill-Seekers? Say goodbye to London in style?"

"And break my own rules?" Leia scratched behind the cat's ears. *But with me leaving in forty-eight hours, do rules matter anymore? Dinner would be nice. And really, am I going to say no to my last chance to see Tarquin in—and hopefully, out of—a bespoke suit?* She sat back. "Okay, on one condition…can we go to that OXO restaurant you mentioned before? I Googled it and the view looks amazing."

Tarquin winked. "You're in the driver's seat, Ginger!"

Sixteen

TARQUIN

"It's Victorian? Hm. And on Sylvester Path in Hackney?" Phone glued to his ear, Tarquin leaned against his office window high up in the Shard, his bird's-eye view taking in London Bridge, Borough Market, and, far off in the crisp early-afternoon sunshine, the London Eye and Big Ben. Immaculately groomed and clean-shaven, he had chosen his navy three-piece suit with its subtle red windowpane check, a white shirt, and a purple tie especially for Leia, wanting to look his best for their last night together. "That's a great location, lots of people on a night out. It's near the Hackney Empire, isn't it?" He took a sip of coffee (his second cup of the day) from his 'I heart the NHS' mug.

"And the Picturehouse. I've heard rumblings about it going on the market since last summer," said Simon, the sound of buzzing juicers in the background forcing him to speak louder. "But the 'For Sale' signs went up at lunch, so I thought I should let you know ASAP."

"Cheers, Si. I'll definitely check it out." Tarquin sat down and pulled up his schedule on his laptop. A blue box with DINNER WITH LEIA owned the end of his day. The rest of his week was dotted with an appointment at the bank, meetings with his architect and project manager, and consults with a structural engineer and a conversion officer. *Maybe go see it Friday?* "A property like that won't hang around long."

"It might be a good replacement for that Spitalfields pub you lost out on."

"Uh, don't remind me." Tarquin sat back in his chair. "That one hurt."

"Well, here's something to ease the pain—*oh, cheers.*" Simon's voice trailed away briefly. "Sorry, Tarq, just paying for my juice. Sooo, this morning Leia said she's going to miss London and wishes she could stay longer. Would that have anything to do with you, Monsieur Balfour?"

Hope so. "We *did* have a pretty spectacular sleepover last night. How's she doing on this glorious Wednesday afternoon?"

"She's good. Scrambling to finish her gown. I don't know if she's coming in tomorrow. I think her sister's taking the day off to hang with her."

Tarquin toyed with a red telephone box keychain on his desk and smiled. The leaving gift for Leia was neither expensive nor unique, but hopefully, it would be a cheeky reminder of their scintillating time together. "What time is her flight Friday?"

"Noon, I think."

Bollocks. "That early?" A sinking sensation filled Tarquin's stomach. *I'm looking forward to tonight, but I'm dreading it, too. We'll just have to make the most of it.*

"Tomorrow is my stock-taking day," said Simon, speaking louder over a passing motorcycle. "I'll be up at six, so I told her she can come over at the crack of dawn if she has last-minute sewing to do…"

Which means leaving mine early. Again.

"…but I won't take it personally if she doesn't. I have a sneaky feeling she might want to spend that time elsewhere."

With me?

"I think she's smitten, Tarq."

"Really?!" His pulse took off with a joyous leap.

"With your cat."

Ah, shit. I fell into that one. "Ha! Very funny." Tarquin couldn't hold back his smile.

Simon snickered. "So, I did the obvious thing; I introduced her to Mrs. Chuzzlewit's Instagram."

Oh, mate. He pawed his hand through his hair. "Si! That account is a joke—started by your Freddie last Christmas!"

The jingly ring of a bell signaled that Simon had entered his shop. "Yeah, a joke *you've* posted to over thirty times. And now Freddie's beside himself—your cat has six times the followers as Moriarty."

"Well, to be fair, Chuzza's prettier than Freddie's cat. Her fluffy stripes, you know, they're more exotic, more photogenic."

"If you say so. Cats are *not* my thing—oh! Hang on." Simon's voice strayed from the phone. "*Sorry, say again?*" He released an exasperated huff. "Sorry, Tarq. Spencer's moaning about her cat only having three followers."

"And she's surprised?" Tarquin cringed as he shifted his coffee mug. "It's hairless and looks like a rubber rat! How can that compete with my Chuzza?"

Simon chuckled. "Listen to you! Keep this up and you'll end up a scary cat-chelor selling Mrs. Chuzzlewit calendars on Etsy. I swear, you love that cat more than most people."

"Can you blame me? She keeps me company, listens—well, sometimes—*and* loves me unconditionally. It's tough to find a woman who offers all that."

A beat passed before Simon responded. "Tarq...I'm really sorry." All the playfulness in his voice vanished. "I wish Leia were staying..."

A familiar ache gripped Tarquin's chest. "Yeah, me too, Si. Me too."

SAY HELLO, KISS GOODBYE

After a late-night feast of lobster and steak high above London in the OXO Tower's restaurant, Tarquin and Leia meandered along the south side of the River Thames, his mind swirling with their lively conversation about favorite childhood books (the *Little Miss* series beloved by Leia, anything Dr. Seuss for Tarquin) and bucket list travel destinations (Leia—Galapagos Islands, Tarquin—Antarctica). They laughed their way through cringe-worthy fashion trends (both chose man buns) and landed on movies they had watched repeatedly.

This is the best night! Tarquin chuckled. "I swear! I was just like Ferris Bueller." His eyes danced past the riverside landmarks he'd seen a million times, each one lit up against the dark, cloudless sky. The air was crisp with a slight breeze, ideal for a farewell stroll.

"Yeah! A rule breaker!" Leia giggled and a puff of warm breath left her lips, floating upward. "You should visit Chicago, explore all the filming locations."

"Oh, I have, actually! Chicago is fantastic. Love the architecture."

"I was born there, you know." Leia's gloved hand swept a piece of hair fallen free from her messy bun behind an ear.

"I thought you were Canadian?"

"I am, but I was born in Chicago to Canadian parents. They lived there when my dad played professional hockey. I have dual citizenship."

He was an athlete? "So, you're a member of the famous parent club, too, then!"

"Yep, but a dad in the National Hockey League is a lot different than a glamorous actress mom." Her eyes skimmed over the top-heavy 'Walkie Talkie' skyscraper across the river. "The only celebs Dad mixed with were other players, which didn't impress me or Saz. You probably met actors, singers…"

"No, not really. Mum took us to events, but it was to put on a show of family unity for the press." Tarquin plunged his hands into the pockets of his long wool coat. "Lots of affairs were going on—first Mum, then Dad. Their marriage finally imploded by the time I was seventeen. That's when I visited Chicago and escaped the mess at home. I tagged along with Harry and his dad Budgie."

Leia angled in with a bemused smile. "His name is *Budgie*?"

"That's his nickname. Professionally, he goes by Harry Manville Senior, but everyone calls him Budgie. He had meetings with several Chicago property blokes, and I must've asked him a thousand questions! Budgie said if I stayed out of trouble and earned respectable marks at uni, I could join his company after graduating. I was chuffed! My grandpa—my mum's dad—was in the building trade, and I've always wanted to follow in his footsteps, despite my father's disapproval."

"Why was he against it?"

"Well, with Nick a showbiz luvvie and Rupert happiest on Orkney, I was Dad's last hope. He's always wanted one of us to join Sports Now, learn the ropes and eventually take over—albeit under the watchful eye of his board of directors." He shook his head. "Look, it's not that I'm ungrateful for the opportunity. I know I'm extremely privileged, it's just...you only live once, you know? I didn't want to blow my shot quibbling over what type of polyurethane to use for footballs."

"Well, that's understandable."

"Yeah, tell that to my father. He holds a grudge like nobody's business. This past Boxing Day, he had guests over to our place on Orkney, and not just family either. The president of the biggest bank in Scotland was there with his wife, along with the owner of Chelsea football club. Dad was pontificating about the Balfour family legacy and proclaimed, in front of me and *everyone* else, that I'm lacking the entrepreneurial acumen to grow my business from the ground up."

"He what?!" Leia stared back, horrified.

"Oh, it gets worse. He also said I'll blow all my money and fall flat on my face within the year."

Her jaw dropped. "Oh, Tarquin! Merry Christmas…"

"I know, right? I was gobsmacked. And then he cheerily asked me to pass the cheese board. Lucky for him, I didn't throw it at him, the daft prick." Tarquin snickered. "So, that's why I cut my hols short, flew back to London for New Year's. I couldn't bear another second in his company. I felt bad leaving Ava, but…"

Leia tsked. "I don't blame you."

"Yeah, well, that's Richard Balfour! No matter what I do, he's always disappointed. Anyway, if it wasn't for Budgie taking me under his wing"—Tarquin caught Leia's raised brow and laughed—"pun *intended*, I'd never have had the confidence to start my own company. I owe a lot to Budgie—and Chicago."

"That's so amazing. Great mentors are hard to find." Leia smiled wistfully as they passed through the riverside passageway on the edge of Hayes Galleria, a former 1850s wharf converted to offices, shops, and restaurants. "So, when you visited Chicago, did you make it to the Art Institute? They've got some great pieces there."

"I did! And I might've imitated Ferris and posed with the sculptures. People stared. I didn't care."

Leia let out a mirthful chuckle. "I kinda did that in New York—in Central Park. I took a single black glove to the rink, channeling the Sara character in *Serendipity*."

Tarquin's face lit up. "Oh, I love that film!"

"*Serendipity*? You sure?" She casually swung her vintage drawstring pouch bag, its elegant beading glinting under the riverside lights. "This one's a rom-com."

"Yeah, with Kate Beckinsale. I love rom-coms."

Leia matched his smile, her eyes in cahoots with her mouth. "Hm. You love rom-coms, soaking in the bath, cooking…you own a *cat…*"

When she puts it like that... He glanced at the HMS *Belfast*, a former warship from the Second World War, now anchored in the Thames as a floating museum. "Whatcha saying there, Ginger?"

"I'm saying, Han Solo, you are full of surprises. It's… refreshing."

"I hope that's a compliment?"

"Well, it's not a dig!"

"Good, I'll take it." Tarquin settled into a smile. "God, I miss New York. Next time I'm there, I'll do the whole *Serendipity* thing. I'll book a room at the Waldorf Astoria, take you for frozen hot chocolate at Serendipity III. Might even buy you a Casanova candle!" He broke into a dirty laugh.

"Hey, I hate to break it to you but most of that movie was shot in Toronto."

"Nooo! Really?"

"Yeah! You know the hotel elevator scenes, where they lose each other? They weren't filmed in the Waldorf. It's the Royal York—in Toronto. And that new age place with the candles? The Green Iguana on Markham Street. Unfortunately, it isn't there anymore."

"Oh." His lips pressed tight. "Shame, that."

"But the place they used for the leasing office still exists. It's on Adelaide. And the engagement dinner and Lars' concert were filmed in Toronto, too. Toronto stands in for American cities more than you realize."

"Lies! It's all Hollywood lies!"

"Just like happily ever afters." Leia tugged her scarf tighter. "Movie endings are the *biggest* lie."

Or…maybe you just haven't fallen in love with the right bloke.

Our happily ever after would make you believe again. It would make me believe again... Tarquin's eyes swept down Leia's purple coat to its hem and her bare legs beneath. *She must be freezing.*

Leia's predicament was the handiwork of a playful Pomeranian she'd met at Waterloo Tube station earlier that evening. Clambering for her attention, the frisky pup's unbridled exuberance resulted in plenty of kisses, a pair of torn tights, and an unexpected pit stop in the National Theatre's toilets where Leia's ripped hosiery took their final curtain call.

A biting breeze darted over the Thames, and Tarquin glanced up from Leia's elegant pointed-toe flats. *I bet she didn't count on it being so chilly tonight. I'd like to wrap her up, keep her safe and warm.* "Are you cold? Your poor legs—we could hail a cab."

"Oh, no, don't bother. This is nothing! We used to walk to school in the winter with bare legs all the time. Teenagers, eh?"

"Canadians are hardier than us Brits, then." He admired the inky night sky, free of snow and rain. "Ah, it's beautiful tonight."

Leia's eyes followed the strings of lights gently curved like twinkly smiles between the riverside's lamp posts. "It really is. It's brisk, but great for walking, especially after such an incredible meal. Oh my god, that lobster..."

"I know. Melts in your mouth, right?"

"And the view?" Leia sighed. "I can see why you love it so much." Tower Bridge loomed in the distance, its towers, high-level walkways, and suspension chains lit up and ready for the perfect photo op. "London's gorgeous. I'm gonna miss it."

I'm gonna miss you. "I bet Sarah would love it if you stayed longer."

"Yeah, she'd *love* a few more weeks of me sleeping on her sofa and ruining her pizza."

"Ruining it?"

"Yeah, with grapes."

217

His eyes bulged. "*Grapes*? On pizza?!"

"YESSS! There's nothing better than a slice straight from the oven with bacon, roasted red peppers, gooey gorgonzola, a splash of honey—and grapes. Mmm! It's the perfect mix of sweet and savory. Don't knock it till you try it! My favorite place in Brooklyn makes it, got me totally hooked."

Tarquin pretended to gag. "Eating grapes is like scoffing squishy eyeballs. I'd have to be off my head to tuck into that."

"C'mon! It's not *that* bad!" Leia gaped. "God, you and Sarah! She says I must've been dropped on my head as a child, altered my taste buds."

"She might be onto something, baby." Tarquin winked.

Leia laughed and jabbed a playful elbow toward his ribs, but Tarquin dodged away just in time. "Balfour, you're *so* gonna get it!"

"I bloody well hope so!" He flashed a flirty smirk and returned to her side as a surge of wind blew across the Thames, ruffling their hair. "Make sure we go out with a bang, eh? Something to remember."

"Yeah," she answered pensively, her eyes lingering over Tarquin's lips. "It would be nice to stay longer, but..." Her gaze rose, roaming to London's City Hall up ahead, a glass globe that leaned away from the river like it was too close for comfort. "I miss New York. It's home."

Unfortunately. Tarquin cleared his throat. "Did you hear back about that museum job?"

"No! I didn't even get a second interview! The one time I'm on holiday and *want* work to call, they don't. I have a hunch my boss is trying to figure out how to let me down easy. You'd think she'd be a pro by now. It's the third time I haven't gotten this position."

"Really? That's taking the piss. Maybe you should quit, just design full-time."

"It has crossed my mind."

"It has?"

"Yeah. I've been saving most of my divorce settlement for a rainy day. Maybe it's time to open my umbrella." She giggled.

I could never tire of her laugh. Tarquin smiled. "I hope you cleared him out."

"Funny, that's what Simon said."

"Do you bump into him often around New York?"

"Not really. He lives in Garden City, a suburb on Long Island, but I definitely *see* him a lot." Leia tightened her purse's draw-strings. "He's kinda famous."

Why are all the women I like into actors? "He's in films?"

"No, he's an athlete—in the NHL."

Oh! Like her dad. "Like father, like former son-in-law. That's so...Canadian?"

Leia nodded. "Yeah, but if I could do it all over again, I'd never have married him."

Ouch, that doesn't sound good. Did Leia stray? Did her husband? He's a bloody fool if he did. "So, you'd erase all those years, those experiences—"

The Spice Girls blasted into song from Leia's coat. "Oh. Sorry!" She winced, digging into her pocket. A quick glance at the screen and she tucked it away. "It's Saz. She's working late—I'll call her later. Sorry, you were saying?"

"Oh, just that you regret being married?"

"I do, yeah. It would've saved a lot of anxiety and heartache, and god knows how many hours in therapy. You name it, I've done it: couples counseling, cognitive behavioral therapy, mindfulness sessions."

"You did all that, plus therapy for PTSD?"

"Yeah. I'm the poster child for therapy." Leia bounced her eyebrows. "Still fancy me?"

219

"Of course! Therapy is nothing to be ashamed of." *Unless you're me. The truth is I'm too ashamed about my depression to even seek help.*

"I totally agree," said Leia. "I mean, I'd be lying if I said I wasn't embarrassed in the beginning. I didn't tell a soul. But then I thought, this is helping me heal, making me stronger. That's *good*, right? So why hide it?"

Tarquin nodded. *And here I am...hiding it, and avoiding therapy because, you know, a bloke who can't man up and sort out his own shit is so attractive. I've been keeping a stiff upper lip, pretending everything's brilliant for so long it's now second nature. I have to be careful, though. I can't let Leia see through my bollocks. Not yet, anyway.*

"But that's the thing—I *know* why people hide it," said Leia, pulling her scarf tighter against another blast of frosty air. "It's that stupid, suffocating stigma."

Exactly! God, I wish I could be comfortable talking about this stuff like she is. "So, did people treat you differently? What about at work?"

"My closest friends have been great, but I still feel uneasy sometimes, especially around anyone I don't know well. You'd be amazed how many are poorly informed or just plain rude."

"I bet." *But that's it—I'm not amazed. I know what people are like, their snide comments, the so-called harmless jokes...that's WHY I've stayed silent, dealt with the lows on my own.*

"I'm using their ignorance to my advantage, though." Leia met his eyes. "For me, it's kinda my litmus test."

"How so?"

"If so-called friends ghost me or business associates choose not to work with me after they find out, then I know they're not evolved enough to be my people."

Wow. She's incredible. "That's a great way to look at it."

"Sarah and I learned the hard way to steer clear of close-minded jerks who clutch onto ignorant and outdated beliefs about mental health or disability." She pulled off her gloves as they passed The Scoop, an open-air amphitheater sunk into the ground beside City Hall. "Sorry! That was a bit of a boring rant!"

"No, rant away! I'm enjoying it!" *Should I tell her my secret? It would be a huge relief to finally spill to someone who understands.* "So, you still go? To therapy?"

"Yep, when things get a bit much. You can't *cure* anxiety or depression, but you can learn how to tame 'em." Leia fussed with her bun, tucking in another loose strand as her smile grew. "So, what were we talking about again? Before I hijacked our conversation?"

Hijacked? No! It's been a breath of fresh air, talking about these things. Tarquin scratched his chin. "Uh, quitting your museum job and...designing full-time."

"Oh, right! Yeah, maybe. I mean, it *is* my goal. Although, right now, I'd miss the industry contacts the Met gives me and all the fashion history at my fingertips. My coworkers laugh—I'm constantly swooning over the vintage fabrics, the craftsmanship. Every day is like Christmas. But to me, they're not just pretty to look at. They inspire me to be a better designer. I'm always learning, trying to figure out how to apply their old techniques to my garments." Her lips softened into a nostalgic grin. "An education like that..."

"Is priceless." *The thought of leaving it behind breaks her heart.*

"Yep." Leia picked at the fingers of her gloves. "But the creative freedom of doing Frill-Seekers 24/7 is almost too exciting to ignore. In a way, working here on Shantelle's gown has given me a peek into my future."

"And do you like what you see?"

"I won't lie. It's scary as hell"—she met Tarquin's lingering gaze and smiled—"but yeah, I do."

"You'll have to text me photos of Frill-Seekers' debut on the red carpet."

"Okay, sure." Shifting aside, Leia allowed a group of exuberant Americans clutching Bridge Theatre programs to pass. "So, what do you have planned for this year? More property acquisitions? A trip or two?"

I don't want to think about this, how empty my life will be without her. On Friday, she'll move on, emotionally, geographically— sexually. I won't hear about her distaste for hot bevvies or how therapy is going, what she likes on pizza or in bed. We'll be strangers again, a brief footnote in each other's story. Tarquin cleared his throat. "I'll be overseeing the church and cinema projects, and Simon gave me a lead on an interesting Victorian pub in Hackney. It would be a great get. I'm a sucker for old boozers. Think I should go for it?"

"Definitely. Snap it up before someone else does."

I wish I could snap her up before someone else does. Lost in her smile again, Tarquin's heart ached. *Two weeks of effortless friendship and mind-blowing sex. Two weeks of Leia never asking for more and me never demanding more. But it's not enough. Not anymore. Tomorrow, I'll leave my bed with the scent of her on my skin, the taste of her on my tongue, and the heartbreaking fear she'll meet someone else, giving them everything—all the secrets, feelings, and dreams I'm not allowed to have.* He looked ahead, hoping he didn't give himself away. "I'm actually seeing it Friday."

"So, I'll be on a plane, and you'll be adding another amazing property to your portfolio. Life goes on, eh?" A hint of melancholy weaved through her words as she looped her bag over her wrist and tugged on her gloves.

Yeah, without you. "I guess life can't be all snooker table sex, ice skating, and unicorns at IKEA."

Leia's chin dipped. "When will you see Ava?"

"Soon. Rupert told her about the unicorn—I reckon the bastard did it on purpose." He chuckled, his eyes combing Potters Fields Park and its riverside cluster of bare trees and sleepy lawns. "It's one way to get me up there. Ava will flood my phone with cute messages until it's in her arms. I'll visit soon and go back again in the fall for the baby's baptism."

"Aw, a new addition. That's lovely."

"Thing is, it won't be all fairy cakes and sandwiches without crusts. It'll probably dissolve into a huge piss-up with Nick shagging some old girlfriend and Mum saying inappropriate things. That's IF she goes. She's not a fan of Orkney."

"How come?"

"She's not much of a nature lover, mother dearest. She gets bored with the limited options for nightlife, and if there isn't a Harvey Nichols within reach, she starts to hyperventilate." A nippy gust of wind blew along the waterfront, bobbing the strings of twinkly lights.

"Well, I hope she visits for Ava's sake," said Leia. "Will you go climbing?"

"Maybe. Depends. Sometimes they get four seasons in one day and the winds can be harsh and relentless. That's why you won't find any trees there."

"You serious? None at all?"

"Well, not *none*, but not many either. The salty gales and short growing season are to blame. The only trees you'll see are sheltered near buildings or in gullies. Oh, but there's the Big Tree, a 200-year-old Sycamore on the main street in Kirkwall. It's withstood bad weather and several misguided attempts to chop it down. It's pretty famous, and locals love it. Maybe one day you can visit and give 'er a big hug."

"Sounds like it could use one!" said Leia. "I like how it's survived despite the odds. No wonder it's beloved."

"Yeah, that's just one of the cool things about Orkney. It really is like nowhere else. I'm lucky I spent my summers growing up there."

"I bet you and your brothers ran wild!"

"You don't know the half of it! My god. So many firsts happened up there, too: my first marathon, my first dive. I did my first climb at Rose Ness when I was nine."

"I'd be so scared to try—even now—but at *nine*?" Leia pressed her lips together. "Forget it!"

"Yeah, but that kind of fear pushes you. It can be invigorating in an odd sort of way. Actually, I used to be scared of heights."

"How'd you get over it?"

"My instructor. He said to think of the rock as a puzzle, and it's your mission to figure it out as you go. He swore my mind would be too busy problem-solving to be scared because I'd constantly be searching for crevices for my fingers and toeholds for support. And he was right. I ended up hugging the rock and felt...part of it. You have to trust it and yourself—or face dire consequences. Not death—we've got safety harnesses—but you can dislocate shoulders, tear muscles..."

"Your well-being is literally in your own hands."

Yeah, like my heart is in yours. Tarquin nodded. "And the sea birds and the ocean waves provide this soothing soundtrack. You can't beat it."

"It sounds beautiful. And you...you're so brave..." Slowing to a stop in the shadows of Tower Bridge, Leia clutched his arm. "And incredibly sexy, too." She swung around, facing him.

"Ooh, why?" Tarquin gently clasped her waist, drawing her in. "Tell me. *Please.*"

"Well"—she curled her arms around his shoulders—"your passion for climbing is a huge turn-on, plus your forearms are to die for."

"You have a forearm fetish?" He contemplated her lips, soft...warm, her mouth irresistibly wet. A throb tingled inside his trousers. *I like where this discussion is headed.*

"It's not a fetish! I just—you know, I like the muscles, veins...leading down to strong, capable hands."

Tarquin leaned closer, tucking a wayward strand of hair behind her ear. "Capable of coaxing one...two...*three* orgasms from you."

"They definitely give a whole new meaning to 'He's good with his hands.'" Leia smirked.

"And here I thought it was because I'm a builder."

"Well, I'm glad you hire people to do the *actual* building for you because if anything were to happen to those hands, womankind would weep." With a heated stare, Leia pressed against him. "Your hips are incredible, too. So flexible."

"It's all down to climbing. All that stretching, leg spreading, opening up." His hands slipped down her lower back to her ass. "I *knew* you liked them."

"You did?"

"Hell yeah. When we're fucking, you grip my hips like it's the end of the world."

"For *that* moment, it is...right?" Leia rocked against him, feeling the growing ridge beneath his coat. Her eyes lit up and she bit her bottom lip, pulling it into her mouth.

Ah. She knows exactly how to tease me. "Touché!" He chuckled.

"You must've seen that book of sexual positions based on climbing."

What? Why isn't THAT in my life? "No, I haven't! But it makes sense. Climbing terminology is strangely sexual."

"Like?"

"Finger-jamming, spreading, nuts, trust the rubber...jugs."

225

"Jugs!" Leia snickered. "That sounds like a teenage boy's wet dream."

"You have *no* idea." He leaned in for a kiss then teased her lips with his tongue. Leia welcomed him in, tilting her head and taking him deeper.

Oblivious to late-night tourists and a raucous herd of drunk office workers jeering as they passed by, they kissed slow and tender, barely pausing for breath. Leia's hands owned the back of Tarquin's coat collar while he squeezed her ass and stroked her back, the hardness inside his boxer briefs aching, longing for a release. *I'm so horny. Thank fuck we're near my flat.*

Leia pulled away, her eyes sweeping up to Tower Bridge. A quiet sigh fell from her lips.

What's she thinking? About our last few hours together? Or is work troubling her? She didn't finish her gown. Tarquin gazed at her, hoping for a sign. *I wish I knew what was going through her mind.*

She grinned and loosened her hug. "Tonight's been so much fun, and I love my cute keychain. I'll probably blush every time I look at it."

Bugger. She's not about to do a Cinderella on me, is she? Hail a cab and disappear? "Hey, the night is still young and so are we! Last I checked."

Taking a step back, Leia giggled. "There's so much I want to do—I wish I had more time. I've only seen Somerset House and the Hayward Gallery."

"The Hayward is awesome. Did you see the *Among the Trees* exhibit?"

"I did! Loved it. The thicket carved out of cardboard and the virtual forest"—she laid a hand over her heart—"incredible. I'd love to go back. I'd love to do so many things. I missed out on afternoon tea, seeing the Palace. Oh! The wax museum."

Tarquin scoffed. "Waxy celebs? *That's* a must-see?"

She stuffed her hands in her pockets. "I know it's tacky and cheesy, but it's fun."

"Creepy, more like!" He laughed.

"Fine, party pooper! I'll check out that bridge instead!" She stuck out her tongue and took off toward the stairs.

Tarquin set off after her and caught up, joining her climb step by step. "You'll just have to come back, then."

"Yeah, one day," she said, voice a little breathy as the soles of her flats met the top step. "This trip is my one last hurrah before I settle down with Frill-Seekers."

She's not coming back. A heaviness pinched Tarquin's heart. *This is goodbye. For real.*

The day's non-stop frenzy of selfie-snapping tourists on Tower Bridge was long gone and only a few vehicles revved past, crossing the river. They strolled along the walkway, and Leia leaned over the west side's parapet, gazing down at the murky Thames. "Jeez, that looks cold."

Not cold enough to make my hard-on go away... Tarquin reached into his coat and tugged at his trousers, discreetly adjusting himself.

She glanced over her shoulder, catching Tarquin's hand fleeing from his coat. A giggle left her lips. "I saw that!" Her eyebrow rose.

"*That*, young lady, is your fault."

"Hmm." Eyes narrowing, Leia took off her gloves and stashed them in her pocket. She stole a sneaky glance to her left, then her right, and pulled him in. "There's no one here, only a few cars. Maybe we should do something about that..." She slipped a hand between the buttons of his coat, rubbing the firm bulge in his trousers.

Ooh! Is she serious? A sneaky hand job?! Tarquin matched her devilish grin. "Maybe we should."

Her fingers curved around him.

Fuck yes! Staring into her eyes, Tarquin sucked in a slow breath, his focus fuzzy, heavy with want.

Leia leaned in, her whisper so close its warmth teased his parted lips. "Want to do me here?"

Whoa! A chuckle of surprise slipped from Tarquin's throat, his arousal tight and throbbing within her grasp. *I didn't expect that!* "You really want—here? Now?" He tilted his head back toward the eastern side of the bridge. "You know, my flat is right there…"

"I know, but *this* London experience is one we'll both never forget!" She grinned, her thumb stroking up and down his hard length with intent.

Oh! God! She's killing me.

"But we can't get caught." Keeping still, Leia's eyes darted down the bridge's walkway. "A mug shot wouldn't be a good look."

Tarquin smirked. "Well, you've already got the first rule of public sex down pat—no sudden movements."

"Hey, my back still aches from last night. I won't be making *any* sudden movements!"

"Good. If we're quiet, we'll just look like a couple kissing on the security cameras." *She might be gung-ho, but…uh, what about condoms? Might be a dealbreaker.* "There's just one problem— protection. I don't have any on me. I know you're on birth control, but…"

"Just this once will be fine," she answered quickly, biting back her smile. "Come on, let's do it." She growled. "I'm so horny I could scream. But don't worry—I won't!"

I can't believe this! "Just let me…" Tarquin wrapped his arms around her, concealing Leia's body beneath his long coat. "You'll have to do most of the work so I can keep what we're up to hidden." He hugged her tightly, his erection poking hard into her stomach.

"This is so naughty!" She giggled, locking her free arm around his waist. "Okay, so I guess I'll lean back against the bridge and then free you from your pants…"

Tarquin ducked his head to meet her eyes. "But are you wet enough for…? I wish I could feel you."

"You will in a sec." Leia fumbled underneath their coats. "Sorry!" She snickered. "This is tough one-handed." She twisted her lips like she was figuring out a difficult math problem. "I'm just moving my panties aside…"

Kill. Me. Now! "I can't believe we're doing this." Tarquin felt his zipper tug downward. *She is such a firecracker. I love it!* "Leia, just so you know, I don't think I'll last lon—"

Leia claimed his lips and kissed him slowly and deeply, her right leg hooking around his right knee as she freed him from his underwear.

I'll never forget this. Savoring her mouth, Tarquin closed his eyes, feeling her wetness, her hand guiding him inside. *Oh, sweet lord!* Pushing into her tightness, hot and slick, Tarquin moaned into their kiss. He rocked slowly with her, feeling her determined finger slip between them.

He snuck a peek down the bridge. *Fuck!* He abruptly left her lips. "Leia," he whispered, nuzzling into her hair, "coppers on the approach…"

"You came in, what, three minutes?" Wearing nothing but his boxer briefs and the scent of sex, Tarquin placed his Rolex on his nightstand. "You sure you're not having me on? Because that didn't feel like your first time in public."

"In my head, it wasn't." Leia popped the front clasp on her black satin bra and shrugged it off her shoulders, dropping it on a chair where her dress lay, neatly folded. "I've fantasized about it a

229

lot!" She crossed Tarquin's bedroom. "With you."

Bring those flirty black panties and that gorgeous ass back here. His thoughts of sliding the delicate satin down her hips and taking her from behind blazed a torrent of heat in his boxers. "You didn't even flinch when that cop car zoomed past." He strolled back to his en suite and dropped a pinky-white bath bomb into the water rising in his soaker tub. It spun and fizzed, releasing swirls of rosy bubbles. "Or when those tourists stood nearby. They were posting on Instagram like mad."

"Well, you did say not to make sudden movements." Leia unwound her bun, letting her blonde waves tumble over her naked shoulders. She combed it quickly with her fingers and opened his bedroom door.

"Where you going?" He walked back into the room, adjusting himself. "Can't be far, dressed like that."

She peered down the hall. "I thought I heard a scratch. Mrs. Chuzzlewit…"

"Ah, I knew she'd wrap you around her little paw. She's probably up in the gallery, attacking her stuffed mousie."

"Mousie?" Leia giggled. "Or enjoying some private time"—she gave him a playful smirk—"away from her fans. I saw her Instagram."

Yeah. Cheers for that, Simon. Fucker.

"Oh, Tarquin—"

"I know! It's daft."

"NO! It's *fantastic*! And hilariously cute." She stepped over her discarded flats and climbed onto his bed. "The fact that you love her so much says a lot about you, Han Solo."

"So, you'll still shag the catstagrammer, then?" His eyes trailed down to her breasts and back up again.

"Like you have to ask! I'm half-naked, waiting to straddle you in that oversized tub."

Cannot wait! He bit his bottom lip and grinned, fighting to carry on the conversation despite the growing distraction in his pants. "So, why don't you have an account? You could show off your travels, nights out, your dresses?" *And keep me in the Leia loop. I hate the thought of wondering how you are.*

"Trust me, my life is not that interesting. Who cares what I have for breakfast?"

"I do! I'm still hoping to find out…"

Leia smiled demurely and broke eye contact, her hands bunching up the duvet. "Maybe we should do something about that."

Ooh, I like the sound of this. "So, who's the rule breaker now, Ginger!"

She gazed up at him. "Well, if we can't break them on our last night…" A subtle shrug lifted her shoulders.

First dinner, now breakfast. Will she put the 'no relationship' rule to bed, too? Tarquin's smile grew. "I'll gladly make you breakfast. What would you like?"

"Pancakes! But"—she let out a ragged breath—"what I really want is to wake up with you, hold you until it's time to say our goodbyes. I mean, if that's okay."

Tarquin's heart hammered against his ribs. "Leia, like you have to ask."

She grinned, snatching one of his bed's pillows. "You better have maple syrup for breakfast and…*other* things."

This is perfect. "What Leia wants…" Tarquin glanced over his shoulder, expecting a mountain of bubbles cresting the curved sides of his tub, but murky pink water rose instead. *Bollocks! It's a dud?* His forehead tensed. "Uh, just a—" He dashed into his en suite and whipped open one of the vanity's many doors. A box of sensually-scented delights drew his impatient hands. *I need bubbles—now. Tonight needs to be memorable.*

"But you're right about Instagram and Frill-Seekers," said Leia, her words nearly drowned out by the roaring water. "I hired a social media company to manage my account, so I can focus on designing."

"Smart." Tarquin raised his voice above the din. "Social media is time-consuming, but it's a necessary evil." He twisted the taps, reducing the flow of water and the noise. "Will you photograph your dresses in a studio or around the city?"

"Around the city, next month. Hopefully, most of the snow will be gone by then." A sigh escaped her emerging frown. "Just the thought of the slush, the minus twenty-degree windchills, my ex being everywhere."

Now's your chance. Say it. It's been on the tip of your tongue all night. Adrenaline sizzled through Tarquin's body. He leaned against the doorjamb, admiring Leia at home on his bed hugging the pillow. "So, why don't you stay? For another week…or longer?"

"I've thought about it. I mean, what *am* I going back for right now? The snow? Hardly. A part-time job where I'll watch some socialite's daughter snatch the full-time position I was told was mine?!" She huffed. "If they're not honoring their promise, maybe I should tell them where they can shove their job!"

That's what I would do. "You know, if you did stay, you'd be here for the Dior exhibit."

"Sarah mentioned that! It's at the V&A, right? God, I'd love to see it, all the sketches, the dresses. When's it on?"

"Early February." Tarquin returned to the bathroom and rifled through his bath bombs, choosing a pink and purple sphere embedded with a small sculpted rose made of soap. He dropped the bubble-maker into his tub, giving it an encouraging nudge. "You could do all the London things you've missed out on—visit the markets, take in the view from the Shard, go for afternoon tea at Fortnum's. You could even hit up the wax museum, ya weirdo!"

Leia nodded slowly like she was checking off her to-do list.

"And still fly back in time for Shantelle's gown fittings." She craned her neck, watching Tarquin wipe bubbles off his hands with a plush towel. "And if you're not sick of me, maybe we could…"

He strode toward her with a confident smile. "I'm the *opposite* of sick of you."

"Great!" Leia tossed the pillow aside. "Well, it's decided, then! I'm calling Violetta right now." Her sunny expression soured. "Tell her I quit!" Jaw clenched, she leaned off the side of the bed and pulled her dainty drawstring bag off the floor. "I know my worth, and I refuse to be screwed over again!"

Blimey, she's serious. Tarquin's grin faltered as alarm bells rang in his head. *And I get it, but hasty, emotional decisions don't often end well. I should know. What if after the exhilarating rush of jacking it all in, she's miserable? Or can't pay her bills? What if it ruins her career?*

Lips tight and brow creased with determination, Leia looked like she was practicing in her head what she'd say to her boss.

Tarquin scratched his temple. *I have to be the voice of reason even if it puts her on that plane home in two days' time.* He sat beside her. "You know, I'm all for telling people who screw me over in business where to stick it, but you said it yourself, this part-time job is more than just a paycheck—it inspires you, gives you access to connections for Frill-Seekers…"

"Uh, yeah…" She slouched, pausing for a beat. "But this hurts, Tarquin. They promised. It was mine this time."

"I know." He swept a strand of hair from her eyes. "It sucks when someone's word means nothing, but I don't think you should be too hasty. You need to think about all the repercussions because once you quit…"

Leia untwisted her lips, letting out a heavy exhale. "There's no going back." She played with the drawstrings of her purse, winding them around her hand. "I guess I don't *have* to do anything right this second. I'm not scheduled to work for another two and a half weeks. I could move my flight and think about it."

"Well, there you go!" said Tarquin. "No quitting necessary, at least not tonight."

A smile snuck up on her cheeks. "So…two more weeks. Think you can handle it—handle *me*?"

She's so into me! "With pleasure!"

Her face shone with happiness. "You know, Tarquin, I'm not sleeping with anyone else…in case, you know…you were wondering."

Oh YES! He couldn't hide his grin. "Neither am I."

"Good, 'cause I hate to share." Leia giggled.

He laughed. "Ah, it's going to be smashing having you here longer. We'll definitely need more maple syrup for all those breakfasts!"

"Yes! I'll steal some from Sar—" Her face fell. "Shit! I forgot to call her back." Leia dug in her bag. "She's working late…she should be up…" With a huff, her shoulders dropped. "Shoot! Do you remember seeing my phone? I thought it was in here, but it's not."

"I'll ring it," said Tarquin, stretching toward his bedside table. "Just let me grab—" The Spice Girls sang out, fighting to be heard beneath Leia's folded dress. "Ah. Sarah beat me to it." He scooped up his own phone, watching Leia scramble half-naked over to the chair. "I'll finish running the bath."

"Add extra ducks for me!" She giggled, lifting her dress and rescuing her phone.

"Sounds good!"

Staring at the screen, Leia's face tensed.

"Go on, answer it. I'm sure she's not miffed—much." Tarquin returned to the en suite. "Say hi for me."

Hitting accept, Leia killed the Spice Girls mid-chorus. "Hey!"

Her tone walked a thin line between cautious and sunny. She flashed a smile Tarquin's way and sat on the edge of his bed.

Give her privacy. Tarquin pulled the door partially closed and dimmed the lights. The second bath bomb fizzed and bubbled, creating a sensual oasis of foamy, jasmine-scented bliss. He streamed music from his phone to the room's built-in speakers, placed a stack of fluffy cotton towels on the tub's edge, and lit several balsam-infused candles, creating a sexy, ski chalet vibe. Sitting on the bench in his bathroom, he smiled to himself. *Every last detail... perfect. Leia's really opening up, starting to trust me. Who knows? Maybe our fling will turn into forever.*

A few minutes later, she slipped into the bathroom, head down and hair up in a messy topknot.

"Come here." Standing up, Tarquin held out his arms. "Did you wake her? Was she cross?" He drew her in, kissing the freckles on the bridge of her nose.

"It wasn't Saz." With a tentative smile, Leia blinked up at him. "It was Violetta."

SEVENTEEN

"Start over, my darling. Be brave enough to find the life
you want and courageous enough to chase it."
Madalyn Beck

LEIA

The next afternoon

Sarah unzipped the lilac-colored garment bag adorned with 'Desjardins' in an elegant French vanilla swirl font and gasped. "He gave you *this*?"

"Isn't it gorgeous?" Leia hung her parka by the front door beside a pair of white garment bags: one protecting Shantelle's almost-finished red carpet gown, the other, the prom dress. "I went in early thinking I'd do a bit of sewing and pick up my stuff, but then Simon walked in with this—for me." She rubbed her slightly puffy, makeup-free eyes, then removed Simon's going-away gift from the bag on her sister's lap. Holding it aloft, she admired the emerald cocktail dress's flattering silhouette and sparkly sequined tulle. "I've been drooling over it for weeks."

"It'll look even more incredible with your red hair. It's the perfect middle finger to Tyler. Look what you're missing, asshole!" Sarah reached out, touching the intricate sequin work. "It feels as decadent as it looks!"

"I couldn't thank Simon enough." Leia hugged the dress against her sweater and jeans, and swayed her hips. The sequins caught a midafternoon sunbeam sneaking through Sarah's front window and threw a kaleidoscope of dappled green dots across the wall. "So, I made him promise he'll let me treat him to dinner next time he's in New York."

"Yeah, with your full-time paycheck. Congratulations, Ley!"

"Thanks. I still can't believe I got it."

"I squealed so loud when I read your message, I woke Jordan." Sarah chuckled. "He sends his congrats, too, by the way. Did you call Dad?"

"Yeah, last night on my way here. He's happy, said he'll visit me this spring and we'll celebrate."

"Lucky," said Sarah pulling out a small purple packet of British chocolate from beneath the garment bag on her lap. "So, how *did* last night go?"

It's been twelve hours and I can still picture Tarquin's face.

Leia's brief happy dance deflated under her sister's question, a wave of angst smothering the burst of giddiness in her chest. "It was incredible. The meal—to die for. We laughed and talked for ages about art and pets and family." She took the garment bag from Sarah and slowly slipped her dress inside. "Then, we strolled along the river and kissed..." Her mind stalled, returning to the bridge. *Our breaths shallow, hips shaking, my gasps muffled in his coat.* She eased the garment bag's zipper closed, careful not to snag any sequins along its upward journey. "Back at his, Tarquin went all out. He had chocolate, fresh strawberries, and sparkling apple cider from Borough Market, and he drew us a candlelit bubble bath. It was cozy and romantic—"

Sarah grimaced. "And you bailed?"

Leia pressed her lips together, a barely audible "Yes" escaping.

"*Leia!*" Sarah pulled a small, curly-shaped chocolate from the purple foil bag.

"I couldn't stay!" With a defiant click of the hanger, Leia left Simon's garment bag hanging alongside the other two. "Not after

I…" She ran her hand through her hair. "I might've…"

Sarah chewed slowly. "What did you do this time?" she mumbled through her mouthful.

"What are you eating?" asked Leia, eyes narrowing.

"Caramel curls covered in milk chocolate. Want one?"

Caramel…Tarquin's fave. Leia's stomach flip-flopped. "No thanks."

"So"—Sarah dove into the bag of candy again—"spill."

Leia sighed and plunked down beside her half-packed suitcase, splayed open on the floor. A ring of folded clothes waiting to be placed inside circled her like a textile fence. "Before Violetta called, Tarquin and I discussed continuing our fling." She winced. "I said I'd change my flight, stay in London a little longer."

A smile lit up Sarah's face. "Aw! You were gonna stay?!"

Leia nodded sheepishly. "You look like Tarquin did—over the moon."

"So, basically, you raised his hopes and then, what? Slashed them all to shit?" Sarah leaned forward, shaking her head. "What were you thinking, tossing *that* out there?"

"I wasn't tossing anything! I meant it. I was going to change my flight after I called you back, but Violetta's name popped up before I could do any of that. I thought she was gonna say the job went to someone else. I didn't expect an offer and a start date!"

"You know, this aggro could've been avoided if you'd just asked for a later one."

"I couldn't!" Leia refolded a Roots sweatshirt from her case that was already perfectly packed. "Remember the grumpy HR guy? He wasn't crabby—he was sick. Violetta said he keeled over after my interview and was rushed to hospital with appendicitis."

Sarah flinched and left the half-empty bag of chocolate on her lap. "Ouch!"

"The hiring process stopped dead. Violetta didn't talk to him

again until he was home a few days later. They both agreed I was
the best candidate and second interviews wouldn't be necessary."

"So why didn't she offer you the job a week ago?"

"Her hands were tied until he returned to the office and pre-
pared the paperwork, and with that delay and the new fashion exhibit launching this spring, they need me ASAP."

"Monday." Sarah pressed her lips together. "So, tough luck,
Tarquin."

I messed up. Leia placed another sweater in her case. "Everything we'd talked about five minutes earlier became null and void."

"Shit. What did he say?"

Leia sat back. "Well, he congratulated me, gave me a kiss. We
hugged. It was lovely, warm, and comforting." *Just like when I told
him about the accident.* An ache swelled in her chest. "But when he
pulled away, he looked like I had cancelled Christmas and stolen all
the presents."

"Oh, my god—you're the Grinch!"

"Don't joke." Leia grimaced, recalling Tarquin's beloved Dr.
Seuss book collection lovingly tucked away in his red phone box.
"It was awful…and awkward. He quickly switched to happy-go-
lucky Tarquin, but it was too late. I knew how he really felt. There
was no way I could climb into the tub and pretend everything was
hunky-dory. I'm not cruel!"

"I know you're not."

"But I could've handled it better. I did a panic blurt, said I had
to go pack my things. Tarquin didn't even try to convince me to
stay over. He offered to drive me home, but…I couldn't take advantage." Leia expelled a heavy breath. "I never wanted to hurt him,
Saz. That's why I was honest, right from the start. That's why I
asked him *twice* if he wanted something more. Both times he said
no."

"Surprise! He lied." Sarah shook her head.

"Obviously. UGH!" Leia bent over and buried her face in her hands. "I wanted sex with him so bad I shrugged off my doubts and went for it. I *let* him get too attached."

"No, you didn't. That's the risk that comes with hookups."

"Thanks! Tell me something I don't know!"

"Well, maybe you should rethink this whole casual sex thing, eh?" asked Sarah. "Because for no strings, you're pretty tangled. I heard you last night, rustling around out here, raiding the kitchen."

Stupid crinkly bag! Cheers, Hickory Sticks. Leia sat up and fought through a yawn. "I was hungry."

"You were freaking out. I know the signs! You can't sleep, you eat crap then look like shit the next morning—"

"Jeez, don't hold back, Saz!" Leia blinked away the watery remnants of her yawn.

"Face it, Ley: you're starting to fall for him. You want the job *and* Tarquin." Sarah crossed her arms, letting her words settle before adding, "And I'd bet my chair on it."

I hate when she says that. She's right and knows it. Leia avoided her sister's self-satisfied stare and sucked in a slow breath. "Okay, so I *might*…feel something." *And I hate myself for it.*

Sarah leaned back with a smug grin. "Called it!"

"What was there to call?! You said it yourself, I'm *starting* to fall for him. But 'starting' doesn't mean something has a middle— or a happy ending." Leia stole the bag of chocolate from her sister's lap. *Curly Wurly Squirlies?* She threw a dismissive look back. "Your whole argument is moot."

"Hmm." Sarah squinted into space and spun their mother's engagement ring, a sparkly amethyst, around her finger.

What is she plotting? With a frown, Leia dipped into the bag of candy, pulling out two squiggly pieces. "Any fleeting feelings I have for Tarquin are totally by accident." She sniffed the chocolate and took a wary bite.

"Feelings don't happen by accident, Ley." Sarah pursed her lips as her comment lingered, ignored by her sister.

These Squirlie things are hard. Leia chewed cautiously, the caramel waging war with her molars. *But they taste pretty good.* "Actually," she maffled, "you might be right about something…" She paused, chewing with closed-mouthed intent.

"Let's let *that* hang in the air, shall we?" Sarah smirked. "I was right!"

Leia rolled her eyes and swallowed, giving her jaw a much-needed rest. "Maybe hooking up isn't good for me. It only worked with Xavi because—"

"He was a self-absorbed dick?"

"Exactly. He made it easy *not* to feel anything for him, and we shared nothing. I don't even know if he's got brothers or sisters, or what he does for fun besides burpees. There was absolutely no investment, no risk—for either of us." She looked into the chocolate bag and gave it a shake, keen for another piece.

"Just how you like it."

It is. "Tarquin's different. He's chatty and playful, interested in other people, and doesn't take himself too seriously."

"Which is pretty rare for someone of his wealth and connections," said Sarah.

Leia nodded. "He's always shown interest in me *and* Frill-Seekers. He's never tried to get me to drink…"

"He's definitely easy to talk to. Plus, he's knee-wobbling hot."

Yes to all of the above. Leia sighed into a slump. Their dinner, their conversation, the unplanned sex on the bridge all teased her, playing on a loop in her head. *Tarquin made me feel appreciated, made me feel safe. He made me feel…loved?* Leia's chin quivered, but she quickly looked down at the foil candy packet in her hands, her hair creating a curtain, hiding the truth from her sister. *I'm not ready for any of this. I can't let myself fall for him any further and break the promise I made to myself.* She flicked the chocolate package with her finger. *Violetta's call was more than a job offer—it was a parachute.*

Sarah swiped her phone from the coffee table. "So, you don't want to date, but you don't want casual sex either?"

"Oh, I dunno." Leia shrugged. "But all this angst is making me hungry." She set the bag of chocolate on the floor and clocked the time on Sarah's DVR. "It's almost two thirty—is it too late for lunch?" *I hope not. I can't binge these Wurly Curlies or whatever the hell they're called.*

"Never." Sarah smiled. "Listen, I know the last few hours have been a clusterfuck, but you can't control how someone else is going to feel, Ley. You *were* honest with him, right? If he chose to think what you two had was more than it really was, well, that's on him— not you." Sarah squeezed her sister's hand. "I just hope all this doesn't make you regret coming over."

"You kidding? I got to be with you." Leia squeezed back.

"Good! Because I don't want London to become another Garden City."

"Tyler's not the only reason I won't go there anymore. You know that."

"Yeah, I know. I just don't want you feeling down about all this. Tarquin's a big boy." Sarah let go of Leia's hand. "He'll bounce back quicker than you can say Banksy. I bet he'll be out tomorrow night, flashing that smile and fighting the ladies off!"

A twinge unsettled Leia's stomach. Was it the wavy caramel chocolates? Or the thought of another woman owning Tarquin's lips, arching her back, meeting his hips? *He'll lose himself in someone who shares her secrets, her present—her future—someone who isn't me.* She swallowed hard. *I feel sick. Better lay off the chocolate.*

Sarah opened her phone contacts. "Those high-flying, wealthy types don't wallow for long. There's nothing his platinum credit card and some leggy model won't fix, trust me."

I hate that leggy model already—bitch! Leia bit her lip, stifling her scowl.

"So…lunch. Want one last pizza? I'll even hold my nose and scatter grapes on it. See, I *must* love you." Sarah laughed, tapping the speaker button on her phone.

Leia perked up. "Glad someone does! Thanks, Saz."

Sarah wheeled down the hall, her voice relaying their order to the pizza place.

Right. I should do yesterday's gratitude entry before lunch arrives. Leia unearthed her journal from a well-packed corner of her suitcase. *This should be easy.* She unzipped the notebook and picked up her pen resting inside.

January 16, I was grateful for:
   1. the beautiful sunrise over Tower Br

Her pen stopped abruptly. *This journal thing only works if I'm honest.* She put a line through it and started over.

January 16, I was grateful for:
   1. ~~the beautiful sunrise over Tower Br~~ morning kisses warm on my neck, fingertips lost between my thighs. Tarquin's kind heart… listening, encouraging, being present despite my messy past.
   2. another great lunch at Simon's thanks to the F&M hamper.
   3. a delicious dinner and easy conversation with Tarquin. Laughing so hard I got hiccups. Ferris and jugs, kisses and secret public sex—a night I'll never forget.
   4. finding out Violetta <u>does</u> appreciate me. I wanted that job so much it hurt.

5. *but my heart hurts, too, saying goodbye. Thanks, Tarquin for making me believe caring men DO exist. For helping me remember the girl I used to be. If we'd met at another time, in another life, maybe we could've had a different ending. Maybe even a happy one.*

Sealing away her secrets and her heavy heart with a quick zip, Leia traded her journal for her phone. After five aborted attempts, she finished her goodbye email to Tarquin, took a deep breath, and hit send.

Eighteen

TARQUIN

One week later

Tarquin slumped in a leather club chair in the dimly lit waiting room, his coat draped across his lap and Leia's email from seven days earlier under his thumb. Beneath his crumpled sweater, his stomach let out a long, snarly growl, furious it had only been fed a diet of champagne and roast beef-flavored Monster Munch potato snacks for the previous seventy-two hours. He scratched his week-old whiskers, now growing wild into a scruffy moustache and beard, and rested his throbbing head in his hands.

I can't have a repeat of last year. I need to get a handle on this! Passing out and missing the meeting with the conversion officer yesterday was so sloppy and unprofessional. Keep this up and I'll damage my reputation—and prove Dad right. He exhaled heavily. *I'd rather run naked down Oxford Street during Boxing Day sales than ask for help, but clearly, I can't do this on my own. Thank fuck this bloke fit me in again on a moment's notice. It's a struggle, spilling my guts. And it's costing me a bomb, but mental wellness is priceless, right? I'll just have to make sure my assistant doesn't spot the receipts. For all she knows, I'm at the gym.*

He nudged his black-framed glasses up his nose and blinked wearily at the aquarium taking up most of the wall he was facing. Striped angelfish gracefully zigzagged through an underwater forest of broad-leafed plants and spikey ferns while the filtration system gurgled and blew an endless supply of bubbles into the tank. Two of the pretty fish hung back in the lower corner, locking lips.

245

Snogging fish? For fuck's sake. Tarquin glared up the ceiling, the dark circles beneath his eyes defying his usual fun-loving demeanor. *Am I the only living thing on this planet who hasn't paired off? This is just another full-on 'Fuck you, Balfour.' You'll NEVER get the girl.*

His gaze fell to Leia's week-old email. He opened it again, poring over the words he could practically recite from memory.

From: Leia Scott
To: Tarquin Balfour
Date: Thursday, January 17, 2019 at 14:56
Subject: About last night

Tarquin, thank you for such an amazing time. I'm so sorry I couldn't stay for breakfast or for a few extra weeks exploring London with you. I'm still shocked about the job offer, but after tossing all night thinking, I believe returning to NYC really is for the best. Phoenix Properties needs all your focus, and the Costume Institute and Frill-Seekers need mine. I would hate to interrupt the great work you're doing in London. I know how passionate you are about saving those beautiful old buildings. You're making a huge difference, giving back to the city you love so much. And when your dad eats his words, it'll feel even sweeter!

I hate goodbyes, especially when it comes to someone as amazing as you. Going into our fling, I didn't expect to feel sad when it ended, but I'll be honest: I do. And I'm not just talking about the mind-blowing sex (although you are TRULY talented in that department!). Tarquin, you're so much more than a 'good shag'. You're incredibly kind, thoughtful, and empathetic, the sweet guy who made my London visit one I'll always cherish. I'm so grateful to have had you in my life these past two-and-a-half weeks.

As for Saz, I think she'll be happy to see the back of me. Our pizza just arrived and she's slicing roly-poly grapes in half, cursing my existence! See what you're missing? Me returning to NYC just saved you from your worst pizza nightmare!

Keep in touch, okay? I'd love to know how your work is going, how you're doing. And next time you're in New York, please call me. The (half-assed) Serendipity *tour and frozen hot chocolate will be my treat, and best of all, no skates required.*

Much love, Leia xo

"Tarquin?"

An American accent stole his attention.

Dex, a tall, gangly fellow with chunky blue eyeglasses and salt and pepper hair slicked off his forehead stood in his office's doorway. With his black and white striped dress shirt, skinny-fit burgundy trousers, and pork pie hat, he looked more like a wannabe jazz musician than a psychologist. All he was missing was a saxophone and a weekly residency in a dingy basement club in East London. "I'm ready for ya."

"Cheers." Tarquin picked up his coat and grabbed his coffee—his fourth of the day—and gladly left the stupid kissing fish behind, taking a seat on the therapist's green couch overrun with matching throw cushions. A small jungle of leafy plants shared the space with photographs of sun-soaked Costa Rican beaches, and a wide window was cracked open just a smidge, allowing brief bursts of the afternoon's chill to mingle with the dry heat pumping from the radiator.

Dex took his own perch, folding his 6'4" frame into an iconic Egg Chair in a retro-tastic dusty blue. Whether it was an original or a design rip-off, Tarquin had no clue and meant to ask, but during his first session three days earlier, he'd gotten sidetracked by the therapist's quirky appearance and mannerisms.

It's so weird! I can't get over how much he looks like Jeff

Goldblum. He must be doing it on purpose. I mean, come on!

Actor doppelgängers aside, Tarquin hoped therapy would work its magic, but one session in, he was finding it hard to connect and open up.

"So"—Dex wrapped his spindly fingers around a pen and balanced a clipboard of notes on his knees—"I last saw you three days ago…on Monday. How've you been doing?"

Excruciating. "Good! Busy. I'm in the middle of purchasing two Victorian pubs. One in Hackney, another in Spitalfields, which I thought I'd lost out on. The original buyer withdrew his offer, so I'm doing everything I can to seal the deal." *If that pillock of a broker would return my fucking calls. I've left five messages already.*

"So, how many projects is that now? On your redevelopment slate?"

"Four and counting. I'm also trying to get my hands on a gorgeous Grade II listed Victorian property in Pimlico…" Tarquin's gaze strayed, landing in the cluster of plants. *Wait. Is that…in the potted fern…a toy stegosaurus peeking out?* A small grin met his lips, his mind hopping from *Jurassic Park* to Leia and his dino rescue in IKEA. "Uh, sorry…where was I?"

The Jeff Goldblum lookalike glanced up from his clipboard. "Pimlico."

"Oh, right! Yeah, it's a rundown B&B-style hotel, but I'd like to refurbish it into a six-bedroom family home. It's got tons of hidden period charm begging to be shown off."

"Making London more beautiful—how rewarding!" Dex wrote something on his papers. "You should be proud, Tarquin. You're doing so well."

I wish. I'm bleeding money right now. He smiled sheepishly.

"Are you taking breaks from work here and there, enjoying a little downtime?"

Not since Leia. "Yep, I've seen my mates a few times." Tarquin picked at the lip of his reusable coffee cup, diverting his eyes and hoping Dex wouldn't spot his unsociable lie. "And I'm heading on up to Orkney next week." *Ava's been so patient, waiting for her unicorn.* "I'm trying to get outside more, but the weather hasn't exactly been kind."

"Not so bad today. No sun. No rain either…" Dex's naughty grin awakened again. "C'mon, grab your jacket!"

What? Eyebrows peaked, Tarquin's gaze bounced to his coat, folded beside his thigh. "Why?"

The therapist slid his clipboard on the coffee table. "Southwark Park is calling!"

In the middle of my session? Tarquin's mouth fell open. "Uh, now…?"

This is just weird…and my head hurts! Wrapped up warm against the midafternoon chill, Tarquin hid his confused frown behind his coffee and meandered along a footpath strewn with mushy brown leaves, soaked from the previous day's downpour. His therapist played tour guide, jabbering non-stop about the gray scenery.

"The park has gone through a lot of change since 1869…"

I don't care about the bowling green or how many trees have knees. Like that's a thing! Damn trees—they make me think of Leia. Tarquin huffed. *So, what's the point of all this, anyway? It's like Dex's playing hooky on my dime, roping me in as his wingman. Sorry, mate, but Ferris Bueller you ain't!*

A few cyclists peddled past and a roving gang of Canada geese waddled up ahead, but the park's faded greenery, closed café, and deserted playground did little to boost Tarquin's mood.

"Isn't this great? We're killing two birds with one stone." Dex side-eyed the geese, honking their displeasure at passing cyclists.

"Chill, guys! I didn't mean that literally." He twisted the cap back and forth on his bottle of sparkling water and snickered to himself. "So! Tarquin! *This* is walk-and-talk therapy! Some clients tell me it's more relaxed and productive than being sat inside."

Yeah, 'cause they don't have to stare directly into your weirdness. Tarquin tugged his burgundy beanie over his cold ears. *Maybe I should change therapists...*

"Back in my office, you mentioned your mates." Dex led the way into a sunken garden with an unparalleled view of the park's lake. Shaped like a semicircle, the commemorative terrace featured benches, vine-entwined pergolas, and dormant flower beds. "Socializing with friends is excellent self-care. It'll help with your other goal, too—inviting love into your life."

Oh, bollocks! He's not going to ask about my parents again, is he? Tarquin trudged down the four shallow steps and gulped his coffee, the lukewarm bitterness intensifying his wince. *Believe me, I get how the whole 'absent mother-thing' makes me crave loving relationships.*

Dex moved aside, allowing a mouth-breathing jogger to trot past before continuing, his voice low, keeping Tarquin's predicament between them. "A committed relationship will be easier to find when you're out enjoying what life has to offer. Speaking of, on Monday you mentioned a date that took place a few days earlier—with Leia, wasn't it?" Dex flashed his Cheshire Cat grin. "Aahh, now *that's* a name, huh!"

Of course he remembered her. She's unforgettable. A tight smile stretched Tarquin's lips.

"Tell me about it," said Dex.

Tarquin spilled all the highlights—except sex on Tower Bridge. A hollow ache swelled in his chest. *I miss her giggle. I miss her.*

"Sounds like a wonderful evening," said Dex, passing a metal sundial missing its shadow due to the afternoon's thick cloud cover.

"But she's gone back to America now. She left a week ago today."

"Oh. I'm sorry. How are you coping?"

Tarquin dragged a hand across the stubble on his chin. "It's been...difficult." Eyes drifting upward, a glint of silver piercing the clouds caught his attention, an airplane circling, waiting to land. "Leia's special. I thought maybe she..." He shook his head, his stare falling to the stone pathway beneath his Tom Ford leather brogues. *Fuck, I hate being vulnerable like this, admitting I'm not some stoic rock of a man who shakes off loneliness and disappointment like a rugby tackle.* He blew out his cheeks. "I've been working all hours, trying not to think about her, but...I can barely think of anything else."

Dex made a sad face. "Let's stop here for a minute." He leaned on the garden's cement railing overlooking the lake. "It's tough, what you're going through. Sometimes we think if we push painful feelings away, we'll be able to deal and move on much faster. But when we shove them aside, they tend to fester and create anxiety, which tricks us into adopting coping mechanisms or self-soothing behaviors that can have dangerous consequences...things like drugs and drinking."

I know this already. I've learned the hard way—multiple times. Tarquin cleared his throat and set his coffee on the railing. "Look, Dex, I know the drill, okay? Yes, I've had a drink or two, but—"

"Only two?"

Shit. Caught out. Tarquin frowned. "Okay, I might've... drowned my sorrows in a bottle of Dom Pérignon Rosé 1959."

"Yowza!" Dex's eyes bulged behind his glasses. "How'd you get your mitts on that? I *know* vintages, and that's a rare beast."

"My Scottish grandfather. He meticulously collected limited-edition champers from around the globe. When he died, he left a magnum to each grandkid, set aside until we turned twenty-one. We were supposed to share them with our future spouses when we got hitched…" A playful smirk bent Tarquin's lips. "*Whoops.*" He did a double take, detecting a sympathetic wince on Dex's face. "But that's it for self-soothing. No drugs, no gambling—that's the old me. Right now, I'm barely making it out of bed, mate. Thank god my office is just a sleep-deprived stumble away from my flat."

"Well, hold up there, cowboy!" The therapist tipped his water bottle in Tarquin's direction. "Overworking is just another un-healthy way to self-soothe. Diving into our jobs so our brains get lost in the minutia while what's bothering us gets buried—that can perpetuate depressive episodes, too."

He's onto me. Tarquin tugged on the cuff of his sweater's sleeve poking out from his coat. His thumb popped through a small hole. *Fuck.*

Dex rested his water bottle on the cement railing. "So, what's the emotion you've been feeling the most since Leia left?"

"That's easy: sadness, hopelessness." Tarquin sucked in a breath and glared at a pair of swans swimming side by side. "My dismal track record with women strikes again."

"How is it dismal?"

Do we really have to go there? Can't we just agree? I'm a fuck-ing failure! "I'm alone, aren't I?" Tarquin snapped back. "I'd call that dismal."

"Well, tell me how you got here." Dex scratched at his pork pie hat.

Flippin' hell. This is like talking about my sex life with some-one's hipster dad. Tarquin exhaled heavily. "I've been with lots of women, okay? I started young. You know, the usual—snogging behind the school at age eight, sex by the time I was fourteen." *I hate this, explaining myself.* "Not to sound bigheaded, but I didn't have to work for female attention. Blame my family's wealth, I suppose."

252

Dex pouted. "Come on! You're an intelligent, fun, attractive fella, Tarquin. There's more to you than your account balance, and you know it."

He shrugged. "But through all the snogging and shagging, I've only fallen for two—no, *three* women."

"Do you fall easily?"

"Yeah...but Leia was different. My dream girl, by name and nature."

"Dream girl, huh? Hmm, you really like this Leia."

"*Like*? Mate, that's the understatement of the century. She's this smart, confident blonde who knows how to have fun. Sexy as hell, too, but she also knows what she wants career-wise and works damn hard to get it. Despite that, she was never all about herself. She was always caring and empathetic, devoted to her sister, and interested in my business—interested in *me*. I didn't have to pretend to be the life of the party or offer to buy her things so she'd like me. And I liked who *I* was with her. I felt good about myself...so good I almost told her about my depression."

"And what stopped you?"

"What always stops me." He snatched his coffee. "Being seen as weak, unconfident—it's emasculating. And besides, everybody wants Fun Tarquin. I don't want to disappoint."

"But you just said you didn't pretend with her?"

"Yeah, but"—Tarquin winced—"I...sorta *did*." He took a long sip, delaying his confession. "I wanted a relationship with her, I knew that right away, but Leia didn't want anything...heavy. I lied so she'd sleep with me. That's why I didn't mention my depression—in case she ghosted me and I was left with nothing. She mentioned once she was in therapy herself, but that sort of made me *more* determined not to say anything. I didn't want to make it all about me."

"Have you heard from her since she left?" Dex nudged his blue glasses up his nose and smiled at the sun breaking through the clouds.

"She emailed before her flight. I drafted a response but didn't send it."

"How come?"

Tarquin shrugged, squinting at the glinting ripples in the lake. "It wouldn't change anything. She'd still be heading back to New York. I'd still be the sad fucker with unrequited feelings."

"Wouldn't it feel good, though? Opening up, sharing how you really feel? Like you are now."

"This"—Tarquin waved his hand back and forth between himself and Dex—"is different. I may feel like a wanker, sharing my secrets with a stranger and admitting my inadequacies as a pretend grownup, but the stakes are low, mate—I don't want *you* to fall in love with me. Telling Leia…" His shoulders rose as he sucked in a breath and let it go. "It's a sticky wicket. Any relief I'd initially feel getting it off my chest would be replaced by more embarrassment and rejection, not to mention a wallop of guilt. I've already swallowed my fair share, playing fast and loose with the truth. At least by keeping quiet, I can hold on to a smidgen of self-preservation." He scratched his whiskers. "But don't get me wrong"—Tarquin lowered his voice as a tour group of seniors admiring the swans loitered by the railing—"I'm not playing the victim here, okay? Because I'm NOT a victim. Leia was honest with me all along. What fucked me up was my own great expectations. They're to blame for how shitty I feel, not her."

"Let's…continue walking." Dex picked up his water and motioned toward the steps leading up to the path, free of chatty pensioners. "So, why do you think you blame your expectations?"

Tarquin scrunched his brow. "I suppose I'm a hopeless romantic? If I fall for someone, I get ahead of myself…fast-forward, picture our future, living together, our engagement, marriage—all of it.

I daydream about how fucking amazing it'll be, you know, us against the world." With each plodding step, Tarquin's thumb pressed harder on the lid of his coffee. "But then reality bites me in the arse. They fall in love with someone else or I do something naff…or like Leia, they don't even *want* a relationship, and my biggest fear slaps me back to reality again."

"And what's your biggest fear?"

"Oh, that's an easy one—that I'll end up alone." Tarquin looked up with a frown, rejoining the path as two joggers wheezed past. "I don't think I'm very lovable."

"Okay, Tarquin, here's the thing," said Dex. "That's your depression talking, stomping on your self-esteem and tearing you down with self-doubt and worthlessness. But I'm here to tell you that these negative statements, these stories we tell ourselves—they are *completely wrong*." He waved lazily at a patch of weather-beaten dandelions hugging the path. "And to top it off, the stories are like those weeds. Left unchecked, they sprout up everywhere. But with cognitive behavioral therapy—what I like to call *emotional herbicide*"—he chuckled—"you and I can identify them when they arise, stifle their growth, and change how you deal with them."

For fuck's sake! I'm NOT going all Sally Sunshine! Tarquin scowled. "So, you're basically saying I should ignore all negative thoughts. Don't worry, be happy."

"No, the opposite! There will be no toxic positivity on my watch, bud! Look, man, it's perfectly normal to have a mix of negative and positive thoughts and feelings. You'll *always* have worries, fears—that's part of being human, no getting around it—but we need to distinguish between what's rational and healthy and what's irrational. I want you to face the irrational head-on, see them for what they really are. If it makes things easier, think of me as your climbing coach, okay? Let's conquer this cliff together, you and me! I can show you how to rise above this and feel better. You in?"

Tarquin took a quick sip of coffee. "Could be interesting."

"Tarquin, it will change your life! We'll practice simple coping strategies you can use whenever negative self-talk or rumination rears its ugly head. In time, you'll feel better, and hopefully, your depression will lift." Dex leaned in conspiratorially. "Heck, we might even get you hitched, too. I *love* a good wedding!"

"Steady on!" Tarquin threw the therapist some dubious side-eye. "Don't start writing your best man speech yet, doc."

Months pass...

February 14, I was grateful for:

1. my Costume Institute job! Today, I helped my boss examine Marie Antoinette's dress!
2. Shantelle's red carpet fittings going well.
3. making it through Valentine's Day at home with tacos and Killing Eve. My mind strayed, wondering what Tarquin was up to: a date, a hookup...
4. chocolate will be on sale in the morning. I need a fix.

March 23, I was grateful for:

1. Sarah cheering me up after Shantelle's news: film reshoots canceling her Promise Unspoken appearance. Self-soothed with pizza and those UK caramel/chocolate things.
2. Tarquin news, finally! Saz had a meeting with him. He asked after me, making small talk, I guess. He never did answer my email. Did it land in his junk folder? Or maybe he was super busy and then it was too awkward to respond a few weeks later? Or worst of all, did I hurt him? God knows that wasn't my intention. I hoped we could stay friends. I'd text him, but what if that leads him on? Shit. What should I do?
3. dying my hair red, so my natural color can grow in. Feel like ME again.
4. Simon stocking three of my dresses in his store and Spencer wants all of them! Ha!
5. hockey season ending soon. Ty's team is out of the playoffs. Hopefully that means no more Tyler on TV until fall.

From: Tarquin Balfour
To: Nick Balfour
Date: Monday, April 1, 2019 at 23:46
Subject: To thine own self be true

Hey Nico, back from Banff yet? Hope your day's been better than mine. I dropped my phone in the bloody sink tonight. I was taking a shirtless selfie in my bathroom mirror. Go on, laugh your arse off. Yes, I've become THAT bloke—phone out, abs flexed, sharing wayyy too much with a woman I barely know.

She's a journalist I met in the pub. We got chatting and drinking, and our banter quickly swerved into a proposition—from her. I haven't slept with anyone since Leia, but I politely declined (breakfast meeting at 8 a.m.). Before I left, she asked me to text her a cheeky photo when I got home—and now my naked message is delayed indefinitely (thank fuck!) whilst my soaked phone kips in a bowl of rice. The bugger better wake up! I've got photos of Leia on there. (And no, Leia's pics aren't nudes.)

What the HELL was I thinking? I know I've always been pretty open sexually, but even in the midst of my most promiscuous romps, shirtless selfies and dick pics were NEVER my M.O., and yet tonight I was stripping off, going the whole hog for this girl who, in retrospect, I don't even fancy. God, sometimes I'm such a tart!

Dex will have a field day with this. We've been working on my 'issues' concerning self-worth and romantic attachments. I've been pushing back a tad, but tonight's phone fiasco made me realize he's not talking bollocks. I should stop pandering for affection; I should be myself. It's the only way I'll attract someone who's into the real me. Like Alex. I never pretended with her. Granted, I could be myself because I wasn't trying to win her over—at least I wasn't in the beginning. She despised me. I had nothing to lose. But with Leia...I was afraid of losing her from the get-go, and surprise—me saying "Don't quit your job" pretty much had her running for the exit.

Anyhoo, I'll keep working on my shit with Mr. Pork Pie hat, see where it leads me.

Hope the Banff Film Festival brought you loads of telly deals. Speak soon, Tarq

From: Tarquin Balfour
To: Nick Balfour
Date: Tuesday, April 2, 2019 at 12:35
Subject: One more thing

Sorry, Nico. Forgot to say, I really appreciate you volunteering to be my agony aunt. And I've got some good news! You've got company now. I told Harry about my depression and he was a champ. Really supportive. It means a lot, you guys listening without judgment. I know I don't say it often, but I love you, bro. Miss you. Give my regards to Broadway and all that.

Cheers, Tarq

April 14, I was grateful for:
1. *getting my Frill-Seekers Instagram up.*
2. *I followed Mrs. Chuzzlewit's Insta (Tarquin didn't follow my Frill-Seekers account, though).*
3. *brunch with Alex. She's casting her play in NYC. Tarquin's name never came up. Saz hasn't mentioned him either, but I don't dare ask. She'll get all sorts of ideas. I hope he's okay. Times like this I wish I had a Facebook account.*
4. *adding eight new designs to my website.*
5. *the cherry blossoms are blooming in Brooklyn.*
6. *Dad booking his flight to visit me next week.*
7. *hooking up with a hot ad exec. The sex wasn't great, but it scratched an itch, I guess.*

May 6, I was grateful for:
1. *happy Saz! Jordan is moving in with her. I'm thrilled.*
2. *catching up on Instagram with my friend Riley.*
3. *having the guts to send Tarquin a Brooklyn postcard. Just something fun to say 'Hi! Happy spring.' Maybe it'll nudge him to email or text me back. I still miss him.*
4. *the Met Gala tonight! People LOVED my dress made from antique bed linens!*
5. *fuckface Tyler was there with some model. I held my own. Didn't punch him or cry in the washroom. Proud of myself.*
6. *Xavi texted after, wanting to hook up. I said no. The ego boost was nice, though.*
7. *late FaceTime chat with Simon about the Gala. Maybe he'll tell Tarquin? Hope so.*

SAY HELLO, KISS GOODBYE

Sloane International
Exclusive and Elite Matchmaking Agency
Featured Listing for June

ROMANTIC LONDON GENTLEMAN SEEKS LIFE PARTNER

Our client, a tall, handsome, London-based entrepreneur in his late twenties, is interested in meeting an intelligent, attractive, stylish woman who is kind, family-oriented, and physically active. She should be confident, trustworthy, loyal, and share his love for fine cuisine, the outdoors, and new adventures. An outgoing manner and desire to partake in lively conversation and fun-loving activities are a must.

He is successful, ambitious, generous, and enjoys all London has to offer. A voracious reader, our client loves to laugh and watch films, and he stays fit by running, rock climbing, and wreck diving. Cooking, attending cultural and sporting events, travel, and socializing with family and friends top his list of favorite activities.

If you are interested in finding a life partner and think this kind, romantic gentleman might be your perfect match, please call or email for a personal interview with Sloane International, quoting profile #June2019244

Sloane International Ltd.
26 Sloane Gardens
London SW1

June 12, I was grateful for:
1. *two stylists repping Met Gala celebs called about dresses!*
2. *my meeting with my no-longer-potential investor. His cash means Frill-Seekers fashion shows and a pop-up shop in Brooklyn. Now, if I could get a second backer...*
3. *hired a back-of-house firm to handle accounting, order and inventory management.*
4. *photos online of the Spice Girls UK reunion tour.*
5. *Alex's play* Thirteen. *I went with Shantelle. I cried. It made me miss Mom a lot.*
6. *post-play tapas and some flirting with a cute guy at the next table. We exchanged numbers.*
7. *finally taking the (silent) hint Tarquin really doesn't want to be friends. I cried about it, then comfort-ate Hickory Sticks and Coffee Crisp bars. Now I feel sad, hurt, and sick.*

July 14, I was grateful for:
1. *Shantelle! She'll wear my gown for* Lost for Breath's *BIG premiere in August.*
2. *a colleague gave me a contact for a vegan leather supplier.*
3. *finding a small property for my pop-up! It's not mine until April, but I'm SO excited.*
4. *my new vibrator. Bought it after another horrible hookup. No more fights over condoms, or selfish guy behavior, just orgasmic bliss! Does everything but make me breakfast.*
5. *my gym session with Xavi. Found out he has a sister and loves country music. Who knew?*
6. *not thinking about Tarquin for the past 2 days until...*
7. *my Facetime call with Simon. We got all caught up. Wish I could visit, see Sarah. It's only been 6 months, but Wilton Way, Somerset House...Tarquin—feels like a lifetime ago.*

SAY HELLO, KISS GOODBYE

From: Tarquin Balfour
To: Nick Balfour
Sent: Tuesday, July 23, 2019
Subject: GET YOUR BLOODY PHONE FIXED!

How long does it take to get a screen fixed? For fuck's sake, Nico! I call bollocks. You just don't want Mum texting you on hols.

I just got back from Orkney this afternoon. Baby Poppy is a belter! All fingers & toes accounted for, plus she's got a quiff of red hair! Fiona is doing well and came home from hospital on Sunday. Rupes celebrated by purchasing a new bull (I knew you'd like that!), and Ava made me take her to Sinclair's for ice cream.

Life has been off the charts. The church redevelopment is storming forward, so London's latest performance space will be hosting all your luvvie friends in no time. And I've got three dates, courtesy of that swanky matchmaker. I'm so chuffed! I'm meeting a Turner Prize winner (!), a foodie/author, and an Olympic rower, so I've pulled out all the stops date-wise. I've booked a cocktails/art exhibit at the Tate, a swish table at The Duck & Waffle (yep, that sinful spot 40 floors above the city), and a kayaking tour along the canals. Hey, maybe one of these ladies will be your future sis-in-law! See, Nick, I AM trying. Moving on from Leia has been tougher than I thought, but I've made my bed... Onwards & upwards.

Speaking of, I've stopped seeing Dex on a weekly basis. We both agree I'm ready. I've learned enough CBT to deal on the daily and have a better handle on things. If I need a top-up, I'll give him a shout. And before you ask, no, I still haven't told Mum or Dad about therapy, so please keep your gob shut, all right? Don't make me regret telling you.

No doubt, you're having a smashing time on your Bahamas bender. Text me when you've got your phone back, you tosser.

Cheers, Tarq

Nineteen

LEIA

New York City, three weeks later, Thursday, August 15, 2019

Pavements sizzled, sweltering tourists searched for shade, and ice cream sellers in Central Park rejoiced as the hazy lazy days of August descended on New York City. Summer wasn't about to loosen its sweaty grip on the Big Apple any time soon, and the heatwave was making everyone, including Leia, a little hot under the collar.

Why haven't we moved? She lowered the window of her Uber, and an airless wall of blistering heat engulfed the air-conditioned sedan. *Gross!* Leia's nose scrunched. *I HATE this weather.* Stealing a peek at the snarled uptown traffic, she kept her phone pressed to her ear as Sarah, energized by her breezy Cornish getaway with Jordan, merrily rambled on about their adventures.

"Ley, we saw *everything*! The beach they used for Nampara Cove, the mines at Botallack. It was a bit of a bumpy ride—my boobs still haven't recovered—but it was so worth it."

Leia's car crept forward, barely making it across the intersection before halting again. *Dammit!* She closed her window and twirled her fingers through her fiery red hair worn high and wavy in a flirty ponytail. *I have no choice. I'll have to hotfoot it if I want to style Shantelle in time for her* Lost for Breath *premiere.*

"Saz, hold on a sec?" Lowering her phone, she leaned toward the driver. "I'll hop out here—thanks." Tote bulging with her stylist kit on her shoulder, phone and garment bags in hand, she begrudgingly traded the cool comfort of the sedan for the suffocating humidity and blazing sun beating down on the northeast corner of

264

Third Avenue and East 48th Street.

God, it's stifling. Three summers in, and I'm still not used to this. No wonder all the old money leaves town at this time of year.

She nudged the car door closed with her elbow and started walking, the delicate lace pleats of her outfit's ivory skirt billowing with each hurried step. The handmade midi dress with its figure-hugging bodice, high neck, and sleeveless silhouette was elegant yet summery, ready for her first public outing as a designer and stylist to one of Hollywood's hottest rising stars.

Okay, no biggie. She took a deep breath, ignoring the intense heat prickling her skin. *It's just the biggest night of my career so far! Let's CRUSH this!*

Picking up speed, careful not to crease Shantelle's gown or the backup dress she'd brought along just in case, Leia slipped back into Sarah's holiday bliss. "So, you saw all the locations for *Poldark*! I wish I could've gone! I bet the sea air was refreshing, unlike this stinky sweat-fest we're having here."

"It was breathtaking, Ley. Gave me serious wanderlust."

Four city workers, t-shirts plastered to their chests from heat and exertion, looked up from a broken manhole, the cause of Third Avenue's early-afternoon gridlock, and gave Leia's long, bare legs appreciative stares as she passed, but their leers went unnoticed.

"See any Ross Poldark lookalikes shirtless and scything wheat?" Leia smiled, her ivory flats whisking her past overheated office workers lumbering back to work after lunch.

"Not a single one," said Sarah, playing along. "But you, dear sister, could've passed for a convincing Demelza, now your hair is red again."

"Maybe. Just don't ask me to make Stargazy Pie!" Leia laughed as she swerved around a pack of wilting tourists, the baking hot pavement and lack of a breeze slowing everyone's progress. "That dish is so nasty—sardine heads poking out, staring at you from the crust!"

"We tried some. It actually tastes good! All yummy custard, onions, and potatoes."

Leia stuck out her tongue. "Two words, Saz: Fish. Heads."

"You don't eat their heads, silly!" Sarah laughed. "Ah, I wish we were still on vacation! I miss Cornwall already! I definitely don't miss work."

"Well, why didn't you take tomorrow off?" Leia caught the eye of two iced lemonade-toting businessmen exiting a coffee shop and zeroed in on their purchases. *I'd kill for a cool drink right now. My tongue feels like it's glued to the roof of my mouth.* "Going in on a Friday after a holiday is either really dedicated or really stupid."

Sarah chuckled. "I would've taken tomorrow off, but I have a meeting booked with Tarquin."

Tarquin? A breath caught in her throat. *She's still in touch? She never mentions him.* Leia trotted to the north side of East 49th Street before the light flipped to red. "Oh yeah? How come? I thought there wasn't anything more to discuss with him."

"There's *tons* to discuss. He just needed some building permits and a few property surveys to come in before we could proceed."

"Oh, good." Leia jagged left and joined the army of pedestrians crossing Third Avenue. "So...how is he?"

"He's good. I would've suggested another day, but his schedule is tight," said Sarah. "He said he's off to the Orkney Islands for a four-day weekend."

Probably wreck diving, seeing his little niece. Yeah, he must be taking a break from being so busy. Mrs. Chuzzlewit's Instagram hasn't been updated in weeks.

Sarah continued. "By the way, did Simon mention anything to you...?"

"About Tarquin's Orkney trip? Why would he?" Leia swallowed, her craving for water testing her patience and pushing her toward cranky-town—population, all of sweltering Manhattan. *The last Simon mentioned him was, gosh, a few weeks ago? Freddie was all aflutter over Tarquin's date with a celebrity chef, Cressida something or other. I Googled her after Simon said they just didn't click.* Leia adjusted her grip on the two garment bags. "Tarquin goes there all the time."

"I don't mean Scotland. Tarquin is off the market. He's got a girlfriend, a new chef on TV, Cressida Davey."

What?! But Simon said—she's his GIRLFRIEND now?! A wave of nausea rolled in Leia's belly. *Damn heat. I need water— STAT!* She weaved through a stream of people on East 49th Street headed in the opposite direction. "Uh, no…he didn't."

"I'm so not a fan. She adds chickpeas to *everything*. So gross." Sarah rambled without taking a breath. "Their taste, their texture— needless to say, I won't be buying *her* cookbooks. She seems nice, though, on TV. Tarquin's cousin is getting married in Kirkwall on Sunday, so she's going up with him."

As his girlfriend. Leia's stomach lurched. *Did Tarquin cook for her—or maybe they cooked together? Did that seal it for him?* She squeezed the canvas shoulder straps of her Met tote. *I bet they're having tons of sex.* Alex's words flashed through her mind—*"He's incredibly passionate and hands-on in the kitchen"*—paired with her own memory, perched on his counter, fingers tangled in his hair, Tarquin's open mouth between her thighs. *God, I miss it—I miss him.* She let out a loud sigh.

"Leia? Earth to Leia? Did you melt into the sidewalk?" Sarah's giggle distorted through the phone.

She shook her head. "Oh! Sorry! It's just—I've got a million things screaming from my to-do list. I'm a bit preoccupied. Uh, can you hang on a…" Breaths coming hard and fast, she lowered her phone and fussed with the high neckline of her dress, the material feeling too constricting, too hot, too much. *I fucking hate this weather!* Wincing, she swept away perspiration from her forehead with the back of her hand and returned to the call. "They must be serious, then, Tarquin and this chef? If he's taking her to meet family."

"I guess…" Sarah paused. "Ley, I thought your infatuation was long gone."

"It is!" Leia blurted. *Isn't it?* "I'm just glad he's happy. *I'm* happy—for him."

"Yeah, me too. Do you want me to say hi for you tomorrow?"

Leia's chest tightened. "Uh, no! *No.* I was just, you know…" *Fuck.* She halted on the sidewalk and closed her eyes briefly, letting a red-faced jogger struggle past. *I threw Tarquin back and Cressida caught him. She's not to blame, I am—no one else. I'm my worst enemy. Scared of love, of giving myself completely to another man, afraid I'll end up hurt and alone again.* She let out a stuttering breath. *Oh, the irony.* Clearing her throat, Leia pinned on a grin and continued on her way. "So, uh, my text last week, did you r—"

"Oh, shit! Sorry!" said Sarah. "I only saw it this morning. I don't know how we did it, but we stayed unplugged the entire time down in Cornwall."

"Ah, right. Well, it was no big deal."

"Leia, *you* looking after vintage Dior isn't a big deal?! C'mon, be honest—did you pee a little when Violetta told you?"

Leia snort-laughed. "Almost. Oh, Saz, it's beautiful. I swear it's the most magical gown I've ever set eyes on, and *I* get to make its custom storage mount! I keep pinching myself."

"For good reason! And to think you almost quit the Institute."

If it wasn't for Tarquin…talking me out of it, making me think twice. "Yeah." A bittersweet ache throbbed in Leia's chest. *He could've urged me to quit, to stay in London, but he didn't. He put my best interests ahead of his that night. How many guys would've done the same?* Her fingers curled tighter around the hangers on the garment bags. *He's a gem, and I'm a fool. I just hope this Cressida woman knows how lucky she is.*

"So, tonight's the night, eh?!" The joy in Sarah's voice roused Leia smile again, the change of subject a welcome one. "On a scale of one to ten, how excited are you?"

"Try twelve! I took the day off so I could make sure everything on my to-do list was taken care of. We've got a few hours, so Shantelle's hairstylist and makeup artist don't have to rush, and I can take my time, have her walk, turn, and sit in her gown, make sure nothing pulls or feels odd. I'm just arriving at the hotel now. The film company is putting Shantelle and her parents up in a suite at the Maxwell."

"Hello, big time!" squealed Sarah. "Look how far you've both come."

Leia swept around the corner onto Lexington Avenue, her eyes drawn across the street. Two gigantic American flags hung still and limp, yearning for a breeze above the entrance to an art deco landmark. *The Waldorf Astoria.* A nostalgia-fueled flutter teased her stomach. *The hotel from* Serendipity, *the one Tarquin wanted to stay in...until I burst his bubble and broke his heart. And mine, too, I guess...*

"You SO deserve this, Ley! Your future starts now!"

Yeah. Yeah, it does. No more looking back. Leia exchanged smiles with the Maxwell Hotel's doorman and escaped inside.

Three hours later, Shantelle fluttered her feathery false lashes behind her cat eye glasses and gulped, her chest rising and falling fast. "Scotty," she whispered, leaning into Leia as they approached the photographers' pen outside Radio City Music Hall. "I can't believe this is actually happening!"

Shantelle's fingers roamed up the symphony of hot pink chiffon of her gown, toying with the tiered sleeves of delicate cerise lace. "Remember all those games? Sat in the stands with Erika? Stuffing our faces with soggy nachos, talking about Eri appearing on *Real Housewives*, me acting, you designing—the two of us having our red carpet debuts together?"

"Green, you mean." Butterflies swirled in Leia's belly. "Tonight's carpet is eco-friendly green! Perfect for *Lost for Breath*'s eco-theme!" *Perfect for my dress!* The moment was the culmination of one of Leia's lifelong dreams, seeing her hard work worn with sass and style in front of the entertainment world's movers and shakers.

Shantelle waved her seashell-hued manicure above her immaculately applied blush and foundation, trying to keep cool in the sticky August heat. "Am I sweating too much? I hope I don't trip. What if I pose funny?"

"You're fine! And you're in good hands." Leia patted her black tote. "I have enough antiperspirant, double-sided fashion tape, and heel liners to fix all of Manhattan!" She stayed a step behind Shantelle, ensuring her Frill-Seekers gown fell properly and didn't reveal any last-minute problems like a popped seam or fallen hem before her friend hit the pack of photographers and reporters. Leia grinned over her shoulder. Mrs. Joy swooned with parental pride, chatting with her daughter's agent while Mr. Joy, phone aloft, captured the festivities live over FaceTime, keeping Shantelle's siblings and grandmother up to date back home in Wisconsin.

"I think I need to pee again!" Shantelle dawdled in her sky-high heels, her hands flitting above her long black hair twisted into an elaborate 1960s-style high bun.

"Shan." Leia tenderly brushed her friend's arm. "Stop fussing. You're beautiful. You've got this!"

Like magic, Leia's calm words soothed Shantelle's distress and swapped her pinched brow for a grateful grin. "God, what would I do without you, Leia?!" She slipped her hands into her gown's pockets. "For one thing, I wouldn't look this stunning! I *never* want to take this dress off—EVER! My ass looks better than J. Lo's! And check out my boobs..." She arched a coquettish eyebrow at the plunging neckline. "My girls are sexy and classy! I must admit, I had doubts when you suggested the deep V. I worried I'd be one sneeze away from nip-slip central, but they're held in place real good!"

"All hail the sticky bra! It's a life-changer." Leia snickered and stepped forward, the heels she'd switched into at the hotel just shy of the green carpet.

"You're a lifesaver!" Shantelle clutched Leia's hand. "Thank you, Scotty! I couldn't do this without you."

"Yes, you could." Leia squeezed back and let go. "It's a shame Morgan couldn't make it."

"Yeah, well..." Shantelle bit her glossy lip and peered past Leia where her mom and dad happily chatted over FaceTime to the Midwest. She whispered in Leia's ear, "Don't tell my parents, but...Morgan and I split three weeks ago."

Split? Three weeks— Leia's head jerked back. *But Morgan's lovely! A cinnamon roll of a guy!* "Oh, Shan..." she muttered under her breath. "What happened?"

Loud squeals from the far end of the carpet disrupted their conversation. Fans draped over the metal barricades cried out for autographs and selfies every time another *Lost for Breath* star joined the press parade. Shantelle did a double take. "My psychic advisor, she recommended it."

Oh, god. She didn't! Leia's face blanched. "What!?" She blurted through a fake smile, plastered on for the benefit of Mr. and Mrs. Joy. *Her family loved Morgan like a son.* "You're kidding, right?"

"No!" The actress let out a rushed breath. "She said Morgan

was holding me back…like, physically."

"How?!"

"One guess—sex scenes. Morgan hates them. I've told him repeatedly, 'They're make-believe, they're part of my job,' but he kept freaking out about Bastien."

Leia peered over her friend's shoulder. *Bastien Soulier.* Dressed in a floral print designer suit, the quirky French actor raked a confident hand through his thick mop of shoulder-length mahogany curls and held court in the middle of the carpet, teasing the baying photographers and hysterical fans with his pouty air of Gallic indifference. Known more for his sensitive musings and love of existential poetry than his pecs, "beautiful Bastien with the f*ck-me eyes" (trademark *The National Mail*) had given Hollywood gossip magazines a huge scoop during his previous film's press junket, announcing his newfound—and fan-criticized—celibacy. With his whimsical *je ne sais quoi*, the twenty-nine-year-old had divulged that by forgoing sex, his on-camera love scenes were indulgent and raw, sizzling with pure, primal instinct.

He's not signing for his fans? Leia curled her lip as Bastien ignored their frantic pleas and lingered just out of reach before sauntering toward Radio City Music Hall's entrance, its open doors dispensing frigid air onto the steaming pavement. *Morgan had good reason to freak out. Shan confided that they had to stop filming their nude scenes twice because Bastien got a raging hard-on inside his flesh-colored modesty pouch. And once, he ejaculated! Blech!* Leia's flesh crawled. *Shantelle might call that make-believe, but I call that real—and really gross.*

Shantelle stared at her left hand and the three-carat pink diamond ring on loan for the premiere from her former employer, Tiffany & Co. "I don't want a fight every time a role requires love scenes. I've supported him through injuries, trade rumors…if Morgan can't support *my* dream, it's time to move on—from hockey and him."

Two months ago, she was talking wedding dresses, hoping he'd propose. Leia exhaled heavily. *Morgan didn't seem controlling. He was a nice guy.*

"Leia, you left Tyler when things weren't good. You understand, right?" Shantelle blinked, eager for approval.

I don't regret my decision, but will she?

"And look! You've rebounded nicely!" The actress grinned. "What I wouldn't give for a steamy sex-fest with a London hunk! Now, why you broke it off with *him* is beyond me. He looked tasty!"

I wish I'd never told her about Tarquin. I should tell her about Cressida later—that'll shut her up. Leia clocked the impatient huff of the film's publicist behind Shantelle's back. "Shan, maybe tomorrow you should give Morgan a call—"

"Shantelle!" The PR guy waved her forward. "You're up."

Leia banished her questions and doubts and gave her friend a soft hug—a tight one could've crumpled her gown. "This is it! You've earned this, Shan! Go, enjoy tonight!"

She squeezed Leia's hand. "Aw, thanks, Scotty—*love you!*" She blew a kiss to her beaming parents. "I'll see you inside!"

"SHANTELLE, OVER HERE!" A slew of photographers beckoned, jockeying for the perfect shot.

Chin up and shoulders back, wearing a cheek-pinching smile, Shantelle pranced toward the noisy crush and posed, fluffing out her gown in front of the *Lost for Breath* publicity backdrop like Leia had taught her.

Look at her, Hollywood's brightest new starlet—in my gown! Leia's heart swelled with joy as she snapped several photos on her phone.

Shantelle followed each photographer's hollered prompt, swiveling left then right before looking over her shoulder with a sassy, confident grin, any hint of nerves long gone.

I did good, Mom. Leia grinned and lowered her phone, blinking back tears. Shantelle began chatting to microphone-toting reporters, boasting about her one-of-a-kind Frill-Seekers gown. *I wish you were alive to see this. You'd be proud.* She sniffed. *I'm finally on my way.*

"Leia, come!" Mrs. Joy paused in her daughter's footsteps. "Shantelle reserved us seats."

"Oh, I'm not staying. My job ends tonight when Shantelle's with the press. And to be honest, I'm dying to kick off my heels and crash on my sofa!" Leia laughed, meaning every word.

"I understand, it's been a long day for you—but tonight's your victory too!" said Mrs. Joy, her husband nodding in marital agreement. "You'll celebrate tonight at home, won't you?"

Yep, with a call to my dad, a take-out gyro, and Ross Poldark on my TV. Leia hugged Shantelle's mom. "Yeah, the night's still young, right?" *Jeez, sound like Tarquin much?* She twisted her grimace into a smile and pulled back, adjusting the bag on her shoulder. "It's been so wonderful seeing you again. Enjoy the film, okay?"

"We will!" said Mr. Joy, joining his wife and the steady stream of passholders entering Radio City Music Hall.

Leia stepped out of the way and scrolled through her pictures of Shantelle, smiling up a storm on the green carpet.

On my last night in London, Tarquin asked me to text photos of my gown at its first premiere, but what's the point now? Heart heavy, she turned off her phone and meandered through the Sixth Avenue obstacle course of TV crews and rubbernecking New Yorkers, her thoughts far away from celebrities and honking taxis. *I can't stop thinking about it—Tarquin has a serious girlfriend. I thought I'd be fine with it when it happened.* She sighed, aimlessly following the flow of pedestrians crossing West 50th Street as she plunged her hand into her tote, battling past her mini sewing kit, portable steamer, and comfy flats. *But here I am, so freakin' jealous of Cressida I could scream!* Her hand resurfaced with her red telephone box keychain. *Dammit! I shouldn't be thinking of him—of her— today of ALL days. Frill-Seekers just made its movie premiere debut! That's what I should be focused on.* Lifting her chin, she chucked Tarquin's London trinket back in her bag and widened her stride. *So, this is it, girl. No more pining for him, no more wistful memories or asking Saz how he is. He's moved on. I will, too. Today I'm done with Tarquin Balfour—for good.*

TWENTY

TARQUIN
Brooklyn, one week later

Taking a large sip of his beer, Tarquin leaned against the Williamsburg Hotel's rooftop bar and squinted through his eyeglasses, the laughter of several bikini-clad women splashing in the pool teasing his attention away from his oldest brother, Nick.

"If you were smart, Tarq, you'd do something like this." Long sleeves of his pink shirt rolled up just so, Nick was immaculately overdressed for their sun-soaked, midafternoon liquid lunch. His navy tie, Hugo Boss suit trousers, and shiny Oxfords belonged in a boardroom on Sixth Avenue, not poolside in trendy Brooklyn. Based in America the past three years, the former child actor, now a lithe six-foot-four inches of square-jawed handsomeness, held the esteemed role of vice-president of TV sales and co-productions for the BBC's Manhattan office. His love of restaurants, boutique hotels, and the latest fashions meant that if something in New York was hip, happening, and expensive, Nick was all over it. "Old pubs and theaters are lovely, but just imagine the money you'd rake in building something new and spectacular like this."

Tarquin yawned beneath his New York Mets cap, his sleepy eyes sailing away from the pool and across the East River. *New York, you sure scrub up nice.* With a bittersweet smile, he scratched his moustache and ogled the Empire State and Chrysler Buildings glinting in the late August haze. *It's strange, being back.* His heart weighed heavy.

"You could still have the vibe of a repurposed building even when it's not," said Nick, sharing a flirty smile with one of the female bartenders. "This place just looks old because of that water tower and the reclaimed bricks. Why bother with all that legit 'heritage designation' stuff when you can *fake* retro just as easily?"

Fake it? Does he even know me? What a twat. "You reckon, Nick?" Battling jet lag and the prickly heat, Tarquin's patience was dangling by a single thread. He glared through his glasses and tugged at the open collar of his baby blue shirt, his fading sunburn-turned-tan a lingering reminder of the previous month's raucous weekend in Orkney. "First, it was the corrugated hardwood downstairs, then the brass accents, and the Brooklyn toile-inspired wallpaper—"

"Oh, man, you saw it, right?" Nick's smile beamed beneath his Tom Ford aviators. "It's got Brooklyn Bridge, hot dogs, and Notorious B.I.G. *in* the design!"

Tarquin plowed his hand into the pocket of his shorts, silently cursing into the midday sun. *Why did I let him talk me into coming here? I agree, this hotel is smashing, but I'd much rather have this go-see on my own without know-it-all here pissing himself about every...single...detail. I should've stayed at my hotel, chilling out with Harry before his club opening tonight.*

"It's the *Where's Waldo* of wallpaper! And a Beastie Boy designed it—"

Oh, for fuck's sake! "Nick, enough! You're doing my head in! How about you leave building development and renos to me, okay? I don't tell you how to make reality shows or whatever the hell it is you do all day."

Nick raised his shades and gave Tarquin a searing dose of side-eye. "Someone skipped coffee this morning! Christ, what's eating you?!" He lowered his sunglasses and dragged several corn chips through a bowl of guacamole. "Oh!" With a mischievous nod, Nick pointed at his brother. "*I* get it."

Tarquin curled his lip, watching Nick crunch his way through whatever ridiculous revelation he'd concocted.

"Sexual frustration, thy name is Tarquin! Aw, baby brother's missing Cressida."

Tarquin toyed with the damp edge of their bar bill. "At least I'm not plastered all over *The Mail* in a sordid three-way kiss-and-tell."

Nick's face soured. "That's old news. Banff happened months ago."

"But it's like herpes, mate—it's the horrible gift that keeps on giving!" Tarquin reveled in his brother's public embarrassment. "Talk about making Mum proud, eh! What was last week's headline again? *Lairds* Stunner Bree Nicked With Stripper—"

"Stop being a tit!" Nick muttered into his Aperol Spritz. "How was I to know the woman Bree brought to her room would sell her story?"

"You could've prevented it."

"And let her blackmail me? No, better to call her bluff."

"And lose big! You always were a rubbish gambler." Tarquin laughed, his cheeks pink from the heat.

"Bree still won't take my calls." Nick raked his hand through his dark waves. "She shouldn't be pissed at me! It's all that hack's fault, paying over the odds for the ridiculous sex tape. It's not like we did anything kinky, for fuck's sake. Three-ways are ten-a-penny these days."

"But *Lairds and Liars* is a hit worldwide, and Bree's a household name in Britain."

"Yeah, well, I'm not. My acting career tanked when my balls dropped."

"Ahh, but you're not just *any* child star, Nico. You're the son of British telly's comeback queen. If I were you, I'd be more careful. If they've sniffed out one salacious story, they'll dig for more—

guaranteed." Tarquin chuckled and sipped his beer. "Come to think of it, I should be thanking you."

Nick narrowed his eyes. "Because…?"

"You've usurped me as the Balfour family fuck-up! My past indiscretions pale in comparison to you landing on the front page of every red top in Britain. Now, I can go to Poppy's baptism in November and watch you take all the flak for a change."

"Hey, don't throw a parade just yet. Knowing Mum, she'll probably forget by then." Nick stared at the mint leaf discarded on his cocktail napkin. "And I hope she's not the only one. If this mess costs me the senior VP position, there'll be hell to pay." He drained his drink and slammed it on the bar, sending melting ice cubes swirling around the bottom of the sweaty glass.

"You think it might?"

"Who knows. I keep getting funny looks in the halls, mostly from junior staff snickering behind my back." Nick pushed his sunglasses up his nose. "From now on, I'm only getting involved with women who've been properly vetted. Like Cressida was for you."

Tarquin raised an eyebrow. "It'll cost ya."

"What was the fee? Ten thousand quid? Won't even miss it." Nick slapped him on the back. "Right. I'll have a wee and then we can head out." With a nod, the elder Balfour strolled off, checking his phone while he weaved through the maze of poolside daybeds crowded with sun-worshipping hipsters.

Tarquin downed his beer and dove into his phone. *1:47 p.m. already?* He yawned. *I should've flown in last night instead of this morning. Can't believe I fell asleep in the shower. I'm so knackered.* Blinking through his jetlagged daze, he scrolled through the day's texts, the only unread message from cat-sitter Freddie: a photo of Mrs. Chuzzlewit sitting on a frowning Simon. *At least Chuzza looks happy. Damn, I really should've grilled Si about Leia, if she asks about me. If I had just answered her email, thanked her for the postcard, things could've been so different. I'd reach out now, but…* He swallowed heavily. *Dex won't be the only one who'll kill me—*

"Tarquin? Tarquin Balfour…?"

He glanced over his shoulder. A short, clean-shaven guy with sandy brown hair worn messily in a topknot leaned in, his eyebrows rising above his Ray-Bans. Unlike most of the rooftop sunseekers, he wasn't flaunting much skin, choosing a black short-sleeved shirt and dark jeans instead of bathing trunks. He clutched a file folder stuffed with papers against his toned chest and clicked a pen non-stop with his thumb. "I just said a quick hey-ho to ol' Nico. He said you were here! Great to see you, man!"

Oh, bugger! Do I know you? Tarquin gave his best breezy chuckle and extended his hand. "Hey! Long time, no see, mate! What've you been up to?" *C'mon, help me out. Drop a name, a place…your job…*

He smacked his file folder on the bar and snapped up Tarquin's hand, shaking it vigorously before letting go. "Oh, the usual, you know?" He spoke rapidly and jittered on the spot like a toy wound up too tightly. His pen-free hand flitted from his puka shell necklace to his stubble-free chin, to his sunglasses as he shifted them onto the top of his head.

Someone's full of beans. "That's great." Tarquin pulled back, a taut smile on his face. *Ah…nope. Even without the shades, I still don't know who the hell you are.*

"So, what about you, man? I thought you were in London."

"I am, but my best mate is launching his private members' club tonight."

"Oh! That's…" Narrowing his gaze, the guy searched the cloudless sky and snapped his pen in a frenzy—*chk, chk, chk*—until something besides his ballpoint clicked. "Bespoke!" His eyes jagged back to Tarquin. "*Bespoke New York*, right?" He laughed apropos of nothing. "You mentioned it, like, last summer."

I did? Tarquin scratched his moustache. *Were we drinking? Gambling? Jeez, it must've been quite the bender if I can't place him.*

"I saw something about it in *Time Out* this week, too. It's that cool red brick building on Greenwich Street...from the 1850s or something?"

"The 1830s." Catching the bartender hovering, Tarquin pulled his wallet from his shorts' pocket.

"Ooh, so close! So, what's my prize—an invite?"

That's...pushy. Will he go away if I say yes? "Sure. Come any time after nine." Tarquin's jaw tensed. "I'll need the correct spelling of your full name...you know, for the guest list." *And my restraining order.*

He bobbed on the spot. "You know, it would be bangin' if I could bring a plus one. I'm trying to impress her. The whole velvet rope treatment would, you know, slay."

The cheek! Tarquin swallowed what he really wanted to say. "Uh, sure...whatever." He tapped his card against the bartender's payment terminal.

"Cool beans!" The guy tossed another glance poolside. "Hey! You can meet babe now."

Oh, brilliant. Removing his baseball cap, Tarquin wiped perspiration from his brow. *I could do without these people glomming onto us tonight.*

"Hey, Leia?!"

LEIA?! Tarquin froze. *No! Can't be.*

He dropped his cap on the bar and spun around, spotting a tall redhead wearing large, Jackie O-style sunglasses and a soaked one-piece, her phone and a long white towel in her hands.

Nope. Not her. His body relaxed. *My Leia is a beautiful blonde.* He slipped his card back in his wallet.

Draping the towel over her shoulders, the woman lifted her

shades and looked up, her sunny blue-eyed sparkle and unassuming smile falling into a stunned gape. *"Tarquin?!"*

He did a double take. *Holy fuck! It IS her!* He sucked in a breath, a sudden veil of lightheadedness tilting him backward against the bar. "Hiya…" His heart skipped a few beats as his gaze swept her body, the drenched fabric of her bathing suit fueling his memory. *Fuck me, she looks incredible, even better than I remember.* Meeting her questioning eyes, he fumbled for words. "I mean, hello…again." *Shit. She's gonna have a go at me. Her email…*

"What on Earth are you doing here in—?"

Leia's male companion jumped in. "Wow! You guys *know* each other?"

"Uh-huh." She grinned, a nervous giggle filling her pause. "Nice 'stache, Han Solo. And glasses, too. They suit you." She pulled her bottom lip into her mouth.

Oh, Christ. I can't breathe when she does that. Come ON, mate, get it together.

"Cheers, Leia." Tarquin broke into a wide smile, fighting every urge to swoop in and hold her tight. *She's not angry! And has red hair!* He leaned in. "You look lovely—as always!"

"Well, *this* is cool!" The guy crossed his arms, biceps bulging. "Leia, I trained Tarquin once last year—he tagged along with his brother."

Oh! He's Nick's TRAINER! Ah, okay. I still don't remember his name, though—not that I care. Everyone else here can just do one. Leia's looking sexy as hell. It's so great to see her!

Tarquin waved a dismissive hand toward the far side of the pool. "You should catch Nick before he leaves, mate." *Yeah, bugger off. Give us some privacy. God, what I'd do to hold her in my arms.* Tarquin's warm gaze didn't waver. No one else existed, not the trainer, not the bartender leaving his credit card receipt—not a soul but Leia. "So, how are you?"

"I'm good. *Busy!* But I'm off today. As you can tell!" Her anxious half-laugh returned. "Time away from the Institute is as rare as a limited-edition Hermès bag these days." She perched her sunglasses on her head and blinked up at him, adjusting the towel on her shoulders. "How are things with you?"

I can't believe she's actually here. God, my heart! It's literally hammering through my chest. Tarquin nodded. "I'm great, yeah! Here on a break. Enjoying the sunshine. Can't complain."

Leia smiled kindly. "Good. I'm glad."

The trainer leaned in. "Uh, babe…"

Her face pinched.

Babe? Tarquin bristled. *She hates that!* His eyes narrowed as the guy touched her arm. *Oh, fuck. At least she used to.*

"Time's a tickin'. We should probably…?" The trainer tilted his head toward the exit and let go.

We? Babe?! She's WITH this guy? Like boyfriend-girlfriend? A burning sensation rose in Tarquin's throat. *Leia, come on! Seriously? He's got a MAN BUN, for heaven's sake!*

She skirted Tarquin's gaze and combed a hand through the ends of her wet locks. "Xavi, you go ahead. I still have to change. But we'll talk later?"

With a lustful stare, Xavi scooped up his file of papers. "You know it!" He winked at Tarquin. "Ciao, dude! Good to see you!" Lowering his shades, he confidently strode away, toned back muscles flexing beneath his tight black cotton shirt.

I can't fucking believe she's with this guy! Tarquin seethed, his glare practically searing a hole through Xavi's departing man bun.

"So…" Leia fiddled with her towel and stepped closer, breaking the palatable silence. "Sarah mentioned business is going well."

Sarah mentioned me? Tarquin's frown lifted. "Yeah, yeah it is! Lots of new properties on the go, but I've always got time for a trip to New York. It's great to be back!" *I know she's going gang-*

busters. Simon said her friend wore a Frill-Seekers gown to a film premiere last month and her phone's been ringing off the hook. "And you?"

"Really good! I have an investor now, so I'll be showing Frill-Seekers' fall/winter collection during New York Fashion Week next February."

I didn't know that! "Leia!" Tarquin beamed. "That's *amazing!*"

"Thanks! It's been A LOT of work. Some all-night sessions over the last week."

Argh! Please tell me those nights didn't involve that man bun fuckwit—

"HEY!" Nick's arm snaked around Tarquin's shoulders. "I can't bloody believe this! Xavi says this stunner is called Leia! Surely not YOUR Leia?"

'Your Leia?' Tarquin's jaw tensed. *Worst fucking timing ever, Nick! Leia will hate that.*

She smirked and eyed up the elder Balfour. "And you must be Nick. I've heard a lot about you."

He dropped his arm from Tarquin's shoulder. "Oh, arse!" He glared at his brother. "The bloody *Mail?*"

"Uh...no? I don't read gossip." Leia pulled her towel tight, stealing another glance at Tarquin, her eyes searching his face. "Well...it's great to see you. I hate to say hi and bye, but I'm meeting a makeup artist about my show"—she woke up her phone— "*shit!* Ten minutes ago!" She scowled at the screen and tapped into her contacts, muttering under her breath. "Please still be there."

She's gonna leave! Adrenaline raced through Tarquin's veins, pushing words from his tongue. "Harry's club opens tonight," he blurted. "You should come!"

"Uh..." Leia's panicked eyes flitted up as she raised the phone to her ear. "Um, okay." She blinked into a subtle grin. "Sounds fun! Text me the info?" She stepped back, her gaze lingering.

"Great! I think you'll like the place." Tarquin's thumbs flew over his screen. "We've kept all its historic character—"

"She's gone, bro," said Nick.

Tarquin looked up. Leia was rushing along the far side of the pool, talking a mile a minute into her phone.

Filmmakers, writers, musicians, and A-list celebrities swarmed the Thursday night opening of Bespoke New York, making Harry Manville's private club *the* hot ticket for young creatives and entrepreneurs. Potential members sipped champagne and dined on sweet potato croquettes, bite-sized Angus beef burgers, and mini gourmet grilled cheese while checking out the welcoming interior of reclaimed wood, vintage-inspired lamps, and tufted wingback chairs spread out over four large floors and a rooftop terrace.

"He's done it again," said Nick, watching Harry mingle with his American clientele. "It's only ten o'clock and this place is already rammed. This crowd doesn't usually head out until eleven—at the earliest—so that's saying something." He did a double take, catching Tarquin tossing back his fourth glass of bubbly. "Hey! Pace yourself, little brother. You'll be sozzled by the time she gets here."

"*If* she gets here."

"She'll come with Xavi."

"That's what I'm worried about." Tarquin blinked, his scratchy contact lenses feeling like a sheet of sandpaper in his eye. *I had to opt for style over comfort tonight, didn't I? Should I head to the loos, switch to glasses? What if I miss her while I'm in there?* He placed his empty champagne flute on a passing tray then tugged at the cuffs of his suit jacket, the one Leia liked, the one he'd worn for their goodbye dinner and secret shag on Tower Bridge. *Seven months later and look at me. I thought I'd moved on, but seeing her was like throwing gasoline on smoldering embers. If I could just speak to her alone, apologize for not emailing back all those months ago...*

He stopped fussing with his Darth Vader cufflinks and pulled out his phone. *Shit. Zero notifications. I can feel her slipping away, and there's nothing I can do about it.* His frown roamed the sea of revelers, their relaxed smiles and carefree laughter doing little to calm the unease rolling in his stomach. A foot away, a flock of leggy models lingered, giving him and his brother approving come-hither glances. "Still nothing from Leia. I hope that doesn't mean what I—"

"Tarq! Relax, will ya? Here. Take this." Nick thrust another glass of champagne at his brother and traded mischievous smiles with their flirty audience. "Christ, do you have to be such a buzzkill?"

"Nick, promise me—when Leia shows, you'll bugger off."

A server leaned in with a tray of bite-sized indulgences. "Pork slider with apple chutney?"

"Uh, no. Ta." Tarquin gulped his drink as his phone buzzed in his other hand.

Finally! He lowered his flute, a flutter of anticipation swooping in his belly as he glanced down.

Surprise! I made it!

The tingly citrus of the vintage champagne soured on Tarquin's tongue. *Cressida?*

TWENTY-ONE

LEIA

It's her. Cressida! My god, she's even more beautiful in real life.

Leia's stomach pinched into a knot. Tarquin, a dozen feet away surrounded by Nick and several friends, offered a wide smile and a flute of glistening champagne to a tall, striking blonde in a summery halter-neck gown.

Shit, shit, shit! Leia's pale pink nails dug into her satin clutch purse as she slouched behind a towering trio of guys furiously debating the latest New York Knicks trade. *This was a BIG mistake.* Peering around the ESPN wannabe sportscasters, she nudged her hair worn loose and wavy away from her face and spied Tarquin moving in for a kiss. Her stare didn't linger. "I-I shouldn't be here."

"Yeah, you should!" said Xavi, stealing two glasses of bubbly from a passing server. "If anyone deserves a night of free fizz and food, you do, Ley." He ogled her curves, resplendent in the sparkly emerald cocktail dress gifted to her by Simon. "Chill, have a drink." He foisted a flute her way and angled toward an incoming tray of phyllo-pastry-wrapped eats. "At least give it an hour, babe."

Why did I tag along with him? Leia flinched. "Would you stop calling me that! I'm not your babe!" she snarled under her breath. "How many times do I have to tell you? We are *not* a thing! We're workout buddies—that's it. And you *know* I don't drink." Backing away, she eluded another eyeful of Tarquin and his gorgeous girlfriend. *I have to get out of here before he sees me.* "This whole thing was a bad idea. I'm going. You stay, have fun."

Xavi pouted above the two full champagne glasses in his hands.

"You're bailing on me? But I told Nick I'd be bringing…"

Leia didn't stick around to answer. A blur of shimmery sequins, she snuck past a cluster of boisterous young actors posing for the party's roaming photographer and bolted outside into humidity so oppressive her airy tulle and crepe georgette dress felt like an iron apron.

So gross! I'll be a puddle of regret before I get home.

She gave a tight smile to the PR rep guarding the guest list and sidestepped Bespoke's velvet rope, squeezing past a clique of designer-draped fashionistas sharing gossip and a dwindling joint. Locking Leia in their sights, the women smirked over their shoulders, trading whispers and laughter as she ducked her head and escaped their pointed stares.

What the hell was I thinking? That Tarquin would be single again? That we'd magically pick up where we left off? You stupid girl! Heels punishing the sidewalk, she hurried along West 11th Street, her clutch coming alive with the muffled vocals of the Spice Girls' "Stop." *He never responded to my email or postcard! He never followed Frill-Seekers on Instagram. What more evidence do I need? Of course he's still with the chef! She's amazing and glamorous and open to love and meeting his family—couple stuff—all things I had ridiculous rules about. And me? I'm the scared idiot who refused to let him get close to me!* The Spice Girls trailed off, then arose again. *Can this day get any worse?!*

She slowed to a walk and tore open the magnetic closure of her purse, the inescapable mugginess rousing beads of perspiration on her skin. *Xavi, take a fucking hint!* She snatched her phone, its glow resuscitating the beads on her dress, sparking a galaxy of emerald green stars orbiting around her. *Saz?* She blinked at the screen, the fury in her heart dying a quick death.

"You're up early." Leia slapped on a smiley face, hoping her voice would lift along with the corners of her mouth. "Isn't it like four a.m. there or something?"

"Yep. I'm tag-teaming coffee and Smarties while I prep for a meeting in Liverpool." The familiarity of Sarah's voice felt comforting and safe like a warm hug. "My train leaves at seven."

"Oh, okay. I'll leave you to it—"

"Not so fast! You can't text 'The Institute let me go' and leave me hanging." Sarah exhaled a heavy breath. "Ley, I'm *so* sorry! What happened and when did you hear? I thought you were off today."

My life is such a dumpster fire. A tingly burn prickled inside Leia's nose. "I was off. Violetta called in the middle of a Frill-Seekers meeting, she asked me to join her for an after-work drink. I thought we'd be discussing my role in our next exhibition, but nope. She let me go instead! Apparently, the operating budget has been slashed and cuts are happening immediately. I'm the last one in, so I'm the first one out."

"But that's ridiculous! You do a great job. Violetta said so last week—"

"But the bean counters don't care, do they? To them, I'm just a name on a spreadsheet with zero seniority." Walking past Magnolia Bakery, Leia fought back tears. *Don't be a cliché. Do NOT cry in the street!*

"This is so wrong!" Sarah seethed, her voice rising through the phone. "They should've axed someone else!"

God love her. There's subtle and then there's Saz. "They did. I wasn't the only one let go. Violetta did say she tried to keep me—"

"That's bullshit. She didn't try hard enough!" Sarah snarled. "Did they give you any compensation?"

"I'll get a small severance package along with a reference. Tomorrow I have to see HR, hand in my ID, and pick up my stuff." Leia sniffed, unable to keep the tears from spilling through her lashes. *At least it's dark out.* Dipping her chin, she hid behind her hair and kept walking. "I was completely blindsided, Saz. I loved working there."

"Aw, honey, I know you did."

"Every day was magical! Always something interesting, something inspiring, and now it's gone. Violetta said it was nothing to do with my performance, but I can't help wondering, maybe I could've done more to make myself, you know, more valuable…?"

"Like hell you could! You were there all hours. Oh, Leia. I'm sorry. I know you're hurting, but look, this layoff might be the best thing that's happened to you in ages. Try to see it as a gift!"

A gift? Leia rolled her watery eyes. *Classic Sarah, going all TED Talk on me. No time to wallow, always trying to fix. Sometimes I think she's actually a guy.* "Jesus, Saz! Can't you just let me be sad for a while?" Leia wiped her damp cheeks and swept her hair off her forehead. "I feel numb and lost, like, where do I even *go* on Monday morning?"

"To the airport! Come here—to London! You can stay with me."

Oh, I would love to run away right now. A frown weighed down the corners of her mouth. "You know I would if I could, but I can't drop everything and take a holiday."

"I'm not saying take a holiday. I'm *saying* stay for a few weeks and work on your dresses"—the clatter of Smarties sliding back and forth inside their box filled Sarah's pause—"away from all that New York industry bullshit. You're free, Leia! You can do Frill-Seekers full-time."

"Yeah. It's sink or swim time, all right. Frill-Seekers has to be profitable or I'm toast. I can't fall back on my Institute paycheck anymore, and my—" The shrill wail of a rushing ambulance erupted a street away. Leia pressed her phone tight against her ear and spoke louder. "Sorry. I was gonna say my divorce settlement will only stretch so far."

"That's why you should come here. Stay with me, catch your breath, and plan your next move."

She makes it sound so easy breezy when life is anything but right now. "I appreciate the offer, but I don't know how I can. I'm right in the middle of Fashion Week stuff. Monday I'm signing the contract for my venue, Wednesday night I'm interviewing models, Friday—"

"For an event happening in February—six months away."

"These things need to be booked months in advance, Saz. If you want good people, you have to grab them early."

"Well, go grab them and *then* come to London. It would be so good to see you! And you know *London* Fashion Week happens here next month, right? You could schmooze, get inspired—hell, you could even stage your own show!"

Is she for real? "You can't just roll into one of the fashion capitals of the world, shove some models onto a catwalk, and call it a show. Fashion Week doesn't work that way." Leia scowled at the gum-stained sidewalk, ignoring the boozy whoops of a herd of red-faced frat boys on a night out. "And even if it did, planning an event from scratch in a foreign location with no contacts, no *nothing*—I doubt it's even possible."

"Okay, sure, it's a bit of a challenge…"

Leia's eyes widened. "*Bit of a challenge?* Can you hear yourself?!"

"Oh, c'mon! You've got friends here. You've got US! Wriggle outside your comfort zone! Plan something on the fly just this once. It'll be FUN!"

"Yeah, 'cause stress, hives, and chaos are a laugh riot."

"Noooo, think of that saying"—Sarah laughed—"if it scares you, it's worth doing!"

The chronic ache in Leia's right knee nagged, each high-heeled step agony. She pulled in a breath. "It doesn't *scare* me, it's

291

just…unrealistic."

"Only because you're a stubborn control freak. Seriously, Ley, what's the worst that could happen?"

"Easy—no one shows up."

"Hey, this is London—have an open bar, people will come."

Leia let out a terse giggle. "I guess."

"And something small here could be your dress rehearsal for New York! You'll learn what works, maybe what doesn't, and you can take that knowledge back for your debut there in February. Plus, London in the fall is heaven for someone like you! So many tree-filled parks. Just wait till you see the changing colors. Jordan could even take you to the Treetop Walkway at Kew Gardens, get a bird's-eye view."

Knee throbbing, Leia slowed to a stop, her mind swirling with London and all its hopeful possibilities: jaw-dropping sights, delicious food, a city of new opportunities and people. *Saz might be onto something.* She bent down and gently rubbed her leg. "Treetops, eh? Hmm." Nervous excitement bubbled up in her chest, dulling the pain. "Maybe London *is* a good idea."

"It's a *great* idea!" Sarah chuckled.

Yeah. Easier said than done, though. "If I did a last-minute show, I'd need to sort out music rights, lighting, hair and makeup, models…the venue—all on my own. Usually, a producer would organize that stuff, but there's no time to hire one. Even *with* plenty of notice, they cost a fortune. I'd need a lawyer for contracts, maybe a PR company for the guest list…" Leia straightened up and started walking again, a slight limp accessorizing her gait. "And I'd have to stage it after London Fashion Week."

"Oh? Can you do that?"

"Yep. More and more designers are doing their own thing. It's a way to avoid getting lost in all the hoopla surrounding the big labels. I'd just have to let my uniqueness shine through and spark enough interest from buyers, editors, and bloggers to make it worthwhile."

"LOVE IT! Steal the limelight, sell some dresses!" Sarah barely paused for breath. "Hey, you might even snatch up a megabucks investor. London is teeming with foreign billionaires right now. They're all looking for the next big thing. I bet you'd have to fight them off!"

Leia snickered. *I do need another investor. I could hire some interns if I had a second backer.* "Don't get too carried away! There's no point spending some fictional billionaire's checks when I'm stuck in New York and contracted to Shantelle. I'd love to come over, but her schedule is bananas and I can't style her US appearances from London. *Lost for Breath* is doing great at the box office here. Everybody wants a piece of her."

"Like who?"

"Tuesday, she has *The Tonight Show*, followed by *Good Morning America* on Wednesday and *Live with Kelly and Ryan* on Thursday. Friday is still up in the air, but there's a product launch she might attend...cosmetics or something. I'm still waiting for her to confirm. There's also talk of a late-night talk show appearance in LA."

"You must be *Lost for Breath* saying all that."

"Sarah!" Leia laughed.

"Now there's a happy sound I've been dying to hear." The smile in Sarah's voice soared through the phone. "So, is that it, then?"

"I dunno."

"Maybe you should ask Shantelle's psychic." Sarah snickered. "She'll know."

Leia's knee twinged again. *Owww. I had to go sexy with heels, didn't I?* She sucked in a sharp breath through pinched lips, ignoring her sister's catty remark. "The studio has me on retainer for two months. I style Shan when she needs me."

"Well, fly back and forth when she does."

"Between New York and London? Uh, I'm a sustainable designer, remember? That's hardly eco-friendly or cheap. And think of all the time I'd waste sat on a plane."

"Fine! Have it your way. Stay there and"—the buzz from a text on Leia's phone cut into Sarah's words—"thought you could use a few weeks away."

"You just want me to bring you new clothes!"

"Well, *yeah*! I'd kill for another skirt. But more than that, I wanna see *you*."

"I want to see you, too!" Leia bit her cheek, considering. "I guess I *could* check with Shantelle, maybe come over when she takes her holid"—Her phone buzzed again. "Sorry. My phone's blowing up with texts."

Sarah snickered. "Shantelle's ears burning?"

"Maybe." Leia lowered her phone. *Tarquin?* Her heart leapt into her throat. *What the hell?* A burst of messages glowed on the screen.

Tarquin: Leia, we should talk.

Tarquin: Meet me tomorrow before my flight back to London?

Tarquin: I'll come to you. Name a place. I'll be there.

Her heart tugged. *What do I do?* Stifling a smile, she wiped perspiration from her brow, her mind drifting back to the pool.

Sunburn on his nose, hair flirting with the breeze, the scent of body wash lingering on his skin... She inhaled a deep breath. *My god, he's perfect. I've missed him, but I didn't realize how much until he appeared in front of me, a serendipitous gift, smiling, laughing, asking how I've been in that irresistible accent. I wanted him then. I want him now. But I can't have him—*

"Leia?!" Sarah sounded tinny and far away. "Everything okay?"

No. Nothing is okay. She returned to the call. "Uh, yeah. It's Tarquin texting. I bumped into him and his brother at a pool in Brooklyn this afternoon."

"Tarquin is *there*? Wow, he gets around!"

"His friend's private members' club opened tonight in Greenwich Village."

"Oh! Sounds fun. Did he invite you?" The rattle of Smarties in their box peppered Sarah's question.

"Yeah. I was leaving the party when you called."

"Before midnight? Must've been a shit one."

"No, it was amazing." Leia hurried across Waverly Place, clogged with cars and bar-hopping twenty-somethings. "Lots of famous faces, great food, but I wasn't into it. I was feeling dizzy, sick…" She wobbled atop her five-inch heels, the pain in her right leg flaring with a fiery vengeance.

"No shit! You lost your job today. I'm surprised you even went, but I guess it was a great networking opportunity."

"I didn't go to schmooze." *Just tell her.* Leia took in a stuttering breath. "Saz, at the pool earlier when I saw him again…all these intense feelings came rushing back."

"Rushing back? For *who*?" Sarah bellowed. "Not Tarquin?!"

"Yeah," Leia answered quietly, her cheeks prickling with heat.

"But months ago, you sat here and swore you weren't into him!"

"I thought it was a crush! I thought it would fade." Leia pressed her clutch tight against her chest. "But it hasn't," she whispered. "Since London, it's taken on a life of its own. I can't stop wondering how he is, what he's doing, who he's with—well…I *did* until

295

you answered that a week ago."

"Cressida…"

"Yeah, the glam girlfriend wowing his family and everyone on Orkney—that stung." Leia glowered at her pedicure—in nude knickers pink—peeking out from her expensive designer heels. "I miss being with him, how much we'd laugh. I miss kissing him. I even miss his stupid *Star Wars* obsession."

"That's a first," said Sarah.

"He never teased me about my name. He was respectful, caring…put my needs before his. I've never had a guy do that before." A lump swelled in her throat. "And what did I do? I sabotaged it. Threw down a bunch of ridiculous rules, pushed my 'I'm fine if you sleep with other people' nonsense, and insisted we could *never* be a couple. I hate myself! I wish I could take it all back and start again." She bit her bottom lip and let it go. "Saz, I'm in love with him. Completely."

"Oh god, *Leia*."

West 11th Street blurred up ahead. "I know, I know!" She wailed into a sob, her fingers whisking away tears. "It's too late. FUCK!"

"So, you *met* Cressida, then?"

"No, she wasn't at the pool. He didn't mention her either. And then, his brother referred to me as '*your Leia*,' so, when Tarquin texted the party info, I felt hopeful, *excited*. I was all, *Yay! He's single again!*" A bad taste soured her tongue. "But he's not. Cressida was there at the club, looking stunning and so *smug*—not that I blame her. I'd feel pleased with myself if I had Tarquin on my arm and in my bed."

"Did you talk to them?"

"No! Tarquin kissed her and I-I couldn't deal. I snuck out before he spotted me." Leia shivered, holding back another flood of tears. "Talk about the perfect ending to a rotten day."

Sarah blew out a long breath. "I'm sorry, hon."

"And you know, I feel like *such* a loser"—words flying, a tightness knotted Leia's chest—"getting worked up over some guy I didn't want to date months ago! I hate feeling this way!"

"I know, but maybe there's a silver lining?"

Oh, please! Leia dabbed the corners of her eyes. "Seriously. You're giving me a *sewing* metaphor?"

"Would you listen?"

"Fine!"

"You being this upset proves something. *You* are no longer afraid of falling in love! Congrats, Ley, maybe you're ready for a relationship."

Shit. I guess...maybe?

"The fact that you're feeling *something* resembling love and longing is *proof*, right?" asked Sarah.

"Well, your so-called proof hurts like hell and I don't like it." Leia let out a trembling breath. "Adding insult to injury, I did it again, bowed to my rotten habit."

"Which one?" Sarah snickered. "Nail biting, humming to your-self? You have so *many*."

"I don't bite my nails! I stopped years ago! No, I'm talking about what I used to do with Tyler—compromising what's im-portant to me. The names and accents may have changed, but I let myself bend *yet* again."

"What are you on about?"

"My dresses! I planned to finish two of them tonight, but a flir-ty smile and an invite from Tarquin, and I was like, *Dresses? What dresses?*" Leia shook her head. "Well, that stops NOW! Frill-Seekers is on the verge of some incredible things, and I refuse to let them slip through my fingers again, not for a guy, not for anything." Waves of anger swelled in Leia's belly, her tone sharp and loud. "Especially now. I'm just getting my momentum back after months of playing catch-up. I lost so much when Brooke—" She halted her rant, spying two women she vaguely recognized outside a bar.

Leia exhaled forcefully, the fallout from the previous year spurring her on. "Stylists are calling again, buyers are interested. It's amazing how Shantelle wearing a Frill-Seekers dress can make me semi-relevant all of a sudden." She giggled nervously. "But I'm not kidding myself. I know people in the industry still trade stories about me." *Like those women outside Bespoke New York tonight.* "Hopefully they'll talk about my designs, too."

"I bet they are, Ley." Sarah yawned through the phone. "Your stuff is too beautiful to ignore."

"So, you see, Saz? There's too much at stake right now. My focus should be on my dresses and nothing else. Whatever I feel for Tarquin…" She lifted her chin, resolve pushing the words forward. "I'm grateful he was in my life for a short time, but it's over and I have to cut those feelings loose. He's moved on and so have I. Frill-Seekers is my one true love, and I'm fine with that."

"Message received and understood. You won't hear another word from me."

It's a miracle. "Thanks."

"But…" Sarah chuckled.

She always wants the last word. "What?!"

"Maybe now you'll see…losing your job, running into Tarquin and his girlfriend—today *was* a gift!"

Leia grimaced and swiped a clammy hand across her forehead. "Yeah, one I'd like to return." She sniffed again, her attention jumping from one unfamiliar building to another where three streets all converged into a six-pronged wheel of choice. *Isn't the M train entrance here? This is West 11th and Seventh, right?* She huffed through a pout. *Shit! I always get lost around here. Try 14th Street, maybe?* Favoring her right leg, Leia hobbled, heading northeast up Seventh Avenue. "I could've done without today's drama."

"Well"—Sarah yawned again—"sleep on it. I'm sure you'll feel better in the morning."

Fat chance of that. "Tarquin wants to see me tomorrow."

A heavy pause hung over the line. "Ley, you can't go."

"I have to—for closure."

"That's a terrible idea! What if he gushes about Cressida? Or wants sex with you *and* her?"

I never thought of that. A breath lodged in Leia's chest. *Shit. Did he lie about liking threesomes, too?*

"I really don't think it's a good idea to go, not when you're feeling so vulnerable," said Sarah.

Leia blinked, avoiding the drunken leers of three prowling Wall Streeters, sweat-stained and ties askew. "Maybe he wants closure, too."

"He's already got it—he's with Cressida!"

Cheers, Saz. Don't even try to sugarcoat it.

"If I were you, I'd take a hard pass on tomorrow. God knows what you'll be walking into." Sarah's scoff was underlined by the rattle of more Smarties.

"No. I *need* closure, and I can't get it if I'm wondering why he reached out after seven months of silence. I mean, what's so important he can't tell me in a text?" Eyes searching ahead, she fought with her bra strap, which was biting into her shoulder. "Saz, can I ask a favor?"

"Name it."

"If I *do* visit you in London, you have to promise me you won't tell Tarquin I'm there."

"He'll probably find out—" Sarah's voice jumped an octave.

"Not from you he won't," Leia fired back. "And I'll speak to Simon. If I'm moving on with my life, I can't let Tarquin be a part of it."

Twenty-Two

TARQUIN

I'm glad I stopped drinking before midnight. This humidity on top of a throbbing hang would've killed me. Tarquin climbed the final stair of the 28th Street entrance to the High Line, an elevated public park and outdoor arts space built above Chelsea and the Meatpacking District. A slight breeze meddled with his hair but did little to alleviate the oppressive midday heat. He whisked sweat from his brow and opened another button on the neck of his shirt, its slightly rumpled white linen tucked neatly into his black shorts. *I love this place, but why'd she choose it? I thought she'd pick a café or a bench in Central Park, something near the Met.*

Tarquin squinted through his shades, his roving eyes zeroing in on a redhead wearing a familiar white lace dress, her straight locks coiffed in a high, swaying ponytail. She strode toward him with purpose, her emotions hidden behind a pair of aviator sunglasses. *She's here!* His pulse took off like a rocket, his smile wide and friendly. "Leia! How are you?"

"I'm good." She grinned, tentatively leaning in like she was unsure what to do. "You?"

"Sun's shining, you're here—life's great!" Tarquin edged closer, kissing Leia on both cheeks.

"Oh!" Her awkward laugh matched Tarquin's and they loosely embraced, his hand flirting with the soft hair at the nape of her neck.

God help me, I've missed this. Leia's subtle perfume triggered memory after sweet memory. *I'd never get tired of waking up with her in my arms, her scent on my sheets...on me.*

She pulled away before Tarquin could get too comfortable.

We barely touched. His heart squeezed into a tight ball. *Bollocks. Am I too sweaty? Oh, shit! Do I smell?* He nudged his rolled-up sleeves closer to his elbows, cursing the humidity.

Leia's gaze lingered on his forearms before reuniting with his face. "Uh, want to…" She glanced away, motioning toward the park's path.

"Have a mosey? Sure. Love this park."

Joining the flow of tourists, they strolled side by side, in no rush to feel the ire of the searing heat. Leia seemed happy but preoccupied, her downward gaze dedicated to her pedicure and barely-there silver sandals.

Tarquin lifted his sunglasses, nestling them in his hair. "I thought my eyes were playing tricks on me last night. One minute, I spied this captivating woman with fiery red hair in a gorgeous emerald dress. Then I blinked, and she was bloody well gone! I swore she was you."

A soft smile pinched her cheeks as she twisted the tip of her ponytail.

"Xavi wandered over and confirmed my suspicion. My god, Leia, you looked otherworldly, like a beautiful absinthe fairy." His appreciative gaze swept her from head to toe. "And your hair is glorious! I love the red."

"It's my natural color."

Tarquin tilted his head. "Blimey! You're really Ginger!" Leia's nod unlocked the words he had wanted to spill for hours. "Well, it's even more bewitching than the blonde."

"Thanks," she mumbled under her breath, her fingers fussing with her right sleeve. "You looked great last night, too." A flicker of a grin warmed her face as she glanced up. "I'd recognize that suit anywhere. I hope the dry-cleaning bill wasn't too high…"

Tarquin laughed. "Worth every penny! You know, I wore it just for you."

Leia's smile slipped away on the light breeze. "Tarquin, why would you say that?" Brows pulling in above her sunglasses, she shot him an incredulous open-mouthed glare. "You have a girl-friend, remember? The tall blonde? She was right there!"

"Cressida." Tarquin shook his head. "No, she's not my girl-friend. Not anymore."

"Shit! You didn't!" Leia halted on the spot, her hand flying to her mouth. "You saw me, then dumped *her*?!" She darted out of the flow of foot traffic and Tarquin rushed after her. "I can't believe this!" she growled. "You asshol—"

"Leia, I'm not a dick." He leaned in, shaking his head. "We split last weekend. Actually, it should've happened ages ago." His hand flitted to his moustache then his temple, looking for a safe spot to land. "It would've saved a lot of tears, actually."

"Oh, classy, Tarquin—really classy!"

"No, the tears weren't hers—or mine." Tarquin gave Leia a stern look. "They were Ava's."

"What?!"

He wrenched the collar of his linen shirt open farther, trying to get some relief from the blazing heat. "Three weeks ago, Cressida agreed to come to my cousin's wedding in Kirkwall. We FaceTimed Ava, told her the news. She went bonkers! She was so excited, jumping around because the lady off telly who makes unicorn cup-cakes was coming to meet *her*! Then, seven days ago, we're waiting for our car to Heathrow, and Cressida threw a strop and bailed. Ap-parently, a boujee foodie festival in the Cotswolds was"—he made quotation marks with his fingers—"more her brand."

"Jesus!" Leia removed her shades, her eyes narrow with fury.

I knew she'd be horrified. "Our split was mutual. Cress drove off to fuck knows where and I flew up to Orkney." He plunged his hands in his pockets and shook his head. "God forbid she misses her umpteenth celebrity schmooze to make a little girl's day."

"Wow, that's…"

"Selfish? Cruel, rude? All of the above?" Tarquin nodded. "Obviously, Cressida and I want vastly different things. She loves being paparazzi bait, adores being recognized out on dates. I despise all that bollocks. I've seen enough showbiz bullshit with Nick and Mum to last several lifetimes." He pressed his lips together. "I didn't invite her last night, Leia. She has a new cookbook coming out and was in town to meet her American publisher. She just showed up, hoping she'd get papped. I will *never* use that over-priced matchmaking agency again. Bleedin' clueless."

"You hired a matchmaker?" Leia squinted into the sun. "That's how you met her?"

He swept his hair off his forehead and peered over her shoulder, his gaze unfocused on the incoming waves of people clogging the High Line's path. "I'm not fucking around, Leia. I'm done with be-ing single." Reuniting with her eyes, he smiled. "I want what Harry has with Lucy, a serious loved-up relationship. I even want to get married one day, have a family." *Question is, does she?*

A tiny breath slipped from her mouth. She blinked, taking him in.

"Cressida is a lovely catch—for someone else. And heaven help me, she puts chickpeas in bloody *everything*."

Leia's expression softened. Tarquin swore she was fighting back an amused grin. "Well, I'm no cook, so I can't speak to that…but I'm sorry it didn't work out."

"I'm not." Tarquin's glance fell to her lips. "The *whole* time I was with her…I wanted you."

A small smile bloomed on Leia's face but stayed only briefly, her focus shifting, landing on the shades in her hands.

What is she thinking? "So, are *you* sorry? About man bun?"

Leia chuckled under her breath. "You mean Xavi? What about

him?"

"Didn't you finish with him last night?"

"Finish?" Her jaw dropped. "Ah, you're joking, right?"

But isn't that why she bolted from the party? "No, that's what he told me—"

"Oh my god! He is SO full of shit! We never *dated*! Ever. We hooked up a few times last year, before I came to London. I haven't touched him since." Leia snapped the arms of her sunglasses closed. "I knew I shouldn't have gone to the pool with him."

I'm so glad you did. I wasn't sure if I should text you, if you'd ignore me.

"Typical Xavi. He takes a friendly gesture and blows it up into something more." She huffed. "So, to answer your question—no! I'm not sorry about man bun. Great, I guess I'll need a new gym."

"Sorry, *not* sorry?" Tarquin gave her a playful wince. "If he called you babe one more time…"

"I told him repeatedly to stop, but…" She shrugged.

"Well, I'm relieved. The thought of you two together, like, *properly* made me want to gouge my eyes out."

"If you thought I was seeing him, why'd you invite me to Harry's party?"

Because I've missed you, and I had absolutely nothing to lose. You already own my heart. Tarquin smiled softly. "Isn't it obvious?"

"Oh. *Okay.* I get it." She nodded into a pout. "You wanted sex."

Tell no lies. "Well, *yeah*."

Her exasperated eye roll yanked him back on course.

"Leia, you're amazing and so sexy—why wouldn't I? But more than that, what I *really* wanted was to see if you'd changed your mind—about me, about us."

Leia's eyebrows peaked. "About *us*?" She blinked, pausing for a beat. "Tarquin, we've been through this before."

"I know, but look at us—here together in the Big Apple, both single. Same ol' Han and Ginger, having a giggle, bonding over our shared distaste of man buns." A brief chuckle left his lips before his demeanor turned serious. *I have to lay it all out there, share my deepest truth like Dex suggested.* "Look, I know this isn't ideal, us living in different cities, but you love London, I'm crazy for New York—why don't we give it a go?"

"What? Like long-distance?"

It killed my parents' marriage, but hey, we're not them! Tarquin's smile grew. "Yeah, why not?!" *Hide nothing.* His pulse pounded, ratcheting up a gear. "I love you, Leia. I'm IN love with you. I have been for months."

Her eyes widened. "You *love*...me?" Leia's gape wandered to the passing throng of overheated tourists. A swallow bobbed her throat. "Wow," she whispered, a hint of a smile playing with her mouth.

It's such a relief, telling her—finally! Tarquin grinned, his shoulders relaxing. *Even if she doesn't say it back, I can work with that. We'll get there, eventually. Together.*

"I...uh, it's just...you sure have a weird way of showing it."

"Yeah, I know—sorry." He laughed. "I'm a bit rubbish this morning. I burnt my breakfast, spilled coffee down the shirt I planned to wear." He enthusiastically gestured between them. "And I meant to grab primroses on my way here, but the flower sh—"

Her glimmer of glee faded. "I'm not talking flowers, Tarquin!" Leia scoffed, the sharp edge to her voice piercing his joviality. "Try *seven months* without a single word from you. Not an email or a text, not even a random 'like' on Instagram. You call *that* love?"

Shit. Tarquin's heart plummeted into his stomach. He scrunched his eyes and plowed a hand through his hair, almost knocking his shades free. "No, but..." Meeting her frustrated frown, he stammered. "I-I *did* write something, a reply to your email. I just…never sent it."

"Why not?!"

"Well, I…uh…" Perspiration beaded on Tarquin's brow as Leia shook her head, the words he desperately wanted to say tangled on his tongue. *Don't panic. Be honest.* He tugged at his belt and tried again, breaking through his wince. "Our last night in London…when you told me about the Met job, I was happy *for you* but gutted for myself." Bowing his head, he wrenched his silver ring around his thumb. "I tried to hide it, but after we hugged…I don't know, somehow, I reckon I gave myself away? You had this look on your face, like you'd sussed me out completely. You knew I'd been lying. You *knew* I wanted more than a friendly fling. Right?"

Leia fussed with the sunglasses in her hands. "I had my suspicions."

"And you were bang-on." He scraped the toe of his pristine white sneakers on the ground. "I was furious with myself, embarrassed, like I'd been caught out." He looked up with a squint. "Nobody likes a liar, right?"

"No," she murmured, letting out a shaky breath. Her eyes fled Tarquin and darted along the curved condominium balconies overlooking the High Line.

"I was afraid to read your email the next day—god knows what you thought of me—but once I did, I was speechless. You were lovely. Absolute class. I felt like I didn't deserve your kindness, not after I lied about my feelings. I'd put you in an awkward situation and I sort of hated myself for it."

Leia chewed her cheek.

"I did sit down and write a response, but thought I should wait a bit, give you some space. And I realized I needed time, too, to deal with a few hard truths of my own. There was only one thing for it— I had to save face, lick my wounds in private, so I left it in my drafts folder. But I swore to myself I'd get in touch once I found the clarity I needed." *All right, old boy, if you're truly embracing this honesty kick, you've got to spill. She can't love you back if you hide the real you.* Tarquin moved closer. "That's why I started seeing a psychologist, hoping he'd help me get there."

Her eyes locked with his. "You went to therapy," she whispered, "because of me?"

"No, I went because of *me*." Tarquin let out a pent-up breath and dipped his chin, his fingers idly tugging the strap of his Rolex. "Despite appearances, I'm not the perpetually cheeky chappie looking for a shagging good time 24/7. Sometimes I feel like a half-assed version of myself, stumbling about in a melancholy funk I can't shake. I become apathetic, withdraw from everyone. I get irritable over daft things." He twisted his lips, his voice growing quieter. "Nothing brings me joy no matter how hard I play or how high I climb. And these intrusive thoughts take over, make me wonder, like, what if I just vanished? Would anyone give a toss?"

Leia leaned in, grasping his forearm. "Yes, they would." The warmth of her hand, its confidence and strength made his heart skip a beat. "Lots of people care about you, Tarquin: your brothers, Harry, Ava...me."

You? He looked up, a sparkle of hope brightening his eyes. "But you know what it's like. Reason does a runner when you're depressed—you can't see what's right in front of you." Leia's nod was the green light he needed to continue. "And it's so flippin' isolating. The thought of anyone finding out, seeing me as this wretched zombie curled up in my trackie bottoms eating Frosties straight from the box...well, that's not the Tarquin Balfour all the ladies and gents want to see."

Leia gave his arm a squeeze and let go. "I know that feeling."

"Right? So, after a few lost days, I'd pack up my pity party for one and get stuck in. Throw on a bespoke suit and act like nothing happened. Like Kiki always says, *'The show must go on, luv!'*"

"Oh, so your mother knows?"

"Does she, heck! But with everything skew-whiff lately"—he shrugged and stopped torturing his Rolex—"I decided enough was enough and reached out for professional help."

"That's great, Tarquin! Really, it's a huge step. You should be proud of yourself." Her gaze settled on his lips. "*I'm* proud of you."

A smile warmed his face. "Cheers, Leia."

"So, how are you feeling? Has therapy helped?"

"Yeah, despite my initial trepidation, it's been bloody great, actually. I've learned a lot, not all of it pretty, but life's messy, right?" His squint strayed to a rowdy pack of teenagers passing by. "I'm not fooling myself, though. I know I'll have to work on this for the rest of my life, but I've never been one to avoid hard graft so...I reckon I'll be all right. As backup, I brought Nick, Rupert, and Harry into the loop."

Leia raised her eyebrows. "Oh? How'd they react?"

"They've been smashing, really supportive..." Tarquin muted his grin and stuffed his hands in his pockets. "While I haven't been. Leia, I feel terrible. I've been a rubbish friend. I'm so sorry."

"I would've listened, you know, helped you." She sighed. "I started to think you hated me."

"Oh god, no! I could *never*. I just needed to deal with my shit before I reached out. I never stopped thinking about you, I never stopped *loving* you." Tarquin bit his bottom lip. "Then yesterday happened and I thought I was dreaming! You! Right *there* with me. I thought my heart was going to conk out it pounded so hard. And that bathing suit..."

She glanced down at her hands and sunglasses again.

Shit. Too honest? He cleared his throat. "But I was bricking it, too. I didn't know how you'd react, if you'd blank me or make excuses and leave. I'm so grateful you didn't." A soft smile curved his mouth. "I'm so grateful you're here *now*. It means a lot, you listening, giving me this chance to explain and apologize." *It feels like the weight I've carried has finally lifted.* He laid a hand on his chest. "I hope somehow you can find it in your heart to forgive me. These past few months have been bloody hard. I've missed you so much."

Leia nodded. "I completely understand struggling with depression." Looking up, she held his eyes for a beat, then blinked away. "The rest, not so much."

His grin melted as his hand fell. "Sorry?"

"Oh, come on, Tarquin." Her glare flew back at him, tinged with hurt and disappointment. "Don't play dumb. You come here claiming you love me, but for seven whole *fucking* months you ignored me, signed up with some elite matchmaking service, and began a relationship with a celebrity chef. Just a week ago, you were planning to introduce her to your entire family!" She huffed. "So, despite all *that*, you expect me to welcome you back into my life with open arms?"

Fuck! Tarquin's heart sank. *The only thing missing from her argument is check and mate.* His gaze fled, skimming the Kasmin Gallery's rooftop garden on their right, its trio of colorful pop art installations by Robert Indiana standing tall amongst meadow flowers and aspen trees. *But wait a minute...if she doesn't want me in her life, why IS she so furious?* He tugged at his bottom lip as his eyes landed on the third sculpture, the red, white, and blue LO stacked atop a VE. *Fuck!* He swallowed hard, adrenaline coursing through his veins. *Because she had feelings for me! And still does...?*

A slight tremor shook her hands as she put on her sunglasses. "You know, my life's great! I have zero emotional drama, no distractions. I can channel all my energy and passion into Frill-Seekers, which is thriving, by the way! Why would I gamble that on you—on anyone?"

Throw it out there. Fighting the nerves rolling in his belly, he took a chance. "Because you love me."

Her mouth fell open and her sunglasses glinted back, cold, detached. "Oh, dream on, rich boy." She crossed her arms and glanced away, shaking her head.

She's in denial. He licked his lips and stepped closer. "Leia, I *know* we shared something real in London. I felt it. You did, too."

A hard swallow bobbed her throat. "It's called sexual chemistry, Tarquin. It's great sex, nothing more."

"But don't you crave, you know, intimacy? Kissing? My god, Ginger, our kisses…" Tarquin leaned in. "Don't you miss feeling so fucking good—with me?"

She pouted downward, her hands seeking refuge in her dress's pockets. "No."

I don't believe her. Fuck, I wish she'd take those bloody shades off! His eyes narrowed. "But our last night in London, our dinner, back at mine…you wanted to stay over, have breakfast—obviously, you felt something for me if you broke your own rules—"

"Tarquin!" Leia looked up. "I didn't come here for a deep dive into my sex life, okay? Or to profess my undying love for you!" Her chest rose and fell, her breaths short and fast. "I came here to wish you well and say goodbye."

Goodbye? The word twisted and knotted in his throat. He sputtered, the heat and crowds suffocating. *I can't lose her again.* He gently touched her arm. "Leia, let's find some shade, somewhere air-conditioned. We can grab a bite, talk—"

"Don't you have a plane to catch?" she blurted, brushing his hand away.

"I'll rebook, move my meetings. Nothing is as important as you."

Leia's lip quivered. She dropped her chin, trading Tarquin's earnest expression for the safety of her sandals. Perspiration glistened on her skin and her fingers poked erratically through the lace of her dress's sleeve, unable to settle. "Look, I'm sorry if yesterday made you nostalgic for"—her voice cracked as her sunglasses slipped down her nose—"whatever you *think* we had, but...it's over."

NO! It can't be! Her declaration twisted like a knife through his heart. "Leia, *please!*" Tarquin caught her eyes softening behind her frames. "You don't mean that." He forced out a staggered breath.

In a single swoop, her fingers evacuated her sleeve and prodded her shades, whisking them up her nose. She sniffed, skirting his gaze.

Wait...is she tearing up? Tarquin bent his neck, closing the distance. "*Leia*, don't do this."

She cleared her throat. "You see, Tarquin, like you, I'm not fucking around either. But the difference is, I *like* being single. I don't want a serious relationship or, god forbid, another wedding." She lifted her chin, defiant. "Go back to London and forget about *us*, okay?"

This can't be happening! A breath-stealing ache squeezed his heart. He edged closer, keeping his hands to himself. "Leia, *please.*" He gasped, fighting back tears. "Don't do this! I know you feel something for me. Why won't you let me in? You deserve to be—"

"I *deserve* to live my life on my terms—not yours!" She hiked the strap of her purse up her shoulder, her tone all business. "I need to get back to work, and you have a plane to catch. Have a safe flight." Without pause, she dashed into the crowd of iced coffee-toting office workers heading toward the glass skyscrapers overlooking Hudson Yards.

Eyes stinging, Tarquin stood dizzy and defeated. Leia's ponytail bobbed farther and farther away until she vanished from view. *The day we met, Leia said she was bad at decision-making. Turns out, where I'm concerned, she's brutally efficient.*

TWENTY-THREE

"Everything you've ever wanted is on the other side of fear."
George Addair

LEIA

London, six weeks later, Friday, October 4, 2019

Wide-eyed guests oohed over elegant finger sandwiches and warm scones as Sarah, sat alone with a second cup of Wedding Breakfast tea in hand, glanced over her shoulder and nudged Leia's phone across the white linen tablecloth. The sisters' visit to Fortnum & Mason's Diamond Jubilee Tea Salon was part of Leia's 'return to London bucket list' and, following their hectic morning at Madame Tussauds, offered a refined respite from waxy royals and pushy tourists.

Leia swooped around Sarah's chair, fresh from her reconnaissance mission across the sun-filled room. She slid into her seat, breathlessly sharing her discovery. "So, that table over there—they call it a cake carriage! How British is that?" Tucking her hair behind an ear, she weaved subtly to Elton John's "Your Song" tinkling from the tea salon's grand piano. "There's a Battenberg, a flourless chocolate cake, a Victorian sponge, and something pineappley. They all look decadent and delicious. I can't choose!"

"Try these first." Sarah swooned over the melt-in-your-mouth mini patisseries on the third (and top) tier of their bone china cake stands. A dark chocolate tart, a mini ginger loaf with a generous swirl of thick icing, a square of raspberry mousse topped with a plump berry, and a tartlet with a green apple crémeux dome competed for taste bud approval. "I thought *they* were the dessert." She laughed. "Which one do you want, Ley?"

"Hmm, not sure. You pick." Leia plucked her linen napkin off the table, noticing her phone's new location beside the low vase of red roses. "Oh! Did you take a photo of me with the cakes?"

"Ah, I didn't. *Sorry*." Sarah added the tartlet to her plate where it mingled with a half-eaten coronation chicken finger sandwich. "But you did get a text from London Fields Brewery."

The Arches event space! Leia's heart skipped.

Sarah licked apple mousse off her thumb and swirled her tea, Fortnum's special blend created in 2011 to celebrate Will and Kate's proposal. "I sorta read it. Hope you don't mind."

She's reading my texts again? Leia pursed her lips and yanked her chair closer to the table. Collecting her phone, she tapped the screen and...nothing. "Oh, you're kidding me. Battery's dead." She looked past their second cake stand, home to pots of Somerset clotted cream, strawberry preserve, and lemon curd, and met Sarah's grin. "So, nosey Parker, what'd they say?" Leia's grimace morphed into a wary smile.

"It's yours! Thursday, November 14th. They'll email the contract this afternoon!"

YES! Leia's heart skipped beneath her sweater. "Ah, thank god! I didn't think I'd find a venue this late in the game. It's just too bad my good fortune was on the back of some poor bride's wedding cancellation."

"Hey, all's fair in love and party planning. So, you nervous?"

Leia pushed out a big breath. "No. Excited and impatient! Six weeks will fly by with so much to do. Get this—Shantelle even wants to take part."

"Really? She'd fly over for it?"

"She's already here. Don't you ever look at my Frill-Seekers

Insta?"

"*Hello*"—Sarah set down her blue and white china teacup—"have we met?"

"Luddite!" Leia scrunched her nose and broke into a grin. "Shan's in London doing *Lost for Breath* press."

"I thought she was lying on a beach somewhere."

"She's supposed to be. The studio ordered her and Bastien to fly over a few days ago. The movie isn't making what they expected here, and they think a last-minute press tour might help. They're certainly not sparing any expense."

"*Oh*, okay—so that's why their faces are parading around the city on the sides of buses!" Sarah contemplated the goodies waiting on her plate. "You can't ride public transport without seeing them."

"Yup. Feels like they're everywhere."

"I'm surprised you could take the day off."

"I'm on call in case of an emergency, but beyond that, Shan's ready to go. I gave her my spare key when I left Brooklyn, so she brought a bunch of dresses with her. We spent her first day planning outfits and accessories and arranging hair and makeup appointments. The tour is busy, but it's not glam. There's no premiere or parties, no schmoozing. It's low stress but high impact—hopefully."

"And no travel for you."

"That's the best part! And I'm getting tons of Instagram content for Frill-Seekers. The PR guy is taking photos all over London. You should check them out. Bastien shows up, too, wearing my moto-style jacket."

Sarah's face brightened in recognition behind her cup of tea. "The wool skirt one? Ah, I LOVE that one!"

"So does Bastien!" Leia laughed. "Shan was wearing hers around New York and he stole it, wouldn't give it back. She begged me, '*Make him one!*' Now, he won't take his off."

"That's great press for you! Bastien shows up in *all* the gossip columns."

"Yeah, he's popular, all right. He was really sweet in Brooklyn during his fitting and gave me a big kiss and posed for photos. He posted one yesterday for Throwback Thursday. It got a shitload of likes."

Sarah swapped her tea for the last bite-sized morsel of coronation chicken. "And what about Shantelle? She sticking around for your show next month?"

"I hope so. If Shan walks the runway, people will definitely take notice. But I'll have to ask her again, see if she's being serious or you know…just Shantelle."

"Pray that Mercury isn't in retrograde when you ask her." Sarah giggled, savoring her sandwich. "I still can't believe *I* get to be a model!"

"I'm relieved you said yes! One model down, nine to go."

"But Simon's helping you search, right?"

"Yeah, and he'll help me backstage on the day." Leia tore off a chunk of clotted-cream-slathered scone. "God love Simon. He also gave me info for three PR companies and suggested The Arches space at the brewery. I'd still be looking if it wasn't for him. I have to let him know I got it once my phone is alive again."

"Here, use my portable charger…" Sarah leaned over the side of her chair, her hand diving into her bag. "He's been such a great friend to you."

In more ways than one. Leia popped the scone in her mouth, her eyes trailing a tall server delivering two cake stands stacked with finger sandwiches, pastries, and jams to a group of Italian tourists, their phones aloft amidst joyful cries of "Bellissimo!" *Simon has stuck to his word. Ten days into my stay and I'm pretty sure Tarquin has no clue I'm here.*

"Shoot!"

Mid-chew, Leia's stare bounced back to her sister, bent over her armrest. "You okay?"

"Yeah, just making a mess…stupid achy wrists." Lifting up her tangled phone charger, Sarah let out a frustrated chuckle. "I fished this out of my bag and upended yours." She left the portable device beside their bottle of sparkling water and dipped back toward the floor.

Leia peered under the table. Her unzipped gratitude journal lay open, splayed against Sarah's left wheel. "Don't worry, I'll get it." Shifting her chair back, a shooting bolt of knee pain curbed her descent. *Great.* Leia winced as her linen napkin slipped to the floor. *Gonna be one of those days, is it?*

Sarah scooped up Leia's journal and pen. "Beat ya, old lady!" She giggled and cradled the book, fanned open to a rippled page marred by ink blotches and blurred handwritten words. "Where'd you write this? Outdoors in a rainstorm?"

Napkin in hand, Leia straightened up. "Uh, no." Her eyes narrowed as Sarah's fingers skated across the wavy paper.

"August 23, Leia Scott was grateful for…"

Shit. Leia's body tensed. *Please don't read that!*

Sarah flipped the page, then a few more, a flurry of blank white sheets parading past her nose. "Ley, you haven't touched this for six weeks. Aren't you supposed to write in here daily?"

Leia relaxed, resting her napkin on the table. "I'd just lost my job, remember? I didn't feel very grateful." With a sharp flick of her hand, she brushed crumbs off her jeans. "My therapist said to start again when I'm ready. I've been carrying it with me just in case. Here"—she reached out—"I'll put it away before we spill tea on it."

Sarah shifted her plate and filled the vacant space with Leia's book. "Do you bitch about Violetta in here?"

What? Leia half-chuckled. "It's not that kind of journal, Saz." *God, enough with the questions. Just give it back!* She kept her expression neutral, hiding her displeasure. *If I make a fuss, Saz will definitely dive in.*

Sarah flicked backward through the sheets until she returned to the crinkly page.

Uh, what's she doing? Leia's stomach rolled, her appetite for cake and banter gone. *Fuck, she can't read that!* "Saz, c'mon. Give it back," she pleaded through clenched teeth, but Sarah had already begun reading the blotchy entry.

August 23, I was grateful for:

1. *reuniting with Tarquin. It felt like home, just me & him.*
2. *we talked & flirted, then he said, "I love you, Leia. I'm IN love with you. I have been for months."*

"Oh. *My god*!" Sarah gasped.

Fighting a lump in her throat, Leia thrust her hand between the two cake stands, snatching the journal. "I can't believe you!" A burning sensation prickled her nose.

Sarah's misty gape followed the book's retreat. "*Ley…*"

"First you read my texts, now this?" she hissed, her volume discreet. Glaring glassy-eyed at the page, stained and rippled by tears shed six weeks ago, a twinge of déjà vu creased Leia's brow. *I sobbed myself into an anxiety attack writing this.* Her chin trembled as the rest of the journal entry blurred beneath her gaze.

3. *Tarquin LOVES me! My heart felt like a red balloon, soaring in the cloudless sky, his beautiful words lingering in the August sunshine. A part of me wanted to breathe them in, feel their warmth, their joy—but I couldn't. My best laid plans pinched & poked, dragging me back down to Earth. Once a skater, always a skater. I stuck the landing & aced my performance.*

317

A sad ache swelled in her chest. *This brings it all back, how much it hurt letting him go.* She whisked away fresh tears and snapped the journal shut, dragging the zipper around its cover, sealing her secrets behind its metal teeth. "Thanks for making me cry in Fortnum's, Sarah." Leia stole a sweeping glance at their neighboring tables, catching the uncomfortable winces and loud whispers from the rapt Italians. *Great.* A blush darkened her pale cheeks.

"He said he loved you?" Sarah leaned forward. "But he was with Cressida then."

"No. They broke up before he flew to New York."

"You never said! My god, *Leia*?! He was single? And in love with you!"

Leia bowed her head, a forlorn huff escaping. "You're not helping."

"Why didn't you tell me?"

"Because look at you!" Leia grabbed her bag from the floor and stuffed the journal inside. "You're swooning. You've practically got cartoon hearts dancing in your eyes."

Sarah pressed her lips together. "And you walked away without telling him how you felt?"

I'm so pissed at her. This is not the time nor the place. Leia blinked, unsuccessfully curbing her tears. *Shit! They won't stop!* Skirting stares from the room, she rooted through her bag, retrieving a tissue. "I went for closure, remember? *You* agreed it was for the best." She dipped her chin. Safe behind her hair, Leia dabbed her eyes.

"Don't put this on me!" said Sarah. "I *agreed* with putting Frill-Seekers first right *now*—not forever. And I would've kept my mouth shut if I'd known you'd be this devastated leaving him behind. Ley, that journal entry screams of regret."

It doesn't scream... Leia choked back a sob, refusing to acknowledge her sister. *This is exactly why I didn't tell her, com-*

ments like that. Her watery gaze roamed their table. *All this expensive food and now I'm too upset to eat.* Balling up the tissue, she dropped it into her purse and reluctantly pinched the dark chocolate tart from the cake stand, placing it in the middle of her crumb-speckled plate.

"So, do you?" Sarah pushed. "Regret walking away?"

Like it matters now. Leia hesitated then plunged her fork into her mini-dessert's rich chocolate ganache. "For the millionth time, Saz…it *wouldn't work*! For lots of reasons. For one thing, he's in London, and I'm in New York."

"But you're here now."

"I'm leaving first week of December. You know that." Leia stuffed a bite-sized chunk of tart between her lips and chewed, its decadent flavor sparking little joy on her tongue. *I can't eat this.* The pianist's twinkly rendition of "Theme from Mahogany" made her pause mid-chew, desperate to change the path of their conversation. With a hard swallow, she forced the mouthful down. "Aw, that movie. Diana Ross playing a fashion designer…I don't care if it's cheesy. I love it, Mom loved it—"

"Mom *never* liked Tyler," Sarah blurted. "Bet she'd like Tarquin."

Leia's face pinched. "Now there's a leap."

"Mom would want you to stay. She'd want—"

"Me to finish my fall/winter collection. Jeez, Saz. Do you ever listen? I *want* to go back. It's home."

"So you keep saying. But why would that rule out trying a long-distance relationship with Tarquin? He's got money. You've got Tyler's settlement. Paying for flights wouldn't be a problem."

Leia remained glued to her plate, avoiding Sarah's intense stare. "He brought up long-distance, too," she mumbled, piercing the chocolate ganache repeatedly with her fork.

"Well, then, why not?"

Leia glared and shot back, "Sarah, you of all people, should know *why*! Tyler's road trips? The away games on Thanksgiving and New Year's Eve? Being alone when I got good news or had a shit day…I spent so much time waiting—waiting for him to get off the ice, to call me back, to come home. Days at a time without a word. And then, the headaches and nausea came, like my body *knew* every single time he cheated." She shook her head. "Separation doesn't make the heart grow fonder, Saz. It makes it wander, shattering promises and trust in its wake. Even now, thinking about all the women Tyler slept with…" Her teeth clenched. "So *please*, don't fight me on the long-distance thing. It's not exciting or romantic. It's torture, and I'll never do it again—with anyone!

"When December 1st rolls around, I'm heading home to finish my collection. And before you butt in—no, I can't do it here. Two of my dresses need vegan leather, which I'm sourcing from a company in upstate New York. I can't assume their practices are sustainable and eco-friendly. I have to actually *go* there, see for myself. And I'll be styling Shantelle, too. The film studio just extended my contract."

"For how long?"

"Through award season and into spring. There's nomination talk for *Lost for Breath*, so they want me on retainer. Where Shantelle goes, I go."

"Well, that's exciting. Frill-Seekers taking Hollywood by storm, eh?" Sarah played with her tea strainer, pausing long enough for Leia's fork to slice through her tart three times, the decimated pieces left on her plate. "But don't you want someone special to share those good times with?"

"I don't like to share, remember?"

"But if Tarquin *was* in love with you, he probably still is."

Saz is like a dog on a bone. "I doubt it." Leia did a double take. "And don't you dare ask him!"

320

"We're meeting next week—"

"Ask him and I'm leaving." Leia's jaw tensed as she dropped her fork and locked eyes with her sister. "I'm serious, Sarah. I'll fly back to New York so fast you'll feel my breeze."

"Okay. *Fine*." Sarah huffed. "I was just trying to help."

"You don't help. You steamroll!" Leia scowled, frustrated their afternoon of fun was souring more and more by the second.

Sarah swallowed the insult and licked her lips like she was buying time, carefully considering what to say next. "I'm sorry you feel that way." She fussed with her napkin, refolding it in her lap. "You know, I'd do anything for you, Ley. I love you to bits. Always have, always will."

Her words wrapped around Leia like a comforting hug. *What is it about sisters that gets under your skin one moment then tugs your heartstrings seconds later?* Leia's face softened. "I love you, too."

"I only push because I want you to be happy, fulfilled."

"I am, Saz. I *love* what I'm doing."

"I'm not talking about Frill-Seekers." Sarah looked up from her lap. "I'm talking cuddles on the sofa after a long day. Flowers 'just because'. Mornings spent in bed talking. All the amazing things love and intimacy bring in moments shared with someone who adores and respects you. And I don't have to steal Shantelle's tarot cards or read your journal to know you believe that, too."

A knot grew in Leia's throat, the aftershocks of Tyler's philandering ways still rippling through her life a year after their tumultuous split. "Sarah—"

"Every day, you take damaged fabrics and lovingly turn them into beautiful dresses. You'd never throw away a torn piece of lace or frayed silk—so why are you doing that with your heart? Yeah, I know it's been shattered into a million pieces, but that doesn't mean you sweep it up and chuck it in a dumpster." She nudged her glasses up her nose. "If anyone deserves a second chance at love, it's you,

Ley. That's *all* I'm trying to say. And if you feel like I steamroll you, well, so be it." With a sniff, Sarah broke eye contact and hung back in her chair, her tea cup hovering by her lips. She stared vacantly out the window as the pianist's version of "This Guy's in Love with You" filled the airy salon.

Restlessness tussled in Leia's stomach. *I know she only wants what's best for me. With Mom gone, I should be listening to her. I need her. We need each other. And my hesitance to share how I really feel isn't honoring our sisterly pact or Mom.* She chewed the inside of her cheek. *Sarah deserves the truth...and I'm tired of running from it.* Leia's fingers flipped the charm on her bracelet over...and over. "So, your question..." She cleared her throat. "The answer is yes."

Sarah blinked back into the conversation. "Yes *what*?"

"Yes, I regret walking away from Tarquin."

Lips parting, her sister lowered her teacup and let out a mournful sigh.

Leia swallowed. "I met up with him to put things straight and say goodbye, but seeing him again...my *god*, Saz. All I wanted to do was kiss him, say yes to everything he suggested, and drag him back to mine."

"So, why didn't you? You're allowed to change your mind, you know!"

"I had to know why he ghosted me. My stupid anxious brain wouldn't let it go. But before I could even mention it, Tarquin said he loved me." Her eyes smiled. "I was SO surprised—on cloud fucking nine! I wanted to scream at the top of my lungs, HE LOVES ME! And I came *so close* to saying 'I love you' back." Leia's face fell. "But then the gravity of it hit me. What if we started something, turned our lives upside down for each other, and months later, it all fell apart?" A sobbed lodged in her throat. "Saz, I don't know if my heart could take it again."

"But Ley, Tarquin's NOT Tyler."

"I know, but don't you see? Tarquin's kind and unselfish, loving—I have so much more to lose." Leia sighed. "And he showed me a different side that day. He was *vulnerable* and shared stuff he's never told me before." She met her sister's eyes. "He has depression, Saz."

"Really?" Sarah's voice jumped. "You'd *never* know."

"He's struggled with it on and off for years but didn't tell anyone until recently. That's partly why he wasn't in touch. He had a depressive episode and couldn't climb out."

Sarah tsked. "Toxic masculinity has so much to answer for. Remember what Mom told us? What she went through with Dad? It took him forever to go see a therapist."

"And that's the thing." Leia nodded. "I *know* it can be difficult for guys. Fuck, most of them won't ask for directions, let alone mental health help. But I get it! I understand the stigma better than most. I've *lived* with it. I felt awful, hearing how Tarquin dealt on his own. He said he planned to get in touch when he felt better, but I can't lie…I wish he'd told me earlier instead of ghosting me for seven months."

"Yeah, but sharing secrets is frightening."

"Tell me about it. I'm the queen of secrets," said Leia.

"Well, then you know how hard it is to share them with the people you love the most." Sarah paused and gave her sister an empathetic smile.

Yeah, there is that. There's still so much I haven't told him. Leia blew out her cheeks. "All these intense feelings, his, *mine*— they scare the hell out of me. They make me doubt everything. What if he was just telling me what I wanted to hear? He's done it before, swearing up and down he was fine with a casual fling when he actually wanted more."

"I think he's learned his lesson, Ley. At least he was completely straight with you about his demons, about his feelings for you."

"Well, I went the other way and lied through my teeth. Instead of accepting his apology and having hot makeup sex, I did what I always do—looked for an emergency exit, this time an emotional one. I picked a fight and lied about my feelings. Then, I stormed off like he didn't matter. But that's just it...he *does* matter."

Sarah leaned forward. "Well, *tell* him, then. Text him."

"I can't. I made it perfectly clear there was no 'us'. I *played a blinder*. Isn't that the saying over here?"

"So you were convincing—so what! You can take it back, you know. Nothing is set in stone."

"And you think he'll forgive me? After tossing his 'I love you' away like trash and blocking him on Instagram?" Leia's heart panged. "Even if he did, it doesn't fix the fact that I'm tied to New York and Tarquin runs a London-based business. Sarah, I meant everything I said about long-distance relationships. I couldn't deal with Tyler coming and going during the hockey season, but at least he had summers off. Tarquin works year-round in the UK. We'd be separated continually with no end date in sight. Just being together when one of us can spare a few days here and there..."

"But isn't he worth it, though?"

A familiar ache prickled the back of her nose. "I've just stopped crying. Please don't make me start again."

Sarah reached across the table and took her sister's hand. "Oh, Leia. You deserve to be happy and to find someone who loves you more than life itself. I want you to have what Mom had with Dad."

Me too. Leia's eyes began to sting. *But I wish I didn't.*

TWENTY-FOUR

TARQUIN

One week later

"Jesus CHRIST!" Lashes clenched, tears dampening his cheeks, Tarquin trembled and expelled a jagged, boozy breath. *God, just put me out of my misery...*

His bleary eyes peeled open. Two surgical masks—blue and blurry—hovered overhead.

"Okay, Mr. Balfour, we're done," said a calm voice behind one of the masks. "You did great!"

Don't feel great. Piercing aftershocks radiated from his right elbow, fueling the storm of nausea bubbling in his belly. *Bleurgh. Make it stop.* His left hand clambered toward his moustache and the two plastic prongs blowing oxygen up his nose.

"You have to keep that on." The other mask gently returned Tarquin's hand to his blue-green hospital gown and its hangover-unfriendly print of swirly dots. "Don't worry, the oxygen is just a precaution."

"Ohh..." His eyelids felt heavy.

"The pain medication will make you drowsy. Try to relax, okay?" She smiled kindly and vanished...somewhere.

Relax? You almost ripped my arm off. His glassy grimace swam haphazardly over the IV line tethered to the back of his left hand, then it swept up the plastic tubing to a metal pole and two semi-deflated bags of liquid hanging like withering fruit. *Blimey. Room's spinning.* Cradling his swollen right elbow, he slumped onto his left side and gently rocked, his desperate sways for comfort wrenching a high-pitched squeak from the undercarriage of the A&E bed.

Where are my glasses? "Hello? Could someone...hey?" His plea barely passed his lips as a chilly draft snuck up his backless gown. He shivered, receding into the murky fog of painkillers, his world warped like a reflection in a funhouse mirror. "Hey..." he mumbled again, fading to black.

"Hey, yourself!"

Huh?! Tarquin's eyes popped open. Beyond the bed's railing, he clocked a blurry visitor in a dress peering around his privacy curtain. *Who's she? Not a doctor.* Her facial features were dreamily out of focus, but one trait was unmistakable.

Long...red...hair.

"Talk about a sight for sore eyes," her playful voice teased.

American or...Canadian! Butterflies soared in his queasy stomach. *Leia!*

Fighting to focus, Tarquin blinked hard and lurched upward, craving a hug, a kiss—*her*. "You're here!" A woozy, pained smile twisted his mouth. "Oh, Leia..."

Her giggle answered back. "*Sure*! I can be her—"

The rumble of an approaching gurney cut her flirt short. Two hospital aides swept past and parked their groggy cargo, a babbling adult male, into the empty examination bay next door.

"Oh, babe! You're back early." With a sheepish smile, the woman ran a hand through her red locks and disappeared behind the neighboring curtain.

Oh... Tarquin's swollen elbow throbbed, halting his breath and decimating his hope. *Seeing things...*

His stare surrendered, retreating to his denim jacket, torn and dirty, discarded on a nearby chair along with his white dress shirt, broken eyeglasses, and cracked phone. Two empty vomit bags left by a nurse lay on top of his hospital blanket just in case. He licked his lips, a low groan burning his throat. *Where is Leia? Why won't she ring?*

"Tarq?" Harry's face crept around the curtain, his eyes widening with concern. "Holy—"

"Fuck!" Lucy blurted from behind her boyfriend, her gape bouncing from the scrapes on Tarquin's face to his half-on, half-off hospital gown pulled down so his swollen elbow wouldn't be constricted. "You look tragic!"

"Looo-seee!" Tarquin smiled woozily. "Hazza!"

"We heard you in the waiting room, you goof." Lucy edged closer, eyeballing the red and purple bruises circling his arm. "Fuuck." She squirmed in her winter coat. "That must've hurt. Is it broken?"

Tarquin gave a half-lidded sigh.

Harry offered a small bag of green grapes, a British tradition when visiting loved ones in hospital. "I thought you might be peckish."

"*Maaate!*" Tarquin hugged the fruit against his chest with his good arm. "Leia loved—she always put these...try it, she said..."

Lucy flinched. "O-kay then! I don't even want to know what *that* kink is."

"Er, don't start! The grapes were meant as a joke," Harry whispered, hiding a chuckle in the collar of his coat. "Tarq *hates* them— well, he used to." Ducking his head, he made a play for his best friend's attention as Lucy leaned over the bed's railing. "Balfy, what happened?"

"I miss her, Haz."

"Yeah, we know, mate. You've talked of nothing else since New York. What were you up to tonight?"

Gazing lovingly at the grapes, Tarquin huffed. "Missing *her*!" He punctuated his declaration with a scrunched face and a frustrated exhale reminiscent of a toddler mid temper tantrum. "What don't you get, man?!"

Lucy recoiled, stepping back from the bedside. "Fuck! Well, *that* boozy vomit breath won't bring her back! Talk about rank." She flapped her hands in front of her face, eyeing the empty sick bags. "If he pukes in front of me, I'm outta here."

Harry ignored his girlfriend's dramatics. "A&E called just as we were leaving Leicester Square. Lucy dragged me to see"—he deferred to his girlfriend—"what was it called? *Lost for Words*."

"Breath!" Lucy corrected. "*Lost for Breath*—just like me right now. Ugh."

"It was good, but I could've done without seeing that French bloke's bare arse."

"You're just envious," said Lucy, swooning. "He's scorching! I'm like '*Ooh la la!*' every time I spot his advert on my bus. You can strip for me *any time*, Bastien!"

Bast...? Tarquin's brows pinched slowly like he was on a three-second delay. *Yeah. The photo...the Brooklyn one in* the Mail. *That's why Leia isn't—she's with HIM! Bloody actor! All over the buses—all over HER!*

"Bastard!" he snarled, his swaying focus surrendering to the ceiling.

Harry rolled his eyes. "*Okay*, fine. I'm a bastard." He leaned in-to Lucy, watching Tarquin mutter to himself. "He's *so* out of it."

"He's legit angry, more like," said Lucy.

"Why?"

She tutted. "Like you have to ask!"

Oh, shut it, you two! Tarquin's weary eyes flickered shut, the sleepy nothingness of the pain medication more desirable than his friends' bickering.

"So I told him a little white lie? It was for his own good and you know it." Harry lowered his voice. "If I hadn't told him Leia was seeing someone, he would've interrogated Sarah—and that's not moving on, Lucy!" He glanced down as his friend. "I'm just thankful it worked."

Lucy crossed her arms. "Yeah, Haribo, your porky worked a *treat*. Dude gets rat-arsed, topples over in the street, and lands in A&E, all purple and puffy." She smirked as Tarquin stirred. "Oh…he's waking up again."

Harry raked an exasperated hand through his blond hair and frowned, studying his mess of a friend stretched out on the bed. Tarquin's expensive blue trousers were torn at the knee and mottled with wet filth. "Balfy, I thought you had a date tonight with that woman you met shopping. Did she leg it?"

Tarquin grunted.

"I guess that's a yes, then," said Harry.

No, it's not. I never even called her. So there!

"So, what happened?"

"I was at Vin'ger…" Tarquin dipped his chin and blinked wearily at the bag of grapes, his pout relinquishing little information. "Drinksss…"

"No!" Lucy chuckled, her brow scrunching sardonically.

Harry leaned on the bed's rail. "Vinegar Yard?" The cheap and cheerful al fresco food and drink venue tucked behind London Bridge Station was a short walk from Tarquin's office in the Shard and his home. "And then what? The Southbank Centre? The nurse said that's where the ambulance picked you up."

Lucy bumped Harry with her elbow, her eyes dropping to the floor and a banged-up skateboard resting wheels-up beside Tarquin's unlaced dress shoes. "Check it. He *was* at the Southbank Centre—the undercroft."

"Oh, you twat!" Harry's face pinched. "Shit-faced noseslides and grinds? Bloody hell! How many pints *did* you have?"

Six? Eight? Don't know. Enough so I felt nice for a little bit. Tarquin scratched his moustache and shrugged, the slight shift firing a blistering bolt of nerve-splitting pain down his arm. *Fucking hell!* He clenched his teeth. "Bollocks!" As he writhed in agony, the grapes slipped through the bed's railing. "I dunno!" he screeched, his chest rising and falling, chasing shallow breaths. "Stop hassling me!" Trembling, he curled into a ball and rocked, each shift accompanied by a mournful whimper.

Lucy stooped. "What a fucking train wreck," she mumbled under her breath, snatching the bag of fruit from the floor.

SCWISSSH! The privacy curtain's hooks whisked along their metal track courtesy of a middle-aged woman wearing baby blue scrubs and a stethoscope around her neck. Her brown eyes flew over her clipboard, ricocheting between Harry and Tarquin before tumbling to Lucy returning from her grape rescue. "Hi, I'm Doctor Fernley. I'm overseeing Mr. Balfour's care tonight. Are you family?"

"We're friends. I'm Harry, Tarquin's 'in case of emergency' person." He smiled. "Hope it's okay, us being here. The nurse said we—"

"Oh, it's fine! He'll relax with you here." She pressed her lips together. "Poor lad, he's been through the wars. He's thrown up twice and keeps asking for Layla—"

"No, nooooo," Tarquin interrupted with an accusing finger, staring at the doctor's graying ponytail. "It's *Leia*. Like *Star Wars*...but hotter."

The doctor's dubious nod pivoted back to Harry. "Ohh, I *see*." She fought back a chuckle.

"No, Leia's real, but they're not an item anymore." Harry set her straight. "He's having trouble moving on, hence tonight's disaster."

"Ah, well, lucky for Mr. Balfour, the Force is with him tonight." Her bad *Star Wars* joke drew a discreet sneer from Lucy. "He's had pain medication and intravenous fluids. They should take the edge off soon." She softly smiled at her dazed patient. "How are you feeling?"

"Not great...sore." He sniveled.

"I'm not surprised, my dear. Resetting a dislocated elbow *hurts*."

Lucy and Harry exchanged squeamish looks. "I thought he broke it," said Lucy, covering her mouth with her hand, grossed out. "So that's why he screamed the place down."

"Yeah, it happens, even with light sedation." Dr. Fernley flipped the papers on her clipboard. "But I have good news, Mr. Balfour. The x-rays and scans show nothing is broken."

"Bollocks," he mumbled. *It IS broken.* Tarquin closed his eyes, the doctor's wordy instructions swirling and fading, sucked into his own tornado of thoughts. *My heart...it's broken so bad and no one cares. It hurts more than my arm...more than anything. But will they fix that? NOPE! I begged—help me! Please! Tell me what to do! I'll do it all. I don't mind what it is. I just want Leia back—* A shaking sensation stirred him out of his drug-fueled Leia spiral. *Er...*

"Tarquin!"

"Wha—?!" His eyes flickered open.

"Balfour, you're the worst!" Harry shook his head. "Did you hear *anything* the doctor said?"

"Erm..."

"She's putting your arm in a backslab, yeah? It's like a cast but doesn't go all the way around."

A cast? His stomach rolled. "I-I can't have a cast!" His panicked eyes bounced from Harry to Lucy.

"Chill, Tarq. It's only for a week or so," said Lucy. "And it's open on one side—in case your arm swells."

Nooo. Can't. He gulped, struggling to push himself up. "I'm going climbing...building a croft on Orkney..." Exhausted, he shakily gave up, flopping back down on the stiff pillows.

"When's he headed up there?" asked Lucy.

"Next month. His niece is being baptized."

Several blinks dropped Tarquin into a deep, closed-eye nod, his chin on a collision course with his chest.

"Pfft!" Lucy bit her cheek. "Wait till he realizes he's out of commission for a few weeks. He's gonna *love* that!"

"We'll go over the doctor's instructions when he's sober," said Harry. "At least tomorrow's Sunday—I can stay with him, make sure he behaves." He patted his best friend's knee. "Tarq? Wake up, mate."

His chin flew upward, but his eyes remained shut. "Leia?! She here?"

Harry's shoe subtly slid into Lucy's boot. She twisted her lips in silent protest. "No, Tarq. Leia lives in New York, remember?"

"I TEXTED her, though." Battling through his fog, he blinked heavily.

"You what?!" Harry scoffed as Lucy snatched Tarquin's phone from the chair.

"I was lonely, missing her...I hoped she'd come." Tarquin deflated into a breathy, mumbled curse, his face crumpling. "Harry, why won't she come? I *need* her."

"Balfy, c'mon, we've talked about this. I *know* it sucks, but you've got to move on." Harry offered an encouraging smile. "Why don't you call that matchmaker again?"

"No! All I want is Leia. *Only* Leia. I love *Leia*."

A chuckle burst from Lucy's glossy lips. "What a wanker!" Her fingers spread over a crack running diagonally across Tarquin's phone screen. "He didn't text Leia—he texted Leyland Carpets by mistake! See?" She held up the phone, the text on his home screen. "They replied, too!" She read aloud.

Leyland Carpets: You miss us? You want us back? Ah, we love you, too, Mr. Balfour! We can't come now, unfortunately, but will Monday suffice? Looking forward to supplying carpets for your pub restoration. Cheers!

"God, he's a right old mess." Harry cringed. "He needs to buck up and forget about her." He leaned in. "Mate, I've been meaning to ask. The other night—at the pub quiz—what was Simon's answer?"

"For what?" Lucy slipped Tarquin's phone into her coat pocket. "The Madonna question?"

Harry gently shook his head and pressed on. "I heard you, Tarq, asking Simon if he'd spoken with Leia."

"Can't…can't I have a private convo?" Tarquin muttered with a sneer.

"Not during the pub quiz, you can't, no," said Harry.

Lucy snickered. "Freddie was SO pissed Si got that *Doctor Who* question wrong."

Tarquin let out a sleepy yawn.

"Balfy!" Harry softly gripped Tarquin's knee, rousing him. "Why'd you go to the Southbank Centre? Were you meeting someone tonight?"

If you overheard me and Si, why are you asking? Tarquin embraced the bag of grapes, a glimmer of clarity breaking through the cloud of alcohol and painkillers.

Lucy tugged on the ends of her wool scarf. "I guess we'll taxi to his and sleep over?"

Fuck. I don't want them sleeping over! Tarquin blinked back into the conversation. "Simon told me nothing. Doesn't matter. I know she's with *him*."

"Who's him?" Lucy's brow furrowed as Tarquin babbled.

Harry shrugged. "No clue." He spoke behind his hand. "I made the guy up, remember?"

Lucy whispered in her boyfriend's ear. "I feel awful. Can't I tell him she's in London?"

"You *know* you can't," he whispered back.

"The trees at the Southbank Centre." Tarquin fought through a hiccup. "I went t'night...to feel close to her. Leia loves trees."

Harry wearily sighed. "What's he on about?"

Lucy's eyes lit up. "Oh, *that's* why he was there! The Hayward Gallery. You know, inside the Southbank Centre? They have a *tree* exhibit—installations, paintings. Cristina in our office raved about it the other day."

Tarquin huffed. "Yeah, but it was closed." *Like Leia's heart.* "So, I thought maybe skateboarding would cheer me up...I paid some kid five hundred quid for his board." His bloodshot eyes searched his best friend's face. "Harry, it's never gonna happen for me"—he hiccupped—"is it?"

"With Leia? I'm sorry, mate, but I don't think so."

He's not sorry. Tarquin sagged in his blousy hospital gown. "Knew it. I'm gonna end up alone. Me and Chuzza...alone."

TWENTY-FIVE

LEIA

Four and a half weeks later, Thursday, November 14, 2019

"So, what do you think?" Sarah rested her arms on her chair's side guards, giving Leia a clear view of the blue silk dress. Its slim cut design complemented her curves and the pencil skirt meant Sarah wouldn't have to worry about excess fabric catching in the wheels of her chair.

"Oh, Saz." Leia covered her mouth with her palm. "You look absolutely gorgeous!"

"See? Told you," said Jordan, admiring his girlfriend. He bent down and kissed Sarah softly on the temple, sparing her makeup. "I have to call work quickly, but I'll be back to help with your second change. Good luck, ladies!" With a thumbs-up, he straightened his tie and ducked through the changing room curtain.

Sarah plucked her phone from her purse. "But are you sure you want *me* to wear this? Honestly, you won't hurt my feelings if you'd rather Shantelle—"

"Shan's got her own dresses. I want *you* to wear this one." Leia crouched in her simple white wrap dress and gave Sarah's hem a little tug, straightening it. "It's one of my favorites."

"Well, shouldn't the star wear it, then?"

I know what she's doing. Leia smoothed the skirt and stood up. "And who do you think you are? If anyone's a star, it's you, Saz! You make this dress sing."

"It's just...I don't want you feeling like you *have* to include me." Sarah pursed her lips. "The fashion world isn't the most inclusive. I'd hate for some snobby, ableist editor to bash your collection because, well, you *know*…"

"If that happens, they can shove their ignorance and suck a bag of dicks! Frill-Seekers is about resilience, starting over, being bold, and *no one* personifies those qualities like you do, Sarah. *You're* the reason I'm a designer in the first place! There is no way in hell I'd do this without you. You're my bestie…and always will be."

Sarah blinked quickly. "Oh, don't make me cry—" Her phone buzzed and glowed in her hand. "Wha…?!" Intrigued, she dove in.

Who is that? Better not be Tarquin—shouldn't be. She hasn't mentioned him since Fortnum's. "Saz, be quick, okay? I need you to line up with the other models." Leia pulled back the curtain an inch and glanced backstage. "Show is supposed to start in ten minutes."

Sarah burst out laughing. "There IS a god!"

What's she up to? Narrowing her eyes, Leia let go of the drape.

"I'm lovin' this!" her sister jeered. "It's from Dad." Fighting back more giggles, she gleefully shared his news.

Dad: I know Leia's got her hands full, so pass along when she's free. Tyler was traded to Arizona.

Leia jolted. "What?! He's leaving New York? But he has a no-trade clause."

"Something must've voided it," said Sarah, her expression full of delight. "Or he waived it for some reason."

"Yeah, I can think of several." Leia twisted her lips and picked up the tote holding her sewing kit. "What else does Dad say?"

Sarah read aloud.

Dad: It hasn't hit the news yet. My buddy in the GM's office swore me to secrecy, so keep this under your hat for now, okay? Love you both. Good luck tonight!

"I can't believe it." Leia let out a happy gasp, relishing the news.

"No more running into him at events, no more gossip!" Sarah stuffed her phone in her bag and hid it under her coat. "You're free of that twatwaffle for good, Ley!"

She nodded and swished open the changing room curtain for her sister. "I can't think of a better 'welcome home' present!"

Leia followed Sarah through the impromptu backstage area of temporary hair and makeup stations and curtained-off dressing rooms. Colorful dresses hung from three rolling clothing racks, each one divided by large tags bearing a single name: Alex, Lucy, Naomi, Joan, and Freddie—all Simon's friends with the exception of Sarah, Shantelle, Riley, and her British boyfriend Ben. They all stood in a casual semi-circle, chatting and fawning over their outfits, their exuberance competing with the upbeat playlist of pop hits spilling through the doorway of the adjacent space. Simon flitted from model to model, doing a final check on seams, hems, and zippers, making sure everyone was runway ready while Spencer lingered by the racks, ready to help anyone needing assistance changing into their second look.

They're all runway-ready...in my dresses! Leia caught her breath. *I have so much to be thankful for.* She paused beside the closest rack and a large piece of Bristol board affixed to the end, its surface papered with a series of numbered photos. The pictures, Leia's 'run of show', showcased each outfit and were organized in the order they would appear on the runway. Poring over it quickly, she looked over her shoulder, studying her real-life models. All, spare Shantelle, were accounted for and waiting in the correct sequence. *Shan's missing again? Where did she wander off to this time?* Leia dropped her tote of supplies on the floor and craned her neck, searching for the wayward star.

"Leia!" Alex waved. Sandwiched between Lucy and Sarah, she looked down at Simon removing lint with double-sided tape from the skirt of her floor-skimming purple dress. "I've been thinking…" Alex met Leia's eyes. "I'd hate to wear this once and then never again. If Mark gets nominated for a BAFTA—"

"He will!" smirked Lucy, running her hands down her pink party dress.

"I'd love to wear this to the ceremony," said Alex. "It's perfect!"

A British red carpet! "Sure!" Leia grinned. "I'll loan it to you."

"Can I *buy* it?"

Tonight's first sale! Leia grabbed her reusable water bottle. "Absolutely. Yeah, that would be amazing!" A glimpse of turquoise caught her eye. *Ah, thank god. There she is!*

"Sorry, Scotty!" Wearing a coy smile, Shantelle skipped into place between Freddie and Naomi, towing a smug-looking Bastien behind her.

"Fuck me!" Wide-eyed, Lucy swore under her breath. She wasn't the only one.

Holy shit! Leia's stare ping-ponged between the actors. *They're together?!*

"Lost track of the time!" Shantelle giggled and Bastien relinquished her hand, brazenly wiping her pink lipstick from his mouth.

Without a heartfelt *Je suis désolé* or *Bonne chance*, he tossed back his crown of curls and strolled through the doorway where fashion editors, buyers, and influential bloggers held court, anticipating Frill-Seekers' runway debut. The backstage monitor popped on, the live feed showing Bastien taking his front-row seat. Several squeals of delight erupted around him.

Leia rescued her jaw from the floor as Simon and the makeup artist, lip brush and pot of gloss in her hand, swooped to Shantelle.

"By the way, Ley…" Shantelle nudged up her glasses as Simon

surveyed her gown for creases. "We have to *talk* later!" She parted her lips, allowing the makeup artist to work her magic.

Uh, I think the cat's out of the bag, there, Shan! Leia felt a soft squeeze of her forearm, and Alex's petite grandmother from Manchester smiled up at her.

Eighty years young, Joan Sinclair had kept everyone laughing during the week's fittings and rehearsals with her ribald tales of backstage hijinks as a dancer/actress in the late fifties. "Thanks again for including me, love." Her rosy grin, silvery pixie cut, and spritely presence easily defied her age by a decade. "I'm usually at the football or on my motorbike, so it's a rare treat, wearing such fancy clothes! In Manchester red, too!"

A motorbike at eighty? God, if I could be half as ballsy now! "You look beautiful, Joan."

Alex leaned in. "Joan practically lives in her David Beckham Manchester United top."

Love how Alex calls her gran by her name. Leia nodded. "Hey, coming from a pro sports family, I completely understand!"

Joan beamed. "That's my girl! Let us know if you get up north. We'll go see a game at Old Trafford!"

The makeup artist and Simon pulled away from Shantelle simultaneously like a Formula One pit crew. "Perfection." He gave Leia a pleased nod.

A headset-wearing member of the venue's staff arrived at Leia's side, clipboard in hand. "We're ready to go. Runway is clear, guests are seated, and cameras are recording. The feed is live on your backstage monitor. When you're ready, just say the word, and we'll lower the lights, turn on the spots, and start your music."

There's no turning back now! Nerves swirled inside Leia's stomach. *Thirteen minutes will be over in a blink. You've got this! Just enjoy it!* "Thank you!" She squeezed her water bottle and exhaled a pent-up breath.

Simon raised a brow. "You okay? Need more time?"

"No, I'm good!" She grinned and studied the eager faces smiling back. "Oh, wow! You all look so incredible!"

"We *feel* incredible," said Freddie, swishing the skirt of his dress. "I've always wanted to be a model, and Si's always dreamed of marrying one!" He laughed as Simon shook his head. "How are you holding up, darling?"

"I'm buzzing on pure adrenaline!" said Leia. "This doesn't feel real."

Riley grinned, her green eyes shining beneath her strawberry blonde bangs. "It's gonna feel real super quick, Ley." She laughed before continuing in her Staten Island twang. "It's packed in there, and they're all here for *you*!"

Tall and slim with an adorable mischievous air, Ben fussed with his unruly dark hair and nodded in agreement. His chiseled cheekbones and sparkly blue eyes were born for the runway—and his Frill-Seekers cerulean shirtdress. "Riles is right. I overheard two ladies raving about your Met Gala gown. I'm no fashion expert, but I reckon you're gonna kick ass tonight."

They're so adorable together. I'm glad we're in touch again. "Well, if I do, it's down to all of you, looking so freakin' gorgeous in my clothes." Gratitude throbbed in Leia's chest. *Time to rally the troops.* "Okay, before we start, I just want to THANK YOU again for starring in my first-ever fashion show. It's so fitting that you're my models. Frill-Seekers is for people just like you—people on the go, on the job, and on the town, people who live with integrity and agency, who crave thrills and adventure but always remember where they came from and never take themselves too seriously. It's a label celebrating uniqueness, second chances, and sustainability, and I can't wait for the experts on the other side of that wall to discover *us*." She smiled, a lump wedged in her throat. "So, be bold and flirty out there, sing along to the songs, and dance your asses off, but most of all, be yourselves…*be Frill-Seekers!*"

A collective cheer and applause erupted from the group as Leia nodded to the event coordinator, who relayed instructions through his headset's microphone.

"Let's treat these folks to the unexpected!" Simon grinned, squeezing Leia's shoulder.

She took her place just inside the door, set down her water bottle, and waved her first model forward. "Lucy?" Alex, Sarah, and the rest of the models all inched ahead in line, a mix of anticipation and nerves on their smiling faces. Each model would wear two outfits and have two trips down the runway. The only exception was Shantelle, who would make a third appearance, closing the Frill-Seekers show by Leia's side.

The venue's lighting softened and its music segued into Leia's fashion show playlist, her three songs chosen for their uplifting vibes and lyrical relevance to Frill-Seekers' mission—to show how beauty and enduring love can be found in the broken and forgotten.

The surging instrumental opening of "Never Can Say Goodbye" by Sheena Easton blasted from the speakers, hushing the guests in the next room. Leia blew out a breath and swayed along to the melody, waiting…waiting until just before the lyrics began. With an encouraging nod, she gave Lucy the green light and off she went, strutting her stuff with a cheeky wiggle and a whole lot of sass.

The last notes of Diana Ross's "More Today Than Yesterday" blended seamlessly into Dua Lipa's "Love Again" as Leia grinned at the monitor's live feed from the runway. Shantelle was sashaying back, finishing her second of three appearances while a beaming Sarah rolled toward the end of the runway, where a cluster of photographers snapped away on a riser. The two rows of seats hugging the sides were full of rapt fashion experts, and the standing area behind remained packed with many a phone aloft, filming the festivities.

Two songs down, one to go...no clothing malfunctions, no runway collisions. Please let us have a clean finish. Leia looked up, catching Shantelle walking through the doorjamb. "Okay, Alex, you're up."

She flashed a grin and danced back onto the runway for her second appearance. Joan, Freddie, Naomi, Ben, and Riley moved forward, awaiting their respective turns. Lucy stood with Jordan, Simon, and Spencer, ready for the presentation's conclusion when all the models would join Leia for her final bow.

Shantelle lingered by Leia's side, fiddling with the ruffled sleeve of her dress.

"You okay?" Leia bobbed her head to the music, her eyes glued to the live feed. "If you need help with your zipper, Spencer can do it, or Simon. Your final dress is on the rack."

"Scotty, there's something you should you know."

Leia spied Sarah about to return backstage. "Is it about your dress? If not, can it wait?"

"Not really." Shantelle stepped closer, giving Sarah space to sweep past in her chair.

"Joan?" Leia beckoned her forward and Freddie took her spot next in line. He casually swayed back and forth, shamelessly eavesdropping.

Shantelle shot him an unamused stare. "Scotty"—she leaned in conspiratorially—"me and Bastien...we're sleeping together."

Leia snorted. "Duh, yeah! I figured as much. He is SO into you."

Shantelle straightened up, ignoring Freddie's smirk. "Yeah, we're moving in together."

"What?!" Leia blurted, her eyes widening, straying from Alex's final walk. *She hated him a month ago!*

"I'm giving up my apartment and moving into his—in Paris."

What the fuck?! Leia's jaw dropped in shock. "Paris?! Shan, but are you...what will—" She stammered, her tongue unable to keep up with the anxious thoughts spiraling through her mind.

I can't believe this! My closest friend MOVING—across the world!

She just bought her new townhouse in Tribeca–what'll happen to that?

Her breath hitched.

What'll happen to our contract?! SHIT!

Reality sinking in fast, Leia's heart raced. She blinked wearily at the live feed and caught Joan dancing and playing up to the audience, reliving her glory days on stage. The fashionable crowd ate it up.

LEIA, FOCUS! Frill-Seekers first, Shantelle's drama later. You're almost done. Keep momentum going, stay in control. She fought the tightness in her chest with several deep breaths and a quick sip of water. "Shan, you go change. Freddie?" She patted his arm. "Once Alex is back, you go."

"No worries, darling!" Sweeping his floppy brown hair from his eyes, Freddie playfully practiced poses in his sparkly blue gown made from two 1970s disco-era dresses.

Biting her lip, Shantelle jumped in again. "I know this changes our contract a smidge—"

"No, Shan. It changes it *a lot*!" Keeping her volume low, Leia's whole body tensed. "Three thousand miles is NOT a smidge!"

"But it won't cost you a penny!" Shantelle clasped her hands together. "I'll pay for your flights between New York and Paris."

"And what about my time, eh?" Leia flashed a tight grin as Alex squeezed past and Freddie bounded onto the runway, his exuberance part Tigger, part Derek Zoolander. "That comes at a cost, too, you know! For me, not you."

"I'm sorry, Leia. I know this is out of the blue, but this afternoon, my psychic said…"

The psychic? Again? Shit! Fuming, Leia rubbed her furrowed brow. "Shan, I love you, but right now, I *really* need you to change."

"I will, but—"

"Shan, NOW!" Leia ordered through clenched teeth. *For fuck's sake! She's going to screw up the end of my show!*

Shoulders slumping, Shantelle skulked past Naomi, Ben, Sarah, and the others, their shared wide-eyed glances silent but loaded.

Shit. Leia chewed her fingernail. *What am I going to do?*

"Ah, I enjoyed that!" Joan, breathless and beaming, ambled backstage, patting Leia's arm before joining her granddaughter, Alex.

Leia watched the two of them, wrapped lovingly in a hug. *Take it from Joan. Be present. Enjoy this. Business crap can wait.*

"Naomi?" She nodded at the stunning actress.

"Cheers, Leia." The long-legged Franco-Indian beauty licked her lips and strode forward like she was playing the role of a famous supermodel. Ben and Riley would follow, and then Shantelle, who was scheduled to close the festivities by Leia's side.

With seconds to spare, Shantelle appeared in a floor-length crimson gown. She weaved her fingers through Leia's. "Sorry, Scotty. My timing is terrible. I just couldn't keep the news secret from you a *second* longer. Please don't hate me?"

Leia offered a consolatory smile as all her models joined Ben and Riley, reuniting with the runway for one final lap. "Of course I don't. If you're happy, I'm happy *for you*. The rest will sort itself out, somehow."

"Thanks, Ley! Okay, you ready to show London who's boss?"

"With pleasure!" Leia squeezed Shantelle's hand and they claimed the spotlight, side by side, the cheers and applause growing louder with each step. Lucy, Alex, Joan, Sarah, et al. hung back in front of the white backdrop with its Frill-Seekers logo, celebrating together as one proud family.

Reaching the end of the runway, Shantelle beamed and let go of Leia's hand, clapping enthusiastically for the designer along with all the appreciative fashion fans filling The Arches. "They love you, Leia! Just look at 'em!"

They're all still here! A pleased giggle burst from Leia's throat as her bright eyes surfed the crowd, sweeping past cheering strangers, well-dressed fashion bloggers, and a tall, dark-haired stranger whooping up a storm with an unlit cigarette bobbing between his lips. But it was the clean-shaven gent beside him, dimples framing a huge smile and arms filled with a massive bouquet of primroses who stole the show for Leia.

TWENTY-SIX

TARQUIN

"I've told her, you know, Tarq—*countless* times. She's a bloody *natural* on the catwalk!" Tom Chadwick-Smythe waved his lit cigarette with a flourish in front of his loosened tie. "And modeling jobs are a nice little earner between acting gigs. I should know—I've strutted my stuff a few times! But wifey doesn't want to hear it." The one-time roommate of Alex and Harry plowed his free hand through his unkempt brown hair. Rakish with a mischievous glint in his blue-green eyes, Tom's glory days of one-night stands premarriage to Naomi were legendary and life-changing. "She thinks adding 'model' to her CV cheapens her acting cred, but hey, us thesps have to pay the piper somehow."

And his baby mamma. His son must be, what? Three, four by now? I wonder how often he sees him. Tarquin nodded politely, wishing he was stuck with anyone but Tom, who he'd always found a bit exhausting. He cradled the bouquet of primroses in his arms and stared at Tom's gold wedding band as the actor scored another glass of free red wine from a server. *Who'd have thought? Here I am, envious of what Tom has. Well, except for the child support...*

"And really, what's the difference between acting and modeling? You're still on display. You're still being ogled by strangers. Actually, when my new play starts in December, I've got a scene where I'm..."

Fuck, he sounds like Mum, prattling on about show business. Eyes glazing over, Tarquin zoned out, absentmindedly massaging his right elbow. Five weeks post-dislocation, the pain, plaster back-

346

slab, and sling were history, but stiffness and daily rehab were his new normal. He glanced away, his attention wandering the large space teeming with exuberant fashionistas and press waiting for Leia's reappearance. *Where the fuck is Harry? Backstage, maybe? He's in for an earful. So is Lucy. What were they playing at? Not telling me Leia was in London...*

Wrapping up his long-winded ramble, Tom cleared his throat. "Anyway, I knew *you'd* understand, mate!"

What? Tarquin snapped back into the conversation. "Yeah. Of course. Absolutely!" He chuckled, pretending he'd heard every word.

"Actually, speaking of people who don't *listen...*" Tom interrupted his crooked grin with a long, satisfying drag on his cigarette.

Is he having a go at me? Wanker!

Tom puffed a parade of one, two, three smoke rings into the air, to the annoyance of a passing blogger. "I talked to my sister last week."

Okay. I'm done. Tarquin coughed. "Mate, you *know* you can't smoke in here!" Wincing, he batted at the smelly vapors. *Was I this annoying before I kicked the habit?* He looked away and caught Alex's eye. *Lex! SAVE ME!* he signaled through gritted teeth, flashing a glare toward Tom.

Confusion flickering on her face, she squeezed past several glittery drag queens engrossed in a conversation with a magazine editor famous for her orange bob and scathing fashion reviews. "Tarquin! And *Tom*?"

"Miss America! A pleasure as always!" Tom ground his cigarette into the floor with his shoe and did a double take over Alex's shoulder. A frowning Naomi clutched her coat and waved him impatiently toward the exit. "Ah, gotta go! The sitter costs an absolute bomb!" Tossing back his fifth red wine, he smacked Tarquin on the back then fobbed off the empty glass to a befuddled blogger passing by. "Laters!"

Alex snickered as Tarquin held back a laugh. "Well, *that* was awkward. Cheers, Lex."

"You shaved…finally!" Her eyes teased. "Hot date?"

"Hope so." Tarquin smiled back, taking in Alex's black and white wrap dress. "You look pretty. So, how was it, strutting your stuff for the fashionable masses?"

"I loved it!" She squeezed her phone. "I was nervous at first, but once I got out there with Lucy, I was hooked!"

"It looked like you were having a grand old time. Where's Mark? I half-expected to see him shaking his arse up there with you."

"He's working late, rehearsals for a BBC radio play."

"Ah." Tarquin smiled. "Good for Keegan."

Alex glanced at the flowers in his hands. "I didn't know you were coming."

"Yeah, about that…"

"Tarquin, I'm sorry, but I was sworn to secrecy. We all were." She winced. "How'd you find out about the show?"

"Shantelle, of all people."

Alex's eyes widened. "Oh! You know each other?"

"No, but she found my work number online, called me up. Shantelle thought I should know Leia was in London. Nice of her, eh? An actress I've never met cares more about my love life than my dearest friends."

"Oh, Tarq. It's not like that!" Alex bristled, whisking her hand through her blonde bangs. "I *wanted* to tell you. So did Leia's sister."

"Wanted but didn't." He shook his head, forcing a half-smile. "You know, I had a meeting with Sarah a few weeks ago. Was Leia already here?"

Alex grimaced and nodded slowly.

Shit! It's official. Leia despises me. He dragged his hand over his mouth and looked away. "Talk about misreading the room, eh? Leia wants fuck all to do with me." *Not that I blame her.* Bowing his head, he glared at the flowers. "Guess I don't need these any-more." Defeated, he lowered the bouquet. "Where's the nearest bin?"

"Tarquin…" Alex pursed her lips.

"There's another bloke, right? The actor in the front row? Harry said she's seeing someone."

"No. At least, not that I know of." Alex blinked up at him, sympathy in her eyes as she reached out, squeezing his upper arm. "Look, it's not like Leia forced us to sign non-disclosure agreements! All she asked was that we keep quiet about her being here. She was worried if you found out, you'd call, and she wasn't ready for that."

Tarquin's brows lifted. "Wasn't ready? But Leia walked away from *me*."

"Maybe she realized she made a mistake."

What? His breath caught in his chest. "Did she say something?" Tarquin edged closer. "Alex, I *need* to know."

She played with the tiny Vespa charm hanging on a dainty chain around her neck and let out an exasperated huff. "Okay—but you can't tell her I told you!" Alex sized up her immediate vicinity, ensuring Leia wasn't anywhere to be seen. "She asked me a few days back if you were seeing anyone. I said you weren't."

Seriously? She asked that?! His eyes gleamed. "And?"

"And—that was it!" Alex added nonchalantly, like she feared her disclosure created false hope. "Naomi showed up for her fitting and Leia changed the subject."

He exhaled heavily, a frown dragging his lips.

"But for what it's worth, I think she's lovely. You two would be great together."

"Mind telling Leia that?" He smiled wistfully. "If we could be half as happy as you and Mark...I want that more than anything. I want *her* more than anything."

"Then *talk* to her." Her gaze flew through the thick crowd, searching, only to circle back with a grimace. "It might be a challenge tonight with all these rabid fashionistas vying for her attention, but hey—you're a risk-taker, right?"

This feels like the biggest risk of my life. "I don't want to scare her off, though. I did that once and well, here we are."

"But if you never tell her..." She shrugged, glancing down at her lit-up phone. "You *will* lose her."

Tarquin rubbed his stubble-free chin. "Maybe I should just listen and let her talk? Take my cues from her?"

"Maybe." Alex opened a new text from Mark.

The addictive feel-good vibes of "Groove is in the Heart" by Deee-Lite bubbled from the speakers, and a pink-cheeked Freddie claimed a corner of the room for an impromptu dance party. Eyes peeled for Leia, Tarquin swayed along to the euphoric anthem, his determined expression slipping into a confused wince. "Lex"—he slouched into Alex, her thumbs typing away—"what's with Si's dance moves? Look at those elbows—they're lethal! He'll take someone's eye out! I hope Freds has health insurance."

Alex snorted and hit send. "You think that's bad? You should've seen him at Tom and Naomi's wedding!" She looked around at all the happy faces chatting, dancing, enjoying cocktails. "Leia must be thrilled by this turnout. The standing ovation was incredible, all the cheers and applause growing louder all around us."

Tarquin adjusted the flowers in his arms. "Yeah, Leia deserves every second. I'm so proud of her."

"Well, good! You can tell her yourself." Alex's shining eyes shifted to the left.

Leia. Tarquin's pulse rocketed beneath his white shirt as he admired her loose red waves cascading over the shoulders of her champagne-hued dress, sparkly and low-cut, the ultimate present for some lucky guy to unwrap.

Different dress, same beautiful angel.

Alex nodded. "I'm gonna check on Joan." She squeezed his arm gently, slipping away.

Leia's smile... So many times I thought about her. Tarquin waited. *But let her choose—talk to me or turn away.*

Leia closed the distance. "Hi."

"Hi." He smiled softly. *Blimey, you idiot! Give her the flowers.* "Oh! These are for you." He offered the primroses. "Your show...Leia, it was beautiful, but fun and completely unpretentious. And the music told a great story, too. Congratulations! I'm so happy for you!"

"Thanks." She blushed, looking at the colorful blooms. "How'd you—um, I saw you with Naomi's husband. Did you come together?"

"No! I bumped into him here. Let's just say Mr. Chadwick-Smythe and I aren't the closest of friends." He pressed his lips together. "Shantelle rang me—this morning."

Her brows peaked. "Shan did?" Leia paused, her eyes darting past Tarquin.

He followed her stare to a dark corner and Shantelle and Bastien making out, their hunger for one another unmistakable, much to the delight of several attendees with raised phones.

And Tarquin.

Bloody hell! I was COMPLETELY wrong! That Brooklyn photo in The Mail *of him and Leia...one hundred percent fake news! The press outed the wrong girl!*

An ecstatic grin lit up his eyes as he fought back a chuckle. *Get in, Shantelle!* His gaze shot back to Leia, her baby blues narrowing as she shook her head, the plastic wrap on the primroses throwing shards of color under the room's spotlights.

She huffed. "Shan, Shan, Shan…"

Shit. She's angry. "Leia, it's not her fault. *I'm* the one who showed up uninvited and blagged my way in."

She raised a brow. "So, you sweet-talked the door staff?"

"Uh, *yeah.*" Knots of regret tightened in his chest. *Now my so-called confession sounds like a total stalker move. And on the most important night of her career, too. Badly played, Balfour, badly played.* He pawed through his hair and backed away. "I know. I shouldn't be here. Sorry, Leia—"

"Tarquin, you *still* apologize way too much." Hugging her flowers, Leia smiled. "I'm not mad, Han Solo. And don't even think of leaving!" Her eyes slipped to his lips.

"Okay. I'll stay." His shoulders loosened as he played with the ring on his thumb. "It's so great to see you." *Understatement of the century there, mate!*

"You, too. We have to catch up, but…" Leia looked left. Blazing toward them, the orange-haired fashion editor elbowed her way through the party, a self-important air of expectation riding her crocodile smile. Following in her wake was a cluster of wineglass-toting bloggers and buyers keen for their moment with London's newest fashion crush.

They're queuing up for her—as they should! Tarquin glanced back at Leia, her eyes sparkling with anticipation. *She's waited years for this moment. I can't stand in her way. Let her go.*

"Bravo, Leia, bravo!" The editor planted herself by Leia and Tarquin's side and whipped out her notebook and phone, the fashion world equivalent of staking territorial claim with a flag.

Leia softly brushed Tarquin's arm. "I'll text you later, okay?" She gave him an eye-crinkling grin and stepped away.

But will she?

TWENTY-SEVEN

LEIA

The next day

Just look at him. So perfect and gorgeous and here, despite everything.

Leia sipped her water and stared longingly across the café table as Tarquin stirred a spoon in his coffee, his soft smile lost in the milky swirls.

Why did I suggest meeting at Peggy Porschen? Sure, I want some celebratory cake, but I want him more! Her heart tripped, giddy like it was about to take flight, destination unknown.

Glancing up from the oversized mug, Tarquin caught Leia's ogle and his grin ran wild.

God, help me. Desire surged through her like an electrical charge. Her fingers, her lips, everything turned on, humming with want and the need to touch. *Does he realize what that smile does to me? I feel like I'm lit from the inside. He must see it, right?*

Tarquin tapped his spoon on the rim of the cup and rested it on a napkin. "Someone looks fit to burst…I gather last night was a smashing success?"

"It really was! Did you have fun?"

"I did! Had drinks with Si and Harry, chatted with Sarah, and met Riley and Ben. Hey, did you know Riley used to work for Nico in New York?"

"Really? I knew she worked at the BBC for a bit but had no clue who her boss was."

"It was him. Small world, eh?" He scratched his chin. "Yeah, it was a top night all around. How about you?"

She put down her glass. "I had a great time *and* chalked up six meetings next week—including Selfridges! Their director of womenswear and accessories wants to talk on Tuesday."

"Oh, you beauty! Congratulations, Leia!"

"Thanks! He raved about my dresses and suggested stocking them in their Oxford Street location. Their younger clientele want limited-edition pieces and sustainable brands, so Frill-Seekers fits perfectly."

"Frill-Seekers in Selfridges' flagship store. You must be so chuffed!"

"I'm stoked! Nothing is signed yet, but I have a really good feeling about it." *And you...*

"To think Sarah had to talk you into staging a fashion show in London."

"Sister knows best." Leia grinned back at him. *Turns out, my sister knows best about a LOT of things. I should've taken her advice, called you weeks ago.*

She leaned over her triple-layer slice of vanilla cloud cake. A dainty white macaron crowned its meringue buttercream. "So!" She nodded at the large cup in front of him. "How many is that? Wait! Let me guess: your third?"

Her coffee inquiry earned a chuckle. "My first."

"No way!" She laughed nervously, her eyes skimming the window boxes outside blooming with whimsical flowers in hues of periwinkle and flamingo pink, their bright bliss matching the hopefulness brimming in Leia's chest. "What happened this morning? Late start?" *Please don't say a woman was involved. I'm still kicking myself for letting him slip away last night.*

"Nope. Slept like a baby and woke up on the right side of the bed—for a change." He lifted his steaming coffee, giving it a gentle blow. "Shame I was alone, though..."

"Such a shame!" Leia smiled coyly and hesitated, admiring his lips until they met his cup. "I tossed all night. Barely slept." *And it's your fault! I was so excited, seeing you again.*

Her appreciative gaze drifted down his blue tartan tie. His white button-down showed off his broad chest, and its casually rolled-up sleeves exposed several inches of skin. *Tarquin, you tease! You know I have a thing for your forearms! I've missed them, their corded muscles flexing, holding you above me. What I wouldn't do for that delicious view now.*

Lowering his coffee, a hint of a smile lingered on his mouth. "I wish you'd called me after your interviews were done."

"I wish I had too." *My vibrator couldn't keep up, but you would've.* Leia's gaze flitted up, her burning cheeks complementing the garland of blush roses traipsing across the adjacent window.

Tarquin bounced his brows. "We would've had one belter of an orgasm to make your insomnia worthwhile."

"*Only* one?" Leia countered.

"Ah, I was trying not to brag."

Leia laughed and tugged the soft cuffs of her sweater over her palms. "Well, if anyone deserves to shout it from the rooftops, you do."

"Oh, good. I'll keep that in mind next time I'm inspecting shingles." He leaned in, poring over the table of fanciful cakes. "This is sweet. My Fridays are usually spent on-site, choking on drywall dust and arguing over electrical sockets."

"So, how *is* business?"

"Brilliant, actually! The cinema reno is done, and the church is nearly there. The two pubs and terraced house in Pimlico are coming along nicely, so I'm lining up what's next." He glanced outside onto sunny Ebury Street, a sophisticated thoroughfare of boutiques, pricey terrace houses, and intimate restaurants. "I'm bidding on a property just down the street, actually, and I'm looking at a few others in Bermondsey, Dalston, and Limehouse, too. Can't stop, won't stop!"

"I was going to say! No rest for the wicked." Leia raked her fork through her cake's icing. "I'm lucky you could spare me an hour or two."

"Hey, impatient architects can wait, but coffee? Never." He muted his grin. "Thanks for texting this morning. After everything with Shantelle, I wasn't certain you would."

Her posture softened. "Tarquin, the reason I kept quiet about being here—"

"Leia"—he held his palms up—"you don't owe me an explanation. We weren't talking, we weren't even *friends* anymore, really." He dropped his hands in his lap and blinked downward, contemplating the sea salt caramel cupcake on the plate in front of him but left it untouched. "If I could do things over…"

Leia deserted her fork and her cake. "No, this isn't on you. I was horrible to you on the High Line."

"I deserved every word."

"Whether you did is debatable, but my apology isn't. I'm *sorry*, Tarquin." She sighed, spinning the charm on her bracelet under the table. "I was dismissive and confrontational."

"And I was impatient and selfish. What are we like, eh? If we keep going, we'll cover all the *Mr. Men* and *Little Miss* books."

Leia giggled. "Well, Sarah *does* call me Little Miss Princess and Little Miss Busy."

"Love it." Tarquin sipped his coffee, the conversation sinking into silence.

Leia sampled her cake, the vanilla sponge's sweetness drawing a tempered grin and her fork back for seconds. Tarquin bypassed his dessert and sat back in his chair, straightening the spoon on his coffee-stained napkin as four women laughed and snapped selfies outside the café's pink façade.

He's never this quiet. Leia swept cake crumbs into a pile with her fork. *He looks uncertain, like he's waiting for me to put a label on this—on us. Friends? Lovers? A full-on committed relationship? But how does Tarquin feel? Alex told me he's single, but that doesn't mean he wants more than sex.* She laid down her fork. *There's only one way to find out.* "Tarquin, I know we were joking before about being busy and stuff, but it *is* great to see you. Really."

He blinked up from the table, his eyes soft with longing and regret. "Where else would I be?"

She shrugged with a nervous smile. "Lunchtime pints with Harry? A midday coffee date with a cute blonde?"

Tarquin shook his head. "I do the odd pub quiz with Harry, Si and the gang, but beyond that"—he lifted his cup—"no coffees, no dinners, no dates. I got shot of the matchmaking firm months ago. Wasn't a good fit."

Like he needs help finding women who'll sleep with him. Leia picked at the side seam of her jeans. "But you're having sex, right?"

"Oh, yeah. Quite regularly—but only with myself." Tarquin took a sip.

Well, that's a relief. She smiled.

"What about you?" He returned his coffee to the table.

"Same. No breaking news there."

As he pressed his lips together, the dimples in his cheeks flexed, then disappeared. "Leia"—his voice grew serious—"are you...*happy*? On your own?"

How do I answer that? Nervous knots tightened in Leia's stomach. *If I say no, I'm kinda lying. But if I say yes, will that push him away?* She sipped her water then cleared her throat.

"Well, I'm happy being free of my husband, but for a long time, staying with him felt less scary than being divorced and alone. Better the devil you know, right? Then, something awful happened and I finally cut him loose. I feared I'd never get over it, but with the help of my family and hours of therapy, I'm doing okay—for the most part. I've learned a lot, mostly from making mistakes. At least now I know exactly what I want, professionally…and personally."

"That's great. Good for you." He nodded but something in his eyes surrendered, suggesting he wouldn't press any further.

Would he look this disappointed if he wasn't interested in me? A storm of butterflies swirled in her stomach. *This feels like I'm teetering atop a rollercoaster about to plummet.* She rocked forward, leaving her glass beside her plate. *I need to hang on, ride this through.* Fleeing beneath the table, her hands latched onto the folds of denim gathering by her knees. "So, what *do* I want? Well, I want kissing. Tons of sex. Pancakes with Canadian maple syrup for breakfast. Hot baths filled with bubbles and *Star Wars* ducks, and a sexy British guy to share it all with. But he must love Dr. Seuss and keep a catstagram account, or the deal is off."

A hint of a smile curved his lips. "That's a pretty tall order." His eyes dropped briefly to her mouth.

"Hey, you know me—I always ask for what I want. And more than anything, I want to love and be loved." She shifted in her chair and tucked her hair behind her ear, her hands unable to settle. "I swore I'd never risk my heart again, but sometimes it breaks its own rules." Swallowing hard, Leia blinked into a hopeful grin. "All I know for certain is…I've missed you, Tarquin. I've missed *us*."

He leaned in, breathless. "I've missed you like mad, Leia. Honestly, you're all I think about."

A rush of relief rippled through her, ten long months of tortured yearning and regret soothed by his confession. There was just one more question begging an answer. "So, do you wanna date me and be exclusive?"

Tarquin huffed out a laugh. "Like you have to ask! Come here!" He stretched across the table and she met him halfway, capturing his mouth.

Nervous anticipation melted into pure ecstasy. *My god, I can feel this kiss everywhere!* She threaded her fingers through Tarquin's hair, tugging him closer, allowing his tongue to tease as he gently cupped her face. The gentleness of his caress, his fresh scent, and the determination of his lips spurred memory after memory, and the hope for many more. *He feels so familiar, so loving...so mine. I never want to lose him again.*

A loud *tsk* and a gruff "Get a room!" popped Leia's blissful bubble, and she reluctantly broke their kiss.

"But we have to take it slow..." She giggled, happiness exploding through her as she sat back in her chair and ignored the judgmental side-eye from the next table. "See how it goes."

"Fine by me!" Tarquin's grin wouldn't quit. "I just want to be with you, Ginger—fast, slow, no distance, long-distance..." He picked up his coffee.

Long-distance. The words kicked her in the ribs.

"When are you flying back to New York?"

"My ticket is for December 1st, but I'm thinking of staying—"

"*Here?!*" Glee sparkled like fireworks in Tarquin's eyes as his coffee cup met the table with a loud clunk. "Permanently?!"

He looks like I just said 'I do.' She gave him a wary grin. "Maybe? I don't know. My situation has changed. Shantelle's moving to Paris to live with Bastien."

"Oh, good for her! But how does that affect you?"

"Last month, I signed a contract extension with her through award season. I re-read it last night and realized there's no exit clause."

Anger pinched Tarquin's face. "You're kidding! Your lawyer left that out? It's their job to cover *all* eventualities."

Leia shook her head. "The way it stands now, if Shantelle moves outside the States, I'm legally bound to style her. It doesn't matter if she's ninety minutes away in Canada or seven hours and an ocean away in France—I'm locked in."

Tarquin blew out his cheeks. "That's fucked up."

"I know! My only way out is to break the contract, but I can't. Shantelle would be so upset, and plus, I'd damage my reputation." *Again.*

"But you and Shantelle are friends. Couldn't you work something out? Suggest someone in Paris?"

"Shan is adamant about wearing Frill-Seekers and will only work with a stylist she trusts. If I bailed, I'd feel like I was abandoning her." Crossing her arms, Leia slumped back in her chair. "And really, whose fault is this?" she grumbled, taking the blame. "I was busy planning my show and barely gave the contract a skim before signing—which is stupid because I *know* Shan can be flighty after she's had a consultation with her psychic. If the psychic says, 'Do a 180,' Shantelle changes direction without a second thought."

"She has a psychic on speed dial?"

"Yep, and she told Shantelle Bastien's *the one.* But hey, what do I know? Maybe it *is* true love."

Tarquin took a fork to his cupcake. "They *were* snogging up a storm last night. Even made it into *The Mail.* Frill-Seekers scored a mention, too."

"Really? That's cool...I guess!" She half-smiled. *And strange! Feeling happy about tabloid coverage? That's a first.* "So, I have a choice: flying seven hours to Paris every time Shan needs me—which will be a lot—or staying in London for the foreseeable."

Tarquin's eyebrows peaked, but his expression remained neutral, refusing to sway her decision one way or the other.

"Both options are problematic. Flying between New York and Paris on Shantelle's whim will probably kill me, but uprooting myself from Brooklyn is a massive headache. My entire business, *my life* is based in New York. That said, London has the one thing that Brooklyn doesn't—you."

Tarquin's face lit up like her declaration gave him permission to speak. "Leia, I know moving will be a right ol' nightmare, but I promise, I'll be here for you. Emotionally, financially, professionally—*anything* you need, just ask. You can even move in with me, if you'd like. Save yourself from Sarah's sofa."

And Jordan's snoring. "Tarquin, that's really kind, but it's a bit…"

"Fast? Too soon, right?"

She nodded. "I was thinking I'd rent somewhere."

"That works, too. If you want suggestions…"

"I'd love some. Thanks. I'll still have to fly home on December 1st, though. I'll need to tie up some loose ends, pack some more clothes. Oh, and I have this visit planned with a vegan leather factory, to make sure it's completely eco-friendly."

"You've got so much going on. Can't you take their word for it?" asked Tarquin.

She shook her head. "I'm using the leather for the skirt portion of several dresses in my New York Fashion Week show. If I don't do my due diligence and the material is unsustainable, I can wave goodbye to all credibility. I can't risk it."

"Yeah, that makes sense." He toyed with his plate. "While we're talking obligations, I have one: I'm flying to Orkney tomorrow morning."

Nooo! I just get him back and he's leaving already? Leia fought the urge to bang her forehead on the table. "Oh, lucky!"

"The timing is naff as fuck. I'd much rather take you back to mine, get reacquainted." He licked his lips, his gaze dimming. "But I have to head back to the office after this, finish a few things. It'll probably be an all-nighter."

And not the type I had in mind. Dammit! I guess our reunion will have to wait. "How long will you be on Orkney?"

"A fortnight."

JACQUELYN MIDDLETON

Two weeks?! Leia forced a smile. "Quality time with your family, right?"

"Yeah, though I'd prefer quality time with you! I'm supposed to help Rupert with repairs on an old croft, but I can't do any heavy lifting until I receive clearance from my doctor."

Leia's eyes clouded with concern. "For what?"

"Oh, it's stupid. I dislocated my elbow five weeks ago. I crashed my skateboard doing a gazelle flip." He grimaced. "Drunk."

"You're kidding?!"

"And before you ask, no, I don't usually get blattered and hit up the skate park. It was a one-off."

Let's hope so. "Are you okay *now*?"

"Yeah. My range of motion is still dodgy, but it should return eventually with more physio. In the short term, I can't climb or lift anything heavy. I'd postpone my trip, but baby Poppy is being baptized and Ava's counting down the days to seeing me."

"Aw, what a sweetie."

Tarquin swallowed another sip and licked his lips, his smile growing naughty, beckoning like he was about to throw down a dare. "So, here's an idea. When your meetings are done next week, why don't you fly up? I'll sort the tickets and you could stay with me, see the sights…come to the baptism."

Of fire?! Is that his idea of taking it slow? Leia eased into a tentative smile. "Really? Won't I be intruding on an intimate family gathering?"

"I don't think intimate is what they're going for. Rupert and Fiona booked St. Magnus Cathedral. It's this massive 12th-century Norse church in Kirkwall, imposing as fuck but incredibly beautiful. Dad will be there, Mum *maybe*, plus Nick and a bunch of relations and friends. Fiona is Orkney born and bred so her family are coming in from the other islands. I think seventy people are invited."

I'm dying to be with him, and I'd love to see Orkney—but that's a LOT of family all at once. Leia tucked her hair behind her ear. "Sounds great!" *And slightly terrifying.* She picked up her phone and tapped the calendar. "What day is the baptism?"

"Saturday, November 23. You know, I think Nick's ex-wife is coming, too."

"Nick was married? Does he have kids?"

"No! Nico hasn't fathered any sprogs—at least none that we know of!" Tarquin chuckled as Leia put on a smile and set down her phone. "His marriage only lasted a few months, but his ex stays in touch with Fiona so..." He swirled the last of his coffee around his cup. "Ava likes her auntie, but I think she'll turn inside out if she meets you! A real-life Canadian ice dancer!" He looked up sheepishly. "Don't be surprised if she asks you to do twizzles with her. She doesn't own skates, obviously, but tries to twizzle in her stocking feet."

Oh no, has he told her about me? Leia blanched. *I can't bail and do a Cressida on her.*

Tarquin did a double take and set down his cup. "But don't worry, Ava's *not* expecting you. If it feels like too many Balfours too soon and you'd rather visit another time, I completely understand. We've only been a couple for what, five minutes? I'm just being greedy, that's all." He reached past their desserts and laced his fingers through Leia's, his smile free of expectation. "Time feels precious. I don't want to miss a single second."

"Me neither." Feeling the warmth of his hand wrapped around hers, Leia's heart weighed heavy. *I want to be with him. I want to meet his family, but this soon? What if it's too overwhelming? They live on a remote Scottish island—I couldn't just leave if I wanted to.* She glanced up from the table. "Where do you stay when you visit?"

"Depends. This time I'm staying in the guest house on Rupert's property. It used to be an old stone barn where our grandparents housed livestock, but the roof caved in and it was partially flooded. I started fixing it up a few years ago and it became a passion project for me. I finished it pretty recently and now it's a cozy hideaway with all the mod cons—a gourmet kitchen, a shower room, two bedrooms, two fireplaces. I restored its stone exterior, too, and kept all the weathered character Orkney is known for. It's easily my proudest moment as a builder."

Aw, I'd love to see it. "It sounds gorgeous."

"Hey, it's not going anywhere." He grinned easily without a hint of disappointment. "You'll see it one day."

This man...no demands, no guilt. He's nothing like Tyler. Why am I waffling? Leia squeezed Tarquin's hand. *It would be amazing to see him in a different light...with his family, away from London.* She flashed a huge smile. "Yeah, one day—in a week's time! Book my flight, Tarquin. And tell Ava I'm coming!"

TWENTY-EIGHT

TARQUIN

Orkney, one week later, Friday, November 22, 2019

"Nice to see you, too, Mrs. Norquay. Safe flight to Stronsay!" Tarquin smiled, his gaze fleeing the chatty senior and her husband, landing on the arrivals board.

IsleAir IA099 from Edinburgh 13:10 LANDED

She's here! And so ends the longest seven of days of my life. Heart pounding beneath his sweater, Tarquin blew out a relieved breath and admired his bouquet of Scottish primroses, a small, delicate purple flower with a yellow center found only on the Orkney Islands and the northern coast of Scotland.

"Ahh, such a lovely lad." The silver-haired Orcadian's lilt carried across the small airport as she shuffled through the café's seating with her husband. "His granny would be so proud."

Tarquin rocked back on his heels. *Well, that seals it. No snogging when I see Leia. One kiss here and all of Orkney will know by dusk I have a new girlfriend. Island life—gotta love it!*

The door leading to the tarmac swung open, and a gust of frosty air escorted a brief parade of arriving passengers into the airport. Tarquin exchanged nods with several familiar faces collecting bags from the small U-shaped luggage belt but only one stole his breath.

"Hey, sexy!" Leia abandoned her suitcase and threw her arms around Tarquin's neck, capturing his lips. One sweep of her tongue and Tarquin was a goner.

365

Fuck the rumor mill! Letting her in, he kissed her fast and deep, losing himself in her subtle perfume and the familiarity of her mouth. Leia's fingers slid into his hair, gently tugging, twisting, refusing to behave. *She REALLY missed me!* He reciprocated, gathering her tight with his free arm, her goose-down parka and backpack still chilled from the gales outside.

Leia moaned quietly in their kiss, oblivious to several rubbernecking Orcadians. Nudging each other subtly, their approving grins suggested Tarquin was right—his love life *would* be the talk of the islands by teatime.

I'm so glad she's here. Tarquin broke away, resting his forehead against Leia's. "Welcome to the Orkney Islands," he whispered, and her soft body curved into him, feeling like home.

"That snog was definitely worth four hours of travel!" She kissed him again, chastely this time before gazing into his green eyes like he was the love of her life.

"You've seen nothing yet!" Tarquin gave her a squeeze and let go, offering her the bouquet. "Betcha didn't know primroses grow wild here."

"They're beautiful! And so tiny and purple!" She leaned in for a sniff. "I love them. Thank you!"

Tarquin smiled smugly. "So, what do you think so far? Kirkwall's airport is wee, eh? No bigger than your average storage depot."

Looking around, she studied the open plan terminal, basically one large room with two small check-in areas, an information desk, a tiny souvenir shop, and a cozy seating area hugging the café's counter. "It really is. The plane was teeny, too—only thirty seats." She hugged her flowers and rescued her midsized backpack from slipping off her shoulder.

"We should fly up to Westray," said Tarquin, extending the handle of Leia's suitcase. "The plane is an eight-seater, and the airport is a small waiting room and a toilet!"

"So, how many different islands have you been to?"

"Seventeen or so." Tarquin held Leia's hand as they walked toward the exit, passing tall glass cases displaying Orkney silver jewelry.

"And there are seventy in total?"

"Yep, but most of them are skerries." He caught her furrowed brow. "Small rocky islands, completely uninhabitable...unless you're a puffin."

"Riley begged me to bring her back some puffin souvenirs."

"Just wait to till we go shopping in town." Tarquin swung her hand as they stepped outside. "Puffin-palooza!"

Striding through the small parking lot, a heavy mist dampened Leia's parka, but not her enthusiasm. Taking everything in, she glanced back at the airport as Tarquin stowed her backpack and luggage in the black Land Rover. "Oh, check that out!" She pointed, her long hair dancing in the blustery Orkney wind. "Viking runes! Above the entrance. What does it say?"

Tarquin closed the tailgate and raced to the passenger side, opening Leia's door. "Krimsitir, which in English translates to Grimsetter. During World War II, the airport was a Royal Airforce Fighter station known as RAF Grimsetter."

Leia climbed in the car and gazed at her bouquet. Taming her messy mane, she smiled the entire time, like a little kid embarking on a big adventure.

Someone is thrilled to bits. I hope Mum doesn't change that. Tarquin hopped behind the steering wheel and shivered, yanking his door closed. "There's plenty of wartime history here, along with all the Viking and Neolithic stuff."

"So much to see!" said Leia, clicking her seatbelt. "A week won't be enough."

"We'll pack a lot in. I'll make sure you see all the Orkney highlights: Skara Brae, Maeshowe, the Ring of Brodgar."

"Balfour?"

"Yes?" Tarquin started the car's engine and pulled his seatbelt across his body.

"No, silly." Leia giggled. "I don't mean you. I mean the *village* of Balfour on Shapinsay. Is it true your family owned the entire island at one point?"

"Someone's been researching on Google." Tarquin cranked up the heat as the wipers did a waving swoop across the windshield. "Only the village name remains. We don't even own Balfour Castle anymore."

"But hello, Balfour *Hospital*! Your last name is synonymous with the islands. And you're descended from lairds!"

"Yeah. Balfours have been tied to Orkney for hundreds of years." Tarquin checked the Land Rover's mirrors and pulled out of the parking space. "They came from Fife in Scotland originally—"

"—and changed the course of farming on Shapinsay in the mid-1800s! I've been doing my homework! So, is that where Rupert's farm is located?"

"No, he's in the parish of Stenness on the West Mainland, where we're headed now, you big swot." He laughed, taking a right. The two-lane road sliced through a panorama of never-ending farmland dotted with grazing sheep. "Good news, though: we've got some free time before you'll be overrun by Balfours tonight. Fiona's taking Ava to Poppy's four-month checkup, and Rupert is meeting with the agricultural society."

"I love that photo you texted this morning of you and Ava wearing unicorn onesies."

"The hood makes it, right? With the glittery horn?"

Leia clasped his hand across the center console, giving it a squeeze. "No wonder you're her favorite uncle."

"Well, Nick tries, bless him, but he's never been big on kids, even when he was a sprog himself. Mum says Nico bawled his eyes out when Rupert was born and demanded she send him back! By the time I arrived, he knew Mum loved him most, so I didn't get it in the neck."

"Your mum plays favorites?"

"Shamelessly. Nick is—and I quote—'Kiki's number-one son'. And not just by birth either. His childhood acting, his preference for city living, his looks...they're similar in many ways. Farm-loving Rupert, on the other hand, is the oddball, and I'm the troublemaker."

Leia winced. "That must be hard, feeling second best."

He shook his head. "Not really. After twenty-seven years, I'm used to it."

"How's Ava been with baby Poppy?"

"Really good. She even gave her sister her teddy."

"That's love, that is." Leia's gaze followed a flock of sheep lumbering along a rock fence. "If Ava is teddy-less, she won't be for long. I bought her a Paddington Bear."

Paddington? Alex had one, I think. Tarquin smiled into a nod. "Aw, Leia! Ava will love him."

"I also found her a Tessa Virtue Barbie."

"There's a doll?!"

"Yeah. Dad couriered her over from Canada last week."

I couldn't adore you more. Tarquin's eyes darted from the road, taking in her soft lips turned up in a grin. "You are amazing, Leia Scott! Ava will be doing cartwheels." He lifted her hand, giving her knuckles a sweet kiss. "So, what would Ava's new bestie like to do this afternoon? We could go into town, grab lunch, or go exploring before the sun goes down—your call."

"How early does the sun set?"

"It'll be dark around half three. Today we get only seven hours of light."

"Wow. We are *north*!"

"Yeah, the joys of an Orkney winter. The summers make up for it, though. During the solstice, it doesn't get dark at all. You could sit outside at midnight and read, go for a hike, play golf."

Leia gaped. "That must be so weird."

"It takes some getting used to. That's why everyone has black-out curtains! But it's really beautiful with the sky all fiery oranges and stunning pinks and purples. There's nothing like it."

"I'll have to come back."

Or never leave. He grinned. "The standing stones aren't too far from the farm if you fancy it?"

She gave Tarquin a flirty smile. "Oh, I fancy it, all right—but I fancy you more! Our FaceTime sex this week was epic."

It was. He grinned, remembering how hard he came when Leia writhed and gasped his name, falling apart as she climaxed. *So hot! It's now my go-to for wanking.* Heat rushed south of his belt buckle. *Who needs porn when I've got Leia?*

"But it felt like a cruel tease. Look, engage, but don't touch. And I *love* touching you, tasting you…feeling you deep inside me." Her hand broke away from his, traveling up his thigh. "Ten *hard* months, Tarquin." She stroked the hot tightness bulging the crotch of his jeans. "I'm so wet for you."

Christ! Tarquin groaned and floored the gas pedal. "I'll have us there in fifteen."

The warm glow of the wood crackling in the stone fireplace high-lighted the trail of discarded jeans, Leia's sweatshirt, and Tarquin's sweater scattered across the hardwood floor. The master bedroom took up a third of the old barn's top floor but felt welcoming and cozy with its woven wool throw rugs, traditional high-backed Orkney chairs, and framed photos of the islands' rugged shores. Leia's flowers, a symphony of wild purple blooms in a blown-glass vase, lent an extra homey touch.

Waiting for Leia to emerge from the bathroom, Tarquin left a bottle of lube on the bedside table and eased back into a mountain of pillows. He tore open a condom, the anticipatory ache of finally being together eclipsing all thoughts of sightseeing, family obligations, and the future. All that mattered was reuniting with Leia, body and soul.

A week apart felt like a fucking eternity, and sex over video chat only intensified my hunger for her. I'm craving the sweet indulgence of her mouth, the softness of her curves, her moans feathered against my skin. I want to worship her, cherish her...love her. Forever.

The water taps stilled and Leia reappeared in her black panties, her smile muted as she gripped her small purse.

This isn't the same Leia I was snogging mere minutes ago. Tarquin sat up. "You okay?"

"Yeah." She pressed her lips together and left her purse on a chair. "I just got my period." Letting out a sharp exhale, she dropped down on the bed, tucking her feet beneath her bum. "It's early. I wasn't supposed to get it for a few days, but I guess the air travel messed up my cycle. It happens sometimes."

Is she in pain? "Can I get you anything? A hot water bottle, ibuprofen...your favorite chocolate?"

"Chocolate." She half-chuckled. "Thanks, I'll definitely have some later. I just took a pain reliever." Spying the condom in his hand, Leia gave a weak smile. "Sorry, Tarquin."

"About what?"

Her eyes slid wantonly to his lonely erection, sprung, loaded, and insanely hard. "Getting you all hot for reunion sex and now having to bail."

371

We've never talked about having sex when she has her period. I guess she abstains? He left the condom on its wrapper and moved closer, embracing her in a reassuring hug. "Leia, we haven't had sex for ten months—we can wait a few more days."

"It'll be *four* more days. That's how long it usually lasts." She bit her bottom lip. "But I could give you a blow job right now? Do that thing you like with my tongue?"

"You could, but I'd rather come when I can pleasure you as well."

"*Right.*" Leia sagged in his arms and withdrew. "Of course."

Shit! She thinks I'm one of those blokes who recoil at the sight of period blood. No, no, no. That is NOT me. Tarquin's fingers skated up her thigh. "But if you *did* want to fool around, you wouldn't hear any complaints from me."

She flashed him a *Yeah, right* look, her gaze falling to the pulled back duvet.

"Leia, I love all kinds of sex. When it's during a woman's period, yeah, it's different, but not in a bad way. It feels extra warm, super wet and slick. It's fucking amazing, actually." His penis throbbed. *Yeah, not that I have to tell you that, mister!* Tarquin bent his neck, seeking her doubtful eyes. "But regardless of how I feel about it, how do *you*?"

"I enjoy it—well, I *did*." She sat up. "Tyler and I only did it once. After that, he wouldn't touch me when I was on my period."

Tyler? That's his name? Every Tyler I've known has been a complete wanker. "Well, it's not everyone's cuppa."

Leia tugged at the band of her panties. "No, I mean, he hated it. Tyler's actual words were, '*I'm not sticking my dick in there again. It's disgusting.*'"

Anger swelled in Tarquin's chest. "The cheek of him! Any guy who makes his partner feel embarrassed or unclean because her body is doing what it's biologically *meant* to do should fuck right off! Seriously, like ejaculate isn't messy?! Sex *is* messy. And sticky and weird and...wonderful!" He wrapped his arm around her, pulling her tight. "I'm glad you got rid because Tyler is a daft prick!"

"I won't argue with that." She huffed. "His reaction upset me at first, but ultimately, he lost out on having tons of sex with his horny wife. I get super aroused when I'm on my period. I reach orgasm faster, and they're longer and way more intense."

"Cor, I like the sound of that!"

"I'd leave him with his beers and video games and indulge in some me time in the bath." Leia smirked. "The showerhead always made me come harder than Tyler ever did."

"Now there's an image." Tarquin pressed a lingering kiss on her temple. "I'm so sorry he let you down, Leia."

"Thanks," she said quietly. "Have you slept with many women during?"

"A few, not many. It's always felt quite vulnerable—for them and me—which made sleeping together incredibly intense and intimate. It's not something you do with just anyone, you know?"

Leia nodded.

"That's why Tyler's overreaction baffles me. A husband, of all people, should be loving and understanding, not rudely dismissive or disrespectful. He had one job: to worship his wife."

"Well, to be fair, he was great when we first got together, but..." She shrugged and trailed off into a heavy exhale.

Tarquin brushed her hair away from her eyes. "It must've been tough, having him rebuff your desire for deeper intimacy. You deserve better, Leia."

She caressed his cheek. "That's why I'm with you." Leaning in, she kissed him tenderly. No tongue, no sucks or flirty bites, just a soft, sweet kiss of gratitude and respect.

And maybe even love?

Tarquin's heart galloped ahead, but Leia's words over cake and coffee a week earlier tugged the reins as he kissed her back: *"We have to take it slow."*

She's right. I can't fast-forward or allow my expectations to run riot like I usually do. He vowed he'd let Leia lead. *And you, Balfour? Follow her and enjoy the incredible view.* Her sexy butt wiggle? Totally worth it.

Leia pulled away, a playful glint frolicking in her blue eyes. "Remember I said I get extra horny…"

"Remember? My dick can't forget!" He motioned downward, his erection growing harder by the second. "So, whatcha fancy, Ginger? I can put towels down on the bed, or we could shower together…"

"I'd prefer here. Cowgirl—me on top—if that's okay? It'll let me control how deep you go."

"It's more than okay!"

She smiled. "And you won't hurt your poor elbow, propping yourself up."

Always thinking of others. "Well, in that scenario, the discomfort would be worth it!" Tarquin kissed her quick. "Just gimme a…" He climbed off the bed and raided the en suite's linen closet, pulling out several large towels.

"But…do you have a washing machine here, or would we use Fiona's?" Leia's worried gaze followed him back to the bed. "For the towels…after."

"I've got one." He smoothed the dark towels over the fitted sheet. "We're all set. Don't worry about a thing."

"Tarquin, are you *really* sure? Sometimes girl on top increases, you know…the flow."

He settled beside her and kissed her temple, his mouth brushing her ear. "The wetter, the better, right?" he whispered, erasing Leia's furrowed brow.

Pressing his lips tenderly down her neck and along her collarbone, his fingers curled under the band of her panties but went no farther, waiting for Leia's okay. He didn't have to wait long.

She pulled the fabric from her hips and edged onto her side, yanking the panties down her legs. Folding the cotton material over her pad, she left her underwear on top of her jeans splayed on a chair.

Thanks to that asshole Tyler, I know she'll feel vulnerable about this no matter what I say. Tarquin's heart ached. *But I'll do all I can to help her feel beautiful, comfortable, and safe.* He smiled as she picked up the lube and climbed back on the bed. "C'mere, gorgeous." He kissed her tenderly on the lips. "How do you want me? Slow and gentle? Hard and fast?"

"Hard and fast." Straddling his thighs, she nudged his shoulders back onto the stack of plump pillows. Her chest rose and fell, her determination undeniable. "I want you so bad it's obscene." She dropped the bottle of lube on the crumpled blankets. "I won't last long."

"Nor me." Tarquin's heavy gaze snagged on her breasts, her nipples erect and begging to be sucked. *I've fantasized about this so much over the past ten months, it's surprising I haven't worn out my dick.* He cupped her breasts and gently squeezed, their soft curves, luscious weight...all his and no one else's. *But memory-fueled wanking is nothing compared to her silky fullness in my hands, the grind of her hips against mine, or the intoxicating heat of her, wet and tight, riding me.*

He glanced up, meeting her eyes, dark and primal as she lurched forward, crushing his mouth with hers. Tarquin clutched her waist and greedily drew her into his chest, the desperate caress of her tongue, her sweet taste arousing moans of joyful pleasure and erasing the angst of months spent apart. He kissed her deeper, faster, shifting slightly so the press of his erection gave her no doubt he was ready, leaving it up to her to call the shots.

She drew back, her pouty lips parting in a giggle as Tarquin's hand threaded through her hair, its softness between his fingers, its scent arousing memories of snooker tables and macarons, Tower Bridge and cozy moments holding her in his arms.

"It's good we're not in Rupert's house." She grabbed the lube and squeezed it twice into her palm. "Might get loud!" She snapped the lid closed.

"Bring the noise, Ginger." Tarquin chuckled and leaned forward, leaving a curve of open-mouthed kisses along her jaw as Leia's hand skipped past his abs, her fingers taking ownership of his hot, hard cock. Her confident, slick strokes up and down urged a loud moan free from Tarquin's mouth. "Your hands...ahh, I've missed them. I've missed *you*," he gasped, the ache of anticipation building as she shifted back and bowed her head, her mouth joining in.

Fucking HELL! Tarquin groaned and melted into the pillows as her tongue flirted with his tip and teased around the head while her hands worked their magic. "Ohhh, god!"

With one hand, she gathered her hair out of the way and took him deeper, sucking gently at first before increasing the pressure, her eyes smiling, watching him lose it.

Leia isn't shy about getting me off. Always makes it extra wet and slippery. So fucking hot! His thighs twitched, the wet suction sending shockwaves surging through his body. *If she keeps this up, I'm gonna come, but this is supposed to be about her.* Fingers digging into the mattress, he fought through a strangled gasp. "Leia...?"

Her lashes fluttered as she popped off, her grin rising into a cheeky dare. "Betcha I'll come first." Her hand slid down his shaft and back up again, teasing.

Tarquin met her challenge with a strangled growl. "Come fuck me, gorgeous."

Raising up on his elbow, he reached over, grabbing a new condom from the bedside table. Tarquin tore open the wrapper with his teeth as Leia added more lubricant to her hands and played with his impressive length gliding up...then down...and up, a wanton glint in her blue eyes.

Minx! She loves torturing me.

With Leia's help, Tarquin put on the condom and settled back, enjoying the view.

She spread her thighs and clasped the base of his hardness, slowly immersing its thickness inch...by...inch in her tight, wet heat. Tarquin let out a low gasp as he filled her. She closed her eyes, her lips parting with a moan of overdue pleasure. "Ten months..." she mumbled, her lashes peeling open.

Tarquin sucked in a measured breath and caressed the soft skin of her thighs. "You okay, love?"

"I'm great! *So* great." She rolled her hips back and forth, the slow sensation of slippery friction pulling a groan from Tarquin's throat.

She remembers what I like. She's never forgotten. A surge of love and longing filled his heart as his finger circled soft and slow above her entrance. "Leia, if anything feels uncomfortable, we can stop."

"Nope. Never stop! This feels SO amazing." She shifted back slightly, chasing the perfect angle as she upped her pace, rolling and grinding, lifting and lowering.

Being inside her, hot and slick, sliding in and out, Tarquin praised luck, fate, karma—everything and anything that'd helped him find Leia again. Ten months, ten *long* months of blaming himself, of regretting his choice to lie about his feelings. Would things have been different if he hadn't? He lifted his head, watching where they were so deliciously connected as tingles grew at the base of his spine, the pressure building and building as Leia bounced and gasped, her soft lips turned up at the corners, breaths ragged, her breasts glistening with perspiration.

She's not talking. She's close—but so am I. "Leia, go on," he groaned, his mind hazy with only one thought. *I don't know how much longer I can hold on.* "Win your dare!"

Swiveling her hips, she answered with breathy moans and a crinkle of her nose as she lost control and cried out, tumbling into ecstasy, her body's internal spasms squeezing Tarquin tight.

I can't wait another second. Tarquin let go, exploding inside her, each pulse shaking him to the core. Chasing breaths after her own climax, Leia gripped his hands, coaxing him through until the trembling subsided and he was completely spent.

I can literally see stars...fuck. His arms flopped down on the bed. *Totally. Annihilated. Sex so good you want it with this one person, forever.*

Leia leaned forward and pressed a soft, smiling kiss on the hard lines of chest. "I was gonna say I won, but let's call it a draw."

Still my Leia, still caring, still giving. He reached up, his hands tenderly cradling her flushed cheeks. *God, I love her.*

Time hadn't changed a thing, not for Tarquin.

But what about Leia? They were a couple now, sharing, opening up, being more vulnerable and intimate than ever before.

Does she feel the same as me?

His eyes pored over her blissed-out grin, delightfully messy hair, swollen rosebud lips. *In London you told me, 'I want to love and be loved.' Well, I'm all in. But are you?* He brushed his thumb across her mouth, lips gently parted, breaths calming as she playfully bit his finger. *Will your doubts and fears about relationships fade along with your orgasm?*

Tarquin could only hope.

With a wistful smile, he slipped his hand into her hair as she swept a lost eyelash off his cheek. *I haven't said 'I love you' since*

New York. I desperately want to tell her again. Actually, I'm dying to shout it to the entire world! But she might feel pressured to say it back, and I don't know if she's there yet. I can't risk scaring her off, not when it's only been a week since we found each other again.

Leia giggled, her smile carefree and somewhat relieved. "We've still got it!"

"We never lost it," Tarquin whispered breathlessly. *God, I love this girl and how she makes me feel. My heart is all yours, Leia, and always will be.*

TWENTY-NINE

LEIA

"What do you say, Ava?" Fiona swept her eldest daughter's red curls from her forehead.

"Thank you!" The five-year-old, sat between her mommy and Tarquin, clutched Paddington Bear and the Tessa Virtue doll to her chest, her blue eyes round as saucers and fixed on Leia.

Ava is cute as a button. She has Fiona's elfin facial features and Rupert's freckles. Leia grinned, tearing apart a crusty slice of warm baked bread covered with melting Orkney butter. "You're so welcome! If you'd like, I can make Tessa some extra skating dresses?"

Ava blinked up at her mommy, checking if it was all right. Fiona returned her glass of red Bordeaux to the round farmhouse table and nodded. "It's okay, Av."

"Okay!" The little girl burst into a smile, her shyness easing as she brushed against Tarquin, her tiny arms overwhelmed with toys. "I want blue dwess, please!"

"Great choice!" said Leia. "Blue is my sister's favorite color."

Tarquin beamed and leaned in, kissing Leia on the temple, his affection igniting a subtle smirk of approval between Fiona and Rupert. Ava was oblivious, babbling full speed ahead in a one-sided conversation with her Tessa doll as the family's brown border collie, Bert, wandered over, giving her new playmates an approving sniff.

"Leia, it was so sweet of you to sew the tear in Ava's unicorn," said Fiona. "Bert got hold of it this morning and had a right ol' chew."

"Oh, no problem. I always have a mini sewing kit on me." She smiled at Tarquin's niece. "I'm glad I could help."

"Ava?" Rupert called across the table, cradling a sleepy Poppy sucking on her bottle. "How about two more mouthfuls of dinner?" Russet-haired and slighter in stature than both Tarquin and Nick, the middle Balfour brother wore black eyeglasses and a flush of freckles across his nose and cheeks. His nerdy good looks and family's connections could've landed him on London's most prestigious catwalks, but his down-to-earth countenance and love of nature had drawn him to Orkney where growing barley, raising prize-winning cattle, and caring for his beautiful young family were his true calling.

"Uncle Talk?" Ava ignored her dad and her half-eaten bowl of hearty beef stew and tugged on Tarquin's sweater.

"What's up, Peedie?" He scrunched down and she whispered in his ear, lovingly placing Paddington and Tessa in his lap. "Oh?!" His eyes slid over his empty bowl and curved toward Leia. "Yeah, you're right." He smiled. "Ava thinks you look like the princess in the Disney film *Brave*."

"Wow, that's a huge compliment, Ava!" Leia grinned, scratching Bert behind his ears as he sniffed her purse lying on the floor. "Thank you!" Her eyes shifted to Tarquin. "Peedie...such a cute nickname."

"It's an Orcadian word, means little." He helped Ava sit back down on her chair. "How 'bout you eat one more carrot? Or finish your clapshot. You know, Tessa eats *all* her neeps and tatties. So does Leia." He winked at his girlfriend.

Her forehead creased. "Neeps and tatties?"

"Swede—*sorry*, rutabaga—and potatoes," Tarquin clarified, handing both Paddington Bear and the Tessa doll to Fiona for safe keeping. "The veggies in clapshot." The Orkney side dish looked like mashed potatoes' more colorful cousin, its savory, buttery taste gifted with a zingy kick courtesy of onions and a sprinkle of chopped chives and pepper.

"Yep, Uncle Talk is right." Leia nodded, scooping the last bit of clapshot off her plate. "Vegetables help us *twizzle* faster!" She happily devoured the spoonful of 'neeps and tatties', her new favorite vegetarian dish.

Ava's eyes widened. With a determined smile, she clutched her spoon and fished for carrots in her stew's broth.

Rupert mouthed 'Thank you' and rested Poppy's bottle near his own partially eaten meal. He held his youngest firmly against his shoulder over the white burp cloth protecting his plaid flannel shirt. "So, when are you two going sightseeing?" He patted Poppy's back.

"Might start tomorrow." Tarquin met Leia's eyes, warmth in his gaze. "After the baptismal lunch, maybe?"

Really? He'll cut family time short for me? She nodded, finishing her stew as Tarquin continued.

"It'll be good to get out, get some sea air."

Rupert chuckled. "Get away from Mum, more like!"

"Christ, can you blame them?" Fiona winced, weaving her fingers through the ends of her long brown hair. "Kiki *is* an acquired taste. She scared the crap out of me when I first met her."

Oh, great. Leia gulped.

"To be fair, Fi, you were seven and scared of everything!" said Rupert.

His wife's brown eyes widened. "Babe, she was like Cruella de Vil! She swore a blue streak at my Shelties in the middle of Alfred Street! All they did was sniff her boots."

"I've always wondered"—Rupert shook his head—"what the heck was Mum doing in Stromness that day? She rarely leaves the house when she's here in case she rubs shoulders with Orkney's great unwashed."

Tarquin snickered and laid his arm across the back of Leia's chair. "When Fi met Mum, her hair was dyed half-white, half-black for *Equinox Ten*. She looked a right state!"

Rupert lifted his hand from little Poppy's back. "Star-drive to maximum power!'" He mimicked the cult sci-fi show's iconic salute and resumed burping his baby.

"I'll have to ask Dad if he and Mom watched it," said Leia. "Sounds right up their alley."

"Nick got his first acting role on that show." Tarquin glanced at his brother. "He would've been, what? A little older than Ava?"

The five-year-old looked up from her bowl, chomping through her last mouthful of potato.

Rupert nodded. "Leia, Mum *made* them give Nico a part, whereas Tarq and I were dumped with our nanny du jour at the craft services table. I was four and ate everything I could get my hands on. Good times!"

"I was two and can't remember a bloody thing. Probably for the best." Tarquin swirled his wine around his glass.

"I'm sorry, but the way she raised you boys horrifies me," said Fiona, smoothing Ava's wild hair. "I could never love one child more than another or pit them against each other. That's so damaging."

Leia nodded. The more she learned about Kiki and her questionable parenting, the worse she felt for Tarquin.

Rupert cocked an eyebrow. "You saying we're damaged goods, Fi?" He punctuated his question with a chuckle.

"No, it's just—it's amazing you two don't have it in for Nick! A lot of siblings would be jealous, resentful."

Tarquin shook his head. "It's not Nico's fault. Any argument I have is with Mum, not him." He downed a mouthful of red.

"Yeah…" Rupert paused, checking on Poppy before patting her back again. "Whenever Nick was a spoiled showbiz twat, Tarq and I took the piss."

"Did we ever!" Tarquin snickered. "Nick *hated* being teased."

"Still does!" said Rupert. "Even when he was annoying as hell, I still felt a bit sorry for him. Mum hired a second personal assistant with the sole purpose of dragging Nick from audition to audition. I'd be sat in science class thinking, 'Glad it's him, not me.'"

"Me, too." Tarquin glanced at Ava slurping broth from her spoon. "Can you imagine putting this little one through all that? The public exposure, the pressure? Nick got most of Mum's attention, but at what price? And she wonders why Nico has issues…"

"See!" Fiona's voice jumped. "You *do* think it's damaging! That's why I told her flat out when Ava was born: don't even *think* of playing favorites with our kids."

Rupert made a face. "Well, there's fat chance of *that* happening."

What does that mean? Leia stilled, her squint shifting between Fiona, Rupert, and Tarquin.

Rupert paused, ensuring Ava was focused on her food before directing his explanation to Leia in hushed tones. "Turns out, she's as crap a grandma as she is a mother. If it's not about Kiki, she's doesn't really give a—"

Leia's phone launched into "Stop." She grimaced and yanked her purse up from the floor. "Sorry…"

"Mummy!" Ava dropped her spoon in her empty bowl. "That song!"

"I know, sweetie!" Fiona stood up, collecting her daughter's bowl as Leia sent the caller to voicemail. "We sing along to the Spice Girls in the car all the time. Ava can't get enough!"

"Is it Sarah?" Tarquin leaned in.

"No, it's a US area code. It can wait."

"Leia, feel free to call them back," said Fiona, stacking bowls and plates. "It'll give me a minute to get dessert ready."

"Ice cream!" Ava squealed. "Can I have chocolate *and* apple cwumble?"

"Yes, but only small scoops, Av." Fiona gave her daughter a knowing grin and picked up Rupert's dishes. "Leia, we've got strawberry, vanilla honeycomb, chocolate, apple crumble, toffee with Orkney fudge..."

This family loves its ice cream! "Vanilla honeycomb sounds good."

"It's incredible. All made locally, too." Tarquin joined Fiona, gathering bowls and plates. "I'll help."

"Oh, *sure*! You just want to pinch extra fudge!" Fiona laughed, heading for the kitchen.

"Well, Orkney fudge IS the dog's bollocks!" Hands full with dishes and cutlery, Tarquin kissed Leia on the top of the head and whispered, "Be right back."

"I come, too!" Ava clambered off her chair and raced after her uncle.

Sat alone with Rupert and the baby, Leia flashed a tight-lipped smile. "I'll just see who called." Pressing the phone to her ear, she listened to the rambling message, the voice ducking and diving until it finally revealed its reason for calling. *Shit.* Disappointment pooled in her stomach. *So that's it, then.* She lowered her phone, erasing the recording with a resigned press of her finger.

"Is everything all right?" Rupert kissed Poppy on the top of her head.

Leia rubbed her temple. "It's a supplier I was checking out. I heard about this amazing vegan leather made from mushrooms. It's meant to be softer and more breathable than animal leather, plus it's completely biodegradable—perfect for Frill-Seekers."

"Sounds great!" said Rupert as the baby's pudgy hand grabbed hold of his shirt's collar.

"Yeah, too great, unfortunately. Turns out they're not as environmentally friendly as I thought." Leia glanced up. Tarquin carried a plate crowded with fudge of various flavors and homemade cookies from the kitchen. "Their vegan leather is actually made from polyurethane. They said they hope to incorporate mushrooms and other plant-based materials down the road, but they're not there yet."

Brows peaked, Tarquin placed the desserts in the middle of the table and sat down. "But that woman at the Institute said…"

Leia shook her head. "She was wrong."

"And polyurethane leather is…bad?"

"It isn't as harmful to the environment as animal leathers, but it's still problematic. It's plastic-based and doesn't degrade as easily as true vegan leather," Leia explained as Bert laid his floofy body by her feet. "I know it's considered the lesser of two evils, but I can't incorporate it into my designs with a clear conscience."

Tarquin rubbed Leia's back. "So, what will you—"

"Uncle Talk!" Ava barreled into the dining room, giggling loudly and waving an accusatory spoon. "You ate *allll* the 'nilla fudge!"

"Peedie, that was *our* secret!" Tarquin's naughty chuckle sparked a howl of laughter from his niece.

Honestly, she's the cutest little thing. Leia smiled despite her news.

Fiona followed with five ice cream-filled bowls on a tray. "Ava, shhh! Inside voice."

"Sorry, Mummy." Her large blue eyes followed the ice cream coming in for a landing.

Tarquin muted his grin. "Leia, what does this mean for your dresses?"

"Well"—she sighed—"it's too late to find another supplier. I was at my wit's end when I stumbled across this one. I'll have to start from scratch, do something different with those dresses." A smile broke through her frown. "On the upside, I won't be flying to New York on December 1st."

"But don't you have to sort a few things?" asked Tarquin, helping Fiona hand out the dessert bowls.

"It's nothing that can't wait until I'm back in February for Fashion Week. So, it looks like you'll be stuck with me until then."

"Brilliant!" Tarquin beamed, kissing her quick on the lips as Ava giggled.

Rupert glanced above his spoonful of toffee ice cream. "Any chance you'll up sticks and move to the UK full-time?"

"Maybe." Leia nodded, ogling her boyfriend. "I'm warming to the idea."

The next day

Leia threaded her fingers through Tarquin's as they strolled into the Storehouse for the private baptismal lunch. Dating back to 1880, the iconic B-listed stone building had been completely restored into an airy restaurant and small hotel. Many of the structure's original characteristics—its stone arches, rustic wood doors, and timber beams salvaged from tall ships—remained, earning a smile of approval from Tarquin. He squeezed Leia's hand. "We'll just get something to eat, say hi to a few people, then do a runner, okay?"

He's sweet—and worried this is all too much. But I'm fine. She flashed an encouraging smile. "Or we can hang out, catch up with your friends? I *love* hearing all the teenage Tarquin stories. You were one popular dude."

"Hey, what can I say? Everyone loved my raves. Well, except Grandma, bless her. And her cows—hated the strobes."

"I still can't get over that street rugby game you guys play."

Her hand swooped down her vintage coat, unfastening buttons at lightning speed. "No rules, no field, just hundreds of guys in a scrum, battling through the streets."

"You mean the Ba'?" He grinned with pure joy. "That's a highlight of the holidays!"

"It's bonkers!" Leia giggled, feeling the weight of curious eyes heeding her every move. But like at the baptism at St. Magnus Cathedral, the whispers in the restaurant were good-natured and non-judgmental. Several faces were familiar, including Tarquin's rock climbing buddies, the Balfour cousins who had welcomed her before the service, and his auntie, an eighty-year-old firecracker from the island of South Ronaldsay. She had shuffled down their pew with her walker, chastising Tarquin for keeping his new "wife" a secret. All three laughed it off with the pink-cheeked aunt blaming her dodgy hearing aid for misunderstanding the latest island gossip. Everyone Leia encountered proved friendly and warm, and she loved seeing how Tarquin's friends and family adored him. With each interaction, her initial fears of feeling like a gatecrashing outsider had been swept out to sea on the morning's salty gales.

But Leia still had to meet Kiki, Tarquin's TV star mother.

Is she here? Curiosity wrestled with nervousness in Leia's belly, but she refused to surrender. Nope, her trepidation wouldn't spoil Tarquin's time with his loved ones or send her fleeing for the exit. *The sooner we meet, the better. I hate being on pins and needles, waiting...*

She let out a shaky breath and chased it with another grin, letting go of Tarquin's hand. "Are you warm?" Shrugging off her coat, her navy chiffon knee-length dress drew approving stares from guests and her boyfriend.

"Leia, I know I keep saying it, but you look so beautiful. I swear, I'm the luckiest bloke." He kissed her on the lips and stood back, admiring her as he removed his coat. His gray bespoke suit sealed it: Tarquin and Leia were the most stylish couple on the islands.

He hung their coats up on the rack in the bar then Leia clasped his hand. "Let's mingle," she said, a glint in her eye.

Winding through the crowd, she clocked Rupert in his black suit bouncing Poppy in his arms as he chatted with two well-fed men in bulky Nordic sweaters and his father. Graying at the temples, Richard Balfour looked like an older, more weathered version of Tarquin. Fit and sharply dressed in a tie-less designer suit, he nudged his eyeglasses up his nose and gestured with his hands, hammering a point home. Like father, like son.

"Do you want to talk to your dad? You two barely spoke before the baptism."

Tarquin nodded to a passing cluster of thirty-something guys supping pints and leaned into Leia. "That's because Ava was with us," he whispered. "Dad's not usually that polite in my presence but get a few whiskies in him here and his filter evaporates completely. I'd rather you didn't witness that." He tugged his tartan tie. "It's embarrassing."

And hurtful. Leia gave him a sympathetic nod.

"And…so is my Mum." Weaving through the party, Tarquin met Leia's eyes. "I'm sorry Kiki blanked us at the service." Unlike the loving adoration in Alex's voice when she mentioned her grandmother by her first name, Tarquin's intonation was bitter and cool. "I *know* she saw us."

"Ah, it's okay." Leia lifted her chin, not bothered by the perceived snub. "She was busy with the kids."

"The doting granny act?" He shook his head. "All for show. You know, today is only the second time she's seen Poppy? The first time was over bloody Skype!"

Yikes. Clearly, Kiki isn't a candidate for grandma of the year. "I noticed she ignored your dad at the cathedral."

"They barely tolerate each other anymore. Too many affairs, too many public embarrassments." Tarquin stopped beside the restaurant's back wall decorated with unbound pages of *The Orkney Norn*, a book written in 1929 celebrating the islands' long-lost dialect. Beneath the display, a blue banquette was filling up fast with guests enjoying the buffet lunch of smoked salmon finger sandwiches and mini pork pies. "Dad sees Mum looking down her nose at everyone here and it makes his blood boil. For once, I agree with him. You won't find kinder, more hospitable people than Orcadians, and she treats them like something stuck to the red soles of her Louboutins."

"That's a shame. She's missing out." *Kiki sounds like a passive-aggressive snob—not that I'm gonna tell Tarquin that!*

But Leia didn't have to.

"Mum's a classic narcissist. Self-obsessed, entitled, demeaning, never apologizes." He paused, his brow tensing. "Leia, you should know...she's not very touchy-feely, and she's never liked any of our girlfriends."

None? The jitters in Leia's stomach jumped and twisted, gaining flight. *At least I know what's coming.* She caressed his cheek, hoping to soothe his unease and her own. "I don't need your mom to like to me. I'm dating you, not her."

"I know, but she can be manipulative. She has a way of getting in people's heads. I don't want her to come between us."

Gazing into his eyes, Leia twirled a piece of Tarquin's hair above his ear between her fingers. "She won't." Leia kissed him softly...once, twice, her lips lingering. She spotted Nick, suit jacket off, tie loosened, rounding a nearby table. "So, Nick's marriage falling apart—did Kiki meddle?"

"Yep. Poor sods didn't stand a chance." Tarquin grinned as his brother approached. "Hey, Nico."

"God, can we leave yet?" Nick playfully pouted, his hands full with the necks of two beer bottles and a tall glass of water. "Mum keeps harping on about the *Mail* story."

"You mean the story that WILL NOT DIE?" Tarquin chuckled as Leia softly smacked his arm. "You and your willy keep popping up on the front page!"

Eyes wild, Nick combed the room like the walls had ears and leaned in. "The photos are dark, Tarq!" he whispered. "You can't *see* my junk!" He handed Leia the glass of fizzy water.

She responded with a pained grin and "Thanks." *Tarquin means no harm, but I feel for Nick. Having your private life exposed is no laughing matter. You never know how far the ripples will travel.*

Nick pressed a cold beer into Tarquin's palm.

"Cheers." Tarquin nodded. "At least your drama keeps Mum off *my* arse."

"For now." Nick pointed his beer at Tarquin's. "I figured you'd need something strong, considering Dad's on top form."

Tarquin swooned over the bottle's logo, a menacing Viking with long blond locks, bushy facial hair, and biceps capable of snapping a man in half. "Yeah, today feels like a Skull Splitter day, all right!" He smiled at Leia. "I'll just have the one."

Nick studied the busy room as his baby brother took a long pull on his beer. "So, what do you think, Ley?"

His casual use of her nickname roused a full-on smile. "I like it here! Everyone is lovely and so welcoming."

Tarquin lowered his beer, his eyes narrowing, sizing up something or someone across the restaurant.

"Hmm. Wait till you meet Mum," said Nick. "She's doing my head in. Thank fuck she's flying back to London tonight."

Says her favorite son. No hope for the rest of us, then. Leia exhaled heavily and sipped her water.

Tarquin's squint popped wide open. "Hey Nick, guess who's just arrived?"

Their mom? Leia's eyes darted over her glass, but the raven-haired woman in the Victoria Beckham trouser suit from the cathedral evaded her gaze.

"Where?!" Nick gaped over his shoulder, searching. "So help me, if you're taking the piss…"

"She's talking to Fi's gran." Tarquin nodded toward the left side of the restaurant. "Near the buffet."

Craning her neck, Leia glimpsed a pretty brunette hugging an elderly lady by the bere bannocks and farmhouse cheeses. *Phew! Not Kiki!* The realization calmed the drum solo thrashing in her chest. She watched as the two women ended their embrace and, with a friendly wave, the younger guest slipped away.

Nick's face lit up.

"Go on, mate!" Tarquin smacked him on the back. "Give it a bit more welly!"

"Cheers, bro! Don't wait up for me."

Leia blinked into a semi-confused smile as Nick bombed through the crush. "I'm almost afraid to ask—what's *welly*? And why does Nick have to give more of it?"

Tarquin chuckled. "It means to put in more effort, try harder."

"With his ex-wife?"

"No. Evie, an old girlfriend—the one who got away." Tarquin raised his beer, but the bottle stalled below his mouth. "Bugger." He cleared his throat. "Kiki incoming."

Okay, it's showtime. Leia blew out a breath as the drums returned.

"We don't have to do this," he whispered in her ear, setting his bottle on a table. "Wanna make a break for it?"

Tempting! Leia's muscles tensed. *But if I want to see this side of Tarquin, see how they interact…*

"No, I want to meet her." Licking her lips, Leia abandoned her glass beside Tarquin's beer and fussed with the skirt of her dress.

What's that saying? Expect the worst, hope for the best?

Tarquin gathered her hand in his and smiled lovingly. "Leia, no matter what, it's you and me, okay? Mum's opinion means fuck all." He stepped closer, pressing a kiss in her hair. "If she's too much, squeeze my hand and we're off."

"Got it." She nodded. *But really, how bad can Kiki be?*

A pack of hungry farmers enjoying second helpings of lunch shifted, gifting Leia a clear view. Hollywood thin with a dewy, youthful complexion defying her fifty-plus years, the London-born diva sashayed with purpose through the obstacle course of guests, tables, and chairs like a Best Actress winner at the Golden Globes. A shimmery black evening gown and a matching fascinator of bowing feathers had replaced her designer trouser suit from earlier, but Rupert and Fiona's friends clearly weren't impressed. Shaking their heads, all rubbernecking stopped as they fell back into conversation, ignoring Kiki's unwelcome cameo.

"Tarquin, darling!" Kiki beamed, lowering the half-empty champagne flute in her grip as she leaned in. Her quick air kisses— left, then right—spared his cheeks from her goopy glossy lips. "Don't tell me..." With a flutter of her thick false lashes, she appraised Leia from head to toe. "This must be Lee!"

Close. Leia smiled politely. *Just go with it. Correct her later.* It wasn't the first time someone botched her name. "Hi, Mrs. Balfour. Lovely to meet you."

Tarquin wasn't as forgiving. "Mum, I *told* you—her name's Leia."

"Oh, yes, of course! The *Star Wars* princess! You had *all* the posters, didn't you Quinzie?"

Quinzie? Leia stole a sidelong glance at Tarquin mid-cringe and sucked back a giggle.

"Remember the one with the bikini?" Kiki gulped her fizz and pointed at her youngest son with her phone. "You *loved* that one!"

Tarquin squirmed and let go of Leia, raking his hand through his hair. "Mum, maybe we should grab you some lunch? Champagne on an empty stomach…"

Kiki elbowed Leia. "You know, I walked in on him once. Kecks off, busy wank—"

"Lovely service, wasn't IT?!" Loud and terse, Tarquin cut her off, his glare a stern warning.

Oh, man. So embarrassing. Leia winced. *And drunk?* She stroked Tarquin's back, wishing she could take away his discomfort.

"Oh, yes! It was absolutely preciousssh," Kiki slurred, her voice rising. "Shame it was held here, though! I'd be tickled pink if I never set foot on this WINDSWEPT HELLHOLE again!"

She didn't! Leia flinched as faces stared in their direction, their usual Orkney warmth cooling—rapidly.

Tarquin scrunched his face. "Mum!"

"What?" Kiki shrugged off his plea, her flurry of blinks heavy with disdain. "I'm not allowed to speak my truth?! If it wasn't for your brother…" She swigged her champagne.

"Yeah, well, I'm sure Rupert's grateful you could fit him in."

"Rupert? No! I'm *here* for Nikolai! He's in crisis. He *needs* me…and it looks like I need another glass."

Leia gulped back her shock, keeping a neutral expression while Tarquin grimaced and swept his hair back off his forehead. *This is so fucked up.*

"Nick is an adult, Mum. He can clean up his own mess."

Kiki flounced closer to her son and scoured the party like a hawk hunting for prey. "Where is he?" She tapped a saved number in her phone.

"He left," Tarquin lied, tilting his head. "But Rupes is here with Poppy—you know, your granddaughter? Baptized today?"

"Dammit!" Wrinkling her nose, Kiki dropped the phone from

her ear. "Nikolai's voicemail."

"You could give Poppy a cuddle, show you care…for once."

Kiki threw a dismissive glare around the room. "Spit-up and couture don't mix, sweetie."

"Ah! Silly me." Tarquin's eyes flashed.

"The things I do for you kids. I *should* be in London recuperating! Yesterday nearly killed me."

Do I dare ask out of politeness? Leia glanced at her boyfriend.

"Mum was the special guest at a comic con in Manchester. Meeting fans, posing for photos—*back-breaking* work." His sarcasm hung in the air as he reclaimed his bottle and guzzled the remaining ale.

"It was HELL, Tarquin!" Kiki fired back, trading her empty glass for a full champagne flute offered by a sheepish server. "There was no first-class treatment, no exclusive green room for top-billed guests. They stuck me at a shared autograph table with some chatty nobody from *Star Gazer*." Her glare swerved between Tarquin and Leia, seeking an ally. "You know! *Star Gazer*?! From 1998, barely lasted a season?!"

Leia attempted a sympathetic smile as Tarquin left his finished beer on the table. "Sorry, Mrs. Balfour, I don't. I'm not into sci-fi."

"And your name is *Leia*?" Kiki tsked. "That's ironic."

"And perfect." Tarquin laced his fingers through hers, giving her hand a squeeze. "We immediately had something in common: odd names bestowed upon us by our odd parents."

You know it, Quinzie! Leia shared a grin with her boyfriend.

Kiki muttered something and dove back into her phone.

"Apart from the table drama"—Tarquin pulled his gaze away from Leia—"yesterday must've been ace, meeting all the *Equinox Ten*—"

"Fat fanboys with B.O. and acne?" Kiki cut Tarquin off, rolling her eyes as she looked up. "No, it was ghastly! And don't get me started on their sad cosplay attempts or ridiculous questions about lasers and space bombs. It was all *terribly* depressing."

"And handsomely paid," said Tarquin.

"Contractual obligation! Anyway, *enough*! I don't want to talk about it anymore!" She knocked back her fresh glass of champagne.

"You brought it up," Tarquin mumbled, widening his eyes at Leia. "Change of topic, then. Leia just held her first fashion show in London! Got tons of buzz."

Lowering her champagne, Kiki left a gooey crescent of pink gloss on the rim. "Oh, I know. You're 'the girl who makes clothes out of garbage'. What's that called? Dumpster diving?"

That's a new one! Leia chuckled.

Tarquin delivered a cutting glare. "For Christ sake! She doesn't sew with *garbage*!"

"I don't dumpster dive, either. Although, maybe I should? Might be fun." Leia laughed, shrugging away the oddity of Kiki's ridiculous comment. "My fashions are entirely upcycled, so I take unused fabric, old and damaged clothes, and use sustainable materials like hemp and organic cotton to create beautiful dresses, jackets—anything, really."

Tarquin proudly nodded. "Leia is all about second chances, like I am with buildings." He swung her hand reassuringly. "Just because something is old or broken doesn't mean you toss it away, right?"

Kiki sighed. "Aww, how *sweet*. But wait…Leia, isn't that what you did with Brooke? Simply tossed her away?"

WHAT?!

Leia's stomach plummeted. *How does she…?* Her eyes bulged before she could blink away the surprise. "Uh…" Smile fading, she reached up, tucking a piece of hair behind her ear. "No, I don't think that's…how do you—"

"What am I missing?" asked Tarquin. "Who's Brooke?"

"Darling, you don't *know*?!" Kiki tsked, pointing with her phone. "Brooke is pretty important to Leia."

Breaths lodged in Leia's chest. "She *was* important." *Fuck! I DO NOT want to get into this here!*

Tarquin scratched his temple, his gaze hopping between his mother and his girlfriend. "Leia, who is she?"

"Tarquin, I was going to tell you—"

"Going to?" Kiki feigned surprised indignation. "My god, you've obviously not told my son about the *twins* either!"

Shit! I should've told him. Why didn't I tell him? Leia dipped her chin and let go of his hand, her arms folding protectively around her souring stomach.

Tarquin froze. "Twins?!" He blinked slowly, leaning in. "Leia, you have *children*?"

A lump knotted her throat. Shaking her head, she glanced up. All the joy had drained from Tarquin's face. "Your mom's taking *everything* out of context. I can explain, but not here—"

"Explain how? By lying?!" Kiki elbowed her son. "See? These money-hungry trollops latching onto you boys—I'm SICK of it! I had a bad feeling about this cheater."

Tarquin flinched. "What?!"

Shit. Leia closed her eyes.

"I called an old friend in Manhattan," said Kiki, scrolling through her phone. "He's a fashion PR, knows everyone."

And everyone's business, I bet. Anger blazed through Leia as she dug her nails into her sides. *Kiki's using my past as a battering ram, smashing me and Tarquin apart.* She opened her eyes. *Well, she's messing with the wrong woman.*

Leia broke her self-soothing hug and edged closer. "Tarquin, you *know* me." She grasped his hand, her gaze imploring him to listen as she kept her voice low and controlled. "What she's saying, whatever bullshit this PR person told her—it's not what you think."

"No?" Kiki sneered. "So, you're going to *deny* that you spent three weeks in a mental institution last September?"

Oh...my god. Leia's breath hitched. *I was going to tell you, but not like this.*

Tarquin stiffened, his expression somewhere between wariness and worry. "*Leia...*"

He's horrified. Lightheadedness swooped in, swaying the room around her. Leia tightened her grip, holding on, keeping him close. "I needed *help.*"

"And probably still does!" Kiki foisted her phone forward. "Tarquin darling, see..." A tabloid photo glowed on its screen in full, finger-pointing color.

A tall female bowed her head, her face partially hidden under Jackie O sunglasses and the bill of a blue baseball cap. Her long blonde hair was pulled back in a loose ponytail, which splayed over the hunched shoulders of a gray Roots sweatshirt while the ragged hems of her shapeless jeans dragged on the ground. An older man—her father, maybe?—walked alongside, his expression somber and his arm protectively wrapped around her waist as they entered a Brooklyn mental health facility.

Tarquin has seen me in those sunglasses, and that sweatshirt is on our bed at Rupert's farm. Nausea swirled in Leia's belly as he gaped at the photo, tears brimming in his eyes. *He can have no doubts now.*

"Granted, this girl had dyed blonde hair and was known as Leia McClelland"—relishing the destruction she'd unleashed, an unkind grin crept across Kiki's face—"but you used your rich husband's surname back then, didn't you, Leia? Poor chap. He certainly had his hands full with you: depressive episodes, panic attacks, arson—"

"I *didn't* set the fire!"

"Well, you would say that, wouldn't you?" Kiki rolled her eyes. "This girl is *unstable*, Tarquin! Do you really fancy playing house in London with someone certifiable? You'll end up like Nikolai—disgraced in the papers, your reputation in tatters. Or, heaven forbid, she causes any harm to Ava and Poppy. Just saying it sends a shiver up my spine."

Tarquin tensed up, pulling his hand free from Leia's.

Take a bow, Kiki. You've done it. You've used the stigma of mental health to rip us apart. Tears prickled the back of Leia's throat, but she fought them hard. She wouldn't give Kiki the satisfaction of watching her fall apart. "Tarquin, I'm so sorry."

"Yeah. So am I." He swallowed hard and scrubbed both hands over his face, blinking back tears. Throwing a glance to his left, Tarquin's eyes snagged on Rupert clutching Poppy, his brother's brow furrowed, caught up in the confrontation. "Well, Mum, I guess you better keep Ava and Poppy away from me too, then."

"I beg your pardon?"

What's he doing? Leia bit her lip.

"By your definition, I must be crazy, too. I suffer from *depression*, Mum."

Kiki's alarmed stare swept the rapt audience sat on the nearby banquette. "Shh!" Her eyes flew back to her son. "You do *not*!"

Tarquin expelled an audible breath. "Why are you shushing me? You embarrassed, Mum? Ashamed of me? Afraid you'll look bad by association?"

Spying Fiona and most of the party looking on, Leia stuffed her fists into the pockets of her dress. *Tarquin shouldn't have to explain his depression in public. He's been forced into this corner because of me.*

"What on Earth do *you* have to be depressed about?" Kiki sputtered. "I swear, you're just doing this for attention."

"And there it is!" Tarquin nodded and threw his hands in the air. "The reaction I expected. Let's just sweep it under the carpet, shall we? Pretend it doesn't exist? Because growing up, you made it *abundantly* clear that mental health 'failings', as you called them, happened to *other* people." His dark gaze shifted to Leia. "When Nick was ten and had a panic attack on set, she told everyone it was an allergic reaction to shellfish! Classy, eh?"

Leia winced.

"So, after she dismissed Nick so heartlessly, there was no hope in hell I'd ever confide in her."

Kiki scoffed. "I didn't dismiss him! I was *protecting* him."

"Bullshit! You were protecting *yourself*!" Tarquin pointed at her. "All that matters to you is your reputation and wealth. If you really cared, nothing would've been more important than the well-being of your child, but that's not how the great Kiki Balfour rolls."

"That's not true!" she protested, jutting out a sparkly hip.

People are staring. Leia slouched and pulled her hands from her pockets. *Tarquin is so private. He'll be hating this.*

His scowl slid away from his mother, his disgust lifting as he reached out to Leia. "I felt so alone, so lost—until I met this one." Weaving his fingers through hers again, he pulled her close.

"Tarquin…" Leia pressed her lips together.

"Learning about Leia's struggles and how she deals with them helped me find the courage to do something about *mine*. For too long I've been scared of what everyone would say and think. Not anymore. I honestly don't give a flying fuck."

Leia blinked back tears. "I'm proud of you," she whispered, un-locking his soft smile.

It didn't linger. Turning to his mother, Tarquin glared. "Leia means *everything* to me, and I won't stand for you insulting her. Our relationship is none of your damn business, so you can keep your ignorant opinions and poisonous gossip to yourself. I'm not interested."

He's standing up for me—for us. Leia's heart felt fit to burst. Noticing Rupert nodding and Fiona's silently mouthed 'YES!', she broke into a determined grin. "That makes two of us."

Kiki bristled. "You're *actually* choosing this girl over your own family?"

"No, just you." He kissed Leia's hand. "See ya, Mum."

As Tarquin led her through the sea of tables and respectful nods of Orcadian solidarity, Leia glanced down at her fingers entwined with his. *I can't hide any longer. I need to share my whole past even if it ultimately pushes him away.*

Once through the door, Tarquin stopped dead by the bar's coat rack and exhaled a deep, deliberate breath, then offered Leia a frustrated smile. "So. I thought that went pretty well…?"

Leia winced but felt overwhelming love for him, trying to lift her spirits. "Tarquin, are you *sure* you can deal with my baggage? 'Cause I have *a ton.*"

He pulled her into a warm hug, nodding back toward the restaurant. "Who doesn't, Ginger? Who doesn't?"

He jokes now, but how will he feel once he knows the truth?

THIRTY

TARQUIN

Hidden away from family and the cold afternoon rain lashing the guest house windows, Tarquin stepped back from the blazing fire and climbed on top of the king-size bed beside Leia, the conversation from their fifteen-minute drive from Kirkwall still whirling in his head. In the car, Leia had begun to unload, sharing stories about dating Tyler through high school in Oshawa, Ontario, and their idyllic first years in Pittsburgh where he played professional hockey while she attended college. Life for the loved-up pair sounded hectic but exciting and a bright future lay ahead, but seven years into their relationship and four months after their 2015 castle wedding, the fairy tale began to sour—badly.

"So, Tyler decides to fuck his teammate's wife," said Leia, lying on her side. She tugged the hem of her sweatshirt over her pajama bottoms. "And not just any teammate. The captain."

I knew it! She didn't cheat! Tarquin felt a sense of relief, and then anger. "What a prick! Did he do it more than once?"

"Oh yeah. For three months, they snuck around, screwing in hotels, at home—"

"In your bed?"

"Apparently."

"Jesus!" Tarquin plowed his hand through his hair and grabbed the folded blanket near their bare feet. "When did you find out?"

"January 30, 2016. I remember it like yesterday. Tyler was in Nashville for the NHL All-Star Game weekend. He was FaceTiming me before he left for the rink when his phone dinged with a text.

The color drained from his face and he blurted out: 'Ley, I had an affair.'" She exhaled heavily, her expression more resigned than sad. "I had trusted him with everything. My life...my heart! It knocked me off my feet."

"Understandably!" Tarquin draped Leia with the blanket, covering his own bare legs and boxers as he sank down to lie beside her. "Was the text from her?" He propped himself up on an elbow.

"Yeah. Apparently, Tyler had broken it off with her the week before, but that didn't stop her from dumping her husband. When Ty didn't come running back, she sent that text threatening to tell me. She said she owed me the truth."

"Revenge dressed up as concern—how considerate! And you *knew* this woman?"

"We chaired the wives' Christmas toy drive together." Leia's lips flattened as she plucked a piece of lint off Tarquin's white Henley. "I could barely breathe, let alone speak, but somehow I spit out, 'How could you do this?!' before bursting into tears. Tyler looked mortified and begged for my forgiveness, claiming 'it was just sex, nothing more', but that left me wondering why he'd risk our marriage over something he said meant so little."

Tarquin fumed. "Selfish asshole!"

"He apologized over and over, but I was sobbing so hard I got a nosebleed. He tried to comfort me, but I hung up. Just the sight of him made me feel sick." She sneered, pulling the edge of the blanket higher.

"Did he ring back?"

"Twice, but I ignored him. Eventually, he gave up because he was late for the skills competition."

"Fuck hockey! He should've hopped on a plane and flown home, groveling."

"I was glad he didn't." She glanced down, her fingers busy, twisting her mother's ring. "I called Saz and cried my heart out, begged her not to tell Dad. She was furious with Ty but agreed to bite her tongue. She stayed on the phone with me until I fell asleep. Tyler wouldn't be back in Pittsburgh until Sunday lunchtime, so I had plenty of time to mull over my options."

"Did you leave him?"

"I did—for a week."

That's it? Tarquin kept his expression nonjudgmental. "Can I ask…why'd you take him back?!"

"Tarquin, I *loved* him. And I know that sounds lame considering what he did, but unless you've been in my shoes…" Leia let out a heavy breath. "Have you?"

Pandora. He fiddled with the three buttons below the neckline of his Henley. "Yeah, but it was a new relationship. I didn't love her."

"Well, Ty and I *did* love each other and had been together through high school, my mom dying, him joining the NHL—*a lot* of major life stuff. Neither of us wanted to call time on our marriage…all that history, you know? So, we started counseling and worked on rebuilding our broken trust. We talked about the anger and resentment I felt and why Tyler's hunger for '*attention and validation*' drew him into an affair, and gradually things improved— off the ice. On it, Tyler's affair really divided the team. One day during practice, the captain started a fight with Ty. The coach hit the roof. The dispute landed in the papers, and a week later the team got rid, sending Tyler to New York on trade deadline day."

"Jesus. And just like that you had to uproot everything?"

She nodded. "Right in the middle of the 2015-2016 season. Our five years in Pittsburgh—over. I had to quit my job at the Carnegie Museum of Art, pack up our home, find a place to live in a new city, and arrange our move—all on my own. Trades are a part of life for hockey families, but I never expected to be forced out by a sex scandal. Suddenly, *everyone* in hockey knew about it. Awkward, embarrassing conversations became my new normal."

Tarquin cringed. "Your dad found out, then?"

"Yup. After he swore non-stop for the first five minutes and calmed down, I told him my side of the story. He grumbled but promised he'd respect my choice to stay. Other people weren't as kind, but luckily, the wives and girlfriends in New York were wonderful and supportive, especially Shantelle and Erika.

"The move actually did us a world of good. It felt like a new beginning, like when we got married, except now we had counseling appointments scheduled side-by-side with date nights and work obligations. In the fall, we bought a beautiful apartment in Garden City, and I started my Master of Arts at the Fashion Institute of Technology, plus a part-time job at the Costume Institute. I also began an internship at a major fashion house. That's where I met Brooke Perry."

Tarquin shifted off his elbow and inched closer, laying his head on his pillow. "That's the woman Mum mentioned."

Leia nodded. "Brooke was their women's ready-to-wear designer and we clicked immediately. She introduced me to buyers and marketing gurus and shared really great industry advice—stuff you can't learn in school. By spring 2017, she'd become more than a mentor to me. She was one of my closest friends. Brooke would hang with me, Erika, and Shantelle, invite us to fashion events, and the four of us would take turns throwing dinner parties." Leia giggled. "Don't tell anyone—I ordered in!"

"Hey, at least your guests didn't go hungry. Things were good, then?"

"Yeah! Professionally and socially, everything was really coming together. It felt like our time to shine. Tyler's season was going great, and I was designing for a paying client or two in between research on my Master's thesis. Erika asked me to be her matron of honor, and Brooke became pregnant. Watching her belly grow, I got really broody, and Tyler and I decided to try for a baby. I've always wanted kids, and I was so excited. Every month, I looked forward to missing my period, but every month, I was disappointed."

She wants kids! Tarquin gently rubbed Leia's arm. "I'm so sorry, love. That must've been heartbreaking."

"I was gutted. Tyler seemed disappointed, but he just took it as a challenge to try harder to knock me up. No guy wants to think they're firing blanks, right?"

"That's true."

"Then, December rolled around, our second Christmas in New York. Tyler injured his shoulder in a game and fell into a real funk. It didn't help when Brooke gave birth to twins in January."

The ones Mum spoke of? Tarquin's eyes widened.

"Yeah, *those* twins—two boys." Leia sighed. "Tyler knew how badly I wanted a baby, and it just wasn't happening for us. We were happy for her, but…" She shrugged. "On top of that, our apartment was mid-reno, and Ty was struggling on the ice. He complained about me working all the time and said I should put my fashion label on hold. He wanted me home more…"

Yeah, barefoot and pregnant, I bet. Tarquin scowled. *Heaven forbid she has a career of her own and doesn't baby him 24/7. Bloody Neanderthal.*

"…which was ironic since *he* was away more than he was home. The team was always on a road trip." Leia stretched her legs under the blanket. "Anyway, last year around Valentine's Day, rumors started to fly: Tyler and puck bunnies, Tyler and models, Tyler and a Vegas sportscaster. I felt nauseous. If the stories were true, he was fucking his merry way across North America."

"Did you confront him?"

"Yeah. He denied everything and said the rumors were started by the woman back in Pittsburgh, stirring up trouble again. I *wanted* to believe him."

SAY HELLO, KISS GOODBYE

"Did you?"

"Yes and no. I had no concrete proof of anything going on but"—she sighed—"my gut was telling me otherwise, you know? And Riley didn't help. She was adamant he was untrustworthy—and that pissed me off. How could she be so judgy when she didn't even know him, not like I did? So, I froze her out. Barely spoke to her."

That's a bit extreme. He fought back a grimace, but it was too late. Leia noticed.

"Yeah, I know! I was a complete *bitch*. Riley had my best interests at heart, and I repaid her with attitude and rudeness." She winced. "And karma didn't forget—it swung back around when Tyler began blowing hot and cold. One day, he'd be all loving and attentive. The next, I'd wake up to the silent treatment. Sometimes, he wouldn't even say good morning. And when he held me, it felt…different." Her eyes, dull and defeated, strayed downward, her hands restless beneath the blanket. "I didn't have to ask why or wait for him to tell me. I *knew*."

"What did you do?"

"Prescribed a taste of his own medicine."

A pained expression washed across Tarquin's face. "You slept with someone?!"

"Just the once, to hurt Tyler like he'd hurt me." Leia fussed with the blanket and shifted up on her pillow, her glance drifting back. "You look disappointed."

"No, it's just—I get it. There were extenuating circumstances." *Can I say the same?* Tarquin's stomach rolled. "Leia, I have to tell you something."

Her brows squeezed together.

"I've never cheated"—he inhaled and exhaled quickly—"but I've been the *other* bloke."

Leia stiffened, her jaw slack. "What?! Really?"

"Yeah. Four years ago." He grimaced. "It was a one-off. I shagged the wife of an English football player."

Eyes wide, she leaned away. "*Oh?*"

Bollocks. Is this a mistake, telling her? Cheeks burning, Tarquin averted her piercing gaze. "We met at a house party, both tripping balls on mushrooms, and started something we shouldn't have. Afterward, she scribbled her number on a cocktail napkin, but I never called her. I wasn't interested in being her bit on the side, or a homewrecker."

Leia blew out a breath and sagged against him. "Thank god for that!"

"Drugs were not my thing, and after that night"—Tarquin squinted as he stroked Leia's shoulder—"I never touched them again. I still can't watch her husband play footy without feeling terribly guilty."

"We all make mistakes." Leia drew back with a rueful smile, then bowed her head. "But at least you didn't break your marriage vows. I was so disgusted with myself, I didn't share my dirty little secret with Tyler or anyone. *Well*, until Erika's rooftop party in June three months later."

"What changed?"

"One of Tyler's rumored puck bunnies showed up on the arm of another player. I asked Ty about her, and of course, he denied even recognizing her. But I saw the letchy way she leered across the bar. Tyler was lying to my face—again. Rage consumed me, and I starting drinking—a lot."

Tarquin's brow creased. "When a non-drinker drinks…"

"Yep. Wasn't pretty. I got wasted *fast*. And then, shit got real when I stumbled into the washroom, catching Tyler dick-deep in puck bunny."

Tarquin cringed. "Fuuuck!"

"I went *ballistic*. Swearing, swinging for them, tears racing down my cheeks. They scrambled to get dressed, and our fight spilled out into the bar. That's when I blurted out my own indiscretion." Leia cleared her throat. "I'll leave it to your imagination how ugly *that* was. Blame Ty, blame the drink, blame my hormones—my period was two weeks late."

Was she pregnant? Tarquin opened his mouth but closed it quickly, not sure what to say.

She pulled her knees up, wrapping an arm around them. "The next morning, I kicked him out." Her voice thickened. "My period came a day later and I was devastated all over again."

Tarquin stroked her cheek. "Oh, Leia."

"I dunno if it was that or the public shame, but something shook Tyler that summer. He went to counseling for sex addiction, and by August, we were talking again. He emailed me contact details for two women in his agent's office who wanted dresses. I let him store his Porsche in my underground parking spot again."

Tarquin gaped, raising a brow. "Is that a euphemism? Leia, tell me you didn't take him back *again*?!"

"No! Not *back*!" She pouted and tugged at the ends of her hair. "I let him stay over once or twice." She blinked up from her fingers, catching Tarquin's huff. "I was lonely! Missing sex, and Ty was there. In a weird way, it felt safer being with him than hooking up with some random guy off an app."

I'd rather you chose the rando!

"So, anyway, Erika's wedding weekend rolled around. It was a massive deal, a who's who of NHL players and their glamorous wives. Riley and Shantelle were there. Brooke, too, but she'd recently broken up with her guy, a goalie with New Jersey. It was a bit awkward. He was there with some woman, and Brooke was alone with their eight-month-old twins in tow."

Leia smiled. "Those twins...I *adored* them. I swear I spent more time with them than Brooke that day. Tyler, too. Watching him, I saw what our future could be: him, me, our babies—my dream. I thought, *If we keep trying, we could have this life.* After dinner and dancing, we went back to my hotel room and made love all weekend, staying in bed until we had to check out Monday morning. Tyler headed off to play in a celebrity golf tournament and I caught a lift home with Brooke and the twins, smiling to myself the whole way. When I got there, our concierge was in a panic and said he'd tried to reach me, but my phone was off. Turns out, some asshole had broken into my building's parking overnight and torched some cars, including Tyler's Porsche."

"Holy shit!"

"Yeah, it was bad. A bunch of vehicles were damaged beyond repair. The fire marshal gave me clearance to sift through Ty's for anything salvageable, but all his stuff was either charred or water-damaged. I checked his glove compartment before leaving and found a scorched pouch containing the car's user manual. I popped it open and my heart stopped. Inside, Tyler had photos of Brooke's twins and two birth certificates naming him as their father."

Tarquin jerked. "Oh! My GOD!"

"I know, right. So much for Tyler firing blanks, huh?"

"Oh, Leia." He pushed his hair off his forehead. "You must've been crushed."

"I felt dead inside, like someone stabbed a pair of scissors through my heart." She flashed a false smile. "My mentor, *my friend* screwed my husband and gave birth to his kids! Kids *I* always wanted."

With friends like that... Tarquin shook his head. "She sat at the wedding, watching you—with them!"

"Not just her—Erika too! They both knew those twins were Tyler's, and neither one said a word. It felt like the biggest 'Fuck you' ever."

"How'd you know Erika was involved?"

"A handwritten note from her was with the photos and certificates. She wrote it on February 3, 2018—one month after the twins were born—urging Tyler to do the right thing and pay child support or Brooke would get lawyers involved."

"Do the right thing!" Tarquin sneered. "The *right* thing would've been telling his wife! What a fucking asshole! And I'm sorry, but this Erika person isn't much better."

"Oh, don't worry. We're no longer friends." Leia's expression soured. "So, I left the burnt-out car, waved thanks to the firefighters, and rushed upstairs, trying to keep it together till I was in my apartment. Once I'd slammed my door shut, the dam broke. I bawled for a good two hours before I could call Saz, but just hearing her voice, I lost it again. Saying the words out loud didn't help either." With a grimace, she squeezed her eyes shut, then opened them again, her slow blink accompanied by a weighty exhale. "I've never felt so alone in my life."

I'll never let her feel that way again. Tarquin's heart ached as he brushed her hair away from her eyes.

"Saz offered to ring Dad, so I could have a shower and be ready for Tyler's arrival. The minute he walked in, I stuffed the birth certificates in his hands and landed a right hook."

Tarquin smirked. "You punched him?! Damn! Bastard got his."

"He really did." Leia bit her lip. "I broke his nose. Blood splattered everywhere."

"Your parents should've named you Rocky!"

Leia half-laughed. "The one time kickboxing classes came in handy. I think I was just as surprised as Tyler. He sputtered and turned on the waterworks, said he'd only slept with Brooke once. Nice, eh? Tyler got Brooke pregnant with a single, meaningless fuck. So, turns out, I was betrayed by my husband *and* my body."

I wish I could make all this hurt go away. Tarquin gathered her in, pressing a kiss on her forehead. "I'm so, so sorry."

"I was too when the police showed up."

Tarquin flinched. "What?! The fucker *rang* them?"

"No, our elderly neighbor did. She heard our shouting, called 911. You should've seen Ty—putting on the charm, smiling above the blood stains on his shirt. He told the cops he tripped over my throw rug and hit the wall. They fawned all over him, and of course, Tyler ate it up, signing autographs and sharing locker room stories. He was so smug. I wanted to claw the entitled smirk right off his face. As soon as the police were gone, I ran into the bathroom, grabbed his toothbrush and the smelly cologne he'd left the week before, and threw it at him. Told him to get the hell out of my life— for good this time. And then…I fell apart at the seams. Cried into my pillow for days. Didn't shower, couldn't eat. Meanwhile, the lovely Brooke took our story public."

"You've got to be kidding!"

"If only. Hitting the gossip rags did *exactly* what Brooke had hoped: forced Ty to open his wallet *a lot* wider. On her blog, she also painted me as a social-climbing, talentless gold digger who used *her* fashion connections to grow my label. She publicly disparaged my designs, too—said I lied about their sustainability. The only saving grace was my business wasn't called Frill-Seekers at the time. I could change the name and start fresh, and pray my reputation was salvageable."

"Unbelievable!" His voice rose. "You're the innocent party."

Leia shrugged, her eyes weary as she tugged on the blanket. "You'd think, right? But then she told Manhattan's top gossip columnist that I was a vindictive bitch who forced Tyler to withhold financial support for his twins."

"Bollocks! You love kids. You loved *hers*!"

"I know! But she was connected. People believed her. In their eyes, I was this horrible wife keeping Tyler's babies at arm's length while I counted his pennies and used everyone around me for professional gain. To them, I got what I deserved. And what I got, besides a broken heart, a destroyed marriage, and a ruined reputation, was a complete invasion of my privacy. Gossip bloggers and paparazzi hounded me relentlessly. I mean, who doesn't enjoy a dishy sex scandal swirling around a pro athlete, two fashion designers, and cute twins? We were total clickbait."

"Sold to the highest bidder."

Leia nodded. "My panic attacks came back. I couldn't deal, so I had to throw the wolves off my scent. Shantelle helped me move from Garden City to Brooklyn and I dyed my hair blonde, hoping the press wouldn't recognize me, but obviously from the photo your mom found, I was wrong.

"All the stress piled up. I lost weight, had daily migraines and bed-soaking night sweats. Every swallow felt like razorblades slicing my throat, and the fatigue was nothing like I've ever experienced. I could barely lift my head off the pillow. Dad freaked out and flew down from Canada, took me to a blur of doctor's appointments and tests."

Concern clouded Tarquin's expression as he held her hand under the blanket. "What did they find?"

"Mononucleosis, the 'kissing disease'—or as Saz called it, 'Tyler's bastard of a parting gift'. It's a virus, so they prescribed bedrest and nothing else. You literally have to wait it out, which gave me lots of time to adopt a new hobby: beating myself up. I was a bad wife, I had worked too much, I had ignored the warning signs— I *deserved* this fate. And as my blame game spiraled out of control, a new tabloid claim would pop up, reinforcing all these negative thoughts in my head."

Leia's thumb slowly swept across Tarquin's hand. "I sank into a really dark place. Everything made me cry, nothing gave me hope. Dad was worried, so he called my doctor, and she spoke to my psychologist. They both agreed admittance to the mental health unit was best for my recovery. It would be safer, more private than at home or with a friend. And let's face it, I didn't really have a lot of friends left. Just Shantelle, really."

"Not the other wives?"

"Dropped me. I was a cautionary tale to be avoided."

"What about Riley? You seem close?"

"Oh, we are *now*. Back then, she was dealing with her mom's cancer, and honestly, she owed me nothing. Months later, I apologized for being so awful. She's become a really good friend."

Acknowledging when you've been wrong takes courage. I'm proud of her. Tarquin squeezed her hand. "How was the hospital?"

"Scary. Lonely. They watched me like a hawk, which felt unnerving. And I *hated* giving up control. I had no say in what I ate, who I talked to, when I slept. They put me on medication, took away my phone, and limited my access to TV. My entire existence was scheduled by someone else. Basically, a micromanager's worst nightmare!"

Tarquin smiled kindly. "If you weren't depressed before…"

"Right?" She laughed. "But in some ways, it was good to just *be*. I read a lot, attended countless therapy sessions, and let myself grieve for what I'd lost and the future I'd never have. Then, slowly but surely, I felt stronger and healthier. I was still scared about the future, but…"

"Hey, who isn't?" Tarquin gave her a reassuring nod.

"Coming home to Saz and Dad definitely helped, though. I could have pizza! Go swimming! Just hang out with them in my place. I still felt bruised, but at least I wasn't blaming myself anymore. By December, I was divorced, working on Frill-Seekers, and in London for the holidays."

"And shopping in IKEA, where you rescued my phone." *And stole my heart.*

"One of my best spur-of-the-moment decisions!" Leia's warm

smile dimmed. "Unlike keeping my past from you. I should've told you all this ages ago. In a way, what happened today was partly my fault."

Tarquin shook his head. "No, Leia, it wasn't. Today was signature Kiki. She loves twisting facts and gets off on making others feel uncomfortable and inferior. It's like she gets a little hit of dopamine every time she stomps on someone's self-esteem. Usually, she saves the belittling for smaller, more familiar audiences—me and Nick or Rupert and Fiona—but occasionally she can't help herself and goes rogue like today. There's no telling what will trigger her."

"Well, see? If I'd told you about Brooke and the hospital..."

"Didn't you just say you've stopped beating yourself up?"

Leia pressed her lips together as the amber flames in the fireplace crackled and danced.

"Look, if I'd known about Brooke and everything you've endured, Mommie Dearest would've found something else to use against you. Seriously, I'm not kidding when I say she's hated all our girlfriends. Narcissists want all the attention, all the time. Girlfriends and wives just steal the limelight." Tarquin cupped her chin. "I'd rather cut off all contact with her than allow her venomous behavior to damage what we have. You're so precious to me, Leia. I won't stand for it."

She smiled fondly. "I'll always have your back, too. But that's why I feel sick about you announcing your depression to the world like that, just to defend mine. No one should be forced to share their most private struggles before they're ready. You didn't have to do that."

"Yeah, I did, and I'd do it again in a heartbeat. I'd do anything for you." Tarquin lifted her hand to his lips and softly kissed her knuckles. "And while I *am* nosey by nature and would love to know every single thing about you, I completely understand why you were hesitant to open up about Tyler and the chaos he brought into your life."

Leia blinked up from their entwined hands with a tentative grin. "I wanted to tell you so many times, but 'I was in a mental hospital' isn't something you drop into casual conversation, you know? Sharing my struggles with depression is always a huge step, but being put behind closed doors? It feels like asking someone to scale a mountain."

"Good thing I'm an experienced climber, then."

Leia half-laughed. "But you *see*, right? I couldn't open up about the end of my marriage without going *there*. And it's not that I'm ashamed of it—I don't really think it's that. Those three weeks brought light back into life. But still, my past is *a lot* to unpack. It's a big ask for a partner to take on or understand."

He kissed her hand again and held it against his shirt, his heart beating beneath their bond. "So, it's complicated and messy. Leia, I'm sorry for all the pain you've been through, but what matters is *today*. Right now. This. *Us*."

"Well, that's how I feel, too. But I worry, though, once you have time to think…"

"What? You think I'll change my mind?"

"Maybe," Leia whispered.

"Not a chance." He kissed her on the nose. "I can't guarantee sunny days or pizza with grapes, but I can promise this: I'll never hurt you."

A soft smile pinched her cheeks as her eyes glistened. Diverting attention, she glanced over at Tarquin's perfectly arranged photos on his bedside bookcase.

He followed her gaze, and his younger self grinned back. Shirtless in swim trunks holding a surfboard, he stood shoulder to shoulder with a sunburnt Harry. In another framed shot, the teens held glow sticks aloft in a sea of dry ice, lasers, and dancing revelers.

"I love your photos," said Leia. "You look so happy and care-free…before life got all complicated."

"Yeah. Occasionally, I catch myself thinking, who *was* that kid and where'd he go?"

Leia snuggled closer. "I miss the old me sometimes, but I don't miss my old life." She let go of his hand and captured a piece of his hair, twirling it around her finger. "This one is so much better…the one I share with you."

Share? Does this mean no lingering 'Let's see how it goes'?

Leia took a large breath, her tearful eyes gazing into his. "I love you, Tarquin."

She loves me! Joy and gratitude swelled through his heart. "Oh, Ginger." Tarquin caressed her cheek. "You don't know how long I've waited to hear that! After today, I thought I never would."

"It'll take more than Hurricane Kiki to scare *me* away." She kissed him tenderly and pulled away, opening her eyes as her hands pressed against his chest. "It was so hot, you standing up for me." One hand slipped lower under the band of his boxer briefs.

Oooh, yes. I'll definitely stand up for you now. Tarquin sucked in a breath. "I'll always put you first, Leia."

"What have I done to deserve you?" Her mouth claimed his again and he let her in, the sweet strokes of her tongue and her wandering fingers raising more than his spirits.

THIRTY-ONE

LEIA

Alone and cocooned in a cozy blanket on the edge of Tarquin's bed, Leia looked up from her gratitude journal, a smile blooming on her face. *This trip was exactly what I needed.* The past six days had been filled with passionate sex, island hopping, and family bonding, and Leia had loved *almost* every minute. Kiki drama aside, the Balfours, Orkney, and Tarquin were firmly ensconced in her heart.

I'll never forget Tarquin doing what Tyler never did: sticking up for me—for us. That sealed it. Tarquin Balfour IS my guy!

Picking up her pen, she wiggled her toes in front of the fire, its roaring blaze masking the blustery winds whistling through Rupert's farm equipment outside. *Tomorrow afternoon we'll be back in London, back to real life, and I am SO ready!* Humming happily to herself, she dove back into her journal entry.

November 27, I was grateful for:

1. *this glimpse into Tarquin's life. Everyone here has a funny Tarquin story, like the one where he was housecleaning drunk and naked after a night out! Such a neat freak! I swear, they love him almost as much as I do!*

2. *rockpooling on Birsay Beach with Tarquin & Ava, finding elusive 'Groatie Buckies'. Other places call them cowrie shells, but the Orkney name is so freakin' cute.*

3. *the ride on Tarquin's boat— he named it* Leia *5 years ago! — around the Bay of Kirkwall. After, we shopped (puffin goodies for Riley!) and I hugged Kirkwall's 'Big Tree'.*

4. visiting the village of Balfour on the island of Shapinsay. Balfour Castle looks like something out of a fairy tale. His family doesn't own it anymore, so we couldn't go in.

5. Shan's call. I'm off to Paris 2x next month to dress/style her for two industry events.

6. my past. It's not the prettiest, but I wouldn't be with Tarquin if my life had played out differently. For the first time in ages, I'm looking forward to the future.

She glanced up, finding her boyfriend, all messy hair, Clark Kent eyeglasses, and flirty dimples, leaning against the doorjamb, a glass of freshly squeezed orange juice in his grip. *Ooh, coming to save me again, naked Superman?* Her appreciative gaze slipped down his happy trail. *Hmm, I'm not the only one who wishes we were still in bed.*

"Good morning, gorgeous." Tarquin raised the glass. "I brought you some sustenance while you sketch. You know, if something urgent has come up, I can make breakfast while you work."

How he can say that with a straight face... Leia smiled and closed the book. "Aw, thanks. It's nothing work-related, though. Just my gratitude journal."

"Oh, really? Is this a new thing?" He stepped over his discarded boxers and Henley, placing her glass on the bedside table just shy of his latest gift for her: a special *Little Miss* book celebrating Ginger Spice.

"I started it last Christmas. It was my therapist's idea. I found it tough at first, finding things to be thankful for when I still felt broken and bruised, but writing down all the good stuff in my life helped me see things differently. It helped me focus on what I *did* have instead of what I didn't." As Leia zipped the journal closed, her eyes leisurely swept down Tarquin's body and hovered over his erection, bobbing hello. *Talk about a wake-up call. Every morning without fail, lucky me!* She smiled brightly as her gaze flitted up, meeting his. "And it turns out I have a lot to be grateful for."

"You and me both." He scratched his temple. "So, do you ever write about me?"

"Sometimes…"

"Hmm, I must be doing something right, then!" He licked his lips as Leia slipped free from the blanket, naked except for a pair of lavender panties. "Do you write daily?"

"I try to." Leia stretched, leaving the journal beside her juice. "But this is my first entry since late August."

"Late August? What was—" His face fell. "Oh! High Line?"

With a nod, she flung open the duvet and shifted to Tarquin's side of the bed, inviting him into her fort of blankets and pillows.

"So, you *did* miss me!" Tarquin slid in beside her, and Leia cocooned the sheets and duvet around his nakedness. He rolled onto his side, facing her, his bliss tipping toward concern. "But all jokes aside, why did you stop journaling?"

"Regret, sadness, longing…there wasn't much room left for gratitude." She swept her fingers along his furrowed brow and back again. "I thought walking away from you was for the best, for me and my career, but it broke my heart."

Tarquin hugged her close.

"And to top it all off, I'd lost my job at the Institute the day before. Budget cuts."

"No! You *loved* it there! I assumed you just quit because Frill-Seekers was getting too big."

"Nope. Being let go hurt, but in retrospect, it was the push I needed." She lifted her chin. "If they'd kept me, I wouldn't have come to London, wouldn't have held my fashion show. I wouldn't be *here* now with you."

He softly kissed her. "I owe those bean counters *several* pints!"

Leia giggled, her fingers swirling in the fine auburn hair on his sculpted chest. "We both do."

"Bless." He squeezed her tight, kissing her forehead. "God, this week flew by. Fancy a little more sightseeing on our last day?"

"How many hours of light do we have?"

"It's around nine o'clock now, so we'll have about six. We'll have to bundle up, though. It's sunny but blustery out there. Or if you'd prefer, we could stay in..." He kissed her lips and down her neck, his sharp, warm puffs of breath skating over her skin. "Pick up where we left off last night." His erection poked her stomach.

Tangled together in the shower. He can't get enough. Want tingled between her thighs. *And neither can I. God, you'd think we'd be all out of orgasms by now.* "This morning, you mean." She smirked and brushed a lazy finger along his jaw, the coarseness of his stubble pricking her skin. "We didn't climb back into bed until quarter to two!"

"Worth it, though! So wet and steamy. Jesus, Leia. I was so worked up, it felt like my balls would blow when I came." Eyes still on her, he bent down, taking her peaked nipple into his mouth for a long, slow suck.

He's SO bad! She sighed. *He knows exactly what this does to me. He just knows.*

And so did Leia. Months of separation did little to erase what they'd learned about each other in London. Tarquin went wild whenever Leia nibbled his shoulder or kissed near his belly button, and every time her tongue flirted with the ridge of his penis, his eyes would roll back and curses would fill the air. In bed, in the shower—it didn't matter where Leia and Tarquin fooled around; their subtle dance of give and take never felt conditional or expected. It felt natural, respectful.

Loving.

This man! Leia arched her back, asking for more. *I swear he's God's gift to womankind. The things he can do with his tongue!*

Tarquin flicked and pressed her nipple, teasing Leia into a dizzy puddle of bliss, her nails digging into his shoulders. "You repaying me for last night?"

He glanced up, his gaze heavy and mischievous. "Don't you want me to?"

"Oh, I do! But…"

"*Butt*? You mean…*this* gorgeous butt?" Tarquin slipped his fingers into her underwear, grabbing a handful of her ass as he closed his mouth around her breast again for a vigorous suck, the sensation rocketing straight to her core.

Goose bumps pebbled her skin as she gasped through a giggle. "You're insatiable and silly, and I'd love orgasms for breakfast, but we really should…" Her eyes lazily flickered, fighting the pleasure building within in.

He sucked harder and slid his hand around Leia's hip and between her legs. All her thoughts of silliness, sunlight, and sightseeing faded away like a north island mist, replaced by countless sighs and uncontrollable tingles worthy of a glowing gratitude entry.

Her breaths shortened. "I love your mouth on me," she gasped, writhing beneath him, desire soaking her panties as his fingers circled and teased.

Tarquin relinquished her breast with a soft kiss. "I can tell. You're so deliciously wet, begging for more." He nudged his glasses up his nose. "I know you'll taste amazing."

Shifting between her thighs, he kissed his way along her stomach, stopping just shy of her underwear, which he peeled away slowly, his leisurely pace a cruel tease. But the wait was worth it. Panties gone, his fingers gently parted her, his breath warm and ragged as his tongue stroked across her, sparking a surge of tingly shivers firing through her body. She twitched with each lick, her hands ravishing his bedhead, grasping, tugging, refusing to let go.

I want this. I want him, more than anything. Leia moaned as

Tarquin glided two fingers inside her. "Deeper, Tarquin." She bucked instinctively against his hand and bit her lip as he circled her slick center with his tongue, his fingers plunging harder, faster, intensifying her need, taking her higher and higher until she broke.

Sucking in a breath, Leia stiffened, letting out a loud moan as the orgasm ripped through her, unraveling body and soul. She fisted Tarquin's hair, riding each explosive pulse until she whimpered with relief. Wilting into a pool of dizzy satisfaction, her open-mouthed gaze meandered over the wooden beams crossing the ceiling.

Tarquin eased himself up onto an elbow. "Ah, Leia. What were you saying about breakfast?" He flashed a satisfied smirk. "You still peckish?"

For you, always! She panted. "I was just"—she waved a floppy hand in the air—"you know, want to make…most of our last day."

"I'd say we're right on track."

Her eyes drifted down, landing on his erection. Still hard. Ever patient like his owner.

I can't leave him like this.

"I can make you pancakes with hash browns before we go sightseeing." He caught her looking at his crotch. "Don't worry about him. So needy!"

Leia giggled. "I'm more than willing."

"Nah, let's wait. Save some fireworks for later, eh?"

"Okay, I'll make you a deal: play tour guide for me this morning, and I'll play *Return of the Jedi* for you tonight."

His adorable face scrunched in thought. "Play? You mean, *watch*?"

"No, Tarquin. Play. Guess who made herself a gold bikini."

"Clothes! Now!" He scrambled out of bed, leaving Leia in fits of laughter.

"Saving the best for last!" Windblown but smiling brightly, Leia placed her hand on the fifteen-foot, lichen-spotted standing stone and closed her eyes. "I realize the magical time travel stones in *Outlander* weren't on Orkney, but just humor me, okay?"

Tarquin laughed as his girlfriend got up close and personal with the Ring of Brodgar, a prehistoric stone circle dating back to 2500BC. Of the original sixty stones, only thirty-six remained, their weathered facades bearing witness to untold mysteries. He stepped back and tilted her phone, fitting Leia perfectly in frame. "I've been here hundreds of times but still get goose bumps. This circle is older than both Stonehenge and the Great Pyramids of Egypt—how's that for a total mindfuck!"

NOO! I knew they were old, but...! Leia's stomach rolled and her eyes popped open. "Shit!" She pulled her hand away. "And I'm touching it?!"

"You're fine! The heritage officer said we could." Tarquin glanced above her phone. "I guess it's a good thing you were blissfully unaware the Stones of Stenness are even more ancient."

"And you're telling me now?!"

Mid-laugh, the ping of a text dragged Tarquin back to her screen. "Oh, it's Shantelle—another jubilantly smug photo from sunny Mauritius."

A biting gust forced its way down the cuffs of Leia's parka. "Fruity cocktails, a barely-there bikini, and Bastien on the beach?" *I miss my mitts.* She shivered, her pink cheeks stinging.

"Yeah." Tarquin nudged up his eyeglasses. He paused for a moment, his coat ruffling against his thighs. "Bastien is treating Shantelle to sun and sand, and here I am tormenting you with wind and rain. Oh, and let's not forget my mum!"

And I've come out the other side knowing you're the one. Leia smiled, adjusting her scarf. "Like I need a sunburn and more freckles. I'm happy *here*, Tarquin. Besides, Mauritius doesn't have ancient stone circles."

She settled back into her *Outlander*-inspired pose, but her red locks and the chilly gales pushing northeast weren't cooperating. She gathered her tangled tresses and leaned into the rock again, closing her eyes as Tarquin snapped a burst of cheesy photos.

"Got some great ones!"

Leia opened her eyes. "Eh, didn't work—I'm still here." Laughing, she bounced over to Tarquin. "I kid! I *love* Orkney!" She threaded her hands around his arm and hugged him tight as he scrolled through the photos on her phone.

"See? I took a bunch."

"Ooh, they're perfect! I'll send some to Saz and Shantelle when we've got wi-fi again." She kissed Tarquin on a chilled cheek and traded her phone for the hat and mitts in her pocket. "Cheers, Han Solo!"

Leia's delighted gaze strayed beyond the parade of stones. "*This place*…clean air, deep blue seas, gorgeous scenery. The sky goes on forever! Honestly, Orkney feels like another world. The ancient sites are amazing, obviously, but I'm just as fascinated by the ruins dotted all over the islands."

"The old houses and farm buildings?"

"Yeah." She tugged on her cotton beanie, taming her wild hair. "Roofs gone, grass overgrown, only their stone walls remaining. They're beautiful…but in a melancholy way."

Tarquin nodded. "Most were built in the 1800s. We call them tumbledowns."

"I like that!" She slipped her hands into her red and white Canada mitts. "Don't you wonder: who lived there, and why'd they leave?"

"All the time. Every house has its story, some tragic, some not." Tarquin blew on his hands and rubbed them together. "Life can be tough here. The remoteness and unpredictable weather aren't for everyone, but it's still a smashing place to live. That's why I bought a few old houses and tumbledowns to work on."

"Really? You're going to bring them back to life?!"

"That's my plan. Orkney has given me so much—it's time I reciprocated."

Leia looped her mitt-covered hand around Tarquin's cold fingers. "You're *amazing*, you know that?"

"Well, I try!" He laughed as they strolled toward the next stone, standing tall fifteen feet away.

Leia eyed up the enormous stone looming ahead. "The history geek in me still can't believe we walked around Skara Brae. An actual prehistoric village! Can you imagine, Tarquin? Building houses now that people will pay to visit five thousand years later?"

"Nope!"

"And how organized were its settlers? Their houses had stone dressers and shelves! Maybe you can trace your neat freak genes all the way back to there!" She giggled.

"Hey, what can I say? Orkney has a lot to answer for where I'm concerned. So, what tops your list of favorite Orkney experiences?"

"Oh god, there are so many things. I loved that tiny tidal island!"

"The Brough of Birsay?"

"Yeah! Although, the whole time I worried the tides would rise and the causeway would vanish."

"It happens." Tarquin shrugged. "People have been stranded with only the seals for company."

"Now *they* were cute! I could've watched them for hours. I really enjoyed St. Margaret's Hope, too—such a pretty village—and the Italian Chapel blew my mind."

"I think it does for most people. I remember visiting as a kid and Grandma saying it was made from Nissen huts and scrap metal. I thought she was having a laugh, but she told me about the Italian POWs who built it, and I was gobsmacked. If I didn't want to become a builder before…"

"Right? Talk about resourcefulness. I mean, who makes intricate hanging light fixtures from corned beef tins?" Leia's eyes widened. "You'd never know they were cans!"

"Gotta love it!" said Tarquin. "Upcycling circa 1943!"

Leia nodded. "It really is remarkable. And the paintings and the tiny metal heart in the floor…" She swooned, plopping her mitt on her chest. "That made me tear up, thinking about the Italian soldier at the end of the war who left his heart behind for the Orkney girl he loved."

Tarquin pulled her close and kissed the top of her head. "Breaks your heart, doesn't it?"

"Yeah. I felt the same way at Betty Corrigall's grave on Hoy, buried alone in the middle of nowhere, just sky and wind for company."

"The loneliest grave in the UK."

Such a tragic story, a young, pregnant girl shunned by her community. Leia leaned on his shoulder. "I'm glad we could pay our respects."

Tarquin let go of Leia's hand and wound his arm around her shoulders like he knew she needed comforting. "Ava is still raving about her adventures with us. She absolutely *adores* you."

"Aw." She smiled wistfully. "I adore her, too! Such a sweet girl. Talented, too."

"Oh, yeah. Sorry about that. I love Peedie to the moon and back, but blimey! Fiddle playing 'Twinkle, Twinkle, Little Star' at breakfast yesterday…"

"But she was so enthusiastic!"

427

"Painful, more like! Ears bled, Bert howled—it sounded like she was strangling Mrs. Chuzzlewit."

"It wasn't that bad!" Leia playfully pushed on his chest. "Like you can talk! I've heard you play your drums."

"So, my style *might* be considered experimental..."

Leia's burst of laughter sailed away on the wind. "What style?" she teased, giving him a squeeze. "Look, I don't care how good you are, just as long as you have fun."

"Thank you! And I don't mean to sound like a dick about the fiddle. *I know* Ava enjoys it, bless her. I just wish she'd save the impromptu gigs for when I don't have a stompin' hangover. That pub lock-in was wild as balls. I haven't been that drunk in ages."

"I knew you'd had a good time with your friends when Fiona said she found you in her kitchen at 3 a.m. cleaning up—nude!"

"Absolute lies! All the important dangly bits were covered by her apron."

"If you say so." She giggled. "I'm just glad you had fun. Ava and I did, too. I can't remember the last time I bounced on a trampoline, played with stuffies, or flew a kite. I taught her how to make s'mores, too."

"I have to tell you, Leia...it made my day yesterday, hearing about you mucking in like that."

"Ah, it was no biggie." Leia met his grin with her own. "I love kids." *And I'm so glad you do, too. Maybe one day we could have our own? I so want that.*

"You and me both, Ginger." Tarquin's gaze glowed with happiness like he could read her mind. They were on the same page, wanting the same things, the same future.

But what if I can't get pregnant?

A breath caught in Leia's chest. She blinked and cleared her throat, glancing away so Tarquin wouldn't spot any concern on her face. "These winds, eh? I'm glad they weren't like this when we were walking along the cliffs at Yesnaby."

"In the summer, Scottish primroses grow around there."

"So it's even more picturesque—wow. And that sea stack, Yesnaby Castle? But hearing about you climbing it…"

"I didn't slip!"

"That's not what Nick said!"

Tarquin bit back a laugh. "So, how'd you like stooping ninety degrees to enter Maeshowe?"

"Nice change of subject, Balfour." She swung his hand. "Yeah, I was relieved to reach the end of that tunnel without banging my head."

"You were pretty hunched over."

"My knee was thrilled when we stood up again inside the chambered tomb."

Concern tightened Tarquin's embrace. "You should've said. How's it now?"

"It's fine. The Viking graffiti inside was worth a little pain."

"I'll tell you a secret: I leave a little graffiti in every build and reno I do," said Tarquin. "Under a sink, behind a closet door. 'I was here.'"

"You don't include your name?"

"No. I'd rather be mysterious. Keep 'em wondering, *Who is this joker?* Kinda like Banksy."

"Right, so you're the new Banksy now, are you?!" Leia laughed, cuddling into him. "Well, I've loved everything we've done this week, but my favorite was seeing you with your family and friends, and hearing their stories. They *love* you here, Tarquin. Orcadians have GREAT taste." Leia swore a blush deepened the pinkish hue of his chilled cheeks.

"True, they do." He grinned above his wooly scarf. "Because they think the world of you. I couldn't love you more, Leia Scott."

Now who's blushing? Leia's shivers dissipated in the warm, fuzzy feelings hugging her heart.

"You know, I *was* going to call you…after my fashion show. See if you'd give me another chance."

"Yeah?"

"Yeah." Leia tucked a skyward strand of hair behind an ear, but another gust flirted it free. "Things were so hectic in the run up to the day, I had to keep my focus. But then you appeared and…"

"The rest is history, right?" He kissed her cheek.

They crossed the ditch circling the ancient stones and joined the main pathway leading to the small parking lot. The fading purple heather growing wild around the ancient site waved goodbye as the wind sighed through the bowing grass.

Leia's eyes swept the horizon, taking in the Loch of Stenness on one side of the stones and the Loch of Harray on the other. "It's so beautiful here." She gasped, her gaze locked on the breathtaking sunset, its warm oranges and dusty blues descending in the distance behind the hills on the island of Hoy.

"If we're lucky, we might see the northern lights after dinner," said Tarquin. "Orcadians call them the Merry Dancers."

"Love it." *And him. I already feel lucky. Everything that's happened here has made me love him even more.* Butterflies flittered in her stomach. *Why wait?* She glanced up at him, his hair playfully tossed by the wind. "So, at risk of sounding premature, I don't want to go home."

He chuckled. "Yeah, Orkney has a way of casting its spell."

"No offence to Orkney, but that's not what I mean." She stopped on the path and pulled him close, their warm breaths mingling. "I want to stay in London…permanently. I mean, I want to be with *you*."

Tarquin's mouth gaped, his eyes blinking in disbelief. "Oh. My. God! Leia, I'd love nothing more! But what about Fashion Week and your pop-up shop in Brooklyn?"

"I'll fly back for both. The pop-up runs for all of April, so maybe you could join me for a bit? Help me pack up my apartment?"

"I'm so there! But are you sure? You know I want us to be together, but I'd never pressure you to up sticks and move. You did enough of that for Tyler."

"I know, but you're not him. Tarquin, you are the kindest, most supportive man I've ever known." She pulled him closer. "I love London. Saz is there, and Frill-Seekers is getting lots of good PR. I know you mentioned before we could have a long-distance relationship, but I just don't think I can cope with that again. Ty and I were apart so much."

"No, I *totally* get it." Tarquin's brow furrowed. "But is it even possible? How would you be able to emigrate and work?"

"I can get a UK Ancestry visa. If you're Canadian and have a grandparent who was born in the UK, you can apply that way."

"Moving, though—it's huge. I'd hate for you to have regrets."

"Like I did in New York?" Leia gazed into his eyes. "I let you go twice before, Tarquin. I won't let that happen again."

He broke out into a smile. "Blimey! I'm *speechless*...for once!"

This will probably fix that. "So, can I move in with you?"

"Of course! I was going to ask but—oh, Leia! London is going to be smashing! We can re-decorate the flat, change up the furniture. Hey, we can turn one of the bedrooms into a Frill-Seekers workroom with dress forms and sewing machines. I'll do anything for you, Leia. Just name it."

She chuckled warmly. "Tarquin, I'm not making over your flat! All I want is *you*—and maybe a date to Simon and Freddie's wedding next month."

"What the lady wants, the lady gets." He pulled her in for a sweet kiss.

THIRTY-TWO

TARQUIN

London, Saturday, December 21, 2019

Strings of fairy lights and silver garlands twinkled like glittery smiles across the large windows of Alex and Mark's plush London Fields apartment, mirroring the joyous grins of Simon and Freddie's wedding guests. The black-and-white-themed celebration was deep in champagne-soaked speeches, the first by a bubbly Alex (Simon's best woman) and the second by Freddie's best man, Mark. Overcome with emotion, the Irish actor ran a hand through his dark hair and playfully cursed under his breath before flashing a teary, eye-crinkling grin at the newlyweds. "Yeah, you got me, Freds."

Digging into the front pocket of his tuxedo's trousers, Mark whipped out a folded fifty-pound note, and Freddie jubilantly snapped the wager from his best friend's fingers. Laughter burst from all corners of the room while a few guests whisked away happy tears, including Leia.

Tarquin set down his boulevardier and leaned in close, plucking a neatly ironed handkerchief from inside his tux jacket. "You okay, love?" he whispered over their half-eaten apple pie butter tarts, the dessert a nod to Simon's Canadian heritage.

"I am. Thanks." Leia accepted his offer. "I *always* cry at weddings." She laughed faintly and carefully dabbed her eyes with his white cotton square.

Does tonight bring back memories of her own? Tarquin gazed at his girlfriend in her floor-length bias-cut white dress and softly rubbed her back, hoping his loving caress might soothe any bittersweet déjà vu. She gave him a reassuring grin and he reluctantly looked away, surveying their table of eight. Sarah and Jordan, Harry and Lucy, Spencer, and Alex's larger-than-life grandmother Joan (who walked Freddie down the aisle) sat captivated by Mark's heartfelt tribute.

"So, please join me"—Mark raised a huge grin and his glass of champagne—"in a toast to this beautiful couple."

Tarquin, Leia, and all the guests held their flutes aloft in a fizzy celebration of love and hope.

Mark licked his lips and lifted his glass a touch higher. "To Freddie and Simon!"

"To Freddie and Simon!" Tarquin and Leia echoed in concert with fifty delighted voices.

"That was gorgeous." Leia sniffed, lowering her glass as Mark was consumed at the head table by a rowdy, laughter-filled man hug. "So sincere and charming."

Truly. Kudos to Keegan. Tarquin sipped his champagne. The noisy Freddie-Simon-Mark tangle of arms claimed its next victim, swallowing up Alex and her black party dress (a Frill-Seekers original) in its fumbling embrace. *It's funny how life turns out. Eighteen months ago, it was me and Lex. Now, she's back with her soul mate, and I'm here with mine.* He reached over to Leia and claimed her hand resting in her lap with his handkerchief as the DJ launched into Madonna's "Cherish", a favorite of Freddie's. *I hope we're just as happy as Alex and Mark. And Simon and Freddie.* Smiling, he weaved his fingers gently through hers. *Together in London.*

Leia squeezed back. "Tarquin, what's the name of Mark's TV series?"

"*Lairds and Liars*," Lucy blurted, stealing a forkful of Harry's tart. He knew better than to challenge her brazen dessert theft. "There are four seasons with a fifth coming in the spring. I'm still reeling from last season's cliffhanger, the absolute fuckers."

Spencer winced in sympathy over the rim of her champagne. "We've *got* to have a viewing party when it's back on."

"YES!" Lucy swallowed and bounced in her chair. "We should cosplay! Simon's already working on something for Freddie." Dropping her fork on her plate, she hitched up the bodice of her white dress and leaned over Harry's plate toward Spencer. "It's the uniform that bloke from Inverness wears."

"Ooh, I HATE that guy!" Spencer seethed. "What he did to Mark's—"

"*Spoilers, sweetie!*" Lucy shot Spencer some cutting side-eye and glanced across the table at the Scott sisters.

Leia smiled at Sarah on the other side of Tarquin. "We better catch up, then! I think we're the only people on the planet who haven't seen this show."

"Mark *is* pretty cute." Sarah stared as he chatted with Ben and Riley a table away.

Joan jumped in. "He's a lovely lad, and he treats our Alex like a queen."

Leia locked eyes with Tarquin. "Don't worry—he's got nothing on you, Balfour! You'll always be *my* movie star."

"C'mere!" He pulled her in for a huge kiss as Freddie and Simon hovered, all loved-up smiles and boozy glee.

"Lovely jubbly, the gang is all here!" Freddie beamed, fiddling with his bow tie. "Oi, Tarq, sorry to cockblock…"

Cheers, Freds. Mid-kiss, Tarquin opened one accusatory eye.

"…but I must hug Leia before I get too trollied."

Leia's giggly snort broke their kiss. "Freddie"—she chuckled—"you *already* thanked me for fixing your hem. Twice."

"But, you SAVED me, princess!" Freddie nudged his glasses up his nose as Simon shared a joke with Jordan. "How horrific would it have been to say 'I do' to my darling fashion designer hubby with one trouser leg flapping on the floor like some disheveled clown?"

"Nice one, Ley. Do you always travel with a needle and thread?" asked Lucy.

Leia laughed. "Just a small sewing kit." Tarquin draped his arm along the back of her chair. "Blame the day job."

Freddie's eyes narrowed as he swept his floppy fringe off his forehead. "There was something else I wanted to thank you for..." He peered across the room.

Tarquin followed his search. Alex was laughing alongside Simon's parents, all three nibbling on colorful Smarties and Rockets.

Freddie snapped his fingers. "*That's* it! The sweetie table. Cheers for the Canadian treats, Ley."

"Yeah, I may have pinched a few." Lucy snickered, revealing a small bag of ketchup potato chips hidden in her bag.

"Brilliant!" Tarquin chuckled, meeting Leia's eyes.

Harry scanned the bag. "*Ketchup* flavor? Ah, so that's why you nicked three—"

"Shh! I didn't take them all!" Lucy protested.

"I'm glad they're popular," said Leia.

"Yep! Si's fam feel right at home because of you! I must admit, I can't leave that cornucopia of Canuck fabulousness alone either. Come on, who *isn't* partial to a sneaky Mr. Big!"

"Freds is so partial he married 'im!" bellowed Simon, a tipsy playfulness saturating his voice.

Tarquin, Leia, and their friends laughed as the wedding coordinator spoke with Mark near the cake cutting table.

"Ooh, and we're so glad Freddie did!" Joan nodded, acknowledging Ben and Riley passing by holding hands. "Aw, bless 'em! True love! You can't beat it." She smiled and leaned in, confiding in Tarquin and Leia. "Do you know, I married Alex's granddad when I was only eighteen? Our parents were dead set against it, but we eloped and did it anyway!" She stroked her thumb gently over a cherished wedding ring on her left hand, lost for a moment to her memories. "Thirty-five wonderful years, we had, almost to the day. And in all that time, no regrets, no doubts. We were just *meant* to find one another, and it's as simple as that..." Joan's voice drifted off, becoming quiet as Madonna gave way to "Wonderwall".

Meant to be. Glancing at Leia, Tarquin took a deep breath and shifted closer, his eyes softening, brimming with gratitude. *That's you and me. You saved me, gorgeous.*

Leia gave him a teary sigh and reached out to hold Joan's hand, but as she did, Alex's grandmother met Leia's rapt expression with a nostalgic smile and a conspiratorial wink. "What I'm saying is— *when you know, you know!*"

"Amen to that, Joan. Amen to that." Tarquin grinned as he raised a respectful glass in her honor. "To true love, then?"

The youthful gleam returned to Joan's eyes as she lifted her champagne and joined in the toast with Leia and Tarquin.

As the conversation continued around the table and the Oasis classic resonated through the room, Tarquin lowered his glass, his heart full and hopeful. He shared a happy glance with Leia as she took a festive sip of her bubbly then wrinkled her nose. *The truth is, I'd happily propose to her right now if I didn't fear it was too much, too soon. Moving countries, moving in with me—that's already A LOT.*

She abandoned her champagne and swayed in close, caressing his clean-shaven chin and pressing a kiss on his temple. Tarquin responded in kind. He softly brushed his fingers along her neck and met her lips with a long, tender kiss, the taste of celebration still on her tongue.

"I love you," she purred against his mouth.

"I love *you*. So much."

Leia smiled into another kiss then gently pulled away.

I want her, and only her. Tarquin's eyes lingered lovingly over her white silk dress. *For as long as we both shall live.*

A loud, high-pitched symphony of cutlery against glass rose from Tom and Naomi's table an elbow away, demanding the new-lyweds kiss for all to see.

Simon winced over his shoulder. "Oh, Tom, not again." His eyes cut back to his new husband. "It's so tacky!"

Freddie raised his brows, ever hopeful. "But it's *tradition*, Si!" He smiled sweetly, the trio of sparkly Christmas trees behind him lending a romantic glow. "I love all that stuff."

Simon's expression softened. "And I love you. Come on, let's give the people what they want!" He brushed Freddie's cheek ador-ingly and kissed him, slowly, passionately.

Loud whoops and applause rose around the room as Tarquin re-filled Sarah's champagne and Leia opened her drawstring purse, pulling out her phone.

"I have to tell you, Tarq..." Sarah admired the fizzy bubbles rising in her glass. "Dad wants us to have a *Star Wars* marathon over the Christmas break. Original trilogy, of course!"

"Oh, TOP idea! I'm in!" The round table quaked as Tarquin set down the magnum of champagne. "Although, Ginger will..." He did a double take.

Leia swallowed and flipped her phone face down in her lap.

Uh-oh! "Bugger! You *saw* it, didn't you?" He winced comical-ly, throwing Sarah a sidelong glance. "I *may* have borrowed some of Leia's new fabrics for Mrs. Chuzzlewit's Instagram photo this morning..." He pulled out his phone from his jacket pocket, photo at the ready. "See? She looks like a nun! A very miserable, *una-mused* nun."

Sarah squealed with laughter. "Ooh, doghouse for you, Tarq. *Never* touch the fabrics!"

The Spice Girls burst forth in all their sassy glory from Leia's phone. Her eyes swept around the table. "Sorry! Uh, just..."

"Saved by the bell," Tarquin murmured with a chuckle.

Sarah swallowed another mouthful of champagne. "Ley, just send it to voicemail."

"I have to take it." She hit accept and pushed back her chair, pressing the phone to her ear. "Hi, just gimme a moment?" Smiling tightly, she lowered it to her chest and squeezed Tarquin's shoulder. "Won't be a minute."

He snickered, eyeing her dessert. "For the sake of your apple tart, you better not!" His cheeky gaze swung up to meet her. "Love you!"

Leia hesitated as if she was treasuring the moment. "I love you, too."

She twisted away and sped toward the hall, the staccato click-click-click of her silver heels on the hardwood lost in another round of tinkling champagne glasses, merry laughter, and "Wonderwall" strumming its last gasp.

LEIA

God, I feel sick. Leia's stomach plunged like an elevator snapped loose of its cables. *How is this happening?* Shoulders shaking in the evening chill, she paced wildly, fighting back sobs as the muffled voice glued to her ear finally took a breath.

"*Three* other women?!" Leia gasped into her phone, her manic steps crunching the frost-licked grass on the edge of London Fields. "You think you know someone—" A knot choked her throat and sudden tears swelled in her eyes, breaching her lashes.

The life she had so lovingly stitched together wasn't just unravelling. It was ripping apart.

Her watery stare vaulted upward. The jolly Christmas lights and steamed-up windows of Alex and Mark's second-floor apartment framed happy silhouettes, swaying and flailing, their frenetic dance accompanied by Saint Etienne's "No Cure for the Common Christmas". A mix of spirited accents and raucous laughter—*Tarquin's laugh?*—cut through the music, and Leia's heart splintered into a thousand little pieces.

"Leia, I'm *so* sorry…I really didn't have a choice." Breathy and pained, the voice on the phone released a woeful sigh.

"No! This isn't your fault. *None* of it is, okay? Please believe that," Leia begged through chattering teeth, her bare arms prickled with goose bumps. "And don't worr—"

"Sorry! Have to go! They're giving me evil stares."

Leia flinched. "Uh, okay. Talk tomorrow?"

"Promise. Love you, Ley, bye."

Three beeps signaled the caller was gone.

What am I going to do?! Dropping the phone from her ear, Leia gasped, and her rapid breaths set free a torrent of hot tears down her cheeks. She pressed the back of her other hand against her mouth and gulped. *It's Simon's wedding. How do I even…?*

She swung away from the happy glow of the reception and trudged deeper into the adjoining park, her white dress dragging through a half-frozen puddle clogged with leaves, their edges furry with ice. "Oh, NO! Fuck!" she barked between sobs, fisting the material and hiking it above the sludge. Her hasty inspection revealed no grass stains or splotches of dirt. *So, my dress isn't ruined—but what about my relationship?!* She glared into the dark stillness of the barren trees, cursing loving boyfriends and unfaithful partners and everyone in between.

"Ginger, *there* you are!"

Tarquin. Leia's breath bottled in her chest. She peered over her shoulder. *He can't see me like this.* Swiping away all teary evidence, she blew out her cheeks and stuffed her phone in her dress's pocket, where her fingers tangled with the fabric measuring tape from her mini sewing kit. *So that's where it went.* She bunched it up with a nervous twist of her fingers and thumb.

"I've been looking all over for you, then I spotted you through the window." Tarquin's tone was boyish and champagne-soaked. "Spencer's a good laugh, but she pogos to bloody well everything! I need my dance partner. I need *you!*"

Leia painted on her best 'Everything is awesome' grin and slowly swiveled, finding Tarquin's smile firing on all cylinders, eyes shining, dimples teasing, her winter coat draped over his arm. *So adorable and considerate. God, I love him.*

Her shattered heart soared, and for that moment, everything felt carefree and bright—until her hand raked over the phone in her pocket and reality swooped in, hurling those fluttery swoons into a spiraling nosedive.

"You'll be proud of me!" Tarquin chuckled. "I didn't lay a single finger on your apple tart, although I *was* tempted." He unfurled her purple coat, swaddling her shoulders in the welcome warmth of its wool.

Always thoughtful and charming. "Thank you." Her mouth flickered with a genuine smile as he kissed her forehead, careful not to muss up her elegant up-do. But the brief press of his lips on her cold skin rippled through her body, whirling all the grief and sadness around inside her.

Tarquin pulled back and rubbed his hands together, blowing on his skin. "Why'd you come out here? It's bloody *freezing!*" A shiver surged through him, and the shoulders of his unbuttoned tux jacket rounded as he shook. "Brrr! My nipples could key a car!"

So goofy! Leia snort-laughed. *No one makes me crack up like he does.*

Wasting no time, he wound his arms around her, and Leia surrendered, snuggling into him, savoring his warm, loving embrace. *Tarquin is everything I've ever wanted.*

"See?" He pressed his chest against hers. "My nips are lethal weapons!"

She giggled through a shiver, thwarting more tears. "Hey, you're in luck—I have nipple covers in my bag."

Tarquin's laugh vibrated through her body. "That's my girl! What would I do without you, eh?" His voice danced, all light and playful, overflowing with joy as he gently swayed, stroking her coat-covered back. "I've said it before and I'll say it again, I'm the world's luckiest bloke! You are my everything!"

Her heart panged, suddenly mourning for the day he might propose, the minute she'd say 'I do', the moment their newborn was placed in her arms. *It's all going to slip away—I can feel it!*

"So, why'd you fancy a solo stroll in the park?"

Loosening her grip, Leia stepped back, her eyes poring over his black bow tie and white shirt. "It was so noisy in there. Then I couldn't get good reception…" She tugged the cozy coat around her neck, but her trembling wouldn't stop.

Tarquin protectively wrapped his arm around her shoulder. "Come on, let's get you inside—"

"Wait!" A puff of warm air escaped her tight lips. She stiffened, heels digging into the winter-beaten grass. "Tarquin, I have to tell you something."

Worry creased his forehead. He swung around, facing her. "It's the phone call, isn't it? Who rang?"

"Shantelle. She'd texted me six times during the speeches, but I didn't see them. My phone was in my purse. When I didn't answer, she called."

"Did something…bad happen in Paris?"

Bad doesn't even begin to… Nausea rolled in her stomach. "Bastien has been cheating on Shantelle. She left him and called me

441

from the plane. She's flying home to New York."

Tarquin's throat pulsed. "Your contract…" The sobering words tumbled from his lips, collapsing his happy-go-lucky smile, stealing his effervescence. "You're leaving."

A sob dislodged from deep inside Leia's chest. "I don't *want* to! But I can't back out. Shantelle is homesick and heartbroken, couldn't stop crying. She feels awful about…" Leia stammered, tears clouding her eyes. "She apologized like twenty times."

"Oh, Leia! Come here." Despair quivered Tarquin's voice as he gathered her in, kissing her forehead, her hair, her damp cheeks, as if committing Leia to memory. "We'll think of something, okay?" He squeezed her tight then cleared his throat like he was trying not to cry. "Uh, what about…maybe you could go just for award season and Fashion Week? Then come straight back."

I wish. "It's a bit more complicated than that." Leia shuddered, her fingers skimming along one of his silk lapels. "Shan called her agent this afternoon, and he said the studio wants me to style her, plus two co-stars from her next film—all in Frill-Seekers." She eased back from his chest and looked into his eyes. "One of them is Victoria Angel."

Tarquin's mouth fell open. "Bloody hell! She won an Oscar this year!"

"I know! The other actress, Charlotte, was just nominated for a Golden Globe. And all three of them need a permanent stylist on call for most of next year."

Tarquin ran his fingers over his lips, the corners twitching then rising into a smile. "That's amazing, Leia! Oh my god, talk about a 'big break'. This is everything you've been working towards."

So why does all this feel like a nightmare? She buried her face in his neck. "I'd have given up everything for this a year ago, but it doesn't come close to being with you. We've been making plans, putting down roots. Now, that life is up in the air until god knows when." Tears toppled down her cheeks and fell onto his silk bow tie, dappling the fabric. "I feel like that Italian soldier on Orkney, leaving his heart behind."

"Aw, my beautiful girl." He tucked a wisp of her hair behind her ear. "You're not leaving it *behind*. You're leaving it with me for safekeeping. I'll fly out, come see you. You know I'd travel to the ends of the earth if it meant spending five minutes with you."

He's not getting it. She lifted her head and wiped her eyes. "Tarquin, we've talked about this. You *know* I can't do long-distance."

"But it would be different with me. You're my priority, and everything else comes second."

"I know and I love you for that, but it's *never* that easy—living in different places, separated by five time zones and an ocean. It takes its toll, the loneliness, the anxiety…"

Tarquin paused, lost in thought, the muscle in his jaw tensing. "Yeah." He let out a staggered breath. "Yeah, I can see that. And to be honest, distance played a huge role in my parents' split. It's hard to build a life with someone who's never there."

Her face crumpled. "And I won't ask you to wait for me."

"You know I *would*, though, right?"

"You can't, Tarquin. It's not fair to you. I'd feel so guilty, making you put your life on hold for something that might never happen. So much can change in a year. Look at the last twelve months we've been through already." The park blurred as she held him tight. "But at the same time, I know I'd *die* if you fell in love with someone else. I want to be the one you kiss before you fall asleep."

"Oh, Leia. I want that, too." Tarquin let out a mournful sigh. "So. What are we gonna do?" He leaned his head against hers and sniffed, pausing for a moment. "I guess there's only one thing for it."

We're breaking up. Tears poured down Leia's cheeks, her

whole body aching and reeling, feeling like it was buckling in on itself. *THIS is why I can't fall in love. It decimates me, every time. It turns my heart to dust.* She nuzzled into his neck, dreading the moment they'd kiss goodbye and forever part, walking away from what might have been.

Tarquin's breath flirted with her hair. "I'm coming with you," he whispered.

WHAT?! How? Breaths stuttered in Leia's chest. She pulled back, blinking in disbelief. "But your life…it's here."

A tender smile curved his lips as he stroked her waist. "No. It's wherever you are."

He says that, but the seams just don't line up. "But…what about your business? Tarquin, you can't bring London with you."

"I could manage everything from Brooklyn." His green eyes glowed. "Video-conferencing these days is almost as good as being there, and I've got great staff who really don't need muggins here micromanaging their every move. My second-in-command is gagging for more opportunities to scope out properties on his own so…why not? Once in a while, I'd have to fly back and check on things, but otherwise…yeah, let's do it! Bring on Brooklyn!"

"But you're so hands-on."

"Oh, I can be hands-on in New York. My green card is still valid, and my contacts from working for Budgie are solid." He smiled confidently. "I know it sounds mad, but in a way, I know the New York building scene even better than London's. Plus, they *love* a British accent over there!"

He needs to think about this. Leia pouted and toyed with a button on his jacket. "But you'll miss Ava and your family."

"I sure as hell won't miss Mum." He snickered. "But as for Ava, that's what planes and FaceTime are for." He stroked her cheek. "Leia, *you* are my life. *You're* my priority. I let you go twice before. I'm not doing it again."

A smirk hitched the corners of her mouth. "Sure, use my own words against me."

"Well, they're *brilliant* words."

"You actually want to do this? For real?" Leia held her breath and fidgeted, her hand nervously slipping into her pocket.

Tarquin smiled. "Do I tidy up drunk?!"

She laughed tearfully and shimmied on the spot. "I can't believe you're coming with me!"

"Believe it. Leia, I want to build a life with you, and I don't care if that's here, New York, or on an island in the North Sea with no trees. I'm all in."

Goose bumps peppered Leia's skin, but they had nothing to do with the cold. "Thank you." She looped her arms around his neck, overwhelmed with love.

I'm all in, too—and boy, am I gonna prove it to him tonight.

Leia couldn't stop smiling. "You know...you're the sweetest, kindest man I've ever met. You've my best friend. You're my heart."

He leaned in, gazing into her eyes. "And you're mine, Leia."

"I love you."

Tarquin raised a cheeky brow. "I know."

I know! Leia squealed and broke out into a sly grin. "Well, it *does* feel like Planet Hoth out here!"

His jaw dropped. "Ooh! I KNEW it! You *have* seen *The Empire Strikes Back*!"

"Yeah, yeah. Doesn't mean I enjoyed it!"

"We might have to work on that."

"No. We don't." Leia giggled. "But I don't mind you loving it. In a way, *Star Wars* brought us together."

She kissed him softly and swept a finger along his jaw before pulling away, her hands lowering, clasping a handful of dress. Lifting it a few inches above the ground, she shakily kneeled.

Tarquin's brows pulled in. "Uh, Leia…what are you…"

She clasped his hand. "*I know.*"

"Sorry?"

Butterflies swooped and swirled in Leia's belly. "Earlier, Joan said, 'When you know, you know.' And I do." She smiled up at him, her eyes glistening with happy tears. "Tarquin Octavius Balfour, will you marry me?"

"Blimey, Leia!" Tarquin squeezed her hand. "Like you have to ask! Yes! Yes! A million times YES!" His smile shone brighter than the Shard at New Year's.

He wants to marry me! Her heart leapt, giddy with unbridled joy. She let out a delighted giggle. "I have something for you."

His eyes widened. "Seriously? You bought a ring?!"

"No, but"—she fished the fabric measuring tape from her pocket—"maybe this can do for now?"

"Ah, love it! Resourcefulness, thy name is Leia!"

"Well, if Italian soldiers can make beautiful lights out of corned beef cans, I can create a ring from sewing supplies."

Tarquin chuckled as she started winding the thin strip of fabric around and around his left ring finger. "But, Ley, do blokes actually *wear* engagement rings?"

"Some do!" She tucked the end into one of the layers of fabric. "Ta-da! We're engaged!"

Tarquin marveled at his hand like she had given him a rare, priceless gem. "Now, come here, future wifey." He bent down and helped Leia up. "You need a kiss worthy of a—" His happy gaze soured as it skirted her outfit. "Oh, bugger, your dress."

Leia clutched her coat, slipping from her shoulders, and glanced down. A knee-sized blob of mud and several grassy smudges soiled the white silk. She shrugged. "I don't care. It was worth it! Kiss me!"

Tarquin leaned in and cupped her face, his mouth gently claiming her lips. Leia curled her arms around his neck and urged him closer as her tongue teased, eliciting a groan of pure pleasure from her fiancé.

"Oh, Leia." He sighed. "I'm going to buy you the most beautiful diamond—and don't you dare say no! I'm so going to spoil you, my future Mrs. Balfour."

"I can't believe I proposed to you—Mr. Scott!"

He threw his arms around her, lifting her up. "Hey! I got a great idea! Let's do it tonight?"

"Get married?"

"Yeah! Why fanny about? The vicar's still at the party! You're in this beautiful white, albeit *muddy*, dress"—he chuckled, setting her back on the ground—"and I'm in a tux. We already look like a bride and groom!"

Leia ogled their outfits. "Oh, my god, we do! But I'd hate to steal Simon and Freddie's thunder." She pressed her lips tight as something tiny and wet landed in her lashes. "Plus, I'd want Dad here. And I'd really like Ava and Poppy to be our flower girls."

He nodded. "There is that."

"Let's not tell anyone. At least for a bit?" Leia grabbed his hands and kissed him. "Keep it just for us?"

A smile played with his lips. "Ooh, that's hot! A secret fiancée!"

She gazed into Tarquin's eyes as a sprinkling of snowflakes danced between them. Her face lit up, all glowing and sparkly, like Alex and Mark's Christmas trees back in their warm apartment. "It's *snowing*! You said it never snows!"

"It doesn't, not really...but I put in a word with Mother Nature, just for you." He leaned in, kissing her on the lips again and again until Leia pulled away laughing. "Sorry, but I just can't stop *snogging* you! It's so amazing! Leia, we're *getting married*! We're moving to *New York*! Two things I did NOT expect to say when I woke up this morning!" He chuckled. "How soon do you have to be back?"

"Right after the holidays."

"So we could still do Christmas and your birthday here, then? With Sarah and your dad?"

"Or on Orkney?" Leia bit her lip. "Maybe Jordan could rent a car and the three of them could take the ferry over?"

"Great idea! We could show them all the sights."

"You could play Santa for Ava and Poppy, and I'd get to watch that weird male bonding ritual you call the Ba'."

"Admit it." He thrust out his chest. "All that Orcadian testosterone turns you on, doesn't it?"

Leia giggled. "What am I going to do with you?"

"I can think of a few things." Tarquin winked.

EPILOGUE

"The more grateful I am, the more beauty I see."
Mary Davis

LEIA

One year and ten days later, Thursday, December 31, 2020

Leia sipped her apple soft drink and looked up from her gratitude journal, the bistro in Brooklyn's IKEA bustling with happy shoppers tucking into meatballs and pink cream cakes. In the mix of dark winter coats and wooly hats, she spotted Tarquin, parka unzipped and his arms weighed down by two large blue and yellow shopping bags. *What didn't he buy?* She giggled.

"Sorry, that took longer than I thought." Tarquin delicately rested his haul on the floor then scratched a hand through his hair. "I forgot the play tunnel for Mrs. Chuzzlewit, and then had to double back and pick up that cute circus tent for Ava and Poppy."

Leia flipped her journal closed and nudged it aside, watching Tarquin strip free of his coat. "You do realize Fiona is gonna kill you, right?"

Smiling mischievously, he neatly folded his parka over the back of his chair. "Where else will they stash all the stuffies and dolls you gave them this summer?"

Leia shrugged as Tarquin sat down. "So I spoiled our flower girls…" She reached across the square table and grasped his hand, her thumb flirting with the platinum band on his ring finger. "It was a beautiful day, wasn't it?"

"The best. One of the longest days of the year, too, which was fitting. I never wanted it to end." His dimples deepened as he angled closer. "I love you, Mrs. Balfour."

"I love you, too, Mr. Scott." Leia leaned over her apple drink and Tarquin's milky coffee and greeted his lips with a quick kiss. "I know it's only been six months, but do I get to call myself an honorary Orcadian now?"

"If a Balfour family wedding in the Italian Chapel doesn't seal it, I'm not sure what does." He squeezed her hand before he let go.

Leia matched his grin. "I'm glad we could get married there. Sarah and Dad are still talking about its beautiful paintings. I know Mom would've been smitten, too." Her expression muted. "Tarquin, I'm sorry your mom wasn't there."

He shook his head and picked up his cup. "Don't be—I'm not. I was relieved when you agreed not to invite her. She would've shown up in some sequin-encrusted monstrosity, moaning about the wind or Dad's relatives, and made our day all about her. And frankly, that sweet little Italian Chapel is too wee to accommodate Kiki's inflated ego or her over-the-top dramatics." Raising his brows, he glanced out the window and sipped his lukewarm coffee.

"Saz thought she'd crash the ceremony and make a scene."

"Nah, I knew she wouldn't." He licked his lips and leaned back in his chair. "Over the years, she's missed important footy games, both my Eton and uni graduations. I'm not *entirely* convinced she was there at my birth." His chuckle slipped into a decisive nod as he swirled the coffee in his cup. "I'm not saying I'll never speak to her again, but she needs to apologize first. A simple 'I'm sorry' would go a long way toward restoring family harmony, but I'm not holding my breath. Nico, Rupert, Fiona, my cousins…they're all still pissed about how she behaved at Poppy's baptism."

Leia gave her husband an empathetic smile and glanced down at her simple platinum wedding band and diamond engagement ring, the round one-carat gem hugged on each side by a tapered baguette stone. Tarquin had promised her the biggest rock on the market, but she preferred the simplicity of something smaller, more elegant. *Kiki was so wrong about me. I'm about as far from a 'money-hungry trollop' as they come.*

She winced and ran a finger along the edge of her journal. "Have you spoken to Harry about tonight?"

"Yeah!" Tarquin shifted forward, placing his coffee on the table. "He called while I was in the queue. Simon and Freddie just checked into their hotel, and Mark and Ben are out running some last-minute errands for Alex. Oh, and she'll bring Lucy and Riley over to ours around three to pick up their dresses. They promise they won't dillydally—they know you and I have special dinner plans before meeting them all at Bespoke."

Leia beamed. "Two years, Tarquin! Where did the time go? The blackout feels like yesterday."

"Happiest day of my life, meeting you." He smiled fondly. "I'm glad we came here today."

"Well, it's tradition, right? A lunchtime drink in IKEA on New Year's Eve. I know London was out of the question because of your Tribeca development and my holiday pop-up shop, but maybe next year? Return to the *real* scene of the crime?"

"What Leia wants, Leia gets." He cracked a smile and lifted his coffee, raising it in a toast.

"How many is that, then?"

"Coffees? My first. It's always a one-coffee day when I'm with you, Ginger."

"I thought you had some this morning. You were up so early." She downed the last of her apple drink.

"No. I had to go for a run, didn't I? Can't let those grape-riddled pizza slices give me a dad bod."

He picks off the grapes—the only healthy bit! Leia giggled and parked her empty bottle on the table. "To me, you're sexy no matter what. It's your heart I fell in love with."

"No—really?" Pouting playfully, he sat up and smoothed his hands slowly down his chest. "Not my pecs? Or my abs?" He hiked up the left sleeve of his sweater. "My forearms? You do *love* a bit of forearm!" He bounced his eyebrows.

He has me there. "Yes, Tarquin, I think they're hot, but honestly, it was y—"

"Got it!" He twisted in his chair, pointing behind him. "My arse!"

Leia laughed. "Now you're being one!"

He chuckled and tossed back the dregs of his coffee, the corners of his mouth still curled upward.

She glanced at him lovingly and dipped inside her purse, pulling out her London phone box keychain. "So, Han Solo with the amazing ass and forearms, you ready to head home?"

"Yeah, let's get going. But first, I'm just going to grab a few of those raspberry drinks to takeaway—never see them anywhere else." He pushed back his chair and swooped down, gifting Leia a soft, chaste kiss.

"Mmm, more, please." She opened her eyes. *I cannot wait for tonight!*

"Soon! I'm just keeping it PG." He tilted his head to the side. "Kids at the next table." With a grin, he pressed another quick kiss to her forehead and straightened up. "Be right back."

Leia's gaze lingered, following her husband's butt until he disappeared in the bustle of coats and scarves and blue and yellow shopping bags headed for the counter.

Happy New Year, Tarquin.

If someone had told Leia during the London blackout that in two years' time, she'd be blissfully married to the posh guy with the *Star Wars* ringtone, have Hollywood A-listers as regular clients, and be trying for a baby, she would've laughed and said, 'What the hell

452

are you on?' But sat in the bustling IKEA bistro in Brooklyn, her heart swelled with happiness. She opened her journal and picked up her pen.

I don't have to wait until tomorrow to know what I'm thankful for today.

Smiling at the page, she pressed pen to paper.

December 31, I ~~was~~ AM grateful for:
1. *our two-year 'meet cute' anniversary.*
2. *True love with the kindest, sexiest, most wonderful man I've ever known.*
3. *Peeing on a stick this morning & watching two miraculous little lines appear (then doing it again just to be sure!).*
   I can't WAIT to tell Tarquin tonight.

ACKNOWLEDGEMENTS

Thank you so much for reading *Say Hello, Kiss Goodbye*!

This novel was supposed to be released a year earlier, but after the unexpected and premature death of our beloved Schipperke, Zoey, I had to step away and grieve. For me and my husband, Zoey was our world, our little girl, and her loss broke us. For months, I was unable to read, let alone write (both, my therapist tells me, are common signs of deep grief), and I decided to give my heart time to heal. I'm still not quite there yet, but at least my writing mojo returned, and now here I am with another book I'm really proud of.

I'd like to thank the kind, generous souls who were there for me in the immediate aftermath of Zoey's passing: Heather & Bill, Val & Tony, Jason, Therasa, Maria, Sheila, Gabby & Rosie, Sally & Bruce, Michal, Vicki, Charlotte, Cristina, Esther, Nicole, Kristin, Alison, Lynsey, Simone, Sally T., Len, Rose-Anne, Charles, Tammy, Alicia, and Susan. I cannot express how grateful I am for all of you. Your hugs, messages, and cupcakes were so appreciated during this most difficult year of my life. Love you all.

Much cheaper than a plane ticket, I hope *Say Hello, Kiss Goodbye* feels like a sweet escape. London owns my heart (40+ visits and counting), while New York is my first travel love (and home of my meet cute with my British husband!). Scotland's Orkney Islands, however, are in my blood. I'm proud of my Orcadian ancestry and treasure the time I spent on the Mainland, South Ronaldsay, Lamb Holm, and Hoy in 2018. It's *really* weird setting foot somewhere for the first time and feeling like you've come home.

I'm proud to be an own voices author, too. I've had anxiety, panic attacks, and depression since I was a kid, and I'm grateful to have this platform to inform and (I hope) help remove the stigma around such issues. Mental health matters today and every day.

One of the themes of *Say Hello, Kiss Goodbye* is gratitude, and I'd like to thank the following people for their support and help.

To my husband, Darren, this year has been unlike any other. I don't know how I would've carried on without you. You're my best friend, my anchor, my nacho-maker, my editor, my book designer, and Zoey's dad. Always. xoxo

Katrina, sending all the love to you for the gift of Charlie. I love our Floof Dragon to the moon and back (even if he did chew my cherished *Grease* soundtrack from the '70s).

Michal, remember telling me your story about being stuck in IKEA during a blackout? And now it lives on with Leia & Tarq. Thank you for being so awesome (I'm glad you made it out okay).

Esther, we finally hung out in London! I know Manchester is our usual stomping ground, but I had a blast researching locations with you. We ate far too many cakes, but it was worth it, right? I'll never see 'cake carriage' without thinking of you. Love ya!

Vicki and Charlotte, my theatre pals, comic con accomplices, and two of the most genuine, funny, and beautiful women I've ever known. I love you both. *Pride* & ladies' toast forever!

Cristina, I so admire your beautiful way with words and am forever thankful that Ben Whishaw brought us together. Thank you for your bookish help. Lots of love (and cuddles for Thorin).

Cheers, hugs, and allll the British chocolate to my brilliant beta and sensitivity readers, with a special shout-out to Jennifer for guiding me through accessibility. Thank you so much!

Nicole Caliva, I love your photo of my Tarquin and Leia. They are the perfect cover stars (and it's even sweeter that they're a real-life couple). Thank you!

Caitlin, you are the most accommodating editor and such a

lovely person. Thank you for your expertise, polish, and for fixing the mistakes I made with lie, lay, and laid (I still don't get it).

Kendra and the Orkney Past & Present Facebook group, your photos and social media posts never fail to make me smile. Thanks for answering my questions about all things Orkney.

BIG thanks to the Grey's Promotion team: Mary, Josette, and Charlotte for helping get the word out! You're all amazing.

Samantha and the team at Frolic, cheers for my cover reveal.

My author friends! I adore your books and want everyone to read them, too! You are all inspiring, talented women, and I'm thankful to have you in my life! Looking at you Nicole Trilivas, Kristin Contino, Marie Landry, Zöe Folbigg, Brenda St. John Brown, Aimee Brown, Rachel McMillan, and Sally Thorne.

Melena, not only do you have some of the cutest kids I've ever seen, you're also a fantastic Keeganites United book club moderator. You always create kickass discussion questions. I'm so grateful for your help and friendship. Thank you.

A heartfelt thank you to all the bloggers, bookstagrammers, booklovers, and social media followers who have read my stories, recommended them to friends, attended book signings, and supported me during my writing journey. Your enthusiasm for happily ever afters inspires me.

Last, but never least, my Keeganites: the members of my Facebook group, Keeganites United. I am so grateful for you sticking by me this last 18 months. When an author's book release gets bumped back (like mine did when Zoey died), it's easy to lose interest and move on, but you didn't. You've cheered me up and kept me going when I needed it the most. Thank you for loving my characters as much as I do. You are the absolute best. xoxo

"Hop on, hold tight, and remember to enjoy the ride."
Mark Keegan's Vespa Rules, *London Belongs to Me*

GLOSSARY

Some people, places, and things mentioned in *Say Hello, Kiss Goodbye* might not be familiar to all readers. Here are a few helpful explanations.

Adaptive reuse: The practice of redeveloping an abandoned building (often one with a heritage designation) and giving it a new purpose. For example, Tarquin repurposing the old cinema with its sky-high ceiling into a climbing gym.

Dead stock fabric: Textile mills and garment factories often end up with extra material they don't use. This 'dead stock' might have been dyed the wrong color, or left over from a production run, or just didn't sell. Design houses are also sources of dead stock. When they create a fashion line and end up with leftover fabric, they usually discard it in the trash, and it ends up in landfill. Sustainable designers like Leia take dead stock, and turn it into desirable garments. Usually, dead stock materials aren't found in large quantities, so the production run is limited (which is great, as you won't find many people in the same dress!).

Smarmy: British word for ingratiating and insincere

St. Clement's: A non-alcoholic cocktail usually made from equal measures orange juice and bitter lemon. The drink is named after the old English nursery rhyme, *Oranges and Lemons*.

Adaptive clothing: Clothing designed for individuals with physical disabilities and/or mobility challenges. Adaptive clothing may feature Velcro, snaps, or magnetic closures instead of buttons, zippers in easy-to-access positions, and material that doesn't rub or scratch.

CAD: Computer Aided Design (or Drafting)

Grapes on pizza: It's not a figment of my imagination! Vinnie's Pizzeria in Brooklyn makes a special pizza with grapes, roasted red peppers, gorgonzola, bacon, and honey.

Grade II listed properties: In England, the government classifies old properties as 'listed' to protect their historical or architectural significance. There are three categories (I, II* and II), which rank their importance. Developers like Tarquin are allowed to alter listed buildings; however, they require written permission from local authorities first before they can proceed.

Sticky wicket: A difficult problem or situation.

Swot: British slang for a person who studies hard and does their homework.

Vegan leather made from mushrooms: Is real! One such vegan leather is made from mushroom caps and is tanned using non-toxic ingredients. Another uses the underground roots of mushrooms. Who knew, eh?

B-listed properties: Like England, Scotland classifies old properties as 'listed' if they are of historical or architectural interest, but they use letters (A, B, and C) instead of numbers.

The Ba': A traditional game of Orkney street football dating back hundreds of years played on Christmas and New Year's Day. Hundreds of men participate and are divided into two teams, the Uppies and the Doonies, based upon whether they were born north or south of Kirkwall's St. Magnus Cathedral. The Ba' has no rules, but the aim of the game is to pass the handcrafted leather ball through the streets of Kirkwall and reach your goal first. It's not unusual for the game to carry on for hours and finish in the dark.

"Give it a bit more welly": British phrase, apparently from the 1970s. Welly is an abbreviation of Wellington boot (aka, knee-length rubber boot). This funny idiom is used to encourage someone to try harder or put in more physical effort.

Groatie Buckies: Tiny (peedie!) white shells that apparently bring good luck—if you have the good fortune to find some!

Peckish: British word for feeling hungry.

Betty Corrigall's grave: In the late 1770s, twenty-seven-year-old Betty Corrigall became pregnant with the child of a passing sailor. Abandoned by her lover and ostracized by the Hoy community, she committed suicide and was buried in an unmarked grave in unconsecrated ground. Betty was finally given a proper burial and a headstone in 1976.

Sea stacks: Steep and often very tall outcrops of rock standing alone in the ocean. Orkney has several, including the Old Man of Hoy and Yesnaby Castle, and yes, brave souls *do* climb them.

Muggins: British term for a foolish person, usually used humorously when referring to oneself.

HEALTH RESOURCES

**If you or someone you know suffers from
anxiety or depression, help is available.**

United States
Anxiety and Depression Association of America
www.adaa.org

Canada
The Canadian Mental Health Association (CMHA)
www.cmha.ca

United Kingdom
Mind
www.mind.org.uk

MEET MY OTHER BOOKS!

My novels are written as standalones.
However, they all take place in the same 'world',
and characters from one book often appear in another.

LONDON BELONGS TO ME
Contemporary coming-of-age story with a touch of romance.
Tropes: friends to lovers, coming-of-age romance,
actor hero/Irish hero, playwright heroine/American heroine
(has open-door kissing scenes but all sex is off the page)

LONDON, CAN YOU WAIT?
Contemporary romance and the sequel to *London Belongs to Me*.
However, it can be read as a standalone.
Tropes: angsty, relationship in trouble, actor hero/Irish hero,
playwright heroine/American heroine,
tragic past, soul mates, second chance, starting over
(open- and closed-door sex scenes)

UNTIL THE LAST STAR FADES
Blurs the line between contemporary romance and women's fiction.
Tropes: angsty, slow-burn, friends to lovers,
Scottish hero, American heroine, tragic past, college
(open- and closed-door sex scenes)

**All titles available in paperback and ebook
from all major retailers.**
***London Belongs to Me* is also available as an audiobook.**

Say Hello, Kiss Goodbye

Enjoyed Leia and Tarquin's story?
Please consider leaving a review on the retailer's website.

Stay in touch!
Follow Jacquelyn:

Instagram: @JaxMiddleton_Author
Facebook: JacquelynMiddletonAuthor
Twitter: @JaxMiddleton
and join her private Facebook readers group
to hear book news first, participate in her book club,
and have the chance to enter exclusive giveaways.

Visit Jacquelyn's website
for book playlists, behind-the-scenes exclusives,
and to sign up to her newsletter.
www.JacquelynMiddleton.com

CPSIA information can be obtained
at www.ICGtesting.com
Printed in the USA
JSHW030357071020
8567JS00001B/3